Love is All

DONNA HEWLETT

OLD FORT PRESS
SAVANNAH, GEORGIA

For my mother, who left this world far too soon.
Thank you for showering me with the many
facets of love that remain the bedrock of my soul.

I love you.

Till God did please to grant him ease. Do end!" quoth I:
"I end with - **Love is all** and Death is nought!" quoth She.

— ROBERT BROWNING
Fifine at the Fair, Epilogue, Verse IV

CHAPTER 1

Thursday, October 11, 2012

Jayne checked her watch again as she stepped out of the flow of morning shoppers making their way along Chicago's Michigan Avenue. The stores had been open for an hour along the Magnificent Mile, yet she hadn't gone into any of them. Until now.

Drawn by the power of chocolate, she stood in front of the Ghirardelli shop. It took a moment for her eyes to adjust from the blinding sun of the street to the shadowed entrance. She glanced next door at her beloved Borders bookstore, its windows now obscured by butcher paper. Doors locked and contents dispersed.

A librarian and book lover, she sighed, mourning the loss. Spending hours among those bookshelves would have obliterated all thoughts of her impending appointment.

Chocolate would have to do instead.

She pushed Ghirardelli's door open and breathed. Pungent yet soft chocolate aromas caressed her nose. The vast range of choices assailed her, from dark chocolates riddled with sweet nectars to crunchy nuts. Anticipation tugging at her throat,

Jayne swallowed as she approached the displays. She indulged in her guilty chocolate pleasures only rarely.

"Two dark chocolate truffles, please," Jayne said as she imagined the crinkling of the wrapping when she would strip the foil away and pop the exquisite morsel into her mouth. Her love affair with chocolate had begun with icing slathered on homemade birthday cakes. It had been only milk chocolate then. As the years passed, she had become a chocolate connoisseur. Okay, a chocolate snob, she thought. Now, it was expensive dark chocolate that satisfied her discerning palate.

The clerk looked at her and asked, "Is that all?"

"Yes, that's it for the chocolate," Jayne said. "But I'd like a black coffee to go with it."

Jayne found a table in the corner of the shop. She pulled the foil gently away and ogled the silky chocolate sheen and inhaled the richness of the truffle before breaking it in half and taking her first bite. Heaven melted in her mouth. The velvety texture played on the roof of her mouth and tantalized her tongue.

As she sipped her coffee, her thoughts returned to the bookstore that wasn't there anymore. *All replaced by Amazon and the convenience of the internet.* She thought of the days before the internet or email. Letters had been hand-written, and tattered pages and worn covers showed evidence of repeated readings of paper books.

She focused on her next bite of chocolate, then licked her fingertips and pulled a paperback from her purse. Kindles or iPads still felt too sterile. Nothing beat the feel of a real book in her hands.

Rummaging through her purse again, she pulled out her red-rimmed reading glasses. Wearing them made her feel her age. Reading trumps vanity, she thought, smiling. She put them on and slid them down so she could look over the rims. *Now I've morphed into a typical librarian.* She suppressed the urge to "shush" the other customers sprinkled around the store.

She opened her tome of Robert Browning's poetry and read *Fifine at the Fair* for the umpteenth time. Browning and chocolate—a perfect pairing.

Jayne glanced at her watch again to see that half an hour had passed. She put her book and glasses into her purse, even though she still had another hour before her appointment at Northwestern Memorial Hospital. She took another deep breath as she left the shop and continued her walk down the Magnificent Mile.

When her daughter Kim had been a teenager, the two of them would shop the Magnificent Mile like starving fashion hounds. Mostly for Kim. Jayne never liked spending money on herself. That had been a fun time. She had been happy when the kids still lived at home.

She paused. That seemed like eons ago. Now, Kim lived a two-hour drive away. They never had time for shopping anymore. *Never made the time was more like it.*

She began walking again, wondering why the heck she had come to town so early. But what had been the alternative? Pacing in her living room? No, this was much better. She wished again that Kim was with her today. An emptiness, deep and aching, almost took her breath away.

The crowds on the street began to thicken. Customers packed the Apple store. If her son John were to be found on the Magnificent Mile, it would have been here. He loved every new gadget. *Technology is making everything I love virtual. Friends, books, magazines.*

The smooth tones of Pink Floyd's *Division Bell* alerted her to a call on her cell phone. Hypocrite, she thought, because despite its bare-bones design, she did love her cellphone. No frills like texting. But it served its purpose.

"Hello," she said after grappling with her purse to find her phone.

"You there yet?" Lynn's voice sounded faint among the traffic noise.

"Yeah, just some shopping first," Jayne replied, reaching up to plug her free ear so she could hear.

"You, shopping?" Lynn questioned.

"Desperate days and desperate ways," Jayne said and laughed.

"Call me after your appointment, okay?" Lynn didn't seem to get the joke.

"Will do," Jayne said and flipped her phone shut. She didn't want to think about the appointment and looked for another way to kill time.

She was passing Saks when a dress in the window caught her eye. Simple, but elegant. She stopped to look at it. Glancing yet again at her watch, she had the time to try it on if she wanted to. *But it's Saks. I never shop at Saks.*

She went into Saks, weaving her way past other shoppers on the escalators to scan the dress racks. Limp dresses huddled next to each other, dripping price tags and attitudes. *What am I doing?* she wondered as she pulled the hangers one by one along the racks, remembering her sister's hand-me-downs.

"May I help you?" The petite blonde salesperson tinged the offer with a curl of her lip that became a plastic smile.

Jayne looked up from the rack, tugged at her coat, and answered. "Yes, I'm looking for the black dress in the window display."

"I'm not sure what's on display," the blonde replied. "They change it all the time, but I can show you some of our little black dresses."

Jayne followed the salesperson. *Why am I even in this store?*

"Here you are." The blonde made a dramatic sweep of her arm. "Enjoy."

The black dresses hung in a line like exclamation points in a bad thriller novel. Crammed together, they all seemed the same.

She looked at dress after dress until, ready to concede defeat, Jayne dropped one to the floor.

Cringing, she looked around and picked up the dress, expecting a sharp rebuke from the salesperson. Instead of shoving it back on the rack, she held up the dress to get a better look.

It's the dress. The perfect size, too. She didn't dare look at the price as she took it to the dressing room, the salesperson close on her heels.

"Please let me know if there is anything else I can do for you," the salesperson said, her plastic smile still in place as she pulled the door shut.

Jayne set her purse on the minuscule shelf and hung the dress on the hook. She still avoided looking at the price tag. Maybe the dress wouldn't look good, but at least her curiosity would be quenched. She piled her coat on top of her purse. She glanced in the mirror as she began to unbutton her favorite blouse, a soft lilac silk with ruffles like a poet's shirt.

After undressing down to her underwear, she couldn't help but take a self-deprecating look at her body. No matter how much she dieted, her small belly bulge remained, sharing the space with stretch marks and a slight muffin top. *Of course, visits to the chocolate shop don't help.*

Her gaze shifted up to her face. Not bad, she thought. Oval face. Eyes she always thought were too big. They made her look perpetually surprised. It's the odd color that makes them stick out, she mused. They were hazel, more gold with flecks of green, just like her mother's. Her pale skin had very few wrinkles, just a couple of frown lines between her eyebrows. Those started in her twenties, so they didn't count. Her black hair, cut in a classic bob slightly below chin-length, skimmed her neckline. It looked sleek only after the daily battle between flatiron and curls. She could feel a couple of curls hiding at the back of her neck. *Overall, it's not bad for a fifty-two-year-old mother of two.*

She carefully removed the dress from the hanger. *Armani*, the tag screamed.

Oh God, I really can't afford this.

But on this day, she decided to indulge. She opened the side zipper and pulled the dress over her head. The fabric floated over her body, skimming her curves. She didn't look at her reflection until she finished zipping.

She inhaled and had to exhale consciously. The cupped sleeves hugged her shoulders. The neckline plunged into a deep V, showing pale cleavage. The empire waist made her midsection shrink, and the slight flare of silky fabric ended mid-knee. Imperfections melted away into a sleek silhouette. She turned. Every angle was the same. Perfect. It was her perfect little black dress.

I really look good. This dress was made for me. It is me.

She knew that Tom would hate the dress. He didn't like her to wear anything low-cut. When they went to business dinners, he insisted she dress conservatively, so she wouldn't outshine the hostess married to a president, or vice-president, he had been trying to impress. Yes, Tom would hate it. Because in it, she did shine.

"How are you doing in there?" the salesperson asked through the door.

"Fine, just fine. Thank you," Jayne replied as she began unzipping.

She slid the dress off and hung it up. Now was the time. She looked at the price tag and gulped. *Oh my God!* She had never spent that much money on anything for herself. Ever. *This is what happens when I have some time to kill and there isn't a bookstore. I get myself into trouble.*

I can't do it, she thought as she got dressed. It would be a waste. She remembered her childhood home, a wooden house tucked in a North Carolina holler, rooms stuffed with brothers and sisters.

But now, we have enough money. We are more than comfortable. But still, Tom wouldn't like the dress. It seemed like his career had become the driving force in his life. His job absorbed the man Jayne had thought he was going to be. Over the years, he had become so engrossed in what he called "getting ahead" and "providing for his family" that he forgot to pay attention to anything outside of work. Their marriage had suffered to the point that they acted more like roommates instead of soulmates. *Maybe we were never soulmates.*

She left the dressing room and hung the dress on the rod by the entrance. Plastic smile extinguished, the salesperson's look said, *I knew you wouldn't buy it.* Jayne made her way to the exit, passing by some lacy shawls.

Maybe a shawl. A shawl would tone down the dress. She thumbed through the flimsy fabrics and found a black and white silk that would complement the dress beautifully.

Her conscience tapped at her. *You'll be adding this to the already outrageous cost. You really don't need this. Your mother would think you're a wasteful floozy.*

But I can afford it, and with the shawl, Tom wouldn't mind it.

But...

She picked up the shawl and returned to the dressing room. Picking up the abandoned Armani, she said to the salesperson. "I'll take these." With her conscience squawking like a Myna bird, she paid for her purchase.

Leaving the store, Jayne looked at her watch again. *Almost time.* She quickened her pace along Michigan Avenue but soon had to slow down to catch her breath. The Saks shopping bag swung slightly, the tissue paper crunching around the dress. *How stupid to go to a doctor's appointment toting a shopping bag.*

Guilt tugged at her. *I shouldn't have bought it. It really wasn't worth it. Maybe I could return it.*

Her conscience continued to grumble. She looked at her

watch again. No more time to kill. Time to get to her appointment.

She continued walking, weaving through the people along the avenue. The bag in her hand seemed to get heavier. She could almost feel her watch ticking against her wrist. Her thoughts zeroed in on what she had been trying to avoid.

It was a second opinion. A hope-filled rejection of her initial diagnosis. There must have been a mistake, like in the comedy she had seen on television about switched records. No use to bother the kids or Tom with unnecessary worry.

Lynn knew. Over the years, Lynn had become her only confidant. They would get together for a drink afterward and laugh at the absurdity.

SHE HAD TIMED her doctor's visit flawlessly. That's all she could think about as she glanced at her watch while the doctor began confirming her worst nightmare, the inconceivable absurdity of her terminal diagnosis. She could hear her heart beating in protest as her breath became shallower. The last vestiges of hope were sucked from the room as her doctor spoke.

"I'm sorry, Jayne," he began as he laid down the papers and folded his hands. "There is nothing we can do."

So much for second opinions, she thought, fighting back tears and trembling. The shopping bag crinkled as she shifted her feet, planting them firmly on the floor.

As the doctor continued talking, she turned her blurry eyes toward his medical degree, etched in filigreed letters and framed with burgundy matting. His bookshelves were full of leather-bound books piled neatly on the top shelves. The easier-to-reach shelves were cluttered with paperbacks and books, lying on their sides and compressed into their limited spaces. She could tell his favorites by the fraying on their spines. She wanted to put them in order, even while words like "radiation," "chemotherapy," and "pain" punctuated her thoughts.

"It's in the final stages," he continued. He turned the computer toward her.

The x-ray on the screen seemed to flicker like a gaudy neon placard. Her ribcage exposed, framing her diseased lungs. *So, lung cancer looks like filmy storm clouds with dark splotches.* Her heart fluttered erratically.

She shifted her gaze and focused on the cherry wood desk and the hourglass engraved with the words "To Our Favorite Doctor." His voice became tinny and distant. *God, is my hearing going as well?*

"We can make you comfortable with medication," he stated. "You may want to make arrangements with a palliative care facility when the time comes."

She looked out the window, framed with a green and burgundy plaid valance. Perfect V-shaped fabric trimmed with burgundy beading. His chair matched the valance. So did hers. The work of a professional decorator, no doubt. Efficiently coordinated and matched.

Everything was very professional, except for the messed-up section of the bookshelves.

"Do you have any questions?" He paused.

"Does it ever get any easier to tell someone bad news?" she asked, her southern accent drawing out each syllable and cracking as her tone pitched the question.

"No, Jayne. It doesn't."

She sniffed and swiped at her nose with the side of her hand.

He stood, took off his glasses, walked around his desk, and sat in the chair next to hers. He leaned over and plucked a couple of tissues from the box on the edge of his desk. Handing her the tissues, he gave her hand a squeeze.

He's very professional, she thought as he looked at her stoically.

"I don't even smoke," Jayne said abstractly while trying to stifle an ironic giggle.

Her fifties were supposed to be the new forties. Her mind swirled with questions. Her nose started running and tears threatened. The fluffy tissue became a wet mass that began to disintegrate in her hands.

"How long do I have?" Her voice shook as she dabbed her eyes with a fresh tissue. She grabbed a couple more and shoved them in her pocket.

"Here," the doctor said as he reached for the mass of used-up tissues. "I'll take that." He stood and walked back around his desk and sat down, discarding the tissues in a wastepaper basket.

He doesn't want me to leave a mess.

"It's hard to say," he postured. "Each case can be different."

Predictable. No answers mean he doesn't know, and he's a specialist. "Please, Doctor," Jayne pleaded. "I need to know."

"Six months to a year."

The silence syncopated her ragged breathing as the clock ticked on the wall.

"Thank you," she said. "Now what happens?"

Her voice echoed in her mind and sounded flat, unnatural.

"I have some medications for you to take for the pain, and you can undergo some radiation treatments to slow the growth of the tumors," he replied as he put his glasses on and pulled out a prescription pad.

His pen delineated her new reality of pill-popping. A cure was beyond its restorative powers.

She hesitated, wondering about the nature of this looming pain. "What can I expect?"

"You'll have difficulty breathing, wheezing, coughing, and some weight loss. You've already started to have some bone pain, and you might have to have your lungs drained if the fluid interferes too much with your breathing. These symptoms will become worse with time."

He sounded like he was reading a list of symptoms from a medical journal.

"Well, I guess the weight loss could be a good thing," she said, trying to grab onto humor to steady herself as she blinked away more tears.

The doctor smiled faintly and stood as she did. The smile did not reach his eyes.

"Jayne," he said as he reached out for her hand, "I'm sorry. Call me if you have any questions, and I'll see you in a couple of weeks or sooner if you need to."

She tucked the prescription into her purse as she left his office and walked into the waiting room. The chairs that lined the walls were empty. *Vogue, Parenting,* and *People* magazines lay haphazardly on end tables, their corners curling.

She left the doctor's office and walked to the elevator. *Radiation.* Images of the snap-crackle-pop of the old Frankenstein movies came to mind. The Saks bag felt ridiculous now. Her hand shook as she pressed the down button. *The doctor said six months to a year, even with radiation.*

Two pregnant women waddled out of the elevator, smiling at her.

Jayne watched them for a moment before entering the elevator. As it started to descend, her heart dropped to her stomach. She grabbed the railing as her knees began to buckle. No more denial now. She pulled herself up as the doors opened to the bustling lobby.

A young man in a tailored suit walked quickly, swinging his briefcase with one hand while he talked on his cell phone. Immediately behind him, a middle-aged woman in walking shoes kept pace. She focused on her iPhone, pounding out messages with one hand while cradling her coffee in the other.

Oncoming pedestrians moved out of her way like the

parting of the Red Sea. All sounds were muffled and tinny as Jayne entered this beehive of activity. It was all so normal. The world went on as usual. Only she had changed.

As she made her way to the train station, the street vendors hawked hot dogs to passersby. Traffic clogged the streets, and impatient cabbies honked their horns as if that would make the light change quicker. Shoppers balanced large bags with "Macy's" and "Nordstrom" in giant letters on their sides. They walked like tightrope acrobats, tilting to maneuver through the crowd. Even though she had her own logo-embossed shopping bag, she didn't belong anymore.

She went with the flow, caught up in a gaggle of people. She glanced at her reflection in the building windows. She didn't look any different.

Finally seated on the L, she stared out the window where the city of Chicago faded into the suburbs. She pulled out her cell phone and scrolled through the list of contacts to Tom's number. Her finger hovered over the button, but she flipped the phone closed and shoved it back into her purse. She stared out the window, shivering.

Just as the doors were closing, a young businessman jumped through the entrance. He yanked on his tie, loosened it a couple of inches, and looked around for a seat. With nothing available, he balanced against a pole and shrugged.

Guess he won't get any extra work done, Jayne thought.

The young man reminded Jayne of her husband. Tom had been the city boy who captured the poor mountain girl's imagination. She had met Tom on one of her visits to her cousin Lynn's home in Asheville, North Carolina. Tom had been gregarious and confident, everything she wasn't.

She couldn't believe it when this dapper young man had paid attention to her. They had married young. He went to school, became an accountant, went back to school, and now was a treasurer in a top Fortune 500 company in Chicago. Yes, she had a beautiful home in Naperville. She had all the material things she could ever want. But that had never been her focus. A small house with a white picket fence would have been just fine.

After another stop, a seat opened. The young man grabbed it, flipped open his computer, and furrowed his brow as he waited for it to come to life. He tapped his foot until the *bing* called to him, and he began typing furiously. Jayne fought the impulse to go over and close his computer and tell him to slow down. *Don't forget what's important. It goes by too fast.*

Jayne closed her eyes. Her husband had become virtually a stranger in the house, even when the kids had been home. She had put everything into raising her children. After the kids left home, she had to do something or go crazy. Lynn had convinced her to go back to school and get her degree. A major in library science with a minor in English had filled the void.

Now what? Am I being punished for some reason?

Tears threatened. She squeezed her eyes tighter and swiped at the corner of one eye.

Her Southern Baptist teachings taunted her. There were supposed to be rewards for those who "do the right thing." There was an order to the world, and she had always followed it. She thought there would be time later.

She opened her eyes as the train came to another stop. A young mother seemed revived by the brief respite of sitting as she ushered her kids off the train. The young girl squealed when her brother gave her a shove. Crumbs littered the seats where the woman and her children had been eating chips, and an elderly couple wiped them off with a tissue before sitting down. Through the din of chatter and engine sounds, Jayne overheard snippets of the couple talking about these "young people today" and shaking their heads. The elderly man made sure to seat his wife comfortably before he sat down next to her. He patted her hand and then continued to hold it as the train started again.

When was the last time she had held hands with Tom?

She thought about her kids, Kim and John. How was she going to tell them she wouldn't be around when they married or had their own kids? How would she tell Tom? They barely spoke anymore unless it had something to do with their jobs or the house. He didn't even seem to notice. She kept it all inside, living through her books and waiting patiently for the future. He had always promised, "We will be set in our retirement. We'll travel and see all the places you've talked about."

God, so much wasted time.

As the train clanked along, the scenery changed from a stream of concrete and red brick into a cascade of autumn-colored trees. Jayne blinked as she took in the splashes of brilliant yellows, oranges, and reds. The last flash of life before the leaves withered, browned, and dropped to the earth.

She searched through her purse and took out her cell phone again. Without hesitation, she hit number one on speed dial to Lynn.

On the second ring, her cousin picked up.

"I've been waiting for your call," she said, echoing a similar Southern drawl. "What happened?"

"It's not good, Lynn," Jayne replied.

"I should have gone with you. Come over here, right now."

"Can't. Tom's coming home early."

"So what?" Lynn huffed. "He can pick something up on the way home for once. I've got plenty of wine in the fridge. I'll be on my way in a few minutes."

Jayne paused for a moment. "All right, I'll call Tom."

She hung up and stared at her cell phone for a moment. *What should I tell Tom?* She had kept her doctor's appointments to herself. She had complained about shortness of breath, but Tom always responded with "probably just allergies" or "you're not as young as you used to be." When her symptoms had gotten worse, Lynn had convinced her to go in for a checkup. That had been about ten weeks earlier.

She had kept her family in the dark, not wanting to worry them needlessly. *Now what?*

She punched Tom's office number.

"What's up?"

Jayne paused. Guilt tugged at the corners of her conscience.

"Jayne?"

"I'm on the L and I can't hear you clearly." She took a deep breath. "I'm going over to Lynn's house, so you'll be on your own for dinner tonight." She waited.

"Why?"

"We just need some girl talk."

"I planned to come home early."

"I know, but you know Lynn. I can't say no to her."

"Yes," he puffed. "You need to learn how. I guess I'll just keep on working and have something delivered."

"Okay, thank you."

"Bye."

She slipped her phone back into her voluminous bag and watched the cookie-cutter houses of the suburbs emerge. Sometimes, she'd complained about all the late hours and time away on travel, but he always said he worked hard to provide a quality standard of living for his family. A house in the suburbs, two cars in the driveway, a full closet of clothing, and two children put through college. That equaled love.

Jayne had always pictured a more romantic view of love. Cuddling on the couch. Watching a classic movie while feeding each other popcorn and washing it down with an exquisite wine. Long walks in the park. Travel to exotic locations. Tom told her that she'd find her version of love only in soggy romance novels and romance didn't pay the bills. She had believed him when she was young, and he was still someone to look up to. Now, she lived vicariously through her books. There had to be more to romance. Too many poets and writers had immortalized their love stories. It had to be real. Attainable.

Her thoughts were interrupted by the computerized voice: "Rosemont, next exit."

She gathered her purse and made her way to the exit. Waves of regret assailed her as she waited for the doors to open. So much time wasted. So many opportunities passed by. Why? What was her purpose for being here? Aren't you supposed to find your purpose before you die?

She stepped off the train. She felt the same physically as she had this morning. The only difference between this morning and now was "knowing" instead of "hoping."

CHAPTER 2

Thursday, October 11, 2012

Jayne scanned the Naperville train stop's parking area, her stomach tightening and lower lip trembling. I'm going to lose it, she thought until she spotted Lynn's red Mustang GT. The sporty car had been Lynn's fiftieth birthday present to herself. Lynn was like that. She plunged into whatever she wanted to and always seemed to come out on top. That's what made her one of the best marketing consultants in Chicago.

"Hey there," Jayne said as she pulled the car door open and threw her shopping bag in the back seat. "Thanks for coming."

"Don't be silly," Lynn said. "Get in and let's rev it up."

The engine roared and Lynn peeled out of the parking lot. Jayne relaxed into the leather seats and inhaled a shaky breath.

"It's official, Lynn." Jayne pulled a wadded tissue from her pocket. "I don't know what I'm going to do. I don't want to be a burden. How do I tell everyone?"

"Honey, I'm so sorry." Lynn reached one hand over and touched Jayne on the arm. "No matter what you do, I am always here for you. Same as when we were kids."

"I know." Jayne sighed as she remembered the childhood

scrapes and teenage melodramas. "I think I already knew it, deep down," Jayne said as she shifted in her seat and blew her nose. Her skin prickled as she coughed deeply and couldn't catch her breath.

"Do you want me to stop?" Lynn asked.

Jayne finally caught her breath and shook her head.

"No, don't stop. I'll be all right." Her hands trembled as she wiped away tears.

Lynn didn't let up on the gas as she turned into her subdivision. Jayne gripped the door handle. Each executive home was angled slightly off the street, offering private views of the trees lining the stream that meandered through the premier backyards. The trees that bordered the beautifully landscaped yards had turned Jayne's favorite shade of autumn red.

Lynn hit the garage door opener and roared into the space. In a single fluid motion, she slammed the gear into park and turned the key to kill the engine.

"Red or white?" she asked as she led Jayne into the kitchen.

"Whatever you have is fine," Jayne replied as she took off her coat and draped it over a chair. She piled her purse and shopping bag on it.

"Jayne, that's the trouble with you," Lynn said. "You never choose what you want. Choose, my friend." She shrugged out of her coat and tossed it over the back of another chair.

"Okay, red," Jayne replied. Her back and shoulders hurt. *Bone aches already?* She concentrated on relaxing her muscles. *Nope, not yet.*

Lynn poured two full glasses of Merlot and nodded toward the living room. "Let's get a fire going."

Jayne's mind buzzed with half-finished thoughts. *Why? What now? I'd better arrange it so ... John would ... Kim doesn't have ...*

Oversized furniture and plump pillows filled the living room. A brown leather couch and loveseat created an *L*-shaped corner, and a red chair angled on the other side created a large open area in front of the brick fireplace. Jayne collapsed into the depths of the loveseat and studied the oil painting over the fireplace. The abstract fusion of deep blue and yellows, with chunky tinges of red firing through the center of the canvas, distracted her for a moment. "Did you buy that at this summer's art fair?" she asked, digging deeper into her thought diversion.

Lynn handed Jayne her glass. "Yeah. It spoke to me." Lynn set her glass down on the end table. "Oh, I forgot the music." She flipped on the gas fireplace, then dug through her purse. With her precious smartphone in hand, she turned on the high-end German sound system nestled on a shelf, then tapped on her phone until the soft beginnings of Pink Floyd's music filled the room. Lynn loved the latest technology. Jayne still listened to CDs.

"To our favorite group," Lynn said as she sat down and lifted her glass. Jayne nodded as she raised hers.

Sipping her Peju Merlot, she savored the flavors of plum, blackberry, and currants. The wine warmed her as she swallowed. Creating a wine this exquisite was an art, she thought. Why hadn't she taken more time to enjoy these simplicities instead of rushing through them to get on to the next mundane something?

"How do I tell the kids?" Jayne asked. There it was. Out loud. Real. Diversion over.

"I don't know."

"I can't believe this."

"I know. It sucks and I don't know what to say."

"Nothing to say."

"I'm not sure what to do next. I had something, but I don't know if it will be right … now." Lynn leaned back and took a huge swallow of wine. She gazed into the fire, a vacant look in her eyes. Her brows furrowed for a few moments and her face tensed.

"Earth to Lynn," Jayne said, trying to break the spell.

"Just a minute," Lynn said as her face relaxed. "I'll be right back." She rose and left the room.

Jayne sank into the couch and let the notes from the song caress her. This music always lifted her, floating and swirling, through the moment unscathed. Out of reach. The notes of the piano subtly reached deep into her conscience. Now, the guitar took over where the piano left off. Soaring effortlessly.

"Pink Floyd and Victorian poetry," Lynn said as she returned with an envelope and handed it to Jayne. "I still don't understand how a southern girl like you can love old poetry and classic rock music at the same time."

"It makes perfect sense to me," Jayne said as she sat up and turned the envelope in her quivering hand. "What's this?"

"I had a friend make the arrangements when she was in London a few weeks ago," said Lynn as she sat down again and picked up her glass. "I thought it would cap off a celebration of the greatest misdiagnosis on earth."

Jayne set her glass down and opened the envelope. She pulled out an airline ticket to London. She looked at the dates and her jaw dropped. "Lynn, are you crazy? Three days until the flight?"

"I bought you a ticket for a European tour," she said as simply as if she were commenting on the weather. "The bus tour is connected to British Airways, so your airfare is covered too. I didn't want to give you time to think yourself out of going. That's why it is such short notice. All part of my surprise."

"What are you talking about? I can't go anywhere now."

"This isn't exactly what I had planned, but still… what better time, Jayne?" Lynn said. "You have always wanted to travel. It can still be something extraordinary. You can use the time to figure out everything. You have your passport from the trip we took to Canada several years ago."

Lynn sat back expectantly and then continued when Jayne

didn't reply. "You've read about these places for years. Your poets were inspired by them. You're always talking about how you and Tom are going to travel the world, when or if he ever retires. What do you have to lose? Isn't it time that you took a couple of weeks out of a lifetime for yourself? Especially now?"

Jayne watched the hearth with its fake logs and dazzling flames while she assimilated the second shock of the day. *European tour? Now? In three days?* She sipped her wine and looked at her crazy cousin. Lynn always did things out of the ordinary. Single and loving it. She was also a woman with a more-than-successful career. From greeting card companies to sporting goods, she could brand and market anything. Consumers responded. She traveled throughout the States to cover her accounts. Jayne had always envied Lynn's independent streak. Lynn had chosen her career over a family.

"I don't know, Lynn. It doesn't seem right."

"Jayne, just do it."

"But what about Tom?"

"Jayne, he's a grown man and can take care of himself."

Jayne gulped her wine and extended her glass. She had a momentary regret for not taking time to savor the tastes, but right now, she needed the numbing power of alcohol more. "I need a refill, my friend."

Lynn didn't take the glass but went to the counter and brought back the bottle. She filled Jayne's glass and topped off her own.

"Well?" Lynn said as she leaned back into her couch.

"But I'm not sure I should go alone." Jayne squeezed her cousin's hand. "Maybe Tom could go with me."

"Right, just like he's gone on all of the other trips." Lynn sipped her wine with one hand and continued to hold onto Jayne's hand.

"Well, you know."

"You have to admit that sometimes you resented him, didn't

you? Just a bit?" Lynn released her cousin's hand and moved toward the fireplace.

"Maybe so," Jayne conceded. "But I chose him. And I was always there for the kids. That was my choice, and I don't regret it."

"I know," Lynn said. "You have great kids." She sat down on the floor and placed her glass on the coffee table.

"And I went back to school." Jayne sipped her wine.

"Yeah, but too late to really have a career." Lynn leaned forward to tuck a pillow behind her back.

"That's important to you, not me," Jayne replied. "I went back after the kids were gone."

"I know." Lynn downed a healthy swig of wine. "Do you remember how mad Tom was after you got your tattoo?" Lynn laughed through a hiccup.

"How could I forget?" Jayne said. "John thought we were all crazy."

"And Tom wasn't at the graduation … putting himself first as usual."

Jayne furrowed her eyebrows.

"A Victorian tattoo," Lynn laughed. "Right on your butt."

"And your tramp stamp!"

"I know. Fitting, right?"

"I still can't believe I did that. I blame Kim. She bought us those drinks after graduation and then kept taunting us, saying we wouldn't do it," Jayne said, laughing.

"I know," Lynn laughed too. "I can still see the look on her face when you stripped off and lay with your butt in the air."

"I love my tattoo," Jayne said.

She swirled her wine, watching the viscous liquid slowly drip down the inside of the glass.

"Now you're going to have to tell Tom," Lynn said as she refilled her drink.

"Talk about a shift in conversation," Jayne replied. "You're ruining my buzz."

"You should have told him from the beginning."

"Maybe." Jayne continued to swirl the dark ruby wine in her glass.

The phone rang and the stilted voice of the caller ID repeated: "Tom Thompson." *Chastising me,* thought Jayne. *Mocking me.*

"Do you want me to get that?" Lynn started toward the phone. "Jayne?"

Lynn didn't wait any longer for a response and picked up the phone.

"Hello, Tom," she said. "Yes, Jayne is still here. In fact, we've decided to make it a girls' sleepover. We haven't done that in years. You don't mind, do you?"

Jayne shook her head and mouthed the words, "No, I'd better go."

"Good, good," Lynn replied, waving Jayne off. "I'll bring her home bright and early in the morning on my way to work." She hung up and turned toward Jayne. "We're all set, my dear."

"Lynn, you're a hypocrite," Jayne said as she pulled her blouse away from her stomach and swiped at her forehead. *If the room is getting hotter, why am I shivering?*

"How am I going to talk with Tom if I stay here?" Jayne added.

"Okay, duly noted," Lynn said as she raised her glass and nodded. "I'm a hypocrite because I really don't give a flip about Tom. He always takes care of himself."

Jayne sighed deeply, which made her cough again.

"Are you all right?" Lynn hurried over to Jayne's side.

"I'm sorry. I know you get sick and tired of being the referee between Tom and me. I'm an ass."

When Jayne regained her breath, she gulped down a healthy

quantity of wine. "I believe I need to be topped off," she said as she handed her half-empty glass to Lynn.

"I'll pop open another bottle," she replied as she emptied the remains into Jayne's glass. She took the empty bottle to the kitchen.

Jayne followed, leaning against the granite countertop. The house had an open floor plan, with the living room leading into a huge kitchen. The countertop curved around a sink. During parties, everyone congregated around the counter and talked during meal preparation. "We haven't done this in ages. Do you remember when we had sleepovers as kids?" She absently traced the patterns in the cold granite with her index finger.

"Yeah, we always had a lot of fun." Lynn smiled as she cranked the wine opener into the soft cork. "Remember when we turned up the stereo so loud that the house shook?"

"How could I forget?" Jayne said. "My first introduction to Pink Floyd."

"Yeah." Lynn pulled on the cork, and it came out smoothly. "My brother's precious record. Remember how mad he was when he found out we'd stolen it?"

"God, do you know how old that makes us sound?"

Lynn came back to the living room and refilled the two glasses. Jayne followed and reached out to take hers.

"Now, with iTunes, iPods, and 'i' everything, kids don't have to steal their siblings' stuff." Lynn laughed and motioned toward the fireplace. "Let's go prop up by the fire." She put her glass on the mantel and scattered throw pillows on the floor. "Make yourself comfy."

Jayne looked at the pictures on the mantel. Lynn looked the same in every shot. Golden blonde hair, thick and perfect. Large blue eyes fringed with thick lashes. Pert body from working out and never having kids.

There were shots of Lynn and her brother, Lynn and Jayne's family from Christmas two years ago, and shots of Lynn in

Texas, California, and New York, with a different man in each. Cowboy hat and jeans in Texas. In California, an athletic, sun-streaked blond. Whether the streaks were natural or manufactured, who knew? A dapper, coiffed Italian man with the New York skyline in the background. Pictures of men that Jayne would never meet, and Lynn had probably forgotten.

Jayne lay down on her stomach and stuffed a pillow under her chest and arms.

Lynn sat down on a pillow and crossed her legs. "I guess we just take it all for granted. We get caught up in the day-to-day crap and let it suck our time away."

"All the moments blur into each other, don't they?" Jayne gazed at the fire. "Guess Shakespeare's right. We spend our lives ranting and raving on our stage of life and the effort seems to signify nothing."

"I don't know about Shakespeare," Lynn asserted, "but that doesn't sound like you. You have two great kids. Kim's a wonderful teacher. And I won't be surprised if John becomes a business tycoon."

Jayne sucked down her wine and pressed her lips together. "It's so unfair." She fought the urge toward a slow decline into a pity party.

Lynn jumped up and picked up her smartphone. "Oh, here it is." She cranked up the sound just as the clocks began to chime in the song. After the cacophony of sounds, the lyrics filled the room, and Lynn began to sway to the music.

"Come on," she motioned to Jayne. "Let's do our air guitar and lip sync."

Jayne shook off her thoughts, got up, and waved her invisible microphone.

Lynn played a mean air guitar with exaggerated movements.

They joined their voices to the band's. Off-key but remarkably right with the words, they looked at each other as the song continued. The words washed over them.

As the song wound down, Jayne bowed to the pretend audience, and Lynn waved her air guitar. The song faded away.

Jayne had heard these words a million times. But now…

Now, they had a different meaning that hit her like a sucker punch.

"The doctor said I have a year … at best. A single, solitary year."

She looked at Lynn and the tears poured out. They hugged each other as another song began. Both shuddered and cried through it.

"Okay," Lynn said as she rubbed her hands across her eyes. "Enough."

"You're right. I will not spend the rest of my time on this earth crying."

Lynn picked her glass up from the mantel and drained it. She handed it to Jayne. "You refill and I'll get some munchies."

Still sniffling, Lynn pulled out chips and salsa from the pantry, along with a bag of pretzels and some crackers. "That should satisfy our salt cravings." She placed the junk food on the counter, then large wedges of Monterey Jack and Baby Swiss cheese from the refrigerator, which she began slicing and placing onto a platter. In a matter of minutes, Lynn arranged a junk-food feast.

Jayne brought the two empty glasses and the bottle into the kitchen, filled the glasses from the new bottle, and sat at the counter.

"Dig in," Lynn said as Jayne handed her a full glass of wine.

"I haven't had chips and salsa in a long time," Jayne admitted as she scooped up salsa on a chip. "I forgot to tell you the good news. The doctor said that I will definitely lose weight." She choked out a thin laugh as she washed down the salty chip and spicy salsa.

"Oh, Jayne," Lynn said, "I'm—"

"Do you remember when we used to raid your mother's fridge in the middle of the night?"

"Yeah." Lynn paused as she fumbled with a slice of cheese and tried to wedge it between two crackers. The cheese fell back on her plate. "I caught hell from her when she found her ice cream stash gone."

"Remember when your brother hid in the closet for hours and jumped out?"

Jayne could almost hear the shrill screams and the satisfied look on Mark's face. His patience had been rewarded, and he still teased them about it. She hadn't seen Mark in ages.

Visiting Lynn and their sleepovers were the only fond memories she had from her childhood. It had been a temporary escape from her straight-laced parents. A house nestled in the mountains of North Carolina. Chores. Church. Strong reserve. They were her roots.

A little lightheaded, Jayne felt the room tipping off-center. *Must be the effects of the wine.* "I'm enjoying our pig-out session here. From now on, we have to pay attention. No more rushing through each day," Jayne said.

"You have a few glasses of wine and now you're a philosopher?" Lynn raised her glass to her cousin.

They both sipped their wine, savoring the mixture of sweet, dry, salty, peppery, and cilantro flavors folded into a subtle wine-infused moment. The music shuffled, and Pink Floyd echoed once again, softly intruding. The irony wasn't lost on Jayne as her favorite song, "High Hopes," filled her soul.

CHAPTER 3

riday, October 12, 2012

The birds chirping outside seemed to have megaphones pressed against the window. Jayne's head throbbed against her pillow. *Who knew birds could be so loud?* Shifting slowly to her back, she wrapped a heavy arm over her eyes and squeezed. Her stomach churned.

Last night, the room had spun like a Tilt-a-Whirl carnival ride. She pried one eye open just as three taps assaulted her ears. Rapid heartbeats pounded in her chest, but the room was back to normal. She put a hand on her clammy forehead as Lynn opened the door, flipping the switch.

The overhead light beamed like the lamp in a lighthouse. Both her eyes opened wide against their will. Windows of pain. Her head pounded in heavy rhythm to her thoughts. *I'm an idiot. I'm an idiot.*

"I thought you might need this," Lynn said. Balancing a tray in one arm, she made room on the bedside table for the tray laden with two cups of tea, a pile of lightly buttered wheat toast, and a bottle of Tylenol.

Jayne struggled up, her head like a lead weight, and stuffed her pillow behind her back. The bed creaked in protest to the shuffling. Or maybe it was her bones … or a combination of both. She fought dry mouth to form words that tasted sour.

"Thanks, you're an angel, cousin mine."

"Nothing close to it."

Lynn picked up a cup of tea and handed it to Jayne.

"I'm afraid this is it. My best breakfast effort," Lynn said as she picked up the second cup of tea and sipped it gingerly. "How do you feel?"

"Like I'm dying," Jayne replied and winced. "As if I didn't have enough to deal with, I had to add a hangover to my list. Not exactly the right choice, was it?" She shook her head but stopped mid-shake as the room spun slightly. She took a hesitant sip of her tea.

"Do you want to stay here today? I can take you home after work." Lynn took a slice of toast and nibbled on it.

"No, I have to get going," Jayne said sluggishly. "I'm scheduled at the library today. I'll be fine once I get something in my stomach and pop a couple Tylenol."

"Okay, I'll see you in about half an hour." Lynn left with a teacup in one hand and her toast in the other.

Jayne's stomach was balled up and her bones really did ache. She reached for the toast and took a bite, waiting to see the result. *Please God, let this settle my stomach. I know it's my fault, but can you see your way to helping me get past this morning without getting sick?* As an afterthought, Jayne wondered whether she had just wasted a prayer that she might need later.

After several tedious bites of toast, a couple of Tylenol, and sips of tea, Jayne's stomach seemed to settle down to a point where she thought she might be able to get up. She swung her feet over the edge of the bed and let them dangle. The bed creaked again. So far, so good.

Jayne had always liked Lynn's guest bedroom. The furniture was dark cherry wood, and the comforter offered a flourish of pink and red roses intertwined with green vines. The room reminded her of a summer rose garden, complete with the comforts of petal-soft bedding. Plus, it had its own ensuite bathroom.

Leaning over the sink, she splashed lukewarm water onto her face. Her nose mocked her by remaining swollen and congested. She reached for the tissue and tried to clear her sinuses.

As she threw the tissue away, her mind drifted back to the doctor's office. She tried to take a deep breath, but her lungs hardened like cement. No matter how hard she fought, the air simply would not penetrate her lungs. *God, and it's only going to get worse.* The effort was like trying to blow up a balloon made of iron. Nothing would give.

She looked at her reflection again. Breathe, breathe, she thought. "Come on, Jayne," she said out loud in quick puffs, "you've got to hold it together." She bent over the sink and concentrated. Finally, the air started filling her lungs. *At least I didn't erupt into an endless coughing fit this time.*

She washed the remnants of the previous day off her face and put some toothpaste on her finger, doing her best to clean her teeth. She would love to hop in the shower, but that would have to wait until she got home. Thank goodness Lynn would be driving, she thought. Mornings were a blur until after a good pelting in her shower, especially after tying one on the night before. She brushed her hair and dressed. The morning ablutions so far would have to do for now.

Hearing Lynn in the kitchen, she took the tray downstairs.

"Good," Lynn said as she looked up from the sink as she rinsed dishes and put them into the dishwasher. "You look like you're hanging in there."

Jayne smiled. Lynn wore a perfectly tailored dark blue suit that hugged her petite curves. She had her taupe briefcase sitting on a chair along with her cashmere coat. Not a shred of evidence of a hangover.

"Lynn, how do you do it?"

"Do what?"

"Recover from a night of drinking without showing it," Jayne said, making her way toward the chair in the kitchen where she had dumped her stuff last night.

"Unfortunately," Lynn replied as she shrugged into her coat, "it's a result of practice. I think I indulge in the forbidden fruits more than you do, my friend."

Jayne went to the pile on the chair, moved her purse and shopping bag to the floor, and slipped into her coat.

"That shopping bag is from a very expensive store," Lynn said as she moved closer.

"Yeah, I had too much time before my appointment yesterday." Jayne laughed and then coughed.

Lynn reached over and rubbed Jayne's back. Then she picked up the shopping bag and took out the dress. "Wow, this is beautiful. Nice going."

"Thanks." Jayne took the dress and shoved the guilt-ridden purchase back into the bag, then followed Lynn to her car.

Lynn pulled into the driveway of Jayne's sleek ranch with the gray stone and golden trim and put the car in park.

"Jayne, think about the trip. It's only a few weeks. Please let me do this for you now." Lynn began to tear up. She swiped under one eye and looked at her fingers.

"Don't cry now," Jayne begged. "I have to face Tom and act normal." She got out of the car and retrieved her purse and shopping bag. Then, she leaned down. "I'll think about it, Lynn. Thanks for everything."

"Ditto, girl. Now, I've got to get out of here and get to work." Lynn put her foot on the brake and put her car in reverse. "Call me tonight."

"All right. Thanks again," Jayne said as she slammed the car door shut. Making her way up the winding path to her front door, she wondered whether Tom had already left for work. The garage doors were closed, so she couldn't tell. A flutter of hope flitted across her consciousness, but it was snuffed out like an extinguished candle as she opened the door.

"Is that you, Jayne?" Tom called out from the kitchen.

"Yes," Jayne replied. "I'm home." She slipped out of her coat and dropped it with her purse and shopping bag on the couch. She found Tom at the kitchen table, in the crook of a bay window, sipping coffee and reading the paper on his iPad.

"Good morning," he said as he looked up. "Wow, you look awful."

"So much for a good morning with that comment," she said as she made her way to the cabinet, retrieved a cup, and poured herself some coffee.

"Jayne, you know I didn't mean it that way," he corrected.

"What can I say?" Jayne replied as she sipped her coffee. "We tied one on last night."

"I'm not surprised," Tom said as his attention shifted back to his iPad. "When Lynn is involved, nothing you do surprises me."

"I know, I know. She's a wild one. But she's my best friend, Tom."

"Well, we'll talk later," he said as he shut off his iPad. "I have to get to work. I have a lot of things in the pipeline. You know the boss. If I'm not getting results at the rate of a supercomputer, then he thinks I'm slacking. I'm not sure how I'm going to manage all of it. We're really swamped."

He put his empty coffee cup in the sink and gave Jayne a cursory kiss on the cheek as he left the kitchen. "Take a nice hot bath and you'll feel better, Jayne." With that parting comment, she heard the front door slam shut. The silence of the house engulfed her.

She sat with her coffee cup poised in midair with her elbows on the table, staring out the window. *Should I tell him now?* There was nothing anyone could do. Sipping her coffee, she wondered what he would do when she did tell him.

Cold realization washed over her, and she shuddered slightly. She could almost hear his reaction. First, there would be shock. Then, a bit of blame. He always blamed her for any action, or even inaction. And then, he would wonder how it would affect his time at the office. She was sure of it. The room seemed to tighten around her like shrink-wrap. The air didn't move.

She dumped the rest of her coffee down the sink and went to the master bedroom. The contrast between this bedroom and her cousin's was remarkable. The furniture was dark and heavy. The curtains and the bedding were dark green with gold stripes. Tom didn't like frills. He never had. She used to think that was what made him so strong, but now she wasn't sure. Sensitivity in a man wasn't such a bad thing. She had come to realize that there was room for both. At least in her mind, but never in Tom's.

She filled the large bathtub and reached under the faucet to let the water pour through her fingers. Transparent like my future, she thought. She dumped some lavender bath salts into the tub. Seeing her nude reflection in the mirror as she stepped into the bath, she thought abstractly that she didn't look like a woman who was dying.

The water caressed her as she sank down. She pressed the button and the jets began to swirl the water, pelting her spine, sides, and feet. She leaned her head back and immersed herself in the luxury. The smell of lavender drifted in the steam that rose from the bath. She inhaled carefully and closed her eyes. Images fluttered by. Soft sunshine on a field of flowers. A hillside peppered with red flowers, standing in contrast to the green grass. Skies the blue of a robin's egg. No clouds in sight.

She opened her eyes and reality hurtled back. When she had started feeling bad, she had agreed with Tom that it must just be the effects of aging. She wasn't in such good shape anymore. She rarely exercised, so naturally, she would be a little short of breath occasionally. After all, she had never been in her fifties before, so how was she supposed to tell the difference?

She had suffered from allergies all her life, so when she developed a cough, she just chalked it up to the wee beasties attacking her sinuses. It was only about ten months ago that she started waking in the middle of the night, unable to breathe if she was lying on her back. She would sit up suddenly, gasping for breath. The first time it happened it had been terrifying. She thought her allergies were triggering asthma. The suffocating lack of air squeezed her lungs painfully. Tom, as usual, had slept right through it. She convinced herself that it had to be asthma. She had put off seeing the doctor because the symptoms just seemed to slowly creep up on her. Anyway, there was always something else more important to do.

And now it was too late.

She finished bathing and drained the tub. In her closet, she chose black pants and a green and black-striped turtleneck. It was a simple but striking outfit that brought out the green in her eyes. Back in the bathroom, she applied base makeup, blush, and other beauty products to help mask the evidence of time passing. Her hand twitched as she applied her mascara. *Steady now, don't poke your eye out.* She finished with a light application of peach lipstick.

In the living room, Jayne sank onto the couch and stared at the cold fireplace with its stone hearth and oak mantelpiece. She reached around to rub her aching lower back and took a deep, ragged breath. Her eyes settled on the bookshelves flanking the fireplace. One side was filled with accounting, finance, economics, and the latest on business tactics. Tom's side. Her side was filled with Victorian and Romantic classic novels and poetry. Her love of England and British literature had started when she was in middle school. First, the Brontë sisters, then Austen. On her shelves, they shared space with Byron, Trollope, Dickens, the Brownings, and Shelley. Sprinkled among those tomes were historical romances and travel books. Her shelves were stocked full, so she had resorted to storing books in closets and drawers. Her copies of Samuel Butler's *The Way of All Flesh* and *The History of Victorian Tattoos* were among her hidden treasures, along with a box full of antique inkwells and quills. Maybe she should stay home, burrow into her bed, and read one of her favorites.

No, she would not hide. She would be strong for the kids. Strong for herself.

She would follow through with her commitment to the library and try to think of her options. Since the kids had left home, getting her degree and working at the library had kept her sane. But they didn't fill the void. Her children had always come first. In any decision.

How do I tell them? It's going to mess up their lives.

Other than Lynn, she decided to keep her illness to herself for a while longer.

It only took her ten minutes to walk to the community library. The quiet wrapped around her like a soft blanket. The only sounds were the slight hum of the computer terminals behind the checkout desk.

The latest books took center stage in the current display, resplendent with autumn colors providing a backdrop for scarecrows and skeletons. Boney hands positioned against best sellers. Maria, a volunteer librarian, whispered, "Good morning," and continued to help the patron checking out a stack of romance novels. Jayne nodded as she entered the office and softly closed the door.

Sheila, the head librarian, looked up from her desk and nodded as Jayne shrugged out of her coat and hung it on the coat rack. Jayne sat down at her desk and flipped on her computer.

"I'm glad the inventory is finished," Sheila said. "What a job! You were great with the spreadsheet."

"What are assistant librarians for?" Jayne quipped. "In fact, I'm tired of being tied to the computer. Do you think I can simply shelve books today?"

"Sure, no problem. Enjoy." Sheila went back to tapping away on her computer keys.

"Thanks." Jayne left the office and went to a cart filled with books.

The first book she picked up happened to be one of her favorites. It was a collection of poems by Browning, not Elizabeth but Robert. She had been introduced to the pair in one of her favorite college courses. The love story between Elizabeth and Robert had immediately intrigued Jayne. The two poets had admired each other from afar based on their poetry. Elizabeth had been bedridden with a lung ailment, but that hadn't stop Robert from romancing her. He literally visited her in her sick room and, through love and determination, helped her regain her strength. Eventually, they married and even had a son. What a real-life story of true love, she thought. And for the first time, she envied Elizabeth. If true love wasn't just the stuff of fairy tales or romance novels, why hadn't Jayne experienced it?

She flipped open the book, squinted, and read the first page that appeared:

"Grow old along with me!

The best is yet to be,

The last of life, for which the first was made:

Our times are in His hand

Who saith "A whole I planned,

Youth shows but half; trust God: see all nor be afraid!"

She quickly closed the book. She had read this poem many times before, but the potency of each word seemed new. Growing old was no longer an option for her. As far as the best that was to come, she doubted that. Having no fear and trusting

God? She would just have to try her best. Placing the book back in the cart, she pushed it along the aisle in an attempt to control her emotions.

She began shelving books almost blindly until she paused when she saw a Frommer's travel guide of Europe. She opened it to the section on Italy and read Frommer's "favorite" experiences: Visiting the Art Cites; Dining Italian-Style; Attending Mass in St. Peter's Basilica; Riding Venice's Grand Canal; Getting Lost in Venice; Spending a Night at the Opera; Shopping in Milan; Experiencing the Glories of the Empire.

Just browsing the list led Jayne to picture the magnificent ruins that made Rome a city that she had always admired. She continued to muse about a gondola ride down Venice's Grand Canal. Her interest in the Brownings had sparked a desire to see Florence, the city they had lived in until Elizabeth's death.

The city where Elizabeth was buried.

"Excuse me?" A twenty-something woman intruded on Jayne's musings. "Can you show me where to find books on the history of economics?"

Jayne replaced the travel guidebook in the cart. "Yes, of course," Jayne replied as she pushed her cart aside and led the patron to the correct section of the library. She then returned to shelving books.

For the rest of the day, Jayne managed to concentrate on entering data into the computer and checking out books. When her short break time came, she took a few books to the office. She heated water for tea, put on her reading glasses, and opened her first book.

She had nicknamed these much-perused volumes her "dream" books. One, *The English Guidebook,* had vistas of Britain. Its pictures of patchwork fields, thatched-roof cottages, and cobblestone streets filled her imagination with thoughts of the generations of people who had eked out meager livings, and walked or rode horses on those same cobblestones. The images were stereotypical, but she loved them. Rain-soaked roads, rolling green hills dotted with gray stone manors, all peopled with imaginary figures from novels and poems. She could imagine Mr. Darcy entering his sprawling estate, or Mr. Rochester riding his horse on the battered country roads.

She sipped her tea and set the book aside, picking up another. This book focused more on history than travel. Tintern Abbey in Wales appeared as she turned the pages and tried to fill in the gaps with her imagination. She mentally fleshed out the remains of the skeletal structure with glorious stained-glass windows and buttresses spanning out to support the walls. She could almost hear the monks' chanting that must have echoed throughout the rafters during its prime.

She traveled from the chapters on Wales to Scotland with its lochs and craggy mountains. The photo of Eilean Donan Castle was her favorite. It wasn't the most famous, but the photo drew her in every time she looked at it. The ruins were nestled on a small island, joined to the mainland by a footbridge. Mountains loomed in the distance, and Jayne inhabited the stark image with the ghosts of men in kilts and women watching sparring matches in the workout field. Bagpipes, wailing their mournful songs, always accompanied any thoughts she had of Scotland.

The thought of bagpipes echoed as she realized her dreams of visiting all of Britain would remain just that—dreams. Images and fantasies that had sustained her for years. Wasted years spent dreaming instead of living.

She had lived when she raised her kids, not needing the dreams as much then.

Setting the book aside, she refused to dive into another pity party. Lots of people hadn't realized their dreams. She was no different.

Her next favorite book offered picturesque views of the Italian countryside. She could see why a lot of her favorite British writers ended up in Italy. Vibrant green fields with fleeting splashes of red flowers. Vineyards snaking through the countryside next to groves of olive trees. Byron, Shelly, Keats, and, of course, the Brownings all used the vitality they found in Italy to stoke their creative fires. There was just an energy that seemed to reach out and engulf her. She pictured Lord Byron, Percy Shelley, and Mary Shelley sitting around the fireplace on a cold night in Ravenna. They had decided to tell ghost stories. *Frankenstein* emerged as the winner of this storytelling contest. What would it have been like to hear its original telling?

She stood, took off her glasses, and dumped her now cold tea in the sink at the back of the office. Then she took her dream books and returned them to their proper places on the library shelves. As she went through the rest of her day, she couldn't shake the possibility that she had a brief chance to turn at least one regret into an opportunity. She thought about the ticket her cousin had given her.

Was it possible?

As her shift ended, she approached Sheila with her tentative decision made.

"Sheila, I need some time off," she said. "I need at least the next three weeks and possibly more."

"What?" Sheila asked as she pulled off her reading glasses.

"I know that it's short notice, but I really need some time. I've never used my vacation days, and Maria can fill in for me. She knows her way around spreadsheets as well as I do."

"What's going on, Jayne?" A frown etched into Sheila's forehead. "Is everything all right?" "Can I do anything to help?"

Jayne shifted her weight from one foot to the other. "No, nothing."

"Are you sure?" Sheila narrowed her eyes. "I'd like to think we have a friendship, not just a working relationship."

"Yes, I know." Jayne nodded. "Believe me, if there was anything you could do, I'd ask. Right now, I just need some time off."

"Take as much time as you want. And, if you need me, please don't hesitate to call."

"I'm sorry about the short notice." Jayne glanced at the floor.

"Don't you worry about a thing. You have been a godsend here." Sheila stood and stepped around her desk. "Hurry back. We'll miss you." She wrapped her in a firm hug.

"Thank you for everything." Jayne turned and left quickly before she broke down.

She arrived home, physically and mentally drained from hangovers, work, and mental jousting. Now that she knew there was a sinister cause to her shortness of breath, aches, and fatigue, they felt more acute.

As she plopped her bag on the couch, she heard the rattle of the prescriptions she had filled on the way home. The grandfather clock began chiming. Another day winding down. She had a couple of hours before Tom got home.

She carried the shopping bag to her bedroom. After hanging the dress in her closet, she draped the shawl on a hook, and folded up the bag, placing it on the top shelf. Stripping off her work clothes, she slipped into her comfy beige sweats.

Crawling into bed should have been soothing as she snuggled under the striped bedding. Instead, repetitive thoughts that she had kept at bay all day accosted her. Squeezing her eyes shut didn't help. How was she going to tell her children and Tom? Life was never going to be the same for any of them.

She covered her head with her arm and squeezed. God, she thought, it's really not fair. A voice seemed to whisper, "Life is not fair. Fair is a place with amusing rides and cotton candy." She tossed and turned, trying to flee from her thoughts. Flipping on her back, she stared at the ceiling. Her limbs seemed to melt into the bed and she inhaled. She tried to inhale again. Nothing. Her lungs turned into liquid, and she wheezed without the ability to bring in fresh air.

Panic consumed her as she sat up, gasping for air. Glimpses

of Tolstoy's fictional Ivan Ilyich, propped up in bed surrounded by pitying loved ones, sprouted from her dark imagination. She slumped over and gave in to a fresh wave of tearful self-pity.

Enough, she thought after a few moments of self-indulgence. She was not going to pity herself out of existence. There was going to be enough of that from others. She resolved to face her future with an awareness that she had never been able to muster before. One precious day at a time. Live every minute left to the fullest. Those would be her two affirmations from now on.

She slipped out of bed and went to the living room for her purse, where she pulled out her cell phone.

She hit speed dial and waited.

"Hello, Mom," Kim said. "I just got home from school. What's up?"

Jayne paused before responding. "Nothing, I just wanted to touch base. How is everything?"

"I'm swamped as usual. I have a ton of papers to grade."

Jayne could hear her daughter shuffling papers while she was talking. "When do you get some time off?"

"Not for quite a while," Kim sighed. "I have some extra projects going on, as well."

"Well," Jayne replied. "I'll let you get to it."

"Okay, Mom." There was a slight pause. "Is everything all right?"

"Fine, dear," Jayne lied. "Everything is fine. I'll talk to you soon."

"Love you."

"Love you, too." Jayne severed the connection and pressed the phone to her forehead. *Coward. Not really. I just need more...*

Then she hit her final speed dial entry and waited.

"Hello, Mom," John answered. "I'm inundated right now. Can I call you back later?"

"Of course, dear," Jayne replied, her heart sinking a little. "I just wanted to say hi and tell you I love you."

"Love you too, Mom," he replied hurriedly. "I'll give you a call later when I get a chance. Bye."

The connection severed immediately.

Jayne went to the kitchen and began preparing dinner. As she pulled the fresh tilapia from the fridge and sprinkled seasoning over the white filets, she continued to think. *What were the important moments of our lives?* She wrapped the fish in foil and placed it in the oven. Retrieving salad makings from the fridge, she splayed out the items and began to mindlessly chop green onions, tomatoes, and mushrooms. Tossing the salad items into a large bowl, she covered it and placed it back in the refrigerator. She would wait until the fish was almost done before putting the vegetables in the microwave.

Sitting at the table nestled in the bay window, she looked outside. Giant oak trees loomed over the summerhouse they had in the backyard. A rose garden filled with flowerless stems, covered with containers to protect them against the winter. The leaves littered the yard with a crispy burnished crust. A brown squirrel made jerky movements as its head darted back and forth. It dug through the leaves to retrieve an acorn, tucked it in its mouth, and ran straight up a nearby tree. Another squirrel bravely came up on the back stoop. It seemed to look straight at her. Its whiskers twitched, perhaps signaling in some sort of code. It stood on its hind legs and cocked its head. Jayne didn't move but kept watching. She wasn't sure who was watching whom. Time seemed to stop as the two surveyed each other. Then, the oddest thought popped into her head. *Will that squirrel still be here when I'm gone?*

She shook her head as the timer for the fish went off and she finished preparing dinner. Almost on cue, Tom came through the back door.

"Something sure smells good," Tom said as he entered the kitchen.

"It's just fish," replied Jayne as she set out plates and utensils.

"Nonsense, you're a great cook. I'll change and be right in." Tom swept past her as always.

So many lost moments, she thought, along with so many missed opportunities. She poured two glasses of iced tea and sat at her place at the table.

"Boy, I'm hungry," Tom said as he sat down and began to pile salad on his plate. "Do we have any of that salad dressing I like?"

Automatically, Jayne went to the refrigerator and retrieved the low-fat ranch dressing.

"Here you go," she said as she handed it to him. "How was work?"

"We're really busy," he said, and then stuffed his mouth full of salad. He swallowed and took a drink. "Dan has asked me to take on the monetary budget for the next quarter in the office. You should have seen Joe. He was livid. He thought he had the project in the bag." Tom laughed and speared a carrot. "If I do a great job, I'm sure I'll get a promotion out of this one."

"So, this would not be a great time to take a break, right?" Jayne asked hesitantly.

"No way," Tom replied as he poked some flaky fish into his mouth. "I'll have to put in a lot of overtime to get this project going. And you know Joe's going to have his goons looking over my shoulders. He's just waiting for me to make a mistake. I'm going to have to do a lot of research and get my team to check and double-check the figures."

The clock sounded from the hallway while dinner continued, punctuated with small talk. Tom simmered with excitement about his new job prospects before leaving the table to go to his study to finish off some work.

Jayne began clearing the dishes, thinking about her options. She could tell her family about her illness now and perhaps start some radiation treatments. Or she could wait until she looked sick and had no choice but to tell them. Guilt started to tug at her. The ringing of the phone interrupted her thoughts.

"Phone, honey," Tom called automatically from his study. She had always hated that. She could hear as well as he could and knew he would never answer it.

"Hello," Jayne said as she picked up the landline.

"Hey, kiddo," Lynn said. "How are you?"

"I'm still here," she said, "for now."

"Have you thought any more about the trip?" Lynn asked. "You only have a couple of days before you need to leave."

Jayne paused. Should she? Her mind drifted back to the pictures she had looked at in the library. So many missed opportunities. Was it selfish? What was a couple of weeks, anyway?

"Who is it?" Tom shouted.

"It's just Lynn," she replied as she put her hand over the mouthpiece. She heard a muffled "oh" in response as she tossed her options around.

"I know," Jayne continued.

"I can hear an excuse coming," Lynn said. "Why wait? You can take this time and think about everything. You can also see the places you have always wanted to see. I really don't see the problem, Jayne."

Jayne waited for the lecture to continue, but silence crept through the calling space. Slowly, pictures of castles, vineyards, and Italian landscapes danced through her mind, filling the silence. The tentative decision gave way like a dam bursting.

"I'm going," Jayne said, not believing the words coming out of her mouth.

CHAPTER 4

Sunday, October 14, 2012

Jayne found an odd sense of contentment in the music filtering through the lobby of the London hotel. She clung to the classic rock music like a child holding her mother's hand. She felt like she was floating in a sea of Jell-O. English accents mingled with French and Spanish, creating a background of white noise. *Maybe this is jet lag.*

Tugging at the bottom of her sweater and smoothing out non-existent wrinkles, she walked through the lobby. Already checked into her room, she was on her way to a meeting for the tour but decided to stop in the hotel bar for a drink. There was enough time. It wouldn't help her jet lag, but it might calm her nerves.

The mahogany bar and dark paneled walls made the atmosphere heavy. She could feel people staring at her as though they knew she had never entered a bar on her own before. As she made her way among the solid, dark wood tables and chairs to a corner, she realized that no one had really noticed her entrance. She could hear her son's voice taunting her: *Calm down, it's just a drink. Get a grip.*

Choosing a seat with her back to the wall, she wiped her upper lip where she felt a bit of moisture and checked the edge of her sweater again. She scanned the menu's list of wines, then flipped to the pages of beer. Nothing she recognized popped out. She stopped scanning when she saw "Nip," described as a mixture of strong barley wine and an ordinary bitter.

The waiter appeared to pour her a glass of water. "The Nip, please," she said with fake confidence, shifting in her chair as if she wanted to burrow into it. She fumbled in her purse for her prescription bottle. The trip had taken a toll on her aching bones. She washed two pills down quickly, ignoring the warning labels. *It doesn't matter now, does it?*

She ran her hand over the smooth surface of the table. Typically British, she thought, just like the photos in my travel brochures and dream books. The wood was worn but shone through many coats of wax. The well-stocked bar was rimmed with mirrors reflecting the bottles on the shelves. Each bottle had a unique shape and color that hinted at a rainbow of tastes. Her leg pumped up and down under the table.

A brown-haired man at the bar cradled a glass of scotch that quickly disappeared. Next to him was a young woman with a tight black sweater and equally tight jeans. She was drinking something light and fizzy in a fluted glass that she took dainty sips from all too frequently. There were a couple of empty seats, and then, a good-looking man frowning over a pint of dark beer.

Her stomach flip-flopped for a moment as she continued to stare. A brown leather jacket that was crinkled with age hung over the back of his barstool. He raked his fingers through his chin-length chestnut hair, flecked with scattered strands of gray. Her grip on the glass of water tightened as she thought about the way the easy waves in his hair fell right back into place. I am going crazy, she thought, but continued looking. One leg dangled down the side of his bar stool, apparently ready to make a quick retreat should someone invade his space.

She coughed slightly as her eyes focused on the man at the end of the bar. His profile was chiseled, with a square jaw and oblique angles. She wondered how he would look if those features relaxed into an unguarded smile.

The waiter returned and set the dimpled pint mug in front of Jayne. By the time she paid and the waiter left, the man at the end of the bar had gone. Too bad, she thought, as her heart sank like it did when she finished a good book. Jayne shook her head and slowly lifted the pint to her lips. She drank and savored the rich mix of barley and hops that tingled her tongue and warmed her throat. As she enjoyed this first sip, she chastised herself for jumping on a plane to fly halfway around the world and ogling a man who just happened to be sitting at a bar.

It had only been a couple of days since she'd had clashed with Tom over the trip. It was right after the phone call from Lynn. She had decided to tell him everything, but his reaction to the trip alone was so over the top that she had kept silent about her illness. Instead, she focused her waning energy on justifying her trip. On Saturday, she had called both kids. Kim immediately thought it was a great idea. But John sounded like a recording of his father. He had asked her if she was sure she could handle being on her own in a strange place, just as his father had. Anyone who had overheard his end of the conversation would have thought he had been talking to an incompetent child.

The rest of the day involved packing. Lynn had come over and helped. Jayne had tried to talk Lynn into coming with her, but Lynn had declined. Jayne had tossed and turned all night. When she managed to go to sleep, dreams of flaming planes and falling from the sky jarred her awake.

Early Sunday morning, Lynn had dropped her off at O'Hare International Airport, and she had flown on her first international flight. Perfectly safe. No falling involved. Now, she sat in a pub in the London Hilton on Park Lane.

She sipped her drink and checked her watch. As more customers entered the bar, the air seemed to become denser. She wheezed a bit, which triggered another cough. She downed the last of her drink quickly and left the bar, following signs pointing to meeting rooms. She fussed in her purse until she found the right piece of paper. The tour group was supposed to meet in the Churchill Room to discuss the itinerary and rules for the trip. They were going to start tomorrow morning in London, then take the ferry across the Channel to France, a more picturesque way to cross than the Eurostar underground tunnel, and then continue on to Switzerland and Italy.

At the door to the meeting room, she heaved a quick sigh. *I can do this.* She felt her nerves tingling and became a little light-headed. *Maybe I shouldn't have had the Nip.*

She shoved the papers back into her purse before she pulled the door open. It was a smaller room with blue and white wallpaper. Chairs were lined up in rows. There were about twenty people already seated. Everyone was chatting, but Jayne didn't understand a word. *Great.* She was about to embark on her dream tour and no one even spoke her language. Talk about doubting a spur-of-the-moment decision.

She saw an older couple sitting in the last row. "Is anyone sitting here?" she asked, her Southern accent more pronounced. Relief washed over her as the gray-haired gentleman smiled and replied in English, with a Midwestern accent: "Nope. Have a seat."

His gray hair looked like it had been red when he was young, and his bright blue eyes twinkled with mischief.

"Please, my dear, sit down," the elderly woman next to him echoed. Her hair was short and a beautiful shade of silver. It accented her features and her petite frame.

"We're the Parks." The elderly man continued. "I'm Floyd, and this here is Emma."

"We're glad to have another American with us," Emma said.

"Me too. I'm Jayne." She sat down and pulled a notebook from her purse as some of her doubts began to melt. Meeting people had never been easy for Jayne. She preferred the solitude of a good book. She mentally repeated one of her new affirmations: "Live every minute left to the fullest."

A few more people entered the room, and as Jayne looked up toward the front of the room, she dropped her pen.

"Here you go, dear," Emma replied as she slowly bent and picked up the pen.

The microphone flickered with static as the handsome man from the bar, with the frown and crinkled leather coat, stepped to the podium.

"Welcome to Hasting's European Tours." He shifted uncomfortably and continued, raking his hair back again. "My name's Mason and I'll be your guide throughout this tour." His voice sounded rote has he itemized the cities. "... London, Paris, Lucerne, Lugano, Venice, Florence, and Rome. Our tour begins at nine tomorrow morning. Breakfast begins at seven a.m., and we'll meet in the lobby at eight-thirty. It'll be a full day, so wear comfortable clothing." He slipped off his coat, tossing it onto a nearby table. He moved from behind the podium towards the first row of seats. "Now, let's all get to know each other." His voice became more natural. His gray-blue sweater fit snugly and accentuated his eyes, which were the exact same color.

"I guess I'll start," he continued. "I was a musician in my former life. I have been with Hasting's Tours for almost fifteen years now. I have degrees in social history and speak eleven languages." He paused and raked his hand through his hair once again. "Now, it's your turn."

The introductions began, and Mason translated flawlessly, first in Spanish, then in another language, and finally in English.

His voice was low and measured. It matched the rest of him. She wondered which language was his native tongue. When he spoke English, it sounded almost perfect. Was he as fluent in all the other languages as well? The introductions were animated with laughs and exaggerated body gestures. He seemed natural with each group.

There were four couples in their mid-thirties from Brazil, who looked like photocopies of each other. The men had short, curly hair grazing the tops of their necks in the back and receding to mid-forehead in the front. They all wore the same shade of khaki pants. Polo sweaters emblazoned with Ralph Lauren logos completed their outfits. The wives were petite with long, shiny black hair pulled back from their faces with decorative barrettes at each side of their heads, right above the ears. They all wore colorful sweaters, and their jeans were tucked into their knee-high boots. It looked like the couples had shopped together to coordinate their outfits just for the trip. They smiled broadly and waved their hands as if pushing the words along to the back of the room. Mason translated from Portuguese that these couples were professionals, two dentists and two lawyers, from Rio de Janeiro. They were on their second tour because they liked the difference between Europe and their own country.

The next group was a mixture from a Spanish tour company. One retired couple was taking their grandchildren on the tour. The rotund grandparents looked like Mr. and Mrs. Santa Claus, while their grandchildren were entering their awkward phases of pubescence. Jayne guessed they were about twelve or thirteen years old.

There was also a young couple, probably in their mid-twenties, on their honeymoon. Even as they introduced themselves, they only looked at each other. Jayne tried to remember whether she and Tom had ever looked at each other like that. Their blue eyes sparkled as they held hands and sat with their taut young bodies touching. He was tanned, his brown hair streaked with blond by the sun. He reached up with his free hand to stroke her long blonde hair. She leaned into his light touch. Their love glowed for everyone to see.

Next, there was Natalie, a college student from Universidad Complutense de Madrid studying religion. She was a plump girl who wore no makeup, and purple-framed glasses balanced precariously on the tip of her nose. Her face seemed to hold a look of perpetual curiosity.

The next row of seats had just one woman about the same age as Jayne. She had long black hair and dressed very European, wearing a tight, low-cut angora sweater and sleek, tapered pants. Her perfume filled the air around her. Ms. Rosa Perez was the only one who stood to introduce herself and told the group that she was an interior designer from Madrid. She spoke in accented English about wanting to "experience Europe in every way possible and had heard wonderful things from her girlfriends about this tour." She looked expectantly at Mason as he translated. Then, she added that she was glad that the group wasn't full of old people who would slow things down. During her introduction, she focused her gaze solely on Mason.

Every man in the room watched Ms. Rosa as she wiggled back down to her chair before shifting their attention to the last row.

"We're Floyd and Emma Parks from Eaton Rapids, Michigan. This is our fiftieth anniversary present from our kids and grandkids." Floyd hugged his wife like a newlywed. "And we're spry and will try not to hold you youngsters back." He winked at Rosa.

Now, it was Jayne's turn. She had always hated these types of introductions, but she plunged in anyway. "I'm Jayne Thompson from the Chicago area, and seeing England and Europe has always been my dream ... a dream of a lifetime." She could hear her Southern accent stretch out the vowels as she spoke.

Mason stared at her. She tried not to sink into those gray-blue eyes. Her breath seemed to catch in her throat. *Had I said something wrong?* She shifted in her seat, broke eye contact, and scribbled curlicues on her notepad. The silence seemed interminable. Finally, Mason translated what she had said, and everyone clapped. Big smiles and exaggerated nodding of heads dissolved her momentary discomfort.

"That's all I have for now." Mason returned to the podium. "If some of you would like to go to dinner, *Galvin at Windows* is a restaurant on the twenty-eighth floor. It has great ambiance and views of Buckingham Palace and Hyde Park." He ran his fingers through his hair as he paused. "For others, I have the Executive Lounge reserved for drinks and hors d'oeuvres. We can mingle and continue breaking the ice."

Jayne listened to his voice as he shifted effortlessly between languages.

"Jayne," Floyd's voice intruded, "why not join us for dinner?"

Jayne turned to face the Parks. "Thanks, but I'm not really that hungry."

"Okay, but the invitation is out there for you anytime during this trip. We don't want you to be alone."

"You're very kind. I'll see you in the morning."

Jayne turned to leave, but Mason had moved to her side. He stood about a head taller than her. He smelled like evergreen and sunlight.

"I know it seems overwhelming," Mason said, looking at the Parks and then focusing on her.

Jayne's mouth dropped slightly. *How could he know?*

"All this translating is confusing at first, but you'll soon get used to it."

Oh, Jayne thought, that kind of overwhelming. Still, the air was charged like lightning bugs flitting erratically.

"Do you have any questions?" Mason shifted his stance and threw his jacket over his shoulder.

"Nope. We're going to check out that restaurant," Floyd replied and rubbed his tummy.

Emma laughed and patted his arm. "I think the Brazilian couples are going that way, too."

"What about you?" Mason asked, as Natalie, Rosa, and the newlywed couple formed a group behind him.

"I guess I'll just get something light from room service," Jayne said.

"That's no fun. Come with us to the Executive Lounge. Mason said it has a great view," Natalie said as she leaned around Mason and pushed her glasses up the thin bridge of her nose with her index finger. Her accent was very heavy, but Jayne understood what she said.

"We could have some girl talk," Rosa said, with a pronounced rolling of the "r" as she moved to stand by Mason's side.

His forehead crinkled a bit as he shifted his position.

Jayne wondered why Rosa had invited her. Girl talk seemed a stretch as Rosa ogled Mason blatantly.

Jayne's affirmations overruled her instinct. *Live every minute left to the fullest. One precious day at a time.*

"Okay, let's go," Jayne said, thinking she'd rather be snug in bed with a room service tray, watching the BBC. Other than Lynn, she really hadn't had close girlfriends. She'd rather curl up with a good book than hang out with people. She mentally repeated her affirmations. Her mantras.

"Follow me." Mason walked to the door with his jacket still thrown over his shoulder. Her eyes slipped down his back to his muscular butt and legs. She glanced away quickly, only to find Rosa taking in the view as well. As Mason pulled the door open, he held it and motioned for everyone to go through. Jayne heard a disappointed sigh from Rosa as she had to relinquish her view.

The group followed Mason to the elevator and filled it. Rosa was closer to Mason than she needed to be. He didn't seem to mind. Natalie was in one corner, while the newlywed couple cuddled in the other. The air in the tight space seemed to congeal. Jayne held back a cough and watched Rosa's shoulder touch Mason's arm. As they arrived, Jayne lost her battle with her cough. It was deep and raspy. Rosa's reaction was to quickly exit and leave everyone behind. Natalie placed her hand on Jayne's back.

"Are you okay?" Mason asked as he held his hand in front of the elevator door so it wouldn't close. The newlywed couple stepped past her and stood by Rosa.

"I'll be fine," she said as she coughed again. She left the elevator with Natalie close behind. "You go on ahead, and I'll catch up."

"I'll stay with her," Natalie volunteered.

Mason nodded and led the rest of the group down the hall. Jayne pulled a tissue from her purse and coughed into it once again. She didn't examine it as she put it in an outside pocket of her purse.

"That did not sound so very good," Natalie said as she patted Jayne's arm. "I hope you are not going to get sick."

Jayne smiled. "Let's catch up with the rest."

They walked down the hall and heard Rosa's voice above the rest, rattling syllables together in Spanish.

"This must be it," Jayne said as she motioned for Natalie to enter first.

Rosa was talking with the newlywed couple, James and Julia, from what Jayne could recognize. They all had drinks in hand. There was a bar at one end of the room and an hors d'oeuvres table at the opposite end. Tall round tables were spread around the center of the room. No Mason in sight.

"I understand the young couple's names," Jayne said to Natalie, "but what else is she saying?"

Natalie listened for a moment and then blushed a bit.

"Is it bad?" Jayne asked.

"Well, she says she doesn't believe in marriage. But she says they have courage to try it. She also says that a group tour doesn't sound like a great idea for a honeymoon."

So much for girl talk, Jayne thought as she looked at the couple. Their faces were frozen. Huge eyes and jaws slightly dropped. Didn't Rosa see the reaction?

Mason appeared in the doorway. Jayne and Natalie moved to the bar and ordered drinks. Jayne ordered another Nip and saw that the bartender was surprised. She smiled and looked back at Rosa and the couple, who had been joined by Mason. They moved to a round table so the newlyweds could put down the plates of food they had been holding.

"Want to go to this table?" Natalie asked with her Guinness in hand.

"I've got an idea," Jayne said. "Why don't you go up to the newlyweds and ask them to join you here and I'll stay with Rosa and Mason?"

Natalie nodded her head. "Nice idea." She walked over and the newlywed couple smiled and moved rather quickly to join Natalie. Jayne had used the intervening time to fill a plate with food.

"Can I join you?" Jayne said as she placed the food in the center of the table. "I brought a little of everything." She picked up a cheese puff and put it in her mouth.

"Sure," Mason said. Rosa nodded as she finished her wine and handed the empty glass to Mason.

He raised his eyebrows but went to the bar for her refill.

"We were just talking about marriage and relationships," Rosa said. "Mason and I agree that they are superficial. They never last. Why not just know that and enjoy as many lovers as you can?"

Mason returned with Rosa's drink and grabbed some bits of cheese from the plate.

"You agree, *si?*" Rosa said as she raised her glass to Mason.

"I've never been married," Mason countered.

"What about relationships?" Rosa asked and tilted her head. "I'm sure a man like you had plenty of opportunities?"

Jayne was beginning to second-guess her own idea. Her face was on fire. She couldn't believe the provocative questions Rosa was asking complete strangers. She glanced at Natalie, who seemed to be having a great time with James and Julia.

"What about you?" Mason said.

"What?" Jayne wanted to sink into the floor. Instead, she took a large sip of her Nip.

"What do you think about relationships?" Rosa asked.

"I believe that lasting love is always possible, even though it may be rare," Jayne replied.

She noticed them both glance at her wedding ring.

"So, what do you do when you aren't on vacation?" Jayne asked quickly, hoping they'd shift to the new topic.

She held her breath.

"As I said before, I'm an interior designer," Rosa said. "I love color and texture. I hope to gain some inspiration from my trip. Lots of inspiration." She moved closer to Mason, who had grown silent.

"That sounds wonderful," Jayne sighed and reached for another hors d'oeuvre. "Mason, where do you call home?"

"Everywhere." He picked up his drink and drained half of it.

"But where do you live?" Rosa persisted.

"I have lofts in Paris and London." He finished his drink in another gulp.

"Interesting," Jayne said.

"Very nice." Rosa rolled her "r" again, leaning forward with her elbows on the table.

"Why?" he asked, glancing at Rosa before shifting his focus onto Jayne.

"I wouldn't have guessed you were from either place." Jayne tried to place his accent and it simply didn't fit.

"I'm not," Mason added as he took a cheese puff. "I'm Canadian."

"I've never been to Canada," Rosa said as she finished her drink. "You'll have to tell me all about it."

Jayne watched Mason's gaze roam from Rosa's face to her cleavage. Then, her heart skipped a beat when he looked at her.

She reached up, trying to smooth out one side of her hair. She downed the rest of her Nip.

"Well, we have a full day tomorrow. We'd better call it a night, ladies," Mason said as he turned and moved away from the table. "Can you find your rooms?"

"No, I'm not sure where it is," Rosa said with a well-practiced pout.

"And you?" Mason nodded toward Jayne.

"No problem," Jayne said. A sinking feeling rose in her stomach as Rosa put her arm around Mason and left the room.

CHAPTER 5

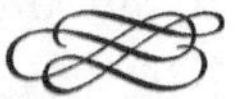

onday, October 15, 2012

Jayne pushed through the hotel revolving door into a damp gray day. The air was thick with mist that looked ready to coagulate into dense droplets. Moisture draped around her as she saw the bus down the street. *The weather is perfect. Perfectly British.*

This was it. Today, her dreams would give way to reality.

She had dressed in layers with brown khaki pants, a starched white shirt, and a button-up sweater with swirls of brown, green, and rust in amoeba-like patterns. Over her outfit, she wore an aptly named London Fog overcoat that hung open. On her shoulder, she carried a large purse with her maps, notebook, and umbrella stuffed inside. She had left her cell phone at home, truly severing her connection for the next couple of weeks. Lynn had insisted on lending Jayne her old iPod, which was neatly tucked deep in her bag.

With her free hand, she pulled at her hair. She had fought her riotous curls, an inheritance from her father, for almost twenty minutes with her flat iron that morning.

The doors on the tour bus swung open like a warm embrace.

She grabbed the railings and looked up into the smiling face of the driver. Deep dimples appeared on the sides of his face, parentheses for his gleaming white teeth.

"Bonjour," he said in his perfect French accent. His blond hair was clipped short, yet shaggy. "How are you today?" he continued, accenting the words in a way only the French could do.

"Wonderful, and you?"

"This English climate is not good for me. You see, I am French," he tilted his head and showed the palms of his hands as he shrugged. "But soon enough, we will be back on the Continent, where the sun will shine again."

She touched the velvety seats as she edged down the narrow aisle and chose a seat in the middle of the bus. She saw a thin sheen of water on the road and thought again about the typical English rainfall. Kim would have enjoyed it. Visions of her as a little girl, nestled by the screen door, listening to raindrops pound on the metal awning, flitted through her mind. A sense of isolation quickly followed, pressing down on Jayne as she turned to watch the bus fill with strangers.

Mason climbed in and spoke to the driver. "Rain or shine, *mon ami,* our tour will go on." Standing beside the driver, Mason introduced him as Jacques and began to outline the day's activities. He was dressed in jeans again, with another tight sweater and the same leather coat.

Jayne thought he dressed a bit young for his age and couldn't help wondering what had happened between him and Rosa last night. She pulled out her notebook and pen. She hadn't slept well. Every time she closed her eyes she thought of Tom or the kids or second-guessed her decision to be here.

Finally, she had gotten up at four a.m. and began writing a letter to her daughter. Hand-written. Old-fashioned. Shaky cursive smeared with teardrops. Full of dreams for a future that Jayne would miss. It was a letter that would never be mailed but opened at the appropriate time.

She had indulged in "why me" again … for a short time. Spawned by the writing. This is the last time, she thought as she resolved to look at each day as a gift to be lived without any more regrets. She hadn't finished the letter but set it aside to work on during her tour. She resolved to write one for her son, as well. The lump in her throat threatened to push out some more tears, so she repeated her affirmations, which had morphed into a single mantra. *Live each day to the fullest, with no regrets.*

Jayne repeated it as she followed Mason's hand movements counting heads. She turned and nodded to the Parks. The young college student smiled and pushed her glasses up while the other members of the group chattered.

As Mason's voice became a background hum, Jayne looked past the condensation dripping down the windows. It was hard to believe she was here, putting herself first for once. When the kids had been involved in sports, theatre, and the many other activities that occupy kids in junior high and high school, Jayne had played cook, chauffeur, costume designer, and whatever roles the kids needed. She had been a good wife and mother. Hadn't she?

The bus began rolling, soon passing the Houses of Parliament and Big Ben. Jayne strained to see the clock tower as the bus turned the corner. One, two … nine times it rang, and goosebumps covered her body. She had looked at so many photos of these facades in her books. Now, faced with the reality, she felt like she had left her body and was floating on a cloud.

The bus stopped and Jayne followed the rest of the tourists who took photos in the rain. She craned her neck, gazing at the tower against the light gray sky. It was perfect. She hadn't brought a camera on purpose. The sights and sounds of rain were etched in her memory. That was all she needed. The experience of the reality and complete separation from home.

The tour passed by Downing Street and continued to Piccadilly Circus. Bubbling excitement made Jayne tap her foot on the floor. The next stop was at St. Paul's Cathedral. Everyone got off the bus and it pulled away to park, leaving behind the smell of exhaust mixing into the rain.

Mason led the group to the beautiful entry of the cathedral. Their subdued mumblings attested to their reverence. Huge carved doors loomed at the entrance of the nave. The Great West Door swung open dramatically to a scene beyond Jayne's imagination. She had seen pictures of St. Paul's, but nothing had prepared her for the beauty of Christopher Wren's masterful artistry. The black-and-white checkerboard floor streamed forward into the vestibule strewn with ornate columns and circular magic. In the distance was the high altar that seemed an eternity away.

"It's beautiful, isn't it?" Floyd said as he and his wife caught up with Jayne.

"Breathtaking."

"The dome is actually constructed in three layers," Mason interjected as he strolled over to them. They walked to stand directly underneath the looming dome.

"Exquisite." Jayne looked straight up into the dome and thought she was glimpsing into a bit of heaven. The golden arches framed scenes of the sublime. "What artistry. Is it painted or mosaic?"

"A bit of both," Mason replied as he moved closer to Jayne. "In the beginning, it was hard to get the right mosaics, so they created paintings. Later, the mosaics were added."

"How could one man have such imagination?" She looked at Mason. "What a gift he left the world."

"Indeed." Mason moved on to the Brazilian members of the group and began translating for them.

"I thought our churches were wonderful," Emma said, her voice subdued. "But this is extraordinary." She clasped her husband's hand, and they walked from under the dome to a circular alcove that housed a marble font. Jayne watched the older couple as they moved in unison. They walked slowly, with a noticeable effort required to bend their stiff joints. Floyd put his arm around his wife as they stood silently in the alcove. Jayne turned away, feeling like a voyeur, and went up a staircase to get a closer look at the dome. Memories of the wood-framed church she had attended in North Carolina came to mind. Peeling paint, rough-hewn pews, and well-worn floorboards accommodated the religious services there.

She had to stop twice as she climbed the spiral stairs that curled along the edge of the dome. Her lungs simply shut down. She sat on the steps until she could continue, praying no one would see her. It wasn't fair. She pushed this thought away as soon as it appeared. When she reached the top of the first level, Mason was there with Natalie and Rosa. The curved gallery spread around her with windows lined with saintly figures. The wrought iron railing glistened, golden even in the dim light from outside.

When she joined them, he said, "Rosa and Natalie both speak English, so I'll switch." Mason smiled.

Jayne thought his smile looked a bit forced.

"I was just telling the ladies about the special acoustics in this area of the dome."

"This is the Whispering Gallery, isn't it?" Jayne had read about it.

"Yes. I'll go to the other side, and you sit right here, Jayne."

Her name sounded a bit foreign coming from Mason. The gentle touch of his hands seemed to burn through her coat as he guided her up a couple of steps to the built-in bench circling the dome. He seated her and told her to keep her head back against the wall and look straight ahead. Before long, he was directly across from her, over a hundred feet away.

"Does this live up to your dream trip of a lifetime?"

She heard the whispered question and jumped. It sounded like he was sitting next to her, whispering in her ear. She turned her head and whispered back, "I could have never dreamed this vividly."

She waited and was satisfied when Mason's eyes met hers for a moment. He didn't move at all. For a moment, they were transfixed, connected by something Jayne couldn't pinpoint. Maybe it was just the majesty of the place.

"My turn." Rosa shattered the brief silence as she pushed forward.

Natalie smiled sheepishly, and Jayne moved to the ledge and gazed at the scene below. Rosa whispered. Jayne didn't hear what she said. She got lost in the geometric precision of the muted pink and green center fanning out in the checkered floor. Swirls of black and white created the foundation for a ceiling with bursts of golds, fuchsias, and blues, a rainbow of celestial phenomena.

It's stunning, she thought as a soothing warmth began to spread throughout her body. *Simply stunning.* Gratitude swelled in her chest as she soaked it all in.

I'm here. I'm really here.

She made her way to the steps before Mason and the others, not wanting them to see her gasping for air. But going down was much easier. She didn't have to fight gravity. Her footsteps echoed with hollow clicks. With each step, she wondered if Tom would have enjoyed the view.

No, he would have been on his iPhone.

She thought about her children all the way down the stairs, out of the cathedral, and into the bus. She began to scribble furiously in her notebook, vision blurred by tears. A salty mix of joy and sorrow. She swiped at them with her finger as the bus began to move.

The tour continued with a stop for shopping along a narrow English high street. Jayne stayed on the bus. She didn't need anything. Her last shopping excursion had resulted in her Armani purchase, which was now neatly packed at the bottom of her suitcase. She hadn't even shown it to Tom. It wasn't the cost that kept the dress a secret. She just couldn't face the criticism of her choice or even the potential lack of interest. *Yes, I am a coward,* she thought. She would probably never even wear it.

She dismissed her thoughts about the dress and watched the local people hurrying in and out of shops. They were simply living their lives, seemingly unaware of the beauty that was just beyond their streets. Their everyday lives blended into routines, routines that seemed to rob them of the splendor of their surroundings and the infinite possibilities each day held.

She realized she was no different.

She looked at her watch as Jacques opened the bus doors. "Time for lunch," he said. "I'll show you where it is."

Jacques led her across the street and down an alley to a cafeteria-style restaurant. In a back room, Mason stood at the head of a long table, addressing the tour group. "We'll go through the serving line in small groups, so we don't overwhelm the place," he said in English, and then translated. He pointed to the Brazilians to go first. It didn't take long before Jayne was in line, Rosa in front of her with Mason behind.

"There are so many choices." Jayne hadn't realized she had spoken out loud until Mason answered.

"If you want something typically English, try the fish and chips with a side of mushy peas."

"Mushy peas?"

"They are like split pea soup with a twist."

Jayne couldn't help but make the connection with pea soup and the movie *The Exorcist,* with Linda Blair spewing green slime all over the place. "I'll skip the mushy peas, but the fish and chips sound good."

"I *thought* you were conservative." Mason teased as he pushed his tray along the rack.

"Mason," Rosa interrupted, leaning around Jayne to look at Mason. "What else can I try? The fried foods will not help my figure."

"They also have broiled fish," he said. "We don't want to change anything about your figure."

Rosa cocked her head to the side and smiled seductively.

They returned to the long table where the group sat. Jayne sat next to the Parks and Natalie, across from Mason and Rosa.

Glasses clanged and silverware clattered as everyone began eating. The smells of fried fish and chips filled the air. Most of the group had ordered the famous English dish. Beer was the beverage of choice to wash down the fried feast. Rosa had opted for the grilled fish and a Perrier.

As the meal continued, the Brazilian couples showed the group their purchases. Silk scarves bearing regal patterns fluttered from hand to hand. One of the wives pulled her sleeve up to display a filigreed gold-and-silver bracelet. The Spanish grandmother showed off an antique brooch of ivory and onyx. Meanwhile, the Parks also pulled open their shopping bags, filled with Paddington Bear and other toys for their grandchildren. The Spanish grandfather laughed when he pulled a twin Paddington bear from one of his grandchildren's bags. Rosa pulled out a hat from her bag. It wasn't a traditional English-style hat with a full brim. It was more modern. Rosa perched it precariously on the front of her head. "What you think?" She posed for the group. "I bought it from a shop that sells hats to royalty."

Everyone was silent as they took in the representation of a bird's nest, woven with intertwined brown and beige ribbons. Errant twigs poked out of random points around the hat.

"Very nice," Floyd said, and his wife nodded her head.

Jayne smiled and focused on her first bite of mushy peas.

They were thicker than pea soup. Hesitating as she moved the spoon toward her mouth, she looked up to see Mason watching her. She shoved the peas in her mouth and washed them down with beer.

"What do you think?" Mason looked like he was choking on a laugh.

"Bitter." Jayne scrunched up her face before taking another drink. "And not at all like split pea soup."

"So, what did you buy during the shopping spree?"

"Nothing."

Mason paused and inclined his head. "Then, what has been the high point for your morning?" He bit into a chip, still looking at her.

"Not the shopping. Not the mushy peas. The Whispering Gallery in the dome."

She looked down at her plate and scraped a chip into the ketchup, noting that the ketchup was also different in England. But she knew he was still looking at her.

After lunch, the next stop was Westminster Abbey. The rain had stopped, and the sun seemed to be fighting a losing battle to pierce the steel-gray sky. Jayne could not take her eyes from the gates of Buckingham Palace as they drove by, while Mason talked about its history. She let her imagination run wild with thoughts of queens, dukes, and horse-drawn carriages. As the bus wound through the streets, she wondered about the monuments standing like soldiers at attention in front of shops whose facades were steeped in the past but now contained modern merchandise.

She realized that this place had always been here. While she had been living her life on the other side of the ocean, people here were doing the same. The difference was the history, she thought. Everything's tinged with the centuries here. Even the mortar holding the stone in place seemed defiant.

The bus pulled in front of a daunting edifice with twin spires reaching toward the heavens. As if on cue, the bells rang out, filling the air with doleful sounds. Medieval chants grew from these notes, she thought, as she followed the group toward the doorway. The hair at the nape of her neck rose and tingled. Above the entrance, chiseled replicas of saints, frozen in time, shared messages beyond human hearing.

Jayne examined the detail and craftsmanship of the outside structure. As she entered, she bowed her head momentarily in deference to those buried in the ancient abbey. The rest of the group craned their heads and whispered to each other as Mason led them through the naves and passages of the abbey, their footsteps echoing like ghosts. Mason's voice reverberated as he pointed to Poet's Corner, where England's famous bards were commemorated by plaques or lay resting in their graves.

The buttresses looked like giant honeycombs crisscrossing to protect the tombs along the sides of the abbey. Plaques, statues, and artwork covered the walls.

Jayne approached a corner where plaques began at floor level and spread upward, out of reach. She knelt and ran her fingers across the fading letters. Tracing and twirling. Although the poets were long gone physically, they still spoke through their words.

She stood and read the names of Dickens, Kipling, Tennyson. Then she found him, her favorite. Her knees trembled. Robert Browning. Lines from his poetry swirled through her mind: *Grow old along with me! The best is yet to be, The last of life, for which the first was made...*

She reached to trace his name and thought it was a shame that he was buried so far away from his wife. Their love story was the stuff of fairy tales. But it had been real, and anchored Jayne's belief in romantic love.

She moved reverently to plaques commemorating other poets and writers, including the Brontë sisters, Austen, Shelley, and Burns. Memories of reading, soothing and familiar, surrounded her with each name. Their words washed over her as her lower lip trembled. She released herself into the moment.

When she came back to her senses, the tour group had moved on and spread out to explore on their own. Their voices echoed off the odd angles of the cathedral, merging into a dull hum. *Or maybe it's the ghost of ancient choruses or chanting monks.* She let her imagination soar as she walked toward the great rose window in the south transept. As she admired the myriad of colors that created the stained-glass masterpiece, the sun shone through it, bringing the artwork to life. The window seemed to open like the petals of a flower swirling with energy. Light danced through the reds, blues, and yellows. She looked around to see if anyone else had witnessed this extraordinary moment. The sunlight vanished just as she turned to leave.

The vastness of the abbey seemed to have taken everyone in different directions. The Parks were nestled in an alcove, whispering softly in each other's ears. The Brazilian couples huddled beside a wall of plaques, reading and translating out loud into Portuguese.

Jayne continued her solitary walk slowly to a huge brass gate and a flight of stairs that separated the main abbey from the Lady's Chapel. No one else was around.

The ceiling looked like finely woven lace that spread from the walls upward. Far from being austere, colorful flags that reflected the hues in the giant stained-glass window lit up the walls. An elaborate latticework of gold and black guarded the tombs. Adorned by angels at each corner of the tomb, gilded effigies of Henry VII and his wife, Elizabeth of York, lay side by side.

Jayne moved closer to look at the faces. Their features were clear. From all the photos she had seen of Henry VIII, she could see family resemblances in his parents, the shape of his father's head and a nose like his mother's.

Jayne stood still in front of the tomb. The effigies were

frozen in time, but the awareness struck her. These had been real people. They had married, raised children, and made daily decisions. Living and basic human instincts had not changed.

"It seems the Tudors flaunted their wealth in death just as they did in life."

Jayne jumped, surprised by the voice behind her.

"I'm sorry I startled you," Mason said as he stepped closer to the tomb.

"I don't know much about these two," Jayne replied. "I know much more about their children."

"Actually, Elizabeth of York was born in Westminster, and her christening happened here in the abbey. She came full circle with her burial here." Mason looked at her and continued, "She began as a pawn in a power struggle and, in reality, was the rightful heir to the throne that her husband gained through conquest."

"Yes, but the fact that they lie here side by side must say something about their relationship." Jayne stared at the two effigies, lying with hands folded in prayer. "It couldn't have been totally mercenary." She looked expectantly at Mason.

He shifted his stance and crossed his arms. She noticed the curve of his bicep as he continued, "Well, they did actually fall in love, but that was the exception more than the rule. She died as a result of childbirth, trying to secure another heir to the throne after the death of Henry VII's brother. She was thirty-seven years old."

"How sad. How did the King react?"

"It's said that he was devastated by her death and paid a great deal of money for a resplendent funeral for her."

"Did he remarry?"

"He thought about it for political purposes, but he died a widower and, as you can see, was buried next to his wife."

"So, love stories are not merely something that fill the imaginations of romance writers?"

"I'm not so sure. You can always find exceptions, but that doesn't make them the rule."

"Yes, but it doesn't hurt to believe in exceptions, does it?"

He uncrossed his arms, angled his head, and ran his fingers through his hair, but didn't respond.

They wandered among the tombs and alcoves toward the predetermined meeting place. It seemed as if more tourist groups had filled the abbey. Their footsteps reverberated, and Jayne wondered about footsteps throughout the centuries and the people who had become history. She thought about the sacrifice that wives made bringing children into the world. Once a woman had a child, her life changed forever.

Jayne looked at Mason, who was walking with her, but staring blankly ahead.

"What are you thinking about?" she asked as another tour group passed them.

"Actually, I'm hoping that everyone will be waiting at the meeting place."

"Oh."

"You sound disappointed."

"No, not really. I'm just so overwhelmed by this place that I can't imagine it ever getting old." She pulled at her coat and adjusted her purse.

"Everything gets old," he said as he checked his watch.

"Does it have to?" she asked.

He stopped walking and just stared at her. She stopped and started to stare back but suddenly found the floor a safer choice. After a few seconds, he started walking again. As they turned the corner, she savored her last glance at Poet's Corner as one of Shakespeare's sonnets ran through her mind:

What's new to speak, what now to register,
 That may express my love, or thy dear merit?
 Nothing, sweet boy, but yet like prayer divine,

I must each day say o'er the very same,
Counting no old thing old, thou mine, I thine,
Even as when first I hallowed thy fair name.
So that eternal love in love's fresh case
Weighs not the dust and injury of age,
Nor gives to necessary wrinkles place,
But makes antiquity for aye his page,
Finding the first conceit of love there bred,
Where time and outward form would show it dead.

CHAPTER 6

Monday Evening, October 15, 2012

Back in her hotel room, Jayne removed her coat and dug through her purse for her pills. She washed her medicine down with a bottle of water and collapsed on the bed. Her legs shook and she labored for shallow breaths. She wasn't sure whether the pills really helped or if the pain was a phantom of things to come. Although physically exhausted, her mind flooded with the magnificence of the cathedral and abbey. She set her alarm so she wouldn't sleep through dinner, then sank into blissful oblivion.

It seemed like only minutes later when the alarm blared.

Is dinner worth it?

Ultimately, she decided that it was.

She struggled up and went to the bathroom mirror. Some curl had fought back from the morning's straightening, making her hair hang in waves. In the choice between hair and face, retouching her face won. She washed her face and put on the minimum of makeup, just enough to hide the circles under her eyes and smooth out her skin tone. Some mascara and a touch of lipstick. *That will have to do.* She picked up her bag and checked for her room key before letting the door slam shut behind her.

On her way to the dining room, Jayne stopped at the hotel's business center to see if she could get access to e-mail. Although she had wanted complete separation from home, she had been thinking about the kids since seeing the tomb of Henry VII and his wife. She pushed on the office door. It opened silently, with no one in sight. She sat down in front of a screen with the backdrop of Tower Bridge, logged on to her e-mail account, and began to write.

My dearest Kimberly,

What an experience! My first day has given me more than I ever expected. The history, the people, the food. Wondrous! I wish you could see this with me. Please don't wait to explore life outside of the United States. Do it now. This coming summer. The experience will open your mind, your life, and your teaching. I love you and miss you more than you will ever know.

Mom

After pushing Send, she composed a similar letter to her son. Then, she sent a short message to Tom.

Tom,

I'm having a wonderful time. I hope you are not working too hard. We will be on our way to Paris in the morning.

Jayne

She found the dining room buzzing with activity. The room reverberated with prattle that sounded like birds chirping. Two of the large round tables had been pulled together by the four Brazilian couples. Across from them were the retired couple with their grandchildren and the young couple on their honeymoon. At another table, Natalie sat with the Parks. Jayne joined them.

The group talked about the day's events as a waiter took drink orders. In broken English and hand gestures, Natalie said that she had enjoyed St Paul's Cathedral. Portuguese undertones punctuated the gaps in conversation as the couples at the other tables conversed. The honeymoon couple clasped hands on the tabletop between them. As the husband spoke, he squeezed his young wife's hand.

Jayne wondered what he had said that resulted in that slight but intimate gesture. *Had Tom and I ever been like that?* Tom had never been one to touch in public. She couldn't remember even holding hands. Her fingers trembled as she sipped her water.

"Everything all right, dear?" Emma asked. "You look a million miles away."

"I'm fine, thanks," Jayne replied as she set her glass back down. She placed her napkin on her lap as Mason and Rosa joined their table.

"Are these seats taken?" Mason asked before pulling out a chair.

Rosa didn't wait for a response as she sat down. Her perfume wafted across the table.

"No, please sit ..." Floyd said as he looked at Rosa and glanced at his wife with a slight smile tugging at the corners of his mouth. "...down."

Mason sat and Rosa edged her seat closer to him.

"How did you enjoy the first day of your tour?" Mason edged his seat a smidgen away from Rosa and closer to Emma.

"Wonderful. Just wonderful. All of it." As Emma responded, Floyd put his arm around her and smiled.

"What an art show," Floyd continued, and Emma concurred with a nod. "The sculptures, the tombs, the architecture. Everything was overwhelming." He squeezed Emma and continued, "And just think, this was our first day."

"The shopping was fun," Natalie exclaimed.

"*Si.* I'm wearing one of the dresses I bought." Rosa stood to give everyone an extended view of her new, form-fitting purple knit dress. Sleeveless with a plunging neckline. Her tawny skin seemed to glisten.

"Stunning," Jayne replied when no one else stepped up.

"What about *your* first day?" Mason asked Jayne as the waiters began serving dinner. The smell of Beef Wellington, mashed potatoes, and green beans filled the room.

"Exquisite." Jayne paused as the waiter served her plate. "Simply exquisite."

As she ate her dinner, Jayne watched the interplay between Floyd and Emma. He didn't eat until his wife started. As she spoke, he listened attentively and nodded in agreement. The couple seemed to finish each other's sentences with flawless ease. Floyd had a witty sense of humor that his wife obviously appreciated. Her head tipped back and she laughed, a staccato, hiccupping laugh. But it was her eyes that showed more than anything. Although her face was withered with age, her eyes twinkled with vibrant love and respect.

Jayne couldn't help but mentally compare their relationship with her own as she scooped up some mashed potatoes, but she didn't taste them as she ate mechanically.

"How long have you been married?" Natalie asked the Parks.

"So long I don't remember not being married," Floyd said and chuckled.

"Stop pulling her leg," Emma chided. "You know exactly how long we've been married." She poked her elbow into his side.

"Fifty years, two months, and eleven days." Floyd smiled as everyone at the table clapped. He bowed his head in acknowledgement.

Jayne wondered if Tom would know the exact date of their marriage as she joined in and clapped. He would certainly know the date, but the months and days?

"How do you stay married for that long?" Rosa asked. "It would get very boring." She shrugged as if trying to get rid of a shiver.

"I guess you just choose right," Floyd said. He looked at Emma and reached over to squeeze her knee.

"Easier said than done." Mason stopped eating and placed his fork on the edge of his plate.

"I think that variety is the way to keep relationships fresh," Rosa said. She looked right at Mason as she spoke.

"Really?" Jayne's eyebrows shot straight up at Rosa's frank talk. "Doesn't that get dull as well?"

"Maybe so," Mason said. He picked up his fork and prodded at the remnants on his plate.

"I guess it depends on the people involved," Jayne ventured and made direct eye contact with Mason.

He paused with his fork in midair, set it back down on his plate, and reached for his drink instead.

"What about you?" Rosa said as she looked at Jayne. "You have a ring on your finger."

"I agree with Floyd," Jayne said as her heart beat faster. "You have to make the right choice." She stopped eating and placed her knife and fork on her plate. Blotting her mouth, she picked up her glass of water.

She looked at the young honeymoon couple again. They were not holding hands any longer, but their chairs were so close that their bodies touched. They glanced at each other often, with looks of longing and love. The young couple leaned across the table and conversed with the grandparents and their grandchildren. Although Jayne could not understand the words, the kids were animated, nodding their heads and flashing their hands around. The little girl nudged her brother and said something, accenting the end of her speech with a slight angling of her head. The young couple laughed along with the grandparents. The boy frowned into his plate and crossed his arms.

What an extraordinary gift these grandparents were giving their grandchildren, Jayne thought. Why hadn't she insisted on traveling like this with her teenaged children? They could have afforded it. Ghosts of her future grandchildren danced through her mind. Shivering and repeating her mantra, she shrugged off the hollow feeling inside. Even if she wasn't going to be there physically, she could give them the gift of insight through her own children. That's what she would write in her notebook throughout the trip. It would have to do. Don't cry, she chastised herself. Don't think about it anymore.

She looked across the table absently to find Mason looking at her. She flushed, feeling the blush spread across her cheeks. Could he hear her thoughts? He looked so intently that she almost believed he could.

Waiters removed their dinner plates, replacing them with bread pudding and coffee or tea. Jayne sipped her tea but didn't touch the dessert.

"Don't tell me you're one of those young ladies that watches her weight," Floyd teased. "It doesn't look like anything I've had before, but it sure tastes good."

"It's bread pudding, Floyd," Emma said with her mouth full.

"I guess I'm not hungry after all that food," Jayne replied, still a bit discombobulated by Mason's scrutiny and her own thoughts.

"Come on," Floyd continued with a smile. "You only live once. How many more opportunities are you going to get to try English bread pudding in England?" He chuckled, spooning up some fluffy pudding and dipping it into the creamy topping. He smacked his lips and said, "Mmmmm."

Jayne laughed at his antics and picked up her spoon. *Maybe he's right. What am I doing letting this pass by?* She slowly plunged the spoon into the middle of the dessert and swirled out a section. She followed Floyd's lead and dipped it into the luscious cream pooled around the giant square of pudding. Methodically, she lifted the spoon to her mouth and succumbed to immense and surprising pleasure. The texture was spongy with bits of fruit to add substance. The creamy topping exploded with sweetness that accentuated the warm bite. Even after she swallowed it, the sensations continued.

"Well worth adding a few pounds, isn't it?" Floyd nodded.

"I'm really not worried about my weight at all." Jayne took another bite, her doctor's words haunting her.

"I always worry about mine," Rosa added without being asked. "But I can't resist temptation." She prodded at the pudding in her bowl and filled only the tip of her spoon with dainty morsels.

Mason stood to get the group's attention. He told them to meet in the lobby with suitcases packed by eight a.m. for the ferry trip across the Channel, and then on to Paris.

"Well, that's an early start," Floyd said.

"Yes, dear, let's get those postcards and get them in the mail, and then call it a night," Emma urged.

"Postcards?" Jayne asked.

"Yes, we want to send our grandchildren picture postcards from each place," Floyd said. "I know there are newfangled ways to send pictures and things, but we're old-fashioned. We just stick to what we know."

"Well, it seems to be working perfectly for both of you." Jayne smiled. "Good night." She moved slightly as the waiter began to clear the table after the elderly couple left.

"Mason?" Rosa accented the second syllable of his name instead of the first as she glanced at the waiter.

"Yes, Ms. Rosa," Mason answered.

"At first, I wasn't sure I would like this type of tour," she said.

"Really, and why not?"

"A bus ... old people ..." she shrugged her shoulders and shifted forward. "But now ...."

"Now?" he prompted.

Jayne felt like an interloper and started to get up.

"Let's order drinks," Rosa said.

"I think I'll just go to my room now," Jayne replied.

"A nightcap will help you sleep," Mason volunteered as he

stood and motioned for her to stay seated. "I'll be back in a few minutes. I have to go and take care of a couple of things."

Jayne sat back down, feeling abandoned as she asked the waiter for a glass of port.

"I will have more of the wine that I had with my dinner," Rosa said, accenting the first syllable of "dinner." She nodded with a satisfied smile that made Jayne think of a cat with her prey within reach.

Rosa repositioned herself at the table, legs crossed and breasts on full display.

Jayne slumped in her seat, not ready to compete. A frumpy image of herself floated through her mind.

"So, what do you think about our tour guide?" Rosa asked.

Jayne paused. "He seems fine."

"He's *muy* fine," Rosa said as the waiter returned with the drinks. "He's gorgeous."

Jayne sipped her port and fought to straighten her shoulders. *Frumpy isn't so bad.*

Mason returned and ordered a double scotch and a beer.

"Has it been that bad?" Rosa sipped her glass of wine.

"Always."

"It can't be that bad," Jayne said.

"Maybe not." His tone flattened. "Nothing ever goes according to plan."

"Why?" Jayne asked, her eyes widening as she moved her hand to her throat.

"Life doesn't work that way," he said and downed half of his beer.

"Just have fun," Rosa said as she raised her glass. "That's how I live my life."

"But I'm not on vacation," Mason said.

"You could be," Rosa said as she swiveled her hips in the chair.

A blush warmed Jayne's face. Again, she felt like an intruder.

Rosa raised her glass and offered an empty toast. "To new friends." She clinked her glass against his as he raised it in response, and then to Jayne's.

"Friends?" he asked with one eyebrow arched.

"*Si*, it always starts with friends." She sipped her wine, her lips lingering on the rim of the glass.

"And I thought it always started with something else." He put his glass down and motioned to the waiter.

Jayne tugged at her sweater and fought some unfamiliar emotions. Confusion? Or could it be a hint of jealousy? Why had he asked her to stay? She didn't know for sure and downed her drink. "I think I'll call it a night." She didn't wait for a response but grabbed her bag and left. She wasn't sure they would even notice her absence.

As she walked to her room, she pushed her confused feelings down and, instead, wondered what Tom would have added to the dinner conversation about making the right choice. She couldn't come up with anything that he would have said. Was she his right choice? What had she based her choice on? Tom had seemed so sophisticated when she first met him. He was so intelligent and filled with dreams of success. She loved listening to his plans for the future and filled in the gaps with her own expectations. Gaps like romance, sharing feelings, even touching. As the years passed, she had realized that Tom's version of success was very different from her own.

She pressed the elevator button and waited.

She thought they had loved each other when they got married. But now what was it? Mutual comfort? Even though Tom hadn't liked public shows of affection, she thought that he would loosen up in private. Another assumption that turned out to be false. Of course, they made love, but the cuddling, light touches, and kisses that should be part of everyday life were missing, leaving an emptiness that left a gaping hole in her soul.

Whatever my marriage is, it isn't like the Parks', she thought as the elevator door opened. The Parks were truly soulmates connected on an intangible level. When she pressed the seventh-floor button and the door closed, the elevator seemed to fold in around her. She hurried off as soon as the door began to open and shoved the room key into the slot with fumbling fingers. When the door slammed shut, she fought for calm. Her mantra wasn't working this time.

She took a quick shower and got into bed. She tried to watch some television, anything to keep her from thinking. It was futile. Leaving the television on, she pulled out her notebook and poured her developing wisdom onto the pages. Turning her own regrets from the past into advice for the future. Fighting tears and heartache as she scratched out each word. Finally, exhaustion prompted her to put down her pen, turn everything off, and attempt much-needed sleep.

Cocooned under sheets and duvet, Jayne tossed as her mind continued to race. She replaced the heavy thoughts of marriage and the future with images of the streets of London, the Thames rushing under the bridges, and the iconic red double-decker buses. Her travel books had come to life before her eyes and trumped her expectations. The pictures couldn't capture the depth and feelings of each place. The colors, textures, and ghostly emotions resonated within her. The history and souls of those who had peopled these places haunted her. The smell of time, of the past, punctuated her memory of these places now. The photos were mere shadows compared to the actual experience.

Giving up on sleep, she piled another pillow under her head. She watched the lights from the street play on her ceiling. London nightlife seemed to be waking. She crossed her arms over the sheets.

For the first time in her life, she had lived every single moment of the day.

Colors had seemed more vibrant. The subtleties of different

languages had created a syncopated backdrop that became magnified in St Paul's Cathedral and Westminster Abbey, a megaphone of sound amplifying the sights. The lifelike statues and memorials that occupied these two places seemed to breathe, but when she had gathered the courage to touch one, the cold, smooth marble destroyed her illusion. She moved her fingers on the duvet, trying to recapture the feeling.

She had taken notes on the tour. *Why?* She didn't know. What she did know was that she would never forget the exhilaration that infused her body during this first day. Experience replaced dreams. Living instead of dreaming.

Her thoughts drifted to Mason. His animated style as he talked about the places the bus passed by had made history come to life. He added humor and insight into the Londoners of today and yesterday. The tour bus had been full of laughter, oohs, and aahs. Yet, when she and Mason had a moment to talk between themselves, he seemed like a different person. His actions after dinner had confused her. There were definitely two sides to this man. Maybe more.

Unbidden, her thoughts shifted to Tom. How different he was from Mason. Jayne couldn't remember the last time she and Tom had laughed at a joke, a television comedy, or anything. Perhaps that's what happens with routine. Then, she thought about the Parks.

She jumped and her heart raced as the phone rang, an odd sound unlike the phones at home. She pulled back the covers and thought it must be a mistake. Panic seized her. Had something happened to one of the kids?

"Hello?"

"Hey there. I hope I didn't wake you, but I wanted to see how your first day went."

Jayne relaxed at Lynn's familiar voice.

"I wasn't asleep." Jayne sat down in the chair by the desk and began to share the events of the day with Lynn. "Mason knew just the right details to share about every place we stopped," Jayne said. "He even showed me how the Whispering Gallery worked. But one of my favorites was a tomb at St. Paul's Cathedral."

She started talking faster, like a child who rushed home from school to share the high points of her day. "The tomb was covered in gold," Jayne said. "There they were, side by side, for eternity. Mason told me the love story and how she died trying to give the King another child."

"What a waste," Lynn replied.

"I didn't see it as a waste. I thought it was true love."

"What does true love have to do with dying to bring another possible Henry VIII into the world? Really, Jayne."

"You genuinely don't think it was love that prompted her to give her husband another heir?"

"Nope."

"You really don't see sacrifice as part of love."

"I guess not. That's why I'm single. Speaking of single, who is this Mason you keep talking about?"

"He's the tour guide."

"What does he look like?"

"He has long hair. Seems to be a kind of free spirit."

"Sounds good."

"A bit of a Casanova."

"Keep going."

"He's got amazing eyes, but they are sad."

"Sad eyes," Lynn seemed to mock. "Only you would see sad eyes. What color are they?"

"Gray-blue. Like slate."

"I'd call those sexy eyes," Lynn countered.

Lynn continued for a while, quickly asking how Jayne felt. "I'll call again in a few days," she concluded. "I have the itinerary."

"I wrote down all the hotel phone numbers, just in case," Jayne said.

"I know. Get some sleep. Good night."

Jayne hung up and crawled back into bed. She tossed Lynn's questions about Mason around, and then her thoughts turned to Tom. He had always been solid. When they were first married, he had promised to provide for her … and he had. They had been a team. She was the stay-at-home mom and he was the breadwinner. There was a connection. It worked. But something had changed as the years went by.

Thoughts churned and cluttered her mind. She fought them off in an attempt to sleep, and in their place, she dreamed of Paris.

CHAPTER 7

Tuesday, October 16, 2012

Jayne breathed deeply, coughed, and focused on taking in every sight from her seat on the bus. She shifted her gaze and craned her neck to capture different perspectives. The modern townhouses intertwined with thatched-roof cottages marked the way towards the coast littered with English vistas. Some of the thatch was cut in intricate edging while others were plain, unadorned. There was nothing like this in either Chicago or her hometown nestled in the Smoky Mountains. She remembered sitting through lectures about England and English Literature that paled in comparison to her current experience.

The bus wove its way from the small towns toward the coastline. The sea foamed in minuscule peaks and undulated softly against the banks. The old town walls stood tall, obstinate against the elements and time. Books transformed into reality with every kilometer. Every fiber of her being pulsed with life like she had never experienced before.

Nothing compared. The streets. Cars. Homes. Her world shifted into the realm of new experiences. No more dreams. She tore herself away from the window, drawn by the need to write in her notebook, recording her thoughts for her kids.

The bus began to slow down, so she tucked the notebook away. As they neared Portsmouth International Port, the harbor itself faded from view, replaced with a paved parking lot packed with people and cars. Horns honked and travelers shuffled forward toward the terminal building.

Inside the building, long lines snaked toward security personnel, who were checking passports, ID cards, and bags. Jayne fumbled through her purse and pulled out her passport. Thank goodness she didn't have to struggle with her large suitcase in addition to her purse. In the morning, she had put the suitcase outside of her hotel room, and it vanished. Would it reappear at her next hotel room?

The rest of her tour group scattered around the terminal and she hoped she could find the designated meeting spot. Approaching the security desk, she dropped her passport, retrieved it, and put it on the desk that was as high as her chin. The security officer began talking rapidly in French.

"Do you speak English?" she asked.

"*Non.*"

"*Anglais, oui?*" She looked him in the eye. "*S'il vous plait?*"

That was the extent of her knowledge of French, and she hoped it was enough.

"Of course, *mademoiselle*," the security officer said, wincing like it physically hurt him to speak English. He told her to put her purse on the conveyor belt, tapped on a keyboard, peered at a monitor, and said, "*Bonjour*," pushing her passport back to her.

She went through the metal detector without making it beep, retrieved her purse, and continued to the loading platform where she saw Mason standing with most of the other members of her group. The sun peeked out from behind clouds and a soft breeze tugged at her hair. The ferries lined up in the harbor like soldiers on parade. They were large and very square, with several decks. Cars drove onto the bottom decks of the ferries, but people stood in yet more lines for boarding.

"Good morning, everyone." Mason addressed the group as they gathered, tucking passports back into wallets and purses. "I think we have a few more stragglers, but let's get in line. Typically, we would be taking the Eurostar, but they're still on strike. Besides, I think you'll enjoy the view while we cross the channel."

Jayne noticed that Rosa, unlike the rest of the group, faced Mason, standing very close to him. She wore tapered-leg pants that hugged her hips. Her low-cut top peeked out from under a cropped leopard-print jacket. Rosa's apparent possessiveness toward Mason bothered Jayne like a fly's buzzing. It shouldn't have, but it did. As she continued to watch Rosa, the buzzing grew more annoying.

The Parks approached Jayne, and she was grateful for the diversion. Both were dressed in crisp layers, complete with matching hats.

So cute. She smiled.

"We thought it might get a bit cold during the crossing," Emma said.

"I think that's very smart." Jayne looked at the ferry and shook her head. "I'm not really sure about this. I used to get carsick when I was a kid. I'm not so good on smaller boats, so I can't imagine how I'll feel on one this size."

"I have some Dramamine, if you need it, dear." Emma patted her giant purse.

"I'll find you if I need to." Jayne had grown fond of the older couple already. She took a deep breath and coughed, tasting the fumes from the boat engines in her mouth. She grimaced and thought the queasiness fluttering in her stomach did not bode well.

The line started moving, and people hobbled onto the ferry like sheep for the six-hour crossing. Once aboard, some passengers went to the deck outside. Others found seats in a cabin with windows lining each side. There was another area where people ordered croissants and tea. The menu previewed the various entrees that were available for lunch during the crossing. Ferry horns blew to announce departures.

Jayne stood by one of the windows when she felt the ferry begin to move. She looked out the window and the view shifted. Her stomach lurched.

If I just sit down, I will be all right.

She found a chair that faced the window. She sat and made the mistake of looking out at the water as the ferry seemed to pivot around. Waves sloshed and tilted. She closed her eyes tightly. Cold sweat beaded above her lip and on her forehead. Several hours of this, she thought. It had only been a few minutes, and she had up to six hours left. The engines roared as the slight smell of fuel reached her nose again. Her stomach roiled like the waves hitting the sides of the ferry. She knew if she opened her eyes, she'd lose it.

"Is something wrong?"

She recognized Mason's voice and instant humiliation mixed with her upset stomach. Her face burned.

"Jayne?"

As his hand covered hers, she realized she had clinched her hands into fists.

"I believe I'm not cut out for ferry rides." She still had her eyes closed. "Right now, I wish those Eurostar people weren't on strike."

"Let me get you some tea and toast," he offered. "That might help."

"Thank you," she opened her eyes slightly. "And, if you don't mind, can you find Emma, Mrs. Parks, for me?"

Mason nodded.

Jayne closed her eyes again and sank down deep into the seat. She laid her head back, pretending she was just sitting in the car on a leisurely ride in the suburbs. Instead, her mind drifted back to her childhood, when she would get carsick as her father drove through the mountains. The moving craggy mountainsides had never failed to make her ill. Her father used to put a bucket in the back seat every time they had to drive for more than an hour. She pushed the memory back, replacing it with an image of a simple car ride with her kids in the suburbs.

"Where is Mason?" A now familiar Spanish accent interrupted Jayne's attempt to be any place but on this ferry.

"He should be back in a minute," Jayne replied, opening her eyes slightly.

"What is wrong?" Rosa continued. "You don't look so good."

"Thanks," Jayne said as she closed her eyes again and put her hand on her stomach.

She smelled tea. Jayne opened her eyes again to see Mason holding a cup and plate. Emma Parks was beside him.

"Oh dear," Emma said as she dug around in her purse and pulled out a pill bottle.

"If you can, come over here to the chair by the table." Mason led the way and placed the tea and toast on a table.

"Here, let me help you," Rosa said as she put her hand on Jayne's elbow, but kept her gaze locked on Mason.

Great. Now I'm the invalid to Rosa's exaggerated nursemaid. Humiliation drenched her from head to toe, just like it used to when she was in high school. The "in" girls had always made her feel inferior.

The roaring of the engines seemed to magnify as she stood, swayed, and was steadied by Rosa. Jayne sat down with a heavy plop, and Mason gave her the cup of tea. Emma sat down in a chair opposite Jayne.

"Can you sit with her for a while?" Mason asked.

"Of course." Emma handed Jayne a pill.

After Jayne swallowed the pill and took a bite of toast, Mason looked like he was going to sit down and join them.

"Mason, you promised me a tour of the deck and around the ferry," Rosa said. She rubbed Mason's arm before she tucked hers around his and kept him from sitting down.

So much for the Florence Nightingale performance, Jayne thought, chastising herself simultaneously.

"Ladies, will you be all right?" Mason didn't move as Rosa inched closer.

"Yes, of course. You go ahead. I'll keep an eye on our girl." Emma smiled and patted Jayne's hand.

Rosa pulled Mason toward the exit.

As the pill started to take effect, Jayne settled into what felt like a trance. She didn't move from her seat. Over the next few hours, she choked down the toast and drank the now tepid tea. She persuaded Emma to rejoin Floyd and enjoy the crossing with him. She felt like a wimp and could hear her father's voice yelling at her to stop being sick so he wouldn't have to stop the car. *Sometimes your body just caves in from under you whether you like it or not.* She knew that now more than ever. When the ferry whistle signaled their arrival in France, she whispered a short prayer of thanks.

On wobbly legs, she joined the rest of her group to disembark. Mason had collected their passports and oversaw their entry into France. The tour bus waited at the edge of the busy parking lot, and Jacques waved from the front of the bus as the group approached. Soon, everyone settled in and they were off to Caen and then to Paris.

Aided by a loudspeaker, Mason told the group that the ferry port was close to the famous Omaha Beach, site of the American landing on D-Day.

Poor soldiers so far from home.

Over 20,000 didn't make it back to the States. She suddenly didn't want to hear any more and plugged in the iPod. Waves of Pink Floyd's *Division Bell* filled her head. She watched the landscape flutter quickly by. There were fields of autumn's burnished browns. The crops were gone. Harvest was in full swing, just like in the States. Amid these fields, sudden patches of green surrounded small dairy farms, made picture-perfect with the addition of cows milling in front of barns. She took out her notebook and began to write as the bus wound its way through the curvy roads and soon arrived in Caen.

Jayne pulled the earpieces from her ears just in time to pick up some local history. Mason had turned into the consummate Frenchman, complete with beret and accent. He was talking about the city that dated back to William the Conqueror. Quaint shops lined the streets and a castle rose like a giant monolith from the hill in the center of the town. Colorful flags lined its parapets and ramparts, and the dark exterior looked daunting.

"William the Conqueror built Chateau Caen over a thousand years ago. The local stone gives the edifice a rather austere appearance," Mason said.

He switched to Portuguese and then to Spanish. Jayne assumed he relayed the same information.

Mason switched back to English and looked directly at Jayne. "Now, what castle would be complete without an accompanying love story? Poor William fell hopelessly in love with his cousin, Mathilda of Flanders. He appealed to the pope, who sent out emissaries. Ultimately, permission for the marriage was granted. Apparently, the cost of marrying one's cousin, according to the Vatican, was the building of two abbeys. One for men, and the other for women. William gladly paid the price to live happily ever after." He smiled at Jayne as he again switched languages.

Her heart skipped a beat in response. *I could lose myself in those eyes.* Quickly, she banished the thought as the result of reading too many romance novels.

The bus pulled into the large parking area. Mason got off the bus but remained by the open door. Everyone was free to explore the grounds on their own for about a half an hour.

As Jayne stepped down, Mason asked, "How did you like my castle story?"

"It appears that love stories are more common than just Henry and Elizabeth. You held out on me." She smiled and looked up at Mason. He was almost a foot taller than her. He had a deep crease in his brow, a result of his continuous frown.

"How do you know it was true love?" His face slowly shifted from the frown to a lopsided smile and an expectant tilt of his head.

She paused, using her arm in a large sweeping motion, and continued her defense. "Look at this palace. He went to the Church and did what it took to clear the way for marriage. They did live happily ever after, didn't they?"

"That's what the history books say." Mason smiled broadly for a change, dimples showing.

Jayne noticed light laugh lines beginning to appear on his face as she remarked, "Touché."

His countenance shifted with the smile, and she thought she'd caught a glimpse of who he used to be.

Rosa lingered by the bus. "Mason. Can we go now?"

Mason's smile diminished perceptibly. He nodded at Jayne as he joined Rosa to walk down the path to the castle.

Jayne watched them for a moment, a slight pang squeezing her insides when Rosa put her arm around Mason's waist. It was nonsense, she knew, and shook it off.

Jayne looked at the grounds and followed a sign that pointed to the castle gardens. They spread out like a giant jigsaw puzzle. She wandered through the maze, savoring the love story she had just heard. She soon found herself in an area replete with flowers in various stages of life. Some roses were withered, their bloom faded from brilliant fuchsia in the middle, to brown edges curling in on themselves. In stark contrast, clusters of other flowers flamed brilliant red or yellow. Smaller purple foliage provided the ground covering. Jayne knew only the names of the most obvious flowers. Roses had always been her favorite. She tried in vain to find a rose that was still in full bloom. It was pointless.

I'm in France. I'm here.

She took a moment just to feel the history. Musty earth. Fragrant flowers. A slight decay, like the pages of an old book, yellowed with age. She savored all of it.

Back on the bus, the tour continued down the road to the next stop. Mason had resumed his role as the itinerant Frenchman. This region of Normandy, the Calvados, was known for its cider, not wine. Jayne had never thought of apple orchards anywhere but in Michigan. She and Lynn had taken the kids there one fall. It had been Lynn's idea to just pull the kids out of school for a week and enjoy the fall colors. They had driven from Chicago to a small orchard in Michigan. They had picked apples, gorged themselves on donuts, and washed it all down with fresh-pressed cider.

The bus stopped briefly at an orchard where everyone sampled the mildly alcoholic cider, unlike the cider from Michigan, and bought apple desserts. The end of the day fast approached, so they loaded back on the bus, pungent with the smell of fresh apples.

Dusk had settled over Paris by the time the bus pulled in front of the Champs Élysées Plaza Hotel in the heart of the city. Jayne's energy was on a low ebb. Adrenaline had fueled her after her bout of motion sickness. But now, her bones ached. Even her skin screamed with exhaustion.

The group had a couple of hours to get dinner and rest, and then they would be off to explore the City of Lights in all its nighttime glory. Mason passed out room keys as they entered the lobby and pointed out the elevator.

Jayne boarded the elevator with Rosa and Mason. As she

located her room, Jayne noticed that Rosa was right across the hall from her, next to Mason's room. Rosa squeezed Mason's arm as Jayne passed. Mason looked at Rosa and stroked her hand lightly. Jayne bristled and shook her head, mentally reprimanding both Rosa and herself.

Jayne's bags were already in her room. She unzipped her pants with a sigh, stripped them off, and hung them over the back of a nearby chair. She decided to skip dinner and get some rest. She couldn't risk falling asleep during the night tour. In just her bra and underwear, she slipped under the sheets, set the alarm, and took a nap.

Much too soon, the alarm sounded. Somewhat refreshed, Jayne ate the apple crisp she had purchased at the orchard as she looked at the view from her window. A vibrant dream spread before her. Lights twinkled from windows and buildings as the city transitioned from languishing daytime to vibrant night. An auburn hue encapsulated the city like a simmering fire. Fueling, not consuming. The City of Lights, she thought. What did those lights illuminate each night? This night? Her night.

Mason had been a bit mysterious about exactly what the night tour had to offer. All he said was for everyone to dress up. Jayne figured this meant it was not going to be a nighttime walking tour. She had brought her little black dress. Lynn had found it in the back of her closet and tossed it into the suitcase with black nylons and high heels. Her perfect little black dress and no shawl.

She pulled her hair up into a bundle of curls, not wanting to take the time to straighten her hair again. Stray tendrils escaped around her face. She took a final look in the mirror. Her skin was alabaster against the black dress. Her makeup was heavier than usual. She wasn't sure she recognized the woman looking back at her. Her eyes glittered with anticipation. She was in Paris. She put on her trench coat, leaving it open, and grabbed her purse.

Everyone was already on the bus by the time Jayne climbed up the stairs.

Mason sat in the front row with Rosa next to him.

"I'm sorry. Am I late?" She looked around for an open seat and saw Floyd point to one across from him and Emma.

"No, I think everyone is just excited and came down a bit early." Mason, with his gaze lingering on Jayne, got up and moved to his seat by the door where he had access to his microphone.

She tugged at an errant curl as she turned away from him and moved down the aisle to her seat.

They drove through the city, and Mason put on his Frenchman mantle, talking about Napoleon, the kings, and the architecture as the bus driver maneuvered through traffic. The Champs Élysées was peppered with people. Artificial lights bathed the buildings in a glow. The lamps spaced among the trees lining the most famous avenue in Paris looked like nesting fireflies. As the bus continued, Jayne saw the Arc de Triomphe appear in the midst of swarming traffic.

"The Arc de Triomphe was built by Napoleon, and the facade illustrates victories in the Revolutionary and Napoleonic periods. Within the Arc is the tomb of the unknown soldier and the accompanying eternal flame." Mason repeated these facts in Portuguese.

The bus slowed as it passed by the monument. The lights shining upward made the monument look like it was floating, mysteriously suspended amidst the bustling traffic. How sad, Jayne mused, to be buried without family even knowing what had happened.

The Louvre entrance was lit up like an ancient Egyptian temple. The lights speared the night sky. Mason announced the group would visit the museum the next day.

The bus proceeded across the Seine toward the Eiffel Tower. Mason continued translating facts, but Jayne was mesmerized by the lattice-worked structure that rose toward the heavens like an enormous torch. Pictures did not do the reality justice. She examined the intricate structure and wondered about the man who had visualized such a creation. She imagined the vision flowing from his mind onto paper and finally into metal. She craned her neck and pushed her face closer to the window as they drifted past the icon and headed along the Left Bank toward Notre Dame.

The Quai des Grandes Augustins ran along the Seine, which looked placid in the moonlight. Building after building fascinated her as Mason shared their histories. Soon, Notre Dame Cathedral loomed near, clothed in the same warm glow of light that bathed the city. The front square towers became beacons of light, and just as the bus neared the side of the cathedral, the bells tolled. *Those lovely bells.* She listened intently as the ringing gave soul to each hour of this magnificent night. The sound touched something buried deep inside her. She looked up at the darkened rose window. When the tolling ended, the emptiness of silence filled the night air.

She looked up and found Mason had stopped speaking and was looking at her. The bus passed by the giant edifice, and life resumed its normal pitch.

Then, abruptly, Mason broke his gaze. "Now, it's decision time. We're going back to the hotel, but for those of you who choose to explore the unique nightlife Paris has to offer, we will proceed to a show at the Moulin Rouge."

"Well, I think we'll call it a night," Floyd said.

Emma nodded.

Some of the others answered in their native languages.

Jayne didn't know what to do. Should she go back and get some sleep? There was a busy day on tap for tomorrow. Or should she explore the nightlife? She tossed the ideas back and forth as the bus returned to the hotel.

The grandparents with their grandchildren got off the bus

along with the Parks and Natalie. The young honeymoon couple also disembarked. Jayne stood up.

"You're not going to miss out on this part of your dream vacation, are you?" Mason asked.

"Well, I am tired," she said as she stood, momentarily immobilized by indecision.

"So, you're going to pack it in with the old folks and kids," Mason taunted.

What was she doing? *Live each day to the fullest, with no regrets.*

"You're right." She sat down and the Brazilian couples applauded. Rosa did not join in the clapping. Instead, she smiled almost imperceptibly and narrowed her eyes slightly.

The bus made its way to Montmartre and pulled in front of the most famous cabaret in the world. The iconic windmill turned slowly, chopping the night air with slivers of twinkling white lights. Not satisfied with advertising the name of the place once in white glowing letters, a round sign emblazoned the name in red neon. The facade flashed and swirled as Jayne descended from the bus, swept forward by the energy of the crowd.

Inside, the ceiling was strewn with fabric reminiscent of the Shrine circus that she and Lynn had taken the kids to years ago. But that was where all similarities to a family-friendly circus ended. Chandeliers spread across the ceiling, and red lamps flickered on every table. Everyone was dressed up. Drinks flowed like water, and some patrons ordered dinner. The air pulsed with possibilities.

The tour group had three tables three rows from the stage. The Brazilian couples occupied two of the tables, leaving Rosa on one side of Mason, and Jayne on the other. Mason helped Jayne with her coat. His gaze lingered on her hair, then scanned the rest of her.

"Ladies, what would you like to order?" Mason asked as he picked up the menu.

"Something decadent," Rosa replied as she touched his hand and ran her fingers down the menu.

"And you?"

"I'll leave it up to you, Monsieur Mason." Jayne tried to imitate a French accent and only accomplished tones of her Southern roots. "Since I can't read a word of French, it really is up to you. I'm not really that hungry."

Mason ordered and soon the waiter appeared with two bottles of wine, one red, one white, and a plate of cheeses, fruits, and bread. Another waiter arrived with a tray of sweet delicacies.

"Voila, we have a plate of decadence and something for someone who is not really that hungry." Mason picked up the bottle of ruby red wine, looked at the label, and poured a sample into his glass. "A Bourdeaux red blend," he said as he raised the glass slowly and sniffed the contents. Then, he swirled the wine in the glass. The liquid shone in the ambient light. He raised the glass and slowly tasted the contents. Jayne watched his throat as he swallowed. A blush suffused her face as she reached up to her cheek with the back of her hand to see if it was hot.

"Exquisite. The blend of Cabernet Sauvignon, Merlot, and Petit Verdot is perfect." He poured some wine for Jayne. "This will enhance the flavor of the cheese and fruit. You can cleanse your palate with the bread. *Bon appetit*." He raised his glass. Jayne raised hers and they toasted. He finished his wine in one smooth motion.

"Now for some decadence." He poured the white wine into his glass and repeated the same tasting. He then poured some for Rosa. "This will be perfect for the sweet tidbits on the tray. Enjoy."

"Always." Rosa leaned into Mason as she took a sip of her wine. Jayne could see that Rosa was not wearing a bra. Her arousal was evident to anyone who happened to glance at her chest.

Jayne ate a bit of cheese and washed it down with a healthy gulp of red wine. It was full bodied and dry, leaving her still thirsty after each sip. She noticed that the label on the bottle read "Chateau du Moulin Rouge" under an impressive seal flanked with griffins.

The Brazilian couples called Mason over. She watched him as he bent over to look at the menu with them. His shoulders were wide and tapered down to a slim waist. His pants hugged his rear end perfectly. As he turned to return to his seat, he almost caught her looking at him. Instead of feeling embarrassed, she found herself enjoying the thought of getting caught. The wine infused her with warmth and maybe a bit of false confidence. After all, she was in France. At the Moulin Rouge.

Precipitously, the lights dimmed and the chatter from the audience diminished. Music filled the room and dancers crowded the stage. Men and women dressed in white tuxedos. Then, suddenly, in one swift movement the female dancers ripped off their pants to reveal long legs and rounded butts. They wore very skimpy thongs.

This isn't so bad, Jayne thought as she continued sipping her wine. The dancers are wearing as much as the dancers in Las Vegas. Of course, she had never visited Vegas, but she had seen shows on television. The number ended and thunderous applause ensued. A man dressed like a ringmaster stepped onto the stage to introduce the next act.

The music resumed, and the stage suddenly filled with topless women wearing sparkling rhinestones and plumages of red feathers, evoking the illusion of a fancy ball gown that fluttered and flowed across the stage. They strutted, sang, and danced with abandon. An array of perfectly formed breasts shimmied in rhythm to the music.

Jayne finished her wine, needing more false courage. Mason refilled her glass. He looked first in her eyes, and then she watched his gaze fall slowly down toward the V neckline of her dress. She was glad that the lights had dimmed because she felt a blush. Her face must have been flaming red. She raised her glass to Mason in false bravado and took a large swallow.

Another number followed based on an Egyptian theme. Again, the women were topless and covered with diaphanous materials of green and gold. Their headpieces were extravagant. They undulated across the stage like a harem entertaining their master.

Before Jayne knew it, she had finished half of her bottle of wine. Mason had a pleased smirk on his face. She thought he was enjoying her discomfort and knew her veneer of confidence was just that ... a veneer. He asked if she wanted some more wine.

"Yes."

Her reward was a slight rising of one of Mason's eyebrows. *God, he has beautiful eyes.*

He filled her glass with some red wine and passed some chocolate éclairs over from Rosa's plate. Jayne then passed some cheese and fruit over, but Rosa refused them, glancing quickly at Jayne.

"Try this pairing with your wine," he suggested.

Jayne picked up the éclair and took a bite. Chocolate filled her mouth along with fluffy cream and crisp pastry. A murmur of pleasure escaped her lips. She followed this sweet sensation with a sip of red wine. She murmured again.

"Pretty damn good, right?" Mason's eyes seemed to sparkle.

"Exquisite."

The next act entered. Jayne sucked in her breath as the most beautiful woman she had ever seen appeared on stage. Her headpiece evoked Medusa with snakes curling out. The dancer wore a thin green cape that was quickly discarded along with the headpiece. A group of men pushed a glass pool on stage, and the dancer climbed some steps and dove in. It looked like something Houdini would have used in his act ... but more sensual.

Within the pool were three giant snakes. Real snakes. Large, yellow-green serpents, undulating. The music crescendoed as the dancer swam seductively and wrapped her nude body within the snakes' coils.

Jayne wiped her forehead and the beads of sweat from above her lips. It must be the wine, she thought as she continued to stare, mesmerized by the woman in the pool. The curves of the snakes mirrored the curves of the woman's pearlescent body. *She's beautiful. Free and sexual. Not in a slutty way, but in an artistic way.*

As the acts continued through the one-and-a-half-hour show, Jayne let herself indulge in the pure sensuality of the experience. She admired the confident women parading across the stage. The audience applauded and appreciated the combination of sexuality and music. She tingled with anticipation as each new act performed on stage.

When the Cancan dancers appeared and that famous music filled the theater, Jayne stood and clapped her hands as wildly as everyone else in the place. The Brazilians stood, wiggling their hips. Rosa flipped her skirt back and forth. When the audience began to echo the shouts from the dancers on the stage, Jayne was one of the loudest. The thunderous applause at the end accented the pumping of her heart.

Instead of being flushed with embarrassment, Jayne let the full flush of excitement course through her body. Her sensations felt magnified. The wine tasted sweeter. Every fiber of her dress caressed her as it swayed. Her skin tingled in reaction.

Mason helped her with her coat. As his fingers brushed across her shoulders, she shivered, but not from cold. He whispered in her ear.

"You look beautiful tonight."

She thought she had imagined it, but the puffs of breath on her neck told her it was real. She breathed in his scent and lingered in the exchange, letting herself get lost in those beautiful gray-blue orbs as he faced her for a moment before turning his attention to Rosa.

As she followed the crowd from the theatre, she tried to remember when Tom had ever complimented her. Made her feel desirable.

Perhaps never.

At least, never in this way.

CHAPTER 8

ate Tuesday night, October 16, 2012

The moon was full overhead, as everyone boarded the bus that seemed to appear magically in front of the Moulin Rouge. The Brazilian couples talked in muted tones and paired off into their seats.

The combination of moonlight and alcohol muddled Jayne's mind just enough. Perhaps this was the "comfortably numb" that Pink Floyd sang about. She giggled at the thought. She sat in the front of the bus and watched Mason help Rosa up the stairs.

Rosa swayed a bit and fell back into Mason's arms. *Boy, if he believes that then he's a fool,* she thought, followed by a somber voice of conscience chastising her. Rosa sat in front of Jayne, and Mason sat beside her instead of in his usual seat at the door. Jacques smiled as he closed the doors, and they were on their way back to the hotel.

Soon, voices silenced, and Jayne watched Rosa rest her head on Mason's shoulder. He didn't move, but he didn't push her away. Jayne shifted in her seat and reached up to a curl that had escaped and tugged at it. She put it behind her ear, but it sprang forward. She gave up the fight as she looked out the window. Her reflection stared back. She looked disheveled, but not in a bad way. Still, she could not compare with the voluptuous Ms. Rosa. The bus pulled up in front of the hotel just as her tiny voice taunted her. *Why are you even thinking about such things?*

Because I'm drunk, she answered.

In the lobby, the Brazilian couples said something to Mason and then nodded at Jayne. Instead of heading toward the elevators, they went back out the door. Jayne must have appeared surprised because Mason answered her question without it being asked.

"They are going out for coffee," he said and smiled. "Do you want to join them, ladies?"

"No way," Jayne said. "I'm enjoying my intoxicated state right now." She put her hand up to her mouth when she realized that she had said this out loud.

"Really?" he said as he lifted an eyebrow. He started walking toward the elevators and pushed the button.

"Mason," Rosa interrupted, "let's go up to your room."

Jayne stiffened with the "your" and focused her bleary eyes on her feet.

The elevator arrived and they all got on. Mason pushed the button and Rosa leaned against him. Jayne moved back to a corner and just watched.

Rosa's breast was on Mason's arm. He had to feel it, Jayne thought, especially after the show they had just watched. How couldn't he feel aroused? Rosa snaked her arm around his lower back, right below his waistline. He didn't move closer, but he didn't move away either. Why did Jayne think he should? Gravity made her feel small as the elevator zoomed up. *Am I sinking into the floor?*

She shifted her focus to the numbers above the door. The elevator seemed to be going far too slowly. Come on, she thought. She pulled at her coat, then she put her hand in a pocket.

The door finally opened and she tried to dart past Mason, but he caught her arm.

"Good night, Jayne," he said and her name sounded golden as he said it.

She turned and replied to both Mason and Rosa, "Good night to both of you."

"*Si*, a very good night," Rosa replied.

Jayne took out her key as she walked to her room. She could feel Rosa and Mason, their sexual tension, behind her. Plunging her key in the door, she looked back to see Mason and Rosa poised in front of the room directly across from her. Jayne hurried into her room, fighting the urge to look back out at the hallway through her peephole. Fighting the unfamiliar inklings of jealousy.

She threw her purse on the seat of the chair, tossed her coat over the back, and undressed. In the bathroom, her face flushed as she washed off her makeup. She felt like the electricity in her body was shorting out. Tingling through her fingertips.

Nestled in her bed, Jayne lay wide awake, reliving the details of the evening. What would Tom have thought? He would have been scandalized by her actions at the end of the evening. She knew that without a doubt. He had never been an overly passionate man. But despite everything, she was still prickling with passion. Sex had always been good, she thought. But she really didn't have any form of comparison. She had only been with Tom.

Reality with Tom gave way to thoughts of Mason. Static electricity under the sheets gave her goosebumps. She wondered what was happening in the room across the hall. Her thoughts kept poking at her. Waking her.

Or, it could have been just the alcohol.

She was tired and should have been deep asleep. Instead, she tossed and turned. Drifting off periodically, only to awaken trying to catch her breath. Wheezing and feeling like she was drowning, she punched her pillows before propping them up.

How could she feel so alive despite that? Moonlight filtered through the window as she drifted off again. Her dreams took flight, transforming her into the woman in Mason's room. Not Rosa.

~

ON WEDNESDAY MORNING, Jayne felt hungover and embarrassed. Her head ached and her mouth felt like a desert. She lingered in the shower, letting the warm water pound against her shoulders and the back of her head. She had foggy recollections of the night and found it hard to face herself in the mirror. She got ready quickly and popped a couple of Tylenol along with her other medications, hoping that she would snap out of it by the end of breakfast. Tea and toast would do the trick.

In the breakfast area, the Parks motioned Jayne over.

Jayne scanned the room.

"Most everyone has already come and gone," Floyd replied to her unsolicited question.

"Oh, am I running late?" she quickly took a seat at the table.

"A bit, but I'm sure they won't leave without the three of us."

Jayne ordered her tea and toast. She couldn't afford to skip breakfast.

"How was last night?" Emma asked.

Jayne blushed profusely as memories peppered her. Rosa and Mason entering his room foremost in her mind. "Wonder-ful," she managed to choke out.

"I'm really looking forward to the museum today," Floyd said.

"Me too," Jayne replied, staunching the thoughts from last

night like a teenager keeping the fact that she made out with her boyfriend a secret from her parents.

They finished their breakfasts and made their way out to the bus parked in its usual place in front of the hotel.

Mason greeted them as they got on the bus. Was it her imagination, or did his smile contain some seductive undertones? Jayne promptly blushed again at the thought, then reminded herself that Rosa was the true source of it, not her fantasies.

It didn't take long for the bus to pull in front of the Louvre, with its giant pyramid entrance. The triangles of glass reflected the sunlight that peeped through the spotty clouds. The group followed Mason through the doors, with Rosa close by his side.

A broad flight of stairs led to different exhibits, from housing antiquities to artwork from all over the world and every period of history. Jayne had looked through so many books containing these treasures that she could hardly believe she was here in the flesh. She bounced up and down on her toes, craning to look around.

Their tour began in the European paintings section. Room after room offered feasts for the eyes. Cinnabar red swirled with Sedona brown to create the folds of a seventeenth-century woman's dress. Tiger's Eye gold accented the lapis coat of an eighteenth-century elite gentleman, posing for eternity with his hunting dogs at his side. Jayne soaked in the sights like someone who had only lived a black and white existence.

Mason stopped the group in front of a French painting of a woman who was simply taking care of her children.

"This is a work by Jean Baptiste-Simeon Chardin, painted in 1740. It might not seem unusual on the surface, but this is one of the few paintings that didn't reflect the extravagant lifestyle of the rich. This woman is not smiling as she indulges in the routine of everyday life. She's a regular person serving an evening meal to her daughters."

The group followed Mason, with Rosa still by his side, as

they went on. But Jayne lingered. She looked closely at the painting. Who was this woman taking care of her children? One child had her hands folded as if in prayer. Was the mother teaching her children to be thankful for their meager meal? It seemed that a mother's role hadn't changed over the centuries. Was routine the only way to live life? No, she realized. Following dreams shattered routine and made life exceptional. She knew that now. Raising children was only part of it.

Jayne moved to another painting by the same artist. This one was called *The Canary* and had been painted in Paris in 1779. The woman in the portrait wore a flowered silk dress. The background of the sitting room was dark, but there was sunlight filtering through the window. The woman had a music box on her lap and her hand was on the crank. She was looking at a canary in a cage in front of the window. The canary appeared very small behind the cage's intricate black wire. The look on the woman's face was hauntingly familiar to Jayne.

"Jayne?"

Mason was suddenly standing by her side, snapping her out of her reveries. "I thought we lost you."

"I'm sorry." She still looked at the painting as it pulled her in.

"He was a talented artist," Mason said.

"He captured her pain," she replied.

Mason paused and looked again at the painting. "What pain? She is in a luxurious room. All the comforts of the age and more."

"She's trapped, like the canary in the cage," she said, turning to face him. "She can only glimpse the freedom that lies outside that window ... and dream."

"Isn't being comfortable enough?"

"No." Jayne took a final look back at the portrait and continued. "I don't believe it is." She followed Mason back to the group.

The tour's next stop was the *Mona Lisa*. Jayne moved closer.

Lodged behind thick, bullet-proof glass, the masterpiece was much smaller than she had anticipated. Apparently, someone had tried to destroy the famous painting. The lights reflecting on the glass made it difficult to see the intricacies of the brush strokes. Disappointment settled on her as she tried to get a good view. Another caged lady.

For the rest of their time in the museum, the group dispersed and roamed about on their own. The Brazilian couples went in one direction and the Parks teamed up with the other grandparents. Rosa and Natalie were with Mason. Jayne didn't want to watch Rosa fawn over Mason, so she decided to venture off by herself.

She ended up in the Near Eastern antiquities area. Egyptian mummies lined one wall. Trinkets, goblets, and pottery were on another. Around the corner, hanging on the wall, was a bust of a beautiful young woman. It was so lifelike that she looked as if she had materialized from the limestone. Jayne read the caption. It was a funerary bust of Ummayat, the daughter of Yarhai of Palmyra, and dated back to the second half of the second century AD. The young girl's hair hung in ringlets that dangled out from an exquisite headdress. Adorned in jewelry, the material she wore hung in delicate folds.

Jayne thought about the parents of this beautiful girl who was obviously struck down so young. *How does a mother survive that?* The girl looked to be about the same age as Kim. Any parent would take the place of their child if given the chance. What an unnatural calamity to survive as a parent. Jayne had seen enough in this area and made her way to another section of the museum.

She found herself wandering through the Michelangelo Gallery, aptly named for the wonderful display of sculptures lining the walls. The marble floor provided a foundation for solid marble bases that held sculptures beyond belief.

"Have you seen the Canova sculpture of Psyche and Cupid?"

Jayne flinched as she turned to face Mason.

He was alone.

"No," she answered.

"It's at the end of this corridor." He led the way, walking just a step ahead of Jayne.

"Where is your entourage?"

"They stopped for lunch and I wasn't hungry."

They approached a magnificent creation in luminous marble. The mythic couple seemed suspended in time.

"Absolutely stunning." Jayne circled the piece, noticing how Cupid's translucent wingtips pointed toward heaven. The light played through the tips, refracting into an aura around the wingspan. She fought the urge to run her hands over the sculpture.

Mason moved to the plaque in front of the statue and began reading, "Canova captured the moment that Cupid found his lady love, Psyche, who was not dead, but had passed out after opening the contents of a forbidden flask. Cupid, the god of love, wanted to marry Psyche, a mere mortal. The gods had a counsel and granted Psyche immortality so the couple could marry. She became the goddess of the soul."

"What a beautiful story," Jayne said as she continued to walk slowly around the sculpture.

"The stuff that myths are made of." Mason walked the opposite way from Jayne so they were across from each other.

"But myths include humanity, don't they? Love is not merely the stuff of the gods, is it?" Jayne looked past the piece to Mason. Their eyes met. Jayne saw a profound sadness reflected in his gaze. Then, a hardness fell back into place.

"It is still a myth," he replied.

What had happened to him that he couldn't see the nuances right in front of him? Jayne looked closely at the sculpture before she continued.

"Yes, myth provided the subjects, but the artist was human.

Flesh and blood just like us. Look at his creation. The swirl of the embrace. Psyche leaning into the caring arms of her love. You can almost feel the breath between them. They are struggling towards life and love. The title of the piece is *Psyche Revived by Cupid's Kiss*. It's a human emotion. They are perpetually suspended on the precipice of a kiss. It's real emotion captured by a human artist. He has really captured the soul and love in this piece. It's beautiful."

Mason walked slowly around the sculpture and came back to stand next to Jayne.

"It is an amazing work of art," he admitted, looking at Jayne.

"Art inspired by love," Jayne replied. "My case for the existence of true love is building."

"If you say so," he replied, still looking at the sculpture with a furrowed brow, but his features were somehow softer.

She shifted her purse on her shoulder. "Where to next?"

"We are off to Montmartre. There are some quaint restaurants there if you're hungry."

"I'm not really hungry."

They walked together away from the sculpture, and Jayne wondered who had damaged Mason's outlook on love and women in particular.

MONTMARTRE, the highest hilltop in and around Paris, had drawn artists like Renoir, Lautrec, Monet, and Picasso. The bus parked at the base of the hill, where steps led up the hillside. The Parks took the funicular along the steps, but Jayne paced herself and remained at the end of the group.

As she neared the top of the stairs, she couldn't seem to catch her breath. *So much for stupid pride.* She gulped and straightened as she saw Mason.

"Are you all right?" he asked as he held out his hand to help her up the last couple of stairs.

"Just … a bit … out … of breath," she managed to puff out.

"Come over here," he said as he led her to a bench.

After a few minutes, she had recovered enough to ask, "Where is everyone?"

"Scattered. Some are shopping for souvenirs. Others are eating. Would you like to join me for lunch?"

"Yes, I think I could use something to eat now." A tingle of excitement ran through her body.

"I know just the place."

He seemed buoyant for a change. She wasn't sure why and wondered where Rosa was. She followed him along the streets peopled with tourists and artists alike. They fell into a natural pace, stopping here and there to view artists' works in progress.

This must be what an out-of-body experience feels like. A mix of numbness and anticipation.

Here she was. In Paris. With a gorgeous man.

On the Place du Tertre, the ghosts of the old masters appeared in the guises of current artists with easels ready to create a masterpiece for any tourist who would pay the asking price. The streets abounded with colorful villas nestled next to each other. Pink alongside yellow. Brown next to red. The villas themselves were artworks in three dimensions.

Mason turned down a narrow alleyway that wormed around to a fuchsia-painted shop covered with red vines. "Here we go."

The quaint bistro was rustic inside, complete with crackled walls and peeling paint. The menu was scrawled on a chalkboard, just in French, of course. The intimate setting could only accommodate a few small tables. A stool and microphone stood in a corner, in front of a beat-up guitar.

"Oh, it looks like they have music here." Jayne wondered what type of music the absent performer would have played.

A shout came from behind the bar as a gray-haired man approached, speaking rapid French and waving his hands widely. Short and stocky. His face had deep lines running down it like mountain crevices. A few customers stopped eating and watched. He hugged Mason and slapped him on the back. Smiling and talking all the while, the man showed them to a table.

As Jayne sat down Mason responded to the enthusiasm until the man hustled to the back of the restaurant. "I'm sorry, but I haven't seen Claude in a long time," Mason explained as he shrugged off his leather jacket and sat down. "I used to play for him."

"That's right. You're a musician."

"Not anymore. I hope you don't mind, but I ordered for us."

"Wonderful. What kind of musician were you?" Determined to find out more, she prodded but was not sure how far she could go.

"I played folk and contemporary music." Mason fidgeted. It was unlike what Jayne had seen of him so far. He usually seemed so together and in control. Guilt tugged at her, but not enough to make her stop wondering. She glanced at the guitar in the corner and then back at Mason. They sat in silence for a few more minutes before Claude appeared again.

"Mason, I know it is usually evening when we have music," Claude said in broken English. He shuffled a bit before he continued. "But would you consider playing something? It's been such a long time, *mon ami. S'il vous plaît?*"

"*Non,*" Mason replied. He shifted in his seat again.

Poor Claude looked like a boy who had been denied dessert. His lower lip protruded slightly. Jayne wondered how many things this obviously well-practiced pout had won over.

She witnessed a few more seconds of warring emotions. Claude was still frozen in his pose. Mason shook his head as he got up and went to the corner. The pout had won another victory as Mason picked up the worn guitar and propped it across his knee. He shifted a bit as he strummed each string to tune the instrument. He ignored the microphone and after taking a deep breath he began to play.

His music filled the room, flowing from his fingertips and fluttering to the rafters. Then he began to sing, in French. Jayne could not understand a word, but she didn't need to. His voice was smooth. Clear dulcet tones tinged with a light, raspy accent. Incredible range. It was a love song. It floated to the ear and caressed the soul. As he continued to sing, he closed his eyes. He was lost, no longer in the café.

So where was he? And with whom? How could a man with such obvious sensitivity become the man she had come to know over the past couple of days? He was truly a gifted musician. Why was he a tour guide?

After he finished, the café erupted in applause. Mason's eyes opened and he nodded his thanks to the crowd. He replaced the guitar reverently and returned to the table as their meal was being served.

The music seemed to linger. Haunting. Somber. Something lost. She couldn't place the myriad of emotions that had deeply moved her. Longing might come close to the right word, she thought. Certainly, poignant.

The waiter set out their food across the table and filled their glasses with wine.

"I didn't recognize the melody. Is it a French classic?" she finally managed to ask.

"No, it's a Mason classic," he said. "Let's eat.

Their lunch consisted of white wine and a unique salad with tomatoes, cheeses, croutons and spices. The chardonnay complimented the salad perfectly. They also had crusty French bread. Mason broke off a hunk and handed it to Jayne.

"Does this meet with your approval?"

"It's delicious." She sampled another sip of wine. "Why did you quit?"

"What?"

"Why did you stop playing?"

"It stopped paying."

"Paying what?"

"The cost was too high." He stuffed a large piece of bread in his mouth. That's the end of that subject, Jayne thought. Still, she found herself wanting to know more. The song showed her that he felt deeply. No one could write something like that and not experience love. She found herself wondering who the real Mason would turn out to be, and what would be the cost of finding out. He had drawn her in with his song.

They were nearly finished with their lunch when Rosa and Natalie entered the café.

"Well, here you are," Rosa said with a slight edge in her voice. "Natalie and I have been looking everywhere for you." She glanced at Jayne and then back to Mason. "You know you could have eaten with us at the museum."

"Yes, I am very well aware of that, but I wasn't hungry then." Mason ripped off another piece of bread. Instead of breaking off a small piece, he bit a huge hunk off and chewed like a millstone grinding grist. He swallowed hard and replied, "We are almost finished, but you are welcome to join us."

Rosa pulled up a chair, but Natalie remained standing. She shifted her feet as she looked down intently at them.

"Please have a seat, Natalie," Jayne said and smiled. The intrusion dissolved her musings about Mason, like being roughly awakened from a beautiful dream.

Natalie sat, but she still looked uncomfortable as she pushed her glasses up on the bridge of her nose.

A waiter appeared, cleared away plates, and asked the newcomers if they wanted anything.

"Just a glass," Rosa said. "I'll have some of what they were having."

Natalie ordered sparkling water.

"So, tell me your secret," Rosa asked Jayne. Her smile didn't reach her eyes.

"What secret?" Jayne shifted in her seat and pulled on the hem of her blouse.

"How did you manage to get Mason all to yourself today?"

"What do you mean?" Jayne tried to act nonchalant as she smoothed the crease in her pants.

"I saw you in the museum and then here."

Jayne's hand shook slightly as she sipped some wine. Her mind tumbled and she couldn't come up with a response to the verbal assault.

Mason cleared his throat as the waiter returned with the glass and sparkling water.

"I'm available to everyone on this tour, Rosa."

"So it appears." She reached across the table and picked up the wine bottle. She filled her glass and took a healthy sip.

"You are married, *no*?"

"Yes, I am," Jayne replied, her Southern accent drawing out the vowels. The guilt card was played to perfection as she looked down at her lap.

"And where is he?" she asked. "Will he be joining you on this trip?"

Mason stood, his chair skidding back several inches. "I think it's time to go to the bus."

Natalie stood in response. "Yes, where are we going next?"

"Notre-Dame."

"Wonderful," Rosa interjected. "Maybe a priest there can help you remember a certain commandment. Maybe the one about not committing adultery?"

In a low, steady voice, Mason countered, "Maybe he can help you remember the scriptures about casting stones, Rosa."

Mason reached over and helped Jayne with her coat. Without looking back or waiting, he guided Jayne out of the café. Her shoulders slumped with regret piled high on multiple levels.

117

CHAPTER 9

ednesday afternoon, October 17, 2012

The cathedral of Notre Dame looked even more daunting in the afternoon sun. Jayne stared at the structure immortalized in Victor Hugo's masterpiece. Twin spires at the front stretched into the sky, and pillars buttressed the back like a spider's sprawling legs.

The group disembarked and gathered at the intricately carved entrance.

"This is the west portal. It's called the Portal of the Last Judgment," Mason began his lecture.

Jayne squinted at the entrance, trying to see each of the intricate carvings individually.

Mason moved forward and swept his hands in an arcing motion. "The bottom portion of the carvings represent the raising of the dead on Judgment Day. Archangel Michael is depicted weighing the souls of the dead. The weight of the souls is calculated by the lives they led on earth, and the amount of love they had for God and their fellow man. You'll notice that to the right of Christ, the deserving souls are led to heaven, and to the left, they're led to the pits of hell."

Mason then pointed to the top extremes of the area. "The gargoyles were not original to the structure and were added in the mid-nineteenth century. They are really drainpipes to protect the masonry from decay."

Jayne looked closely at the faces frozen in the stone extremes of ecstasy and agony. Love of God and fellow man was the criterion. Where did she fall on the continuum? Certainly, her thoughts about a certain tour guide didn't help her cause.

As they entered the cathedral, the resounding toll of a giant bell filled the air. Resonating through the immense structure, it dolefully counted the hour of the day. Jayne stood motionless while most of the others entered the giant brass doors. The notes fluttered in her soul, swaying and pulsating with each heartbeat. She looked up at the tower and saw the slight movement of the bell. If just one bell affected her so profoundly, what would happen when all five bells pealed?

She lingered in the doorway after the last toll, thinking about the joyful and sorrowful events that the bells had responded to through the centuries. From baptisms to funerals. Revolutions and victories. Would anyone notice her death or come to her funeral other than her children? Did she even warrant a second thought? She sighed a shaky breath.

Do the bells know the occasions and alter their tones? No, of course not, she thought as she placed one hand on her chest and felt the subtle rhythm of her heartbeat. *People's emotions add that intangible element to music.*

As if cued by God, the sound of the organ burst through the partially open door. Jayne went in, drawn by the fullness of the sound. It was like the thundering voice of God. The cathedral loomed in Gothic splendor to the heavens, pierced with light from the multifaceted stained-glass windows. Chandeliers hung over the end of each pew, suspended orbs of light further accentuating the darkened interior. The line from Browning's *Pippa*

Passes floated through her mind: "God's in his heaven—All's right with the world."

Jayne saw the Parks sitting in a pew, so she sat beside them. No one spoke. They just sat with eyes and ears open, drinking in the cathedral. As the music continued, the choir added angelic voices. Voices mixed with pipes echoed off the walls and ceiling. The arches and angles played with the sound. It was an experience as close to heaven as possible while still planted firmly in the earthly realm.

After the music ended, no one spoke until they were outside once again. The leaves on the trees surrounding the cathedral quivered in burnt orange and brilliant red. Even the light that filtered through the drifting clouds seemed more brilliant.

"Magnificent." Floyd finally ended the silence.

"I never dreamed," Emma reflected. "I will never forget this moment for the rest of my life."

"Me too." Jayne looked at the elderly couple. They were holding hands again. She could see the lasting effect of what they had just witnessed. She envied their connection. A unique bond she had never experienced herself.

"We lucked out today." Mason intruded on her thoughts. "They usually close when the choir practices, but not today." When no one responded, he continued. "Did you know that the bells in the towers have names? The giant bell that you heard earlier is named Emmanuel. It's in the south tower. The other four bells are in the north tower."

"I can see why Victor Hugo chose this place for his novel," Jayne responded, thinking about poor Quasimodo and the bells.

"Why?" Mason asked. "Don't you think a church is a strange place for a love story?"

"Not when you hear those bells, I don't. If the soul isn't stirred by that, then there is definitely something missing." Jayne thought about what was missing in hers. "Don't you think that the tolling of the bell kind of reflects the nature of love?

There are swings of passion, celebration of good and bad, and a bit of pounding along the way."

"Maybe so," Mason said as he looked at the towers. "I never thought of it that way, but maybe so."

It seemed almost anticlimactic for Jayne when everyone got back on the bus, and Mason announced that they would go to Le Quartier Des Grands Magasins for a while. The bus dropped everyone off in front of a giant department store. Jayne had never seen anything so large. In giant lights, *Galeries Lafayette* blinked amid the extravagant ironwork. The art nouveau design was a stark counterpoint to gothic architecture.

"Can you believe this?" Floyd said.

"I guess it's a real shopping mecca," Emma added.

They entered the structure and stopped as ten floors loomed above them in a circular pattern. High above was a dome with stained glass accents.

"It is a shopping cathedral," Jayne said. "I know some people who shop religiously."

Emma and Floyd laughed. "Where do we start?"

"I don't know, but I hope I can find my way back to the front entrance." Jayne started toward the center of the circle. "You two enjoy yourselves."

Jayne browsed with her daughter Kim in mind. Trembling slightly and feeling hollow, she missed her daughter. *I should have invited her along. Made memories together.*

Stop it. You didn't, so keep writing in your notebook.

She wanted to get her something meaningful. Something that would make Kim want to visit this place herself someday ... someday soon. *Something that will help her remember me.* Jayne looked at the fancy perfumes. They wouldn't last long enough. She saw jewelry in one corner of the perfume counter. She thought about the legacy of Coco Chanel, who had fought her way to the top with hard work and innovation. Jayne looked at some earrings with the famous intertwined initials that trademarked the brand. Kim could keep these and maybe even pass them down to her own daughter someday. Jayne fought the lump in her throat, swallowing hard as she thought about a granddaughter she would never know. She repeated her mantra silently.

The salesperson came over and spoke in French. Jayne snapped out of her thoughts. She didn't understand a word but managed through sign language to show her interest in the earrings. She cradled them in her hand, the diamonds glittering in the light. Kim had always liked designer creations. Jayne looked at the cost and gasped. Tom wasn't going to like this extravagance. Even so, she pulled out her credit card and bought them.

As she walked around each circular floor, she saw Jimmy Choo, Cartier, Hugo Boss, and every other designer name in existence. This was a palace for high-end consumerism. The prices staggered her. She looked for something for John and found a beautiful set of pens. When he became a famous entrepreneur, he could use them to sign his big deals. She talked with the salesperson trying to find out whether the refills could be purchased in the States. Sign language wasn't working now.

"Can I help out here?" Mason appeared by her side.

"Yes, I just want to know about the refills." Jayne was glad to see him.

He translated and told Jayne she would not have a problem with getting refills at home.

"Good." She smiled and finished her purchase, which was incomprehensibly expensive as well.

"You don't seem to have much," Mason said as he walked with her out of the store. "I've seen some of the others with several big bags, and they're still going."

"My purchases may seem modest, but trust me, the cost wasn't."

"Your husband will love the pen."

"It's for my son."

Mason raised his eyebrows slightly. "Oh, well, I'll let you get back to your shopping."

"I'm finished with buying. Now I'm just going to window shop."

"Mind if I join you?"

"Not at all."

They took the elevator to the next floor.

"How do they do it?" Jayne asked as she looked at the rich displays in each storefront.

"Do what?"

"Stay in business."

"Tourists help."

"I know," Jayne said, "but how can they sell that much high-priced inventory every day?"

"Typically, Americans are the biggest spenders," Mason replied. "New York, Los Angeles, and even Chicago come to mind."

"That's true," Jayne admitted. "But the exchange rate makes a difference here. I guess my younger southern girl self who saved her pennies isn't completely gone."

"Don't you like shopping? Most women do."

"Yes, I like some shopping, but I also like a bargain."

"They have sales here."

"I'm sorry, but any percentage off the outrageous prices here is still too high a price for me."

Mason looked at Jayne, his brows knit together and eyes shining.

"What?" She responded to that look by staring into those deep blue-gray orbs.

"Nothing," he said as he shrugged. "I've just never met a woman quite like you before."

"I'll take that as a compliment," she said. "I will confess that the gifts I bought for my children were outrageously priced, but in that case, it was worth it. I want these gifts to last and mean something."

"And what about something for your husband?" Mason asked.

"No matter what I bought for him, he would definitely be put off by the overindulgence of it," she commented.

They kept walking through the extensive shops that were set up like a Middle Eastern bazaar. Fashion designers, jewelry, accessories of every kind. A kaleidoscope of material goods provided a feast for the eyes.

"Follow me," Mason said and grabbed her hand. It felt strong, but soft. Firm. Comfortable. They rode the elevator to the top, and he led Jayne out to a terrace.

Paris stretched out beneath them. In the distance, the Eiffel Tower stood against the backdrop of the powder-blue sky.

"Now this," Jayne said, "is the best thing about the Galeries Lafayette, and it's free."

"Somehow, that doesn't surprise me," Mason said. "I haven't been up here for a long time."

She took a deep breath and tried to take it all in. The place. The man. Her feeling of being special every time she spent a moment alone with this stranger.

Mason looked at his watch and said it was time to head back down to catch the bus back to the hotel.

"Thank you," Jayne said as she passed through the door that Mason held open for her.

"My pleasure," he said.

The group trickled back to the bus. Rosa had purchased so much that Jacques and Mason had to store the bags in the luggage area underneath the bus. The Brazilian couples were close behind her in purchases. The grandparents had spoiled their grandchildren, who were wearing some of their recent purchases. Only the Parks and Jayne had no evidence of large purchases.

She watched the older couple. Floyd always made sure that he seated Emma comfortably before he sat down. They snuggled shoulder-to-shoulder most of the time. When they had toured the city, they pointed out things to each other like excited children.

"Let's count heads and make sure we don't leave anyone behind," Mason said, his gaze lingering on Rosa.

Her legs were crossed with one foot hanging a bit in the aisle. Her sleek black pants were tight all the way down to the ankle, where her feet sported sexy black heels, not at all suitable for either touring or shopping. Her purple cashmere sweater had a deep V-neck. Her earrings were massive and a scarf was draped strategically around her neck, never daring to interfere with the show of cleavage. Everything was on magnificent display.

So, this is his type of woman, Jayne mused. Sexy and extravagant. Forward and confident. Everything she wasn't.

So what? Why are you even thinking this way?

Her tiny voice was at it again.

Why had he spent the time on the roof with me? Because it's his job, silly!

"OK," Mason's voice seemed to boom into her consciousness, "it looks like everyone is here. Let's go back to the hotel. Tonight, you have a free night. There is a band in the hotel restaurant if you want to go dancing. Otherwise, the concierge will get you a taxi to go wherever you wish. Enjoy another night in Paris."

He clicked off the microphone and took his seat. Jayne couldn't help but feel like she would be wasting her last night in Paris. All alone with her room service.

Exhausted from the busy day, Jayne let her room door slam shut. She dropped her bag on the desk, shrugged out of her coat, and lay flat on her back across the bed. Immediately, she knew she had made a mistake because she couldn't breathe. She quickly rolled to her side and sat up, trying to catch her breath. Her lungs were not opening all the way. She switched to measured, short breaths.

The phone rang, so she sat at the desk as she picked it up. "Hello?"

"Jayne, how are you?" Lynn's voice sounded far away. "You sound funny."

"I'm fine," she lied.

"Good, then how's Paris?

"It's wonderful," Jayne replied. "Everything is just beautiful."

"And how's the tour guide? He sounded intriguing, and I have to admit that I've been wondering about him."

"He is very intelligent, and I think the sexy Spanish woman is sleeping with him."

"Really?"

"Yes, she was not happy to see him sharing lunch with me today."

"You had lunch alone with him today?"

"Yes, but it could have been anybody who was the last out of the bus. This time it was just me."

"Really?"

"Lynn, don't let your imagination get away from you. I'm an old married lady with complications." Jayne shifted in her seat. "We went shopping today. You would have loved it. All your favorite designers."

"You're changing the subject."

"You're right."

"Okay, I just wanted to check in with you. I'm following your itinerary and thinking about you every day. Do you still think it was a mistake?"

"No, I am really enjoying every minute of it. We heard the bells at Notre Dame today. It was more than wonderful. I've met an older couple who are just darling."

"I'm so glad. I'll call you again when you get to Italy." Lynn paused. "Or maybe I'll just show up to get a look at that tour guide. Dark chestnut hair, combed straight back, wavy and flowing to his chiseled chin. Sexy streaks of gray. I remember your description in detail. Wonderful eyes. Nice build. Sounds like my type."

Jayne's heart seemed to skip a beat, and her body tensed as she realized that she didn't want Lynn to join her. She wanted to continue on her own.

"Lynn, you never cease to amaze me."

She hung up the phone and then lifted it again to call for room service. Within half an hour, her tray arrived. She feasted on a simple salad and a glass of wine, lingering on her experiences of the day. Full experiences. The joy of living each day to the fullest, with no regrets.

Placing the empty tray outside of her door, she called for room service to pick it up. Then she tumbled into bed.

Just as Jayne was drifting off, a light knock on her door startled her. She sat straight up, her heart racing. Slipping her robe over her shoulders, she looked out the peephole to see Mason. She paused, then unlocked the door and slowly opened it a crack.

"I'm sorry to bother you, but I have something for you."

Jayne opened the door wider and saw that he had something tucked under his arm. She didn't know what to do.

"Where's Rosa?" she asked before she could stop to think about it.

"What?"

"You know … sexy curves … nice pout," Jayne replied as she made an hourglass shape in the air.

"I don't know now. It's a long story," he said. "Why don't you get dressed? I'll meet you in the lobby."

She just stared at him, confusion bouncing around in her mind. *Am I still asleep? Dreaming?*

"I know it's sudden, but it was an impulse for me too. I didn't want to wait until tomorrow with everyone around."

He looked like a schoolboy with an apple for his teacher. She thought for a moment.

Definitely not a dream.

"My hair is a mess. It might take me a few minutes."

"Your hair is wonderful. I'll be in the lobby."

Jayne closed the door. Excitement and curiosity filled her with renewed energy, like a kindergartener getting ready for the first big day at school.

She put on some light makeup and just ran her fingers through her tousled hair. She usually didn't wear jeans, but she decided to slip on the only pair she had brought. Designer jeans that Kim had talked her into buying. She added a silk purple turtleneck and picked up her purse.

She found Mason seated in a corner grouping of plush chairs in the lobby. He ran his fingers through his hair and fidgeted in his chair. The package rested on a table in the center of the grouping. Mason stood as she put her purse down on the table.

"This is for you," he said as he pointed to the package.

"I can't believe you bought me something," she said as she pulled at the twine.

She felt like it was her birthday. She hadn't received a surprise gift in years. Most of the time, Tom just gave her money to buy what she wanted. He had always said that he didn't have a knack for getting the right gift.

"You really shouldn't have."

"I saw it when we were walking down the street. I had to go back to get it."

"We?" she asked.

"Yes, I was with Rosa," he said as he swiped both hands through his hair. "I was beginning to think I had made a mistake with her. Then, I knew it when I saw this. She got mad when I wanted to stop and get it for you." He rubbed his hand across his cheek. "But it was worth it to get this for you."

She undid the twine and ripped at the brown paper. It was an oil painting.

She looked at the depiction of the row of houses she had walked past with Mason earlier in the day. It was the street that led to the café. The painter had captured every nuance. The light filtering through the buildings, the colorful houses, the rust-colored ivy on the walls, and even the lace curtains within the dwellings.

"It's beautiful and thoughtful," she said as tears threatened. "Why?"

"I wanted you to remember today."

"I would have remembered today anyway."

She just looked at Mason, his chestnut hair flecked with gray and a satisfied smile on his face. She didn't know what else to say. Warmth radiated through her chest.

"Let's go out on the town," Mason filled the silence.

"What?"

"I know where we can go."

She paused, wondering if she should, but made the mistake of looking at the painting once again.

"Okay, I'll just take this up to my room and get my coat."

Jayne couldn't believe she was going out with Mason on her own. At night. Her pulse quickened. Her tiny voice started to say something, but this time, she shut it down. She got her coat and felt like a schoolgirl slipping out for a secret date.

The taxi pulled up to *Les Closerie des Lilas*, according to the signs hanging on twin sides of a typically Parisian building. The white lights were like guiding stars twinkling in the night sky. The canopied entrance looked inviting, skirted by trellises and draped in ivy. Tables and chairs sat on the sidewalk behind hedges. It was so French. Part of the terrace was enclosed in glass, while the rest was open. Old-fashioned lamps adorned the outdoor section and reflected against the panes of glass.

"This place is beautiful," she said.

"It is," Mason agreed. "This café was one of the many hangouts for writers from the Lost Generation." He guided her through the glass doorway. "I guess it's one of my favorites, too." A gleaming bar ran along one side of the restaurant, lined with red leather-covered stools. Apparently, the same roof sheltered a restaurant, a bar, and a brasserie.

Mason glanced at her. "Are you hungry?"

"No, I had dinner."

Mason spoke to the maître d', who took them to a table in a secluded corner of the bar. "Wine, café, or hot chocolate?"

"Hot chocolate, please. Coffee will keep me awake all night."

He ordered the drinks and asked, "Are you interested in writers?"

"I'm a librarian," she laughed. "I have lived my life through books." *Until now.*

He gave a slight smile, his dimples briefly appearing as he leaned forward. "I stumbled onto writers and poets because of my job. Lots of tourists enjoy tracing the paths of their favorite writers. At first, I was at a loss. Then, I started reading and now I'm hooked. Now, I believe I'm as well-versed as any English professor."

"Do you have any favorites?" she asked.

Mason's gaze focused on her. "I like the decadence of the Lost Generation, but I enjoy a variety of Victorian and Romantic poetry. It's lyrical. There's music in it."

The waiter arrived with their drinks. Jayne sipped hers cautiously but found it was not too hot. It was rich with a full flavor, unlike the watery hot chocolate at home.

"This is absolutely decadent," she said as she placed her cup back on the table.

Mason sipped his café au lait. "This café was one that

Hemingway and Fitzgerald used to frequent. In fact, it's rumored that Fitzgerald brought a draft of *The Great Gatsby* here for Hemingway to review."

"Fascinating. I wonder where they sat." She glanced around the room, hoping to see the ghosts of these famous authors. Shifting in her seat, she leaned closer to Mason, sinking deeper into their conversation.

"The waiter says that Hemingway used to sit in one of these tables by the bar when he was writing." Mason sipped his coffee.

"You have a Hemingway mustache," Jayne said, handing him a napkin.

He twitched his lips before wiping his mouth.

She laughed out loud.

Jayne rubbed her hand across the table, fingers tingling. "Just think about what was created here." She sipped her chocolate.

"The Lost Generation seemed to thrive here in Paris. What did Fitzgerald say? 'All gods dead, all wars fought, all faiths in man shaken.'" Mason seemed to preen a bit as he finished the quote.

"Impressive," she acknowledged with a nod. "But what a tragic way to look at life. It seems like that attitude would block any effort at being creative. I don't understand it."

"Sometimes, pain can be inspirational," said Mason. "If it doesn't destroy you."

Jazz music filled the room as a band began to play.

"How appropriate," Jayne responded.

"It was a difficult time. Values were tenuous and hedonism ruled." Mason balanced his elbows on the table and clasped his hands together.

"Yes, and their hedonism led to alcoholism and madness. Think of poor Zelda, not to mention Fitzgerald himself."

"Do you have a favorite author?" He picked up his cup and took another sip. This time, he wiped his mouth automatically.

"From this era, I believe I like Hemingway the best," she answered quickly.

"Really? I find that surprising, since his regard for women was low at best."

"I know," Jayne replied. "That's what intrigued me. I explored his life, and loves, and saw a sensitive man who was continuously crushed by love. He only put down on paper his own reality. It's too bad that he couldn't break away from being attracted to that type."

"What type is that?" Mason quirked an eyebrow.

"The destructive type."

The café became livelier as the hour grew later. Glasses clanked. Animated voices rose. Music reverberated. And Jayne sat opposite a handsome man, having a conversation unlike any other she had ever had.

Should I feel guilty?

Her tiny voice was at it again. She pushed the question away with another sip of chocolate.

CHAPTER 10

Thursday, October 18, 2012

The drive from Paris to Lucerne was long but beautiful. The tour stopped at a couple of vineyards in Burgundy and areas in Dijon. It was well worth the early start to include the stops along the way. A short walk down the Rue de la Verrerie took the group back in time. Medieval times thrived along the narrow street. Jayne learned about the famous mustard and all the combinations on display. Impressed, she would never view the condiment in the same way again. The charcuterie and cheeses offered flavors for every discerning palate.

Along the way, Mason morphed from a smooth and arrogant Frenchman, complete with beret, to a somber Swiss citizen. As they passed by pasturelands and country homes, he pointed out the piles of wood in sequestered areas. Each piece of wood was cut precisely the same length and piled with the care of a store-front display case. He talked of Napoleon's exploits and then introduced the medieval city of Lucerne.

Jayne leaned forward when Mason pointed to places on the opposite side of the bus from her. She squinted and took in every moment. The Alps in the distance rose from the earth in craggy peaks.

One of the Brazilian couples uncorked the bottles of wine they had bought in Burgundy. Mason supplied paper cups, and the wine flowed throughout the bus. Jayne had sampled her share of wine during the tastings, so she quickly succumbed to a blissful state.

As the wine continued to flow, the language barrier seemed to dissipate. Some of the Brazilians stood in the aisle to offer toasts. The grandparents let their grandchildren share a few sips of wine. The children showed their distaste with scrunched up faces. Everyone laughed.

The only person who did not seem to be enjoying the moment was Rosa. She sat in the rear of the bus, with a cup of wine and her earphones plugged in. Cold and unapproachable. Ankles crossed like a fence line in the countryside. She stared out the window, but Jayne wasn't sure that she saw any of the beauty the landscape had to offer. Rosa's eyes didn't move; she simply stared into space.

Floyd and Emma sat in the seats across from Jayne.

"Boy, this group has got some personality now," Floyd said. "And it only took a few bottles of wine."

Emma laughed and raised her cup. "May the friendships continue to grow."

Jayne raised her cup in response and reached across the aisle to tap each of the elderly couple's cups. She took a sip and relished the feeling of joy, free from the confines of time. Joy like when her children were young. Joy before it became tarnished by time.

It was evening when the bus pulled up to their hotel in Lucerne. Everyone checked into their rooms and met in the lobby for a short walking tour. The mountains towered in the moonlight around the small city. Jayne walked with the Parks as they followed Mason along the classically Swiss buildings, with heavy wood beams and bright colors. Pungent smells of pine planks and lake water filled the air. Waves lapped gently, reflecting the moon in soft ripples.

In the morning, the restaurants would offer wonderful views of the lake that now glistened in the moonlight. They crossed the lake along the famous Chapel Bridge, one of Europe's longest covered wooden bridges.

"Isn't it wonderful?" Emma asked without needing a response.

"It is something," Floyd said.

The group's footsteps on the wooden bridge sounded like an invading army. Nestled in the peaks of the bridge's roof were old paintings that depicted the history of Lucerne.

"Unfortunately," Mason shared, "the bridge caught fire in the 1990s and some of the paintings were lost. Several have been refurbished, but others were not recoverable."

A stone tower, built in the fourteenth century, rose above the bridge. Jayne mused about the lasting efforts of the hands that had positioned each stone in its place. The builders lived on through what they had left behind.

Mason went on, "It's called the Water Tower, but it had many other uses. It was a storage place for valuables, and at one time it was a place for prisoners who were tortured."

With that eerie information, Jayne's thoughts shifted swiftly to tormented souls and ghostly cries.

Emma seemed to be feeling the change in mood as well. "My word," she said as she squeezed Floyd's hand.

Jayne watched the couple as they walked slowly across the bridge. *They are so cute.*

"They are a wonderful couple, aren't they?" Mason said as he approached Jayne.

He had echoed her thoughts yet again. She smiled.

"They are one of the highlights of this trip," she replied.

It was late, so Mason herded the group back to the hotel for dinner. In the morning, they would head out for the complete two-hour tour of the city, followed by a trip to Mount Titlis and then free time to shop or visit museums.

~

FRIDAY MORNING, Jayne met the Parks for breakfast.

"It's a beautiful morning," Floyd said. "Every day is a gift, isn't it?"

"More than you know," Jayne replied. "Do you mind if I tag along with you two today?"

"Of course not," Emma said. "If you don't mind taking it a bit slow."

"Slow works for me."

They finished their breakfast and met the group in the lobby. The first stop was the Lion Monument, carved into a mountainside. Mason told the group that Mark Twain had remarked about the dying lion of Lucerne in his travel writings.

"Just think, Emma," Floyd whispered. "We're walking the same path as Twain. Think I can capture some of his wit?"

"Shhh." Emma smiled as she patted Floyd's arm. "You're already witty enough. Now, listen."

Floyd snickered like a chastised schoolboy.

Jayne couldn't help but laugh as well and then focused her attention back on Mason.

"The monument symbolized the loyalty and sacrifice of the Swiss Guard during the French Revolution as they defended the king and his family," Mason continued and headed up toward the Glacier Gardens and Panorama.

Jayne and the Parks stayed behind, examining the complexities of the carving. The wounded lion lay on its side. A broken lance protruded from its abdomen.

"How sad to die all alone," Floyd said. "Just look at his face."

"Poor soul," Emma said as she squinted and leaned her head forward for a better examination.

"I can't believe how an artist can take a piece of rock and create something that looks so real. The agony on his face just reaches out and fills the space." Jayne gazed at the lion's mane curled around the face with the mouth slightly open. She could almost hear the sonorous roar. "Look at the muscle definition in the shanks of the beast."

"I like the smooth rock all around the carving," Floyd said. "It shows what was there before the carving. Maybe it all has hidden potential."

"That's very interesting, Floyd." Emma gazed at her husband, appreciation written all over her face.

"Do you want to catch up with the others at the garden?" Jayne asked.

"No, I'd rather go back to the bus," Floyd said.

Emma's jaw dropped and her eyebrows rose.

"I could use a bit of a breather, too," Jayne said.

They returned to the bus.

When the rest of the group came back, they made their way to the town center for a two-hour walking tour. Floyd seemed rejuvenated, but his pace was slower than normal. At an old clock tower, Floyd stayed outside with Emma. Jayne decided to take the steps to the top. She was winded but glad to see the workings of the clock, clicking off the seconds that added up to a lifetime. It had been ticking since 1535. The face of the clock was large enough for fishermen on the lake to read the time. The clock always chimed the hour a minute before the other clocks in the medieval city.

The tour then proceeded to a Jesuit church created in the ornate baroque style. Pink marble looked like a swirled wedding cake trimmed in gold icing. The ceilings were covered with paintings, like a grand palace.

"I wonder what Jesus would think of this place," Floyd commented.

"It is pretty fancy," Emma replied.

Jayne thought that Floyd was being very introspective today.

In stark contrast to the Jesuit church in all its finery, there was a Franciscan church built in the Gothic style.

"Now, this is more like it," Floyd said as he entered the simple church. "These guys took their vows seriously. No gilt rococo in here."

"Yes, I see," Emma said. "Jesus would feel comfortable here."

Jayne listened as the old couple talked. They were so connected. True soulmates. She followed them outside, where they waited for the rest of the group to finish.

"It's really a beautiful place," Floyd said as he scanned the area. The towers of other churches pierced the horizon. Mountains in the background framed the quaint city. Parts of the medieval wall were intertwined with more modern buildings. It was like a living picture postcard.

The group assembled in front of the church.

"Now, we have a choice for lunch. We can go back to the hotel, or we can go off individually to the many cafés in town and then meet back at the hotel to take the bus to Mount Titlis." Mason counted the votes and the "go our own way" votes won. Jayne's jaw dropped slightly when Rosa paired off with the Brazilian couples and Natalie instead of Mason. As everyone scattered, he came over to Jayne and the Parks. "Do you mind if I join you for lunch?"

Something wasn't right, she thought, but she felt a tingle of anticipation despite it. *Calm down. It is part of his job.*

"Of course, you can," Floyd said as he clasped Mason on the shoulder. "Where do you suggest?"

"There's a nice place in the middle of the old town."

"Lead the way." Floyd motioned for Mason to take the lead, and he also pushed Jayne ahead. "A man can't walk alone down these beautiful streets. It just wouldn't be right." He smiled and held hands with his Emma.

Mason and Jayne took the lead into the maze of streets that twisted and turned into the ancient market area. They strolled by charming shops and ancient fountains. Time slowed. There was only now. The moment. Jayne released the tension of thoughts about both the past and future. Her shoulders relaxed as she kept pace with Mason.

"Look at this," Emma said as she pointed and bobbed up and down.

Mason and Jayne stopped and walked back to Floyd and Emma. Whatever was in the shop window had them both enthralled.

"It's cuckoo clocks," Floyd said. "My Emma has always wanted one of those."

"Well, let's see what they have to offer," Mason said as he pulled the shop door open.

They entered the shop as a symphony of cuckoo noises and accompanying songs like Edelweiss filled the air. Miniature birds poked their heads from behind their doors. Little men and women danced around each other on other clocks. Still others displayed country scenes carved into the wood, with men chopping firewood or water wheels spinning in front.

"Does this happen every time someone enters the shop?" Emma's smile radiated her excitement as she surveyed the various clocks filling the walls.

"I don't think so." Mason grinned and glanced at his watch. "It's just that we entered on the hour."

Jayne scanned the diverse scenes on the clocks while Mason translated between the tourists and the shopkeeper.

"But how are we going to manage taking care of it during the rest of the trip?" Emma said, disappointment dripping from her slumped shoulders. "It's going to be too much trouble."

"Oh, Emma," Floyd said. "There has to be a way."

"The shop will take care of shipping it to your home," Mason said. "That way, it will be waiting for you when you return."

"Oh, it's probably too expensive," Emma protested.

"See if they can do that," Floyd said. "Just pick out the one you want, and we'll get it. It will be our memento of our trip. Every time it cuckoos, we'll remember our time here with our friends." Floyd put his arms around Emma and gave her a squeeze.

She examined the clocks and chose one that resembled a Swiss chalet.

"I know exactly where I'm going to hang it at home." She fidgeted about like a kid on Christmas morning.

Mason helped them complete the purchase and they went back out to the bustling street. Mason and Jayne took the lead again, but soon Jayne was the one who stopped in front of another shop. She swallowed hard as she pressed as close to the window as she could get.

"Look at the chocolate," she said, staring at the plates of exquisite chocolate piled in pyramids. "They are works of art." She glanced down and then turned her head toward Mason. "I'm a self-confessed chocoholic. This is just too much."

"Oh, are you in the right place." Mason smiled and put his arm around Jayne's shoulder. She fit perfectly and relaxed into his side. "I know just where we're going to go for lunch now. Is a light lunch with exquisite desserts all right with everyone?"

"We are right behind you." Floyd and Emma still glowed from the purchase of their clock.

Mason led them to Heini's Tearoom, nestled on a corner in the Old Market area. They entered the café filled with decadent displays of chocolates, truffles, and tortes. Jayne inhaled the lusciousness, anticipation making her mouth water.

"This is chocolate heaven," she said as she moved toward the displays.

"They also have some lunch items on the menu if you want to avoid a vast sugar high." Mason got the attention of a waitress, and they sat in a corner by a large window where they could people-watch as they ate.

Mason ordered tea for everyone and a vegetable tray with a dip. Then, everyone but Jayne ordered a sandwich. Jayne munched on the vegetables, but her mind was flooded with choices of chocolate. Dark chocolate.

"I'm sorry, but I have to ogle the chocolates and get a box to take with me."

She left her coat at the table and took her wallet from her purse. She went to the counter that had all the chocolates and began choosing.

"Do you know what you are getting?" Mason asked as he joined her.

"No, but I know dark chocolate."

"If you like, I can tell you what type of dark chocolate it is and the type of filling."

"That would be great." She listened to the descriptions and made her choices as strategically as someone planning a party.

As they returned to the table, Mason asked, "Have you ever had port with chocolate?"

"No, I haven't."

"Then, you have a treat in store." His smile spread across his face and even lit up his beautiful eyes. For the first time on the tour, he seemed to be enjoying himself. He rubbed his hands together and asked if everyone was ready for dessert.

He smiled as he turned toward Jayne. "Do you mind if I order something for you?"

She shook her head and moved her seat closer to the table.

"My dear," Emma said, "I haven't seen you so excited during this whole trip."

"Chocolate has always been my weakness."

"Jayne, I'm looking forward to just watching you eat your dessert to see the look on your face," Floyd said and chuckled.

The desserts arrived. Emma had a light, flaky confection and ordered more tea. Floyd had a fruity covered chocolate and more tea as well. Mason had ordered the same thing for him and Jayne, a large piece of dark chocolate torte and a glass of port.

"First, take a small bite of the chocolate and let it dissolve in your mouth," Mason said as he took his fork and speared a corner of the torte.

Jayne copied his movements and when the chocolate hit her taste buds she moaned. The luscious chocolate had a richness that she had never tasted before. It clung to her senses like ambrosia. *Better than my favorites at the gourmet shop at home.*

"Now, take a sip of port while the chocolate still lingers on your tongue."

Jayne followed the directions and attained instant nirvana. The tastes mingled and accentuated each other. She closed her eyes so she could fully concentrate on the sensation. She opened her eyes when she heard Floyd laughing.

"Yep, it was worth watching." Floyd smiled as he sipped his tea.

"Now, Floyd," Emma lightly chastised but then acknowledged, "It was a sight."

Mason watched her intensely and leaned forward. "Well?"

"Heavenly," Jayne said breathlessly as she leaned closer to him.

He has darker gray flecks mixed with the lighter color of his eyes. His lashes are long and full.

The sensations on her tongue traveled down. Aroused by the combination of Mason and dark chocolate.

"If chocolate can do that, Emma, then we'll have to get some too."

Jayne blushed but took another bite of the torte and slowly let it dissolve. She sipped the port and swallowed. *This pairing is better than sex. Well, maybe not,* she countered as her thoughts drifted back to Mason.

"I'm glad you like it," Mason said as he leaned back and took another sip of port.

Did his voice have a seductive tone? His eyes mirrored something that was beginning to take hold between them. She wasn't sure about it. Her still, small voice was strangely silent. She dismissed any further thoughts intruding on her and her chocolate to savor the rest of her dessert.

After lunch, they walked back through the crowded streets. They paused at certain shops, just staring at the displays. Most shops offered very expensive items. They paused in front of the Rolex store, its windows chock-full of beautifully designed timepieces. Some were encrusted with diamonds, while others were filigreed with gold.

"They are certainly beautiful, but I guess I'm still a prudent southern girl at heart. I've never understood why someone would spend that much money on a watch," Jayne commented. "They all tell the same time."

"That's true," Floyd echoed. "And buying an expensive watch will not give you any more time either."

Jayne stared at Floyd, wondering if he had insights into her that were not of this world. No, she thought, it was a coincidence. She glanced at him again and noticed a sheen of perspiration across his forehead. It wasn't overly warm out.

"Perhaps we should get a taxi to take us back to the hotel," Jayne said, turning toward Mason. She nodded almost imperceptibly toward the older couple. Mason picked up on it immediately.

"Great idea," he said as he hailed a cab.

Emma smiled at Jayne as she climbed in the cab after Floyd.

Jayne sat with them in the back seat while Mason sat in front next to the driver. As they arrived at the hotel, the Parks got out and said they were going to go to their room instead of taking the trip to Mt. Titlis.

"Thank you for sharing your time with us," Jayne said. "I hope we didn't tire you out too much."

"We had a wonderful time with you youngsters," Floyd said. "I will never look at chocolate the same way again."

Jayne blushed again at Floyd's teasing.

"We'll see you tomorrow," the older couple said in unison as they headed toward the elevator.

"Aren't they something?" Jayne said to Mason. "After fifty years, they still love each other. Did you see that in the clock shop?"

"I have to admit that they are special," Mason conceded. "But they are one in a million."

"So, you still want to view life through Hemingway's pessimistic view?"

"Maybe not as much as I did before I met the Parks," he paused for a moment, "and you."

Me? Can't be. I'm not his type. He could have anyone ... anytime.

She looked down, trying to squelch her thoughts.

Soon, the rest of the group began to congregate in the lobby. Their chatter showed how much they had enjoyed exploring on their own. Rosa was with Natalie now, their arms filled with more shopping bags. The Brazilian couples also had been successful at their shopping.

Rosa called Mason over and began spilling out her purchases onto a coffee table in a sitting area. She stretched out her arm to show off a glistening new watch. Jayne stood by and watched as Mason squinted and pulled Rosa's arm closer to see the time. A flutter deep in the pit of Jayne's stomach made her wince. She stared out the window at the waiting bus and pulled at the lapels of her jacket. Maybe she would skip the mountain tour after all.

"Everyone is going to drop off their loot and meet us back down here on the bus," Mason said, returning to her side.

"I think I'll call it a day," Jayne said as she turned to face Mason.

"You can't miss the Alps," he countered. "They're unlike any mountains you will ever see."

Jayne thought for a moment...was she letting another opportunity slip through her fingers? Her mantra returned, prodding her. "Let's get on the bus."

The drive from the picturesque town to the Swiss Alps twisted through the mountains. As they climbed, Jayne realized she had made a mistake by coming on this expedition. Her breathing became labored. They were almost at their destination, so she just concentrated, telling herself she could manage the situation until they returned to the hotel.

Breathe in, breathe out.

She was the last off the bus. Mason had already gotten everyone on a 360-degree rotating cable car that would go even higher.

"I think I'll wait with the bus," she shouted and motioned them to go on.

Mason sent the group on in the cable car. Rosa tried to linger, but he gently pushed her along before he came back to where Jayne stood. "What's wrong?" He furrowed his forehead and placed his hand on her shoulder.

"I'm having trouble breathing," she said. "I think it's the altitude."

It was stupid to come on this excursion. Altitude. Of course.

"Some people have a bad reaction."

She didn't say a word.

"We can take one of the smaller cable cars to the top, stay for a few minutes, and then come back down where you can wait." He waited for her response. "It really is a beautiful sight."

"Okay, I'll see if I can make it."

They boarded a four-seat cable car and began a slow ascent. Mason cracked a window open. Jayne scanned the landscape that lingered below. The lush green pines contrasted against the craggy, snow-capped mountains. Initially, sheep and cows spread across the green landscape. The tingling of the bells that hung on their necks created a diminutive symphony. The cowbells were bigger and made a lower sound than the lighter ringing of the sheep bells.

"The farmers can find their animals by following the sounds," Mason seemed to be reading her thoughts again.

As they continued higher, the landscape shifted from green to rocky beige and white. Jayne's lungs felt heavy and tight, rigid as iron. Her head felt like a balloon floating away as the sounds of the bells faded and heaps of untouched snow began to dot the mountainside.

When they reached the top, Jayne thought she might faint. Mason took hold of her arm and led her to the viewing deck. She gazed at the surrounding tips of the mountains. They looked like they were trying in vain to pierce the heavens.

Her thoughts scattered as she heard laughter coming from just below the viewing deck. The Brazilians were down there frolicking like children. They shouted and threw snowballs at each other.

"Most Brazilians have never seen snow," Mason explained.

Jayne watched them cavort for a moment before her gaze narrowed into a tunnel as she grasped the railing. The sensation of spinning engulfed her.

"I'm sorry, but I really don't feel well. I'll go back alone. You need to take care of the others."

Mason looked at the group and looked back at her. A frown

marring his face. "You're right, but let me get you on the cable car." He cradled her shoulders softly.

Once safely seated in the cable car, she closed her eyes and simply tried to get air into her lungs. She was drowning slowly, floating into a sea of air without being able to take it in. The tightness gripped her, squeezing like a vice. Fear and panic teamed up to add a mental attack onto the physical. Just breathe, she thought. Just breathe.

CHAPTER 11

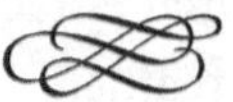

Early morning hours, Saturday, October 20, 2012
For the first time during her trip, Jayne was glad when her head hit the pillow. Usually, she had to fight to get to sleep. She took her pills and propped herself up higher than usual, taking in huge gulps of air that replenished her like water to a desert survivor. With each breath, she found solace, and soon stilted sleep offered an escape from pain and reality.

She dreamed of floating, suspended on a cloud, gazing down at Paris. The city looked like a night sky full of sparkling stars. The world was upside down. There was a gentle knocking sound that became louder. *Was it thundering?*

Jayne tried to open her eyes, but they were heavy. She strived to understand where the sound was coming from and slowly realized that someone was calling her name as the knocking continued. Tom? Her heart began to race. John? Why didn't they just come in? Then, she recognized the voice and sat straight up in bed. She rubbed the sleep from her eyes and yawned. Slipping on her robe, she peeked out the peephole and saw Mason.

"What are you doing?" she said as she opened the door and pushed her hair out of her eyes.

"Jayne, I need your help. Something awful has happened." Mason was pale. His hair was a mess as he nervously ran his hands through it. "Put some clothes on and come with me."

Jayne closed the door, grabbed her jeans, and slipped on an oversized sweater. She plucked her purse off the floor before she ran out the door.

"What happened?" Jayne couldn't imagine anything that would shake this experienced tour guide.

"It's Floyd Parks."

"Oh God." Her heart thumped against her ribcage as she fought the urge to run back to her room.

They hurried to the elevator and Mason punched the button.

"What happened to Floyd?" Fear clawed at her gut. *Not Floyd.*

"Heart attack," Mason said as the elevator opened into the lobby.

Jayne sucked in and then held her breath for a moment.

"What?" She exhaled the question.

"Emma called. Said she got up to go to the bathroom. She knew. Something was wrong. Floyd had been tired. But she kept saying that he hadn't acted out of the ordinary. She's blaming herself."

"It must be a mistake." Jayne rubbed her forehead, shifted her feet, and flipped her purse from one shoulder to the other.

"No, I called the hotel physician." His sullen expression reflected the stark reality.

"My God, I can't believe it."

"He called an ambulance immediately and took them both to the hospital. He speaks a little English. But I need to get back there to help. I thought Emma could use a friend as well." Mason placed his hand on her shoulder.

"Of course. I'm glad you thought of me. I really do like them."

Life had become a nightmarish episode of the *Twilight Zone*. The streetlamps cast a yellowish haze over the empty boulevards, leaving brooding shadows to lurk against the play of light. They hailed a taxi and soon arrived at the hospital.

The walls were pristine white, with that same antiseptic smell in hospitals at home. Stainless-steel carts lined the hallways. A nurse pushed one cart laden with pills in little white paper cups. Greens, yellows, and reds.

It was quiet. Too quiet…Mason stopped at the desk to ask where Floyd Parks was. The situation was bleak and blatantly unfair, and it terrified Jayne, but she fought this negativity as she prayed silently for Floyd to be all right. She fought for calm, her hands the only evidence of her struggle as they trembled.

When they entered the room, Emma sat by Floyd's bed, holding his hand. He was connected to several machines. Wires tangled with IV tubes. He appeared so frail, lying motionless. The Floyd that had been so vibrant over the last few days was a ghastly shade of greenish-gray. His breathing was shallow. The heart monitor bleeped irregularly. Jayne found herself willing it to regain a regular rhythm. Her efforts didn't work.

Emma looked up. "Jayne, I'm losing him. I know it. I can't lose him."

Jayne rushed to Emma's side and hugged her. The elderly woman felt like a child as she leaned into Jayne's embrace.

"Now, Emma, you have to be strong. He's still here."

Jayne tried to sound confident, but fear grew as her hands turned to ice. She didn't want to watch someone else die, but she had to be there for Emma.

"Mason, can you get us some coffee?"

He left the room without a sound, and Jayne pulled up another chair beside Emma. They sat quietly, watching Floyd for a few minutes.

"He was tired, but that wasn't unusual. You know we had a busy day. We had a nice dinner and then Floyd wanted to call the kids. That was unusual because it's so expensive, but he really wanted to hear the kids' voices." Emma paused, her eyes locked on Floyd. "He also took the rose from our centerpiece at dinner and gave it to me. He said he had loved me from the first moment he saw me."

Jayne's chest tightened as she put her arm around Emma.

The heart monitor seemed to be acting up. It beeped and then would skip. Jayne watched the erratic illustration of life on the monitor.

"He was so happy today. We really enjoyed spending time with you. He thought it was too bad you were married because you and Mason looked so good together." Emma smiled faintly. "Floyd likes you, you know."

"I like him, too. And you. I feel like we have known each other much longer than just a few days. Sometimes it happens like that. I'm very lucky to have you in my life now." Frail shoulders cut into her hands as she hugged Emma again.

Mason came back with three coffees. "Just what the lady ordered." He tried to lighten the moment, but it came crashing down when the monitor stopped beeping and rang with a deadly straight-line screech.

"What's happening?" Emma shook, her face drained of color.

"Let's get out of the way," Jayne said as she helped Emma up and moved to the corner.

Doctors and nurses rushed into the room. They were all over Floyd, pumping his chest and checking the machines.

"Let's get her out of here," Mason said, still holding the cups of coffee.

Jayne put her arm around Emma and guided her to the door.

"I can't leave him," Emma protested. "I have to be with him."

"Emma, he wouldn't want you to watch this," Jayne said. "He seemed to always protect you. Do what he would want you to do now."

Emma let Jayne lead her out of the room. The delicate bones of the older woman shook under Jayne's arm.

"See if you can sip some coffee."

Mason handed Emma the cup, but it just shook in her hands.

It seemed like an eternity passed as they stood in the hallway. Jayne couldn't understand anything being said in the room. She was glad in a way. Hope began to fade as dread coiled her stomach into a mass of pure fear. The activity in the room began to slow and quiet. Jayne knew that death had won.

The doctor emerged from the room and approached Emma. Mason put his arm around the older woman as the doctor spoke in German. Emma didn't need a translation. She lost her grip on the coffee and it hit the floor. She looked up at Mason for confirmation.

"He's gone, Emma. I'm so sorry."

Emma ran into the room. Jayne and Mason stayed outside, giving her time to say her own goodbye. They could hear her weeping.

"I feel so helpless." Jayne looked up at Mason and swiped a tear away. He appeared gutted, with dark circles underneath his eyes.

"Me too," he said as he put his arm around Jayne.

She leaned into him, trying to tap into his strength. Was death taunting her, coming so close? She suddenly felt ice cold, as if the fingers of Death were nudging her along. She wrapped her arms around Mason and squeezed him closer. He was warm. Tears flowed.

After about fifteen minutes, Jayne asked Mason to get Emma. She didn't want to see Floyd. She tried to replace the image of him connected to the machines with reflections of him throughout the tour. She knew she could do that only if she didn't enter the room again.

Jayne couldn't face the lifeless body. It was cowardly, but it was her truth right now.

When Mason emerged from the room with Emma, she looked years older. It seemed that Floyd had taken his half of her with him. Jayne got on the other side and nestled Emma between her and Mason.

"I'm going to get you two in a taxi before I take care of everything here," Mason said.

"Thank you." Emma's voice was barely audible.

"I'll take her to my room," Jayne offered. "I have an extra double bed. When you get back to the hotel, can you ask someone to bring her things to my room?"

"Yes," Mason nodded. "I'll take care of the bags and packing, too."

The ride back to the hotel seemed much shorter. As Jayne and Emma entered the lobby, the desk manager handed Jayne a packet. The hotel doctor had been worried about Emma's ability to sleep and left some pills. Emma was quiet, probably in a bit of shock. Jayne guided her to the elevator and up to the room.

"This isn't my room," Emma said.

"I know. You're staying with me."

"Oh."

Jayne pulled out an extra nightgown.

"Why don't you go in the bathroom and change into this?"

"Okay." Emma went slowly into the bathroom, her shoulders drooping and eyes downturned.

Jayne got a bottle of water that was sitting on the desk. She opened it and tapped a couple of sleeping pills from the packet onto her palm.

"Here," Jayne said, handing them to Emma as she emerged from the bathroom. "They will help you sleep."

The nightgown was too big and buttoned up the wrong way. Jayne fixed the buttons on the gown and tucked Emma into the extra bed, then changed clothes herself. By the time Jayne got to her own bed, Emma was resting comfortably.

At least one person in the room will get some rest.

Jayne pulled up the sheets, her mind a tangled web of thoughts.

Just yesterday, Floyd had been walking down the street, and now he was gone forever. There really were no guarantees, she thought. Every day really could be the last day of life. At least she had a warning that her days were numbered. Maybe that made her oddly fortunate. The irony of that thought flitted back and forth as she continued to think about making the choice to live each of her remaining days to the fullest, with no regrets.

Saturday morning at about 9:00 a.m., after Jayne had managed to finally drift off for a couple of hours, there was a soft knock. She went to the door and opened it.

"Room service," Mason said as he entered with a cart. "I thought you two ladies could use some food."

"That is very sweet, but I really don't have an appetite right now," Emma said as she propped herself up in bed. "I feel a bit groggy."

"You need to have something," Jayne urged. "You have to keep up your strength."

"What am I going to do?" Emma was slowly coming back to reality. "I have no idea what to do."

"I'm taking care of everything," Mason said as he pushed the cart into the center of the room. He lifted the covers off the various dishes. There were jams, butter, eggs, toast, yogurt, and fruit. He poured two cups of coffee and pulled a chair up to the cart. "I'm getting a local tour guide to take the rest of the group on a tour that will keep them busy all day. Then, I'm going to make all the necessary arrangements. I'm hoping to get you on a plane home later this afternoon. I just want you to relax with Jayne. Your suitcases are outside the door. Just make sure you are ready when I return."

"Thank you, Mason," Emma said, lifting a frail hand from her grip on the duvet.

Mason left, and Jayne encouraged Emma to eat. Jayne filled a plate with fluffy eggs and a dab of jam spread thinly on toast. As Emma sat in the chair, Jayne sat on the edge of the bed.

"I keep expecting Floyd to come looking for me," Emma said as she struggled to swallow her bite of toast. "I knew his heart was not in the greatest shape, but I thought we had much more time. I would have never come on this trip if I had known. He deserved better than dying in a foreign country."

"You were celebrating your anniversary," Jayne said. "He was very happy. You looked like a young couple in love. Your last day together was beautiful."

"We did love each other." Emma looked at Jayne with tears welling up in her eyes. "Through good times and bad, we always loved each other. That's what marriage is about."

"How did you know he loved you so much?" Jayne couldn't help asking.

"He shared. He always considered my feelings in any decision he made. He listened and compromised. He made me feel like the only woman in his world." Emma tried to drink some coffee, but it went down the wrong way. She coughed.

"I'm sorry," Jayne said. "I shouldn't be asking you such questions."

"It's all right, dear," Emma said and reached her hand across the cart. "Floyd wondered why you were not enjoying this trip with your husband. He was always nosy about things like that."

Jayne was silent and continued eating her toast. She couldn't imagine Tom putting anyone before himself. Even the kids had to schedule things around Tom if they could. If they couldn't, then Tom would not be part of it. Always working in the name of providing for the family. But didn't providing mean more than material support?

"Jayne," Emma leaned forward, imploring. "Don't waste time, dear. Make every minute count. Floyd and I enjoyed every minute. Don't hold back."

Jayne fought her conscience, but then everything came gushing out. "Emma, I don't have time to waste. You and Floyd showed me what marriage could be. I never knew it was possible, but it is.

"Jayne, you have plenty of time," Emma said as she stood up and walked over to the edge of the bed.

"No, I don't." Jayne crumbled into a fetal position on the bed as Emma sat down and began to rub her back. "I only have another year at the most." She broke down, shaking uncontrollably, but managed to squeeze out one more word. "Cancer."

Emma held her like a mother holds her child. Her own mother had always been distant. There were always rules to be followed. Love and discipline were equally cold in her childhood home.

"My poor dear," Emma said as she stroked Jayne's hair. "And you are here all alone."

"They don't know yet," Jayne said as she struggled to sit up and face Emma. "I haven't told my family."

"Oh, Jayne," Emma said. "Why?"

"I don't know," Jayne replied as silence tinged the air. She got up and reached out to Emma. "I'm sorry. I shouldn't burden you with my problems at a time like this. I don't know what I was thinking."

Emma stood and pulled Jayne into a warm hug and whispered, "I had a wonderful marriage and spent fifty years with my soulmate. You've helped me realize how blessed I was, and I will always thank you for that. Don't let my loss affect the rest of your trip. Floyd wouldn't want that, either."

"I'm going to miss you and Floyd." Jayne released from the embrace.

After breakfast, Jayne helped Emma get her suitcase.

"Jayne, you go ahead and get ready," Emma suggested. "I'll sit here and relax for a minute. I'll have to make some phone calls, and I need to figure out what I'm going to say."

Jayne pulled some clothes from her suitcase and went to the bathroom. She didn't take a lot of time. It just didn't seem to matter. She emerged from the bathroom to find Emma sitting at the desk, just staring at the phone.

"Do you need some help?"

"Yes, I can't even make a phone call by myself." Emma had dark circles under her eyes and a pallor that made her eyes seem to sink deep within their sockets.

"Oh, Emma," Jayne said as she placed her hand on the shattered older woman's shoulder and picked up the phone. "We'll just call the front desk and hope that they can do the rest."

After Jayne made the connection with Emma's children, she slipped out of the room. She went downstairs to the business center and got online. She felt a primal need to connect with her own children.

Kim,

Just wanted to reach out and let you know how much I love you. I hope you know that. I am learning so much during my travels. Things I'm writing down in a notebook to share with you and your brother.

I am so proud of your accomplishments as a teacher. Your students love you and you make a difference in their lives. But, darling, please don't put off your dreams until it is too late. Live for yourself as well. Travel. Meet people. Absorb the world. Live every moment as if it were special. You are a major part of my heart and soul. I love you forever.

Tears flowed as she signed off and hit Send. Her hands shook as she started the email to John.

John,

Doing well and just wanted to let you know that I love you. I am learning a lot as I travel and realize my dreams. I know you think dreams are nonsense, like your dad. But, I beg you to think about what you really value in life. Something outside of business. Something that makes you passionate. Passionate to live life … now … in the moment.

Don't get me wrong. I am very proud of your professional accomplishments, but life is more than your job. Don't let time pass you by without noticing what is really important. Don't write this off as your mother lost in her dreams and imagination. I'm living my life right now like I never have before. Don't wait.

I love you. You are part of me always.

The letters became blurry as she signed off and pressed Send again.

She sent another e-mail to Lynn telling her what happened and started to log off when she thought of Tom. She opened a new email and stared at the blank screen. What should she say? Would he care about the news of the death of an old man that he didn't know? Would the fact that Jayne had liked the old man make any difference?

She continued to stare at the computer screen as her mind reeled into the black void. When she died, would Tom be devastated like Emma? Would it make any difference that it was expected? What would it do to her kids? That was the worst part of her entire situation, the pain she was going to inflict on her children.

Someone touched her on the shoulder and pointed to the computer. They obviously wanted access to it.

Jayne quickly typed:

Tom,

Having a wonderful time. Will see you soon.

Jayne

By the time Jayne returned to her room, Emma had finished her phone call and was pacing back and forth in short shuffles, wringing her hands. Jayne opened Emma's suitcase and picked out a comfortable outfit for her trip home. She laid everything out in the bathroom. Emma didn't say a word and followed directions like a preschooler.

As Jayne waited, she heard a knock at the door. Mason entered.

"Everything is set. We can take her to the airport this afternoon, but I need to talk with someone on the other end to get them ready to set up final transportation." Mason sat down on the edge of the bed.

"She just told her kids. I'm sure one of them will take care of things." Jayne sat next to Mason.

"We should try to get her to rest. She has a long trip ahead of her." He opened his hand.

"I think we should have the hotel doctor take a look at her, too." She nestled her hand in his. He gave her hand a quick squeeze and stood up.

Mason picked up the phone and called the front desk. He got the number that Emma had called. He also asked for the doctor.

"I'm going to go to my room to make this call. I don't want her to overhear. Be back in a few minutes." Mason started out the door and then turned. "Thank you for being here for her … and me."

The doctor appeared just as Mason was leaving. Jayne excused herself and went into the hallway while the doctor examined Emma.

After a few minutes, the doctor opened the door.

"I gave her something to help her sleep again. It should wear off before you have to go to the airport. If you need anything else, please call the front desk and ask for me."

"Thank you, Doctor." Jayne went back into the room. Emma was lying on top of the sheets. Jayne put the "Do Not Disturb" sign on the door.

"Do you need anything?" Jayne asked Emma.

"Nothing you can give me, dear. But thank you."

"I'm going to be down in the restaurant. I'll leave the number by the phone. If you need me, just call. Now, get some rest. Mason and I will come and get you when it's time."

Jayne ran her finger down the list of phone numbers. She wrote down the number for the restaurant as well as the number for the front desk, placed them next to the phone, and quietly closed the door behind her.

She met Mason in the hallway.

"Where are you off to?" he asked.

"I thought I'd give her some privacy so she could get some rest."

"I talked with her son and he is going to take care of everything on that end." He sighed and continued, "He sounded like a younger version of Floyd."

Jayne touched his arm.

"I'm going to the restaurant. I really don't want to sit there alone. Can you join me?"

"Of course. I've done everything I can until we go to the airport. We'll stop by the front desk and make sure they know where to find me in case anything comes up." He stroked her hand and then tucked it in the crook of his arm.

The hotel restaurant was not busy. The lunch rush had come and gone. A hostess seated Jayne and Mason at a table near the window. Life outside the window went on, untouched by the loss of Floyd. Jayne stared at the menu.

"So, you can read German or French now?"

"What?"

"That menu is not in English." Mason put his hand, palm up, in the middle of the table.

Jayne closed the menu and put her hand in his.

"I know you liked Floyd. I did too."

Jayne just nodded. The waitress came to take their order.

"What would you like?" Mason asked.

"Anything."

Mason ordered and handed the menus back to the waitress.

"It's hard to come to terms with something like this when it happens so suddenly."

"Do you really think that matters?" she asked as she curled up the edge of a napkin.

"What?" he asked. "You've lost me."

"The suddenness," she replied as she continued to mutilate her napkin. "Does it really matter whether it's expected or it's sudden?"

"I'm not sure what you mean." He reached out and lifted her chin so she had no choice but to gaze into his eyes.

"Is it any less of a loss for everyone left behind if the death is unexpected or expected?" she asked.

"I guess the only difference is that if it's expected, you have the chance to say goodbye." The lines by the sides of his mouth appeared but didn't quite make a full smile.

"You're right. That does make a big difference."

The waitress returned with a soup, sandwich, salad, bread, and a large bottle of Perrier.

Jayne ate but really didn't taste anything. Floyd's death provided a preview for Jayne. "Why is death such a difficult thing to handle?" She paused with her spoon halfway to her mouth, then set it back down in the bowl. "Why is it such a taboo topic? Everyone is going to die."

"I don't know. I think it is part of our hedonism. We can't believe that existence will go on without us, so we avoid thinking or talking about it." He dipped some bread into his soup.

"Maybe we don't talk about it because we don't want to see the pain our leaving will cause others." She poked at her salad and put her fork down.

She pulled at some bread, breaking off a piece. Should she tell him about her own situation? What would he think? She wanted to, but when she tried to talk about it, something shut off. She couldn't do it just now, or perhaps maybe ever. Her hands shook as she put the piece of bread in her mouth.

"At least they seemed to enjoy their lives together," Mason commented. "They were the coolest old couple I've seen in years."

"Yes, you could tell they were really close, and somehow, I don't think it was just because they were on vacation. I think that was the way they lived their lives." Jayne remembered the way the couple always touched each other. Small embraces. Light smiles. The twinkle in their eyes when they shared a special moment. It was real love. It wasn't a dream. It wasn't her marriage, but now she knew it was a possibility.

"If that is true, then they were truly an extraordinary couple."

"They were," she realized.

The rest of their meal passed in relative silence. Jayne pushed her plates away and glanced at her watch.

Mason wrapped up the sandwich he had ordered.

"We'd better go check on Emma," she said.

"Right. Take this sandwich to her. I'll leave you two alone until it's time to go to the airport," Mason said as he stood and came around to help Jayne from her chair. "Thanks again for helping with all of this."

"I wouldn't be anywhere else."

Jayne went back up to the room and found Emma still sleeping. She lay down on her own bed, her mind flitting about, fusing images of Paris, Floyd, life, and death. Her brain felt like a Picasso painting, fragmented with light and dark cubes of feeling. She mourned what she had never experienced with Tom, envied the life Emma had shared with Floyd, and wondered about the mysteries of Mason. He seemed to be a constant amidst the chaos. She had watched the way he handled the situation. His soft hugs and comforting words helped Emma visibly relax.

She didn't know how much time had passed before she heard a soft knock on the door. Jayne let Mason in and woke Emma. The bags were packed, so Mason called the front desk for a bellman. Emma reached out to Jayne, who put her arm around Emma's slumping shoulders.

"Do you want to try to eat something?" Jayne pointed to the sandwich.

Emma just shook her head.

The bellman loaded the bags into the waiting taxi, and Jayne got in the back seat with Emma. Mason sat in the front seat next to the driver. The ride to the airport passed in silence. When they pulled up to the airport entrance, Emma began to shake.

"Don't worry," Jayne said as she patted her hand. "Mason has taken care of everything. You will be fine once you get home with your family."

Emma smiled and hugged Jayne. "I'll never be fine again, but thank you for your friendship. I will never forget you."

"You and Floyd will always be part of me now." Jayne reached into her purse and handed Emma a slip of paper. "Here is my phone number. Please keep in touch."

Emma started to rummage around in her purse, but Jayne stopped her. "Mason already has your number and I'm sure he will share it with me."

Emma squeezed her hand and got out of the taxi. Mason was waiting with the luggage.

"I'm going to help her get checked in and then I'll be back," he said. Mason had a porter take care of the bags. He put one arm around Emma and held her hand with the other as he led her into the terminal. Before long, he returned to the taxi.

"She is safely on her way." Mason slid in the back seat with Jayne. "What a roller coaster day."

"Isn't that what life is like?" Jayne asked.

"Ups and downs," Mason replied as he slipped closer to Jayne.

"Yes, but the downs. You really feel the force of them. It seems the ups feel lighter and shorter." She nestled next to Mason.

"Both have excitement," he said as he put his arm around her shoulders.

"Yes, you just have to be brave enough to purchase a ticket for the full ride." She laid her head against his shoulder, and he responded by doing the same against the top of her head. She exhaled softly.

As the taxi pulled up to the hotel, loneliness crept into Jayne as Mason leaned forward to pay the driver and threw open the door. It was a cold void that she tried to ignore. As they walked through the lobby and entered the elevator, the coldness felt like shards of ice duplicating geometrically. It was more than missing the Parks. She could hear Emma's advice echoing against the isolation. The elevator opened and Mason walked her to her door.

"Are you all right?" Mason asked as he took her card key from her hand and slipped it in the door.

"No," she replied. "I don't know what to do. I don't want you to misunderstand."

"What?" He moved closer to her.

"I really don't want to be alone tonight." She stared at him, wondering what he was thinking. She could hear a slight cry from her strict mother. "I don't want to mislead you. I just don't want to be by myself."

"I understand," Mason said and put his arm around her.

They entered her room and shut the door. Fully clothed, she led him to her bed, where she nestled in his arms. She relaxed as his warmth began to melt the loneliness. They spooned as she heard her mother's voice railing about the impropriety of the situation. Had her mother ever known love like the Parks?

Never, came her mother's stern answer. *But you're a married woman and you're in bed with another man.* The tone of her mother's voice echoed in her mind.

Jayne answered, *Married but not in love.* What was more important? She felt the gentle strength in Mason's arms, which she had never experienced before. His breathing became rhythmic. Sleep came naturally while she was cocooned in the protective embrace, and her mother's voice gave way to Floyd's soothing tones. *Hey, kid, don't listen to her. Live every day like it was your last. My last day wasn't so bad.*

CHAPTER 12

Sunday, October 21, 2012

Sunlight streaked between the drapes and hit Jayne's eyelids. She opened her eyes and tried to move her head away from the beams of light. As she tried to move, she found she was anchored with an arm snaked around her waist. She froze as the reality of the night before slammed into her consciousness. Poor Emma. She shifted and tried to ease out of bed.

"Where are you going?" Mason said, his voice still full of sleep.

Jayne stopped moving. "Bathroom."

"Oh," he lifted his arm and glanced at his watch. "Damn, I better get going."

He sat up on the edge of the bed.

"Oh God," Jayne replied.

"What?" he said as he stood on the opposite side of the bed.

Her face burned as she began to fidget with the duvet. "I can't imagine what you think of me." She ran her fingers through her hair.

"I think that you went through a very emotional day yesterday and simply didn't want to face an empty night alone." Mason stood up and turned toward her. "It's the best night I've spent in bed with a woman in a long time." He rubbed his forehead and pulled a lock of hair behind his ear. "Even without sex."

Jayne stared at him quietly, then quickly looked at the ceiling. The silence pulsed with awkwardness as she glanced down at the duvet and began to fidget with it again. If someone had told her she would be in this position just a few weeks ago, she would have laughed.

"I have to get things ready for our trip to Lugano today," he said as he moved toward the door. "It's not a long trip. I'll see you in the lobby in an hour." He opened the door and left.

As the door clicked closed, Jayne got up and began to get ready. Her thoughts continued to pound at her. She had lain in a bed with another man. But that wasn't the worst part. She had liked it. Not just physically, but emotionally. He voiced her thoughts. Their conversations were natural. Comfortable like a fleece blanket. She had been more herself, more alive with this man than she had in a lifetime with her own husband. What kind of woman did that make her? Why had she done it? Yesterday, her emotions were linked with this man and had made her weak. Maybe that was it. Or maybe it had been shock.

She splashed cold water on her face and stared in the mirror. She didn't look any different. But something deep inside had changed. Guilty, yes. But regretful, no. The two feelings seemed to cancel each other out. He had simply done what she asked. He had understood and been a gentleman. He had listened. That was a first for her.

She dismissed the rest of her thoughts and focused on getting ready. She jumped in the shower, dried, straightened her hair, and got ready to go. She packed her suitcase and placed it outside the door. As she pulled the suitcase into the hallway, Rosa was doing the same from her room across the hall.

"Good morning," Jayne said.

"It must be for you," Rosa replied as she came up to Jayne. "I would have never guessed from your mousy appearance that Mason would want anything to do with you. First that horrible painting and now this."

Jayne's mouth dropped open.

"I find it incredible that you could satisfy his appetites." Rosa twisted her lips and spat out the next few words. "*Eres una puta.*" She pivoted sharply and walked back to her room, her hips swaying in her skin-tight outfit.

Jayne went back into her room. She checked out her reflection in the mirror again. She wore a red cardigan and black pants with black flats. She had a silk scarf twisted around her neck with gold hoop earrings. Her hair framed her face as it always did. *Is this what an adulteress looks like?* She hadn't had sex like Rosa thought, but did that matter? She did have an emotional attachment. Was that adultery?

Jayne dreaded seeing everyone in the lobby. First, there would be the obvious void of the Parks. She had loved spending time with the couple. There was really no one else she could hang out with. Then, she would have to face Rosa again. And finally, she had to face Mason. This dream trip was turning into a nightmare.

In the lobby, Mason shared the news about the Parks. The grandparents shook their heads. The Brazilian couples murmured quietly among themselves. Natalie took her glasses off to wipe away some tears. Everyone slumped and looked down, except for Rosa, who stared daggers at Jayne. Then, the group loaded onto the bus for the relatively short trip to Lugano.

Jayne waited for everyone else to board before she got on

and found a seat that was isolated. The Brazilian couples patted her on the back as she passed. The young newlyweds nodded. Jayne avoided making eye contact with Rosa and Natalie.

As the bus started to move, Jayne stared out the window. The landscape didn't really change much from Lucerne, so she tried to write in her notebook. But instead of writing, she wondered whether she should just go home now. She had already experienced more life in these past few days than she had ever before. Maybe that was enough.

She heard Emma's voice answer, just as if she were sitting in the seat across the aisle. "Floyd would want you to continue. Don't you dare let us down. Finish this trip and enjoy every minute of it."

At that, Jayne began writing in her notebook and continued through the journey from Lucerne to Lugano. She put down thoughts, memories, and her experiences unvarnished. She wrote for her kids. For Kim in particular. The activity calmed her. As she wrote, she ate her chocolates one by one. She let each nibble melt on her tongue. The savory dark flavor was a balm for her soul.

Ensconced in her own world, she remembered the feel of Mason's arms around her. Safe and comfortable. Natural. Who was Rosa to judge her just because she was the one Mason had chosen? The feeling of being envied was new and intoxicating, even if the source was a cheap exhibitionist like Rosa. She squelched her inner voice that sounded much like her mother and continued to bask in her newfound security.

Before she knew it, the bus pulled up to the hotel in Lugano. She looked around when she got off the bus. The town appeared to be very similar to Lucerne, perhaps a bit more modern. Mason came up to her after he had helped unload the luggage.

"You were very quiet on this trip. I don't believe you listened to a word I said." He smiled and fell in step with her as they entered the hotel.

"Well, you know me and chocolate," Jayne said.

"I was thinking about something on our way here, and I have a surprise for you." Mason stopped at the desk and got the door keys for everyone. "Meet me down here as soon as you get settled."

"Mason, I'm really tired. I think I'll just stay in my room."

"You will love this. Trust me. I promise you that you won't get tired. The rest of the group is just going to go shopping again."

Jayne could hear Floyd's voice in the back of her mind.

"I'll be down in a few minutes."

"Great."

Floyd's voice gave way to Rosa's as Jayne slipped her key into the door of her room. Her suitcase was nestled at the end of the bed. She didn't take any time to look in the mirror. *He's waiting for me. For me.* Then, Rosa's words came back. *He had spent this kind of time with her. I'm just the next in line.* Floyd's voice roared back. His voice won this round of conscience as she left her room and doubts behind.

Mason had a taxi waiting outside when Jayne came back downstairs. She hopped in with him and they were off to destinations unknown.

"You have to stop giving me special treatment. People are going to talk, and you might even lose your job."

Mason sat very close to Jayne, their legs touching.

"Why? Has someone complained?"

"No, not complained." Jayne turned toward Mason. "Rosa saw you coming out of my room this morning."

"So."

"I don't want you to get into trouble because of me."

"Don't worry about Rosa."

The taxi pulled up in front of an upscale building that

appeared to be another hotel. They got out of the taxi and entered. Mandhara Day Spa was written on the glass window.

"A spa?"

"This place is exactly what you need after the day you had yesterday." Mason pushed open the door and held it for Jayne.

"But I have never been to a spa in my life." *How did he know about this place? Another abandoned lover, maybe.*

"Then, this is the perfect time."

"But I don't know what to do and I don't speak their language." *Stop it. Don't sabotage yourself.*

Mason went to the front desk and talked with the manager.

"It's settled. They have technicians who speak English, so you can relax and be pampered for two hours. Just follow their instructions and relax."

"How much do I owe them?"

"It's taken care of."

"I can't accept that."

"Please let me do this for you. I'll see you in a few hours."

"Why?"

"Because you are the most amazing woman I have ever met."

He turned before she could say another word and was gone.

Amazing? He had to be kidding. Rosa's "mousy" taunt paired with her own "plain Jayne" feelings. But no one had ever given her a gift like this. A gift of total indulgence, just for her.

Floyd's voice settled the matter again. *Sabotage be damned. Enjoy this gift, honey.*

She looked at the woman behind the desk and smiled faintly. Another woman appeared, and Jayne followed her through the doors swathed in gauzy curtains. A few hours of aromatherapy, light massage, and a simultaneous manicure and pedicure were heavenly. She had never been the focus of such pampering in her life. After a final flourish of a facial and makeup, she emerged from the spa completely renewed and silently thanked Floyd.

Mason was waiting for her outside the spa.

"Wow, you look absolutely beautiful," he said as he came to meet her.

"Did I look that bad?" She pulled at her curls that had been tamed but not straightened. She had never had this much makeup on in her life. He was just staring at her. "Is something wrong?" She shifted on her feet, reaching for her hair, and glanced at the ground.

"No, everything is right … perfect." He hailed a taxi and opened the door. "I have another surprise for you."

"This is really too much," Jayne said as she entered the taxi. "You are definitely going to get into trouble for neglecting the rest of the group."

He spoke to the driver and they were off.

"The rest of the group is indulging in more shopping. If you want to shop, I can take you to them, but I thought you might enjoy this more." He settled back in his seat, his jeans tightly hugging his thighs. His weathered leather jacket felt soft where she placed her hand on his arm.

"You're right." She decided to just take what was offered and stop fighting. Besides, she had enjoyed every adventure with Mason. Even though he professed to be a skeptic when it came to romance, he was proving to be one of the most caring men she had ever met. To her, caring was definitely romantic. And with Mason, she was anything but plain.

The taxi pulled up in front of a museum. At first, Jayne thought that it was an art museum, but when she stepped out of the taxi, she saw the name Museo del Cioccolato Alprose mounted above the door.

"The Alprose Chocolate Museum," Mason translated.

"You are kidding me," Jayne laughed. "A real chocolate museum."

"Of course. The Swiss are very proud of their chocolate." He paid the taxi and held out his arm for her to hold. "This way, my chocolate connoisseur."

As he opened the door, the rich smell of chocolate assaulted Jayne's senses. The air was so thick with it, she was sure that she was inhaling calories just by breathing. If I can just keep filling my lungs with the fragrance of chocolate, she thought, my last breath wouldn't be so bad. She could float to the other side on the solace of chocolate.

In the center of the room, a fountain spewed streams of dark brown chocolate a foot into the air. In a vat at the copper base of the fountain, a single wire slowly teased the texture of the liquid.

"First impressions?" Mason looked at her with a smile tugging at his lips.

"Exquisite." She took his arm and squeezed it. This day was like a perfect birthday, with gift after gift raining down one after the other.

He led her to the desk where they signed up for a factory tour. The back of the museum led to the actual manufacturing facility. The guide, a slim young man with soft brown hair, talked about the history of chocolate that dated back to 1000 B.C. The Mayan and Aztec cultures also cultivated and appreciated the essence of chocolate in its various forms. Finally, the most amazing fact she found out was that Spanish friars and conquistadors had brought chocolate to Spain in the 1500s.

"I think chocolate is eternal," Jayne whispered to Mason as the guide continued the tour.

They observed the modern machinery that stirred and processed the different types of chocolate. There were more machines that created bars and yet others that created unique pieces of the luxurious confection.

At the end of the factory, there was a gift shop, open like Pandora's chocolate box.

Jayne's eyes darted everywhere, trying to decide what to do first.

"How about some chocolate tasting?" Mason said and laughed. "You never cease to amaze me with your reaction to chocolate."

"It's a major weakness, but one I intend to indulge in without a smidgen of guilt."

In the tasting area, Mason pointed out some dark chocolates. There was one bar that was about a half an inch thick and packed with almonds and cranberries. The salesperson snapped off a piece, wrapped it in tissue, and handed it to Jayne.

She bit into the chocolate and was rewarded with a mixture of smooth sweetness and a tart cranberry. She closed her eyes and savored the bite. She kept it in her mouth until the chocolate completely dissolved and then chewed the cranberry delicately and swallowed it. She sighed, contentment spreading from her mouth to her stomach and throughout her body. She opened her eyes as her mind wallowed in the thrill of it … and in being the center of Mason's attention.

Mason watched her intently. "You have no idea what watching you eat chocolate does to me." He continued staring at her. "You remind me of the Meg Ryan character in that iconic movie scene in *When Harry Met Sally,* where she faked the orgasm in the restaurant. Except you are not faking."

She closed her eyes to concentrate on the flavor and hide her embarrassment.

"It's very sensual," he said.

She heard him shift in his chair.

"This is wonderful." She opened her eyes as she took another sample and her face flushed.

She closed her lips, but not tightly. A seductive smile curved the corner of her mouth. She tipped her head back ever so slightly. Her neck pulsed in a slow swallow. As she savored the moment, she watched his eyes glaze over. Power surged through her. The power of sexuality that had been latent ... until now.

"I really shouldn't be enjoying this as much as I am," he said, "but you have somehow broken through and I can't help it. I think I've fallen for you, the good girl, for the first time in my life."

Time seemed to stop, and her mind reeled as her powerful feeling dispelled like a fog in the Smoky Mountains. *Me? It can't be. I'm just plain Jayne. Rosa's your type. It's just the stress of everything. That's what it is.*

"I'm going to pick out some chocolates now," she announced. "My other stash is almost gone."

"I'm not going anywhere."

On tiptoes to ogle the glass display cases, she fluttered about like a bee around honey. Her mind continued to spin around what he said. Some "good girl" she was, because in truth she was a married woman. She wondered what Rosa had called her in Spanish.

Jayne finished her purchase and approached him with her largest bag this trip.

"Do you think you have enough?" he laughed.

"I wasn't sure if there would be any more places like this, so I went a little crazy."

"I'm glad you enjoyed yourself. You deserve it after the last couple of days."

"I can't say I have ever been this relaxed or satisfied in my whole life."

Mason smiled seductively and his body seemed to stiffen. "I can think of other ways to satisfy you."

She dropped her bag of chocolates, quickly bending over to recover them before they tumbled out.

"Since you're so relaxed, are you ready for one more adventure that is not relaxing in the least?" he said as he stood to help her.

"I'm satiated with chocolate, so I'm vulnerable right now. What do you have in mind?"

"Ice skating."

"What?"

"Let's go to the ice rink." Mason rubbed his hands together.

"I haven't been ice skating since I was a kid."

"Then it's time to do it. It's just like riding a bike." He nudged her with his elbow.

"I don't think so."

"Come on. I won't let you fall, or at the very least I'll break your fall."

Mason was acting like a guy on his first date. He hailed a taxi and went to the indoor ice rink. It was not very crowded. He asked Jayne her shoe size and had to ask the rental person to translate the American size 7 to the European size. When he brought the skates over to Jayne, her palms were sweating.

"I'm not sure about this. What if we break something?" She took her shoes off and noticed her shoulders were tightening up.

"We won't. What has happened to your eternal optimism?"

"I left it at the door of the rink." She pulled on her skates.

Mason helped Jayne with her skates first and then he laced up his own. He stood steadily and helped Jayne to her unsteady feet.

"Why aren't you wobbling?"

"I play hockey a lot when I'm not touring."

"Oh," Jayne said as she gripped both his hands so tightly that her circulation seemed to stop.

"Don't worry," he said. "I don't need to feel my hands."

"What?"

"You don't have to hold so tight. I won't let go."

They made their way onto the ice, and Jayne's feet slipped forward. Mason pulled her up and she steadied.

"I'll just guide you around the ice the first time until you get used to it." Mason held her hands and glided smoothly backwards. She managed to relax by the time they got halfway around the rink. At two-thirds of the way around, she started making small strides herself. When they got all the way around, she had loosened her stride and was in sync with him. They circled again, silent and content as he maneuvered around to her side. They held hands and glided around the ice like a scene from an old classic movie. Round and round. In sync. Perfectly in sync.

After about a half an hour, Jayne's breathing was coming up in short, shallow puffs.

"Are you tired?" He noticed her becoming winded.

She fought to take deeper breaths.

"Yes. This has been wonderful. I'd forgotten how free you feel on skates. It's like floating. But I think I've had enough."

They glided to the exit, where they took off their skates and returned them.

"This has been a magnificent day. I can't tell you what it has meant," Jayne said as she softly laid her hand on Mason's arm. Warmth radiated through his sleeve. It had been the most perfect day of her life.

"I've enjoyed it, too." Mason put his arm around her, and they walked out the door where they hailed a taxi.

She held tightly to the warmth that her emotions pumped throughout her body. Wallowing. Burning it into her memory. Living like a heroine in her books. Identifying with Elizabeth Browning instead of envying her.

AFTER DINNER THAT EVENING, the group gathered in a piano bar reserved especially for them. The grandparents with their grandchildren said their goodnights, but the rest went to an intimate space with tables surrounding a grand piano. Candles fluttered in the middle of each table, providing a dim yet warm ambiance. Jayne sat alone at a table close to the piano.

As the pianist entered and sat on the piano bench, Mason made sure everyone in the group had their drinks before he began an impromptu speech.

"As everyone knows, Floyd Parks passed away in Lucerne. It was his wife's wish that we continue with our tour and enjoy ourselves as they would have. Let's raise our glasses to the Parks." He translated for the rest of the group.

Raised glasses glittered in the ambient light. The only sound that could be heard was the slight ring of glasses. Jayne thought about the bells at Notre Dame and how Floyd had enjoyed that day. Mason raised his glass toward her and took a sip, then joined Jayne at her table as the pianist began to play.

"Emma would be touched." Jayne sipped her drink.

"I thought we had to have closure of some kind."

The group raised their glasses many times over the next hour. It seemed that everyone had noticed the older couple. The pianist continued to play soft jazz that filled the room with just enough sound.

The relaxed atmosphere shattered when Rosa, who had been drinking heavily, stood up from the table she shared with Natalie. Jayne was not sure what to expect as Rosa teetered slightly. She raised her glass and spoke in Spanish.

"*Usted piensa que esta mujer es buena? Ella es una puta.*" She spat out the last word.

Jayne raised her glass as well, thinking that it was another toast to the Parks.

"*Vi Mason saliendo de su habitación,*" she continued her speech that now included gesturing towards Mason and then Jayne. "*Él es un hijo de puta y ella es su perra.*"

As the foreign words spewed forth, Mason stiffened. The Brazilians gaped at Jayne, their mouths dropping open slightly. Jayne did not need a translator to know that Rosa was not toasting the departed. She put her glass down and looked at Mason.

"What's happening?" Jayne asked. She didn't know whether the Brazilians had understood, but it was clear that Natalie had. The young girl's face was crimson.

Mason didn't respond but stood up and quickly approached Rosa. Leaning close, he spoke in low, rapid Spanish. She tried to slap him, but he caught her hand.

Jayne knew then that whatever Rosa had been saying was much worse than she had imagined.

Mason took Rosa's glass and put it back on the table. He spoke to Natalie as he gripped Rosa's arm and led her out of the room. Natalie quickly followed.

Jayne didn't know what to do. Everyone was still looking at her. Even the pianist had stopped playing. No one else in the room spoke English. She swallowed the rest of her drink in one huge gulp and pushed away from the table. Before she left the room, she turned to everyone.

"Good evening."

She went to her room, her mind trying to fill in the blanks. She knew it had to be something about her and Mason, but she didn't know how bad. She sat on the edge of her bed and shook from the inside out. Her mother's voice stoked guilt. What a fool I am, Jayne thought. I am just another in a line. How stupid to believe it was anything more than a fling. She glanced around the room and noticed the light on the phone was flashing.

She got up and picked up the phone, calling the operator. She asked what the red light meant, and the operator connected her to a message center.

"Hey, Jayne. You are probably out enjoying yourself. I hope you get this message."

Jayne found temporary relief in Lynn's familiar voice as she continued to listen to the message.

"I have a surprise for you. I'll be meeting you in Venice. I talked with the touring company, and they said as long as you didn't mind, I could share your room. They also said there is plenty of room on the bus, and I worked out a great deal."

Jayne wasn't sure what to think. She was happy to have an ally especially with what had just happened in the piano bar. But something else tugged at the edges of her consciousness.

"See you soon." Lynn's voice seemed to echo and ended with a click.

CHAPTER 13

Monday, October 22, 2012

The next morning, Jayne struggled with exhaustion. She had stayed awake in her room for a while, hoping that Mason would show up and tell her what Rosa had said. But he didn't. She had tried to sleep but ended up staring at the ceiling for most of the night. Guilt and justification warred. *You're a married woman and you slept in bed with another man.* Yes, but that's all we did. It had been a horrible day. *What would Tom think?* Tom doesn't need to know. *What about spending the next day with this other man, and enjoying every minute of it?* I'm on vacation. *What does everyone else think?* I don't care what everyone else thinks. *Really?*

Sleep was impossible amid her noisy thoughts. Instead, Jayne tossed and turned as her mind kept reeling.

She got ready early. Her bones ached. *Probably from the ice skating.* She popped a few of her pills before placing her packed luggage outside the door as usual.

The next stop on the tour would be Venice, a four-hour drive without any stops. The part Jayne dreaded the most was facing everyone on the bus.

If I could just sneak on and hide.

Knowing this was impossible, she opted for a plausible action. She went downstairs early, hoping to be the first one.

She took a deep breath, coughed, and climbed aboard the bus. Jacques greeted her with his usual smile.

"How are you?"

"I've been better."

"Oh, too bad. You're supposed to enjoy the trip. I know you liked the old couple, but they would want you to be happy." Jacques smiled.

"I know. Thank you, Jacques."

"*C'est la vie, madame.*"

She looked down the row of seats and saw only Natalie. She exhaled deliberately as her shoulders relaxed.

"Good morning."

"Good morning." Natalie shifted in her seat. "I'm sorry about last night. Rosa just had too much to drink."

"Do you know what she said?"

Natalie looked down and nodded her head.

"Will you tell me?"

"No, it is too embarrassing, and those words should not be repeated," Natalie said as she looked up at Jayne. "But if you would like to sit with me, I would like that."

"Why won't you tell me what she said?"

"It is no matter what a drunk woman says about you," Natalie said. "We're all sad. The old couple was sweet. We must be happy. They were."

"You're mature beyond your years, Natalie."

Jayne sat down and took out some chocolates and her notebook before shoving her bag under the seat in front of her.

"Want some chocolate?"

"It's a bit early, isn't it?

"It's never too early for chocolate."

~

AS THE BUS continued from Lugano toward Venice, Mason morphed from a sedated Swiss persona to a vibrant Italian, complete with gold chains hanging around his neck and a shirt unbuttoned one button too far. His language became exaggerated and everyone laughed at his antics. Jayne wondered if he was trying a bit too hard to lighten the mood. The thought buoyed her with a tingling contentment.

She glanced around and saw Rosa propped up in the back of the bus. She wore her sunglasses and had a scarf wrapped around her head. She wasn't moving much but had her hand on one side of her head.

Jayne plugged in to Lynn's iPod and gazed at the crystal blue of the lake and the sloping green mountains sprinkled with houses and churches. The bits of fluffy clouds in the sky cast intermittent shadows on the terrain. Houses lined the coast of the lake. The multi-tiered structures accented the coastline with splashes of color. Earthy terra cotta. Lemony yellow. Tawny peach. She wondered about the people living in those homes, facing such beauty every morning of their lives. Did they appreciate it? Or did it just become normal and lose its intensity over time? She couldn't imagine how anything so beautiful could become mundane.

The bus wound its way through the mountains. She admired the abundant beauty nature had provided. The light seemed to change as the journey continued. When they crossed the border into Italy, Jayne could see what had attracted artists and poets to the area. Something was different. The only thing Jayne thought it could be was the light. It seemed to shift and change. Like a painter's brush, adding bits of almost imperceptible color to unleash emotion, the light opened the countryside in vivid layers. *Floyd would have liked it.* After soaking it all in, Jayne took out her notebook and began to write.

The time flew by until the bus plunged into heavy traffic, signaling their arrival in Venice's mainland. Jayne put the iPod away and offered Natalie more chocolate. Jayne looked around the bus, and everyone who caught her eye smiled back. She sat up straighter in her seat as the bus pulled into a parking lot by the water.

Jayne gulped at the sight of the water taxis bobbing up and down at their docks. She hadn't thought about how she was going to get to Venice. *Of course, it would be by boat. Wonderful.* She remembered how kind the Parks had been on her last ordeal with a water crossing.

As everyone got off the bus, Mason waited for Jayne.

"Don't worry about this boat ride," he said. "It isn't very long."

"I'll just keep my eyes closed," she replied.

Mason smiled and followed her off the bus. He purchased tickets for the group while Jayne stood alone. Whenever she made eye contact with some of the other group members, they smiled. But they weren't friendly smiles. They were sympathetic smiles. She shifted her focus and tugged at her coat. The water sloshed against the taxi and the smell of seawater assaulted her nose. Her stomach knotted.

Mason herded the group on board the water taxi. Everyone talked and pointed. Jayne lingered on land as long as she could.

"Come on, Jayne," Mason held out his hand. "I'll sit with you as soon as I take care of the luggage."

She took his hand and walked onto the boat.

"Just focus on something solid on the horizon. That might help."

Mason left. Jayne's stomach began to feel queasy. She closed her eyes and tried to pretend she was on the bus and the movement was just the tires rolling along the road. She still had them closed when she felt Mason sit next to her. The motor revved up and the smell of diesel flooded through the open windows.

She reached over to hold hands with Mason. Then, she visualized the horrid ordeal with Rosa and just squeezed her hands together in her lap.

Mason pulled her hands apart and cradled one in his warm hands.

"People are going to talk," Jayne said, her eyes still closed. She tried to pull her hand away. "They are going to believe what Rosa said ... whatever that was."

"Everyone is on your side. They are European and South American. They don't judge in the same way. Especially when they know the attack stemmed from pure jealousy."

"How do you know?"

"Because I talked with each one of them and told them how you helped me with the Parks' situation. They saw how close you were getting with them. Just because they don't speak your language doesn't mean they don't understand. They are not judging you. Certainly, no one is judging you as hard as you are yourself."

Jayne opened her eyes.

"I've always done that."

"Isn't it time that you stop?"

The question echoed in her mind. She squeezed his hand and closed her eyes again.

"Tell me when we're there."

She heard a soft chuckle in response.

"You must open your eyes."

"Why?"

"You don't want to miss this."

She slowly opened her eyes and zeroed in on the city.

"Incredible. I can't believe that it's sinking."

"Unfortunately, yes."

"What a shame," she said as she concentrated on the spires of the cathedrals. "Certainly, modern technology can do something."

"Yes, but it's expensive." Mason shifted in his seat.

"We spend money on wars without a second thought. And this is worth saving." Jayne looked at some of the smaller manmade islands around the main one. Focusing on the horizon seemed to help settle her stomach … a little.

"You do realize that this place was created in response to war, right?"

Jayne smiled at Mason and nodded.

The water taxi docked, and the group disembarked and followed Mason to their hotel. Jayne looked around, and with each step, couldn't believe she was walking on a manmade island that was centuries old. She kept her steps light in an unconscious effort not to add extra weight to the pylons. She laughed as she caught herself and resumed a normal stride.

The hotel was positioned on the side of a canal, facing the water with another island in the distance. Mason proceeded to hand out keys.

"Someone must have made a mistake," he said as he handed Jayne her keys. "There are two for your room."

"No, there's no mistake."

Mason's forehead creased and he tilted his head slightly.

"Someone is joining me." Jayne enjoyed Mason's obvious discomfort. He looked intently at the offending keys and shifted his stance. One hand swiped through his hair.

"Oh."

"I'm sure the information will be in your e-mail when you check it."

The corners of his mouth turned down slightly. Jayne couldn't stand to tease him any longer, but she did enjoy his now familiar habit of running his hands through his hair.

"My cousin, Lynn, is joining the tour."

"Oh." Mason's tone was totally different now as he stood taller. "Good, that's great." He handed over the two keys. "Well, she's not here yet or there would only be one key. After you check out your room, meet me here in the lobby."

"All right." Jayne sought out her room, found her luggage already there, and gazed out her window. The waves undulated softly and reflected the azure sky. The sun sprinkled flashes of light on each ripple. She smiled as she turned away from the beautiful view.

The group was supposed to meet back in the lobby, so Jayne quickly freshened up and headed back downstairs. Her head filled with the books she had read with Venice as their back-drop. Now, she was where Romantic poets had sought solace. Excitement vibrated in every nerve. There was a lilt in her step, almost like the skip she used to do as a child when she was on her way to a special event.

She scanned around the lobby. *Have I missed it?* Her shoulders slumped. No one was there, so she went outside to find the group congregated around Mason. She exhaled softly. He looked like a new-age guru with his flock. He held a hat high above his head, turned upside down, and reached into it. He pulled out a slip of paper. He gave the hat to Natalie and read.

"Our winner of the gondola ride is ..." He paused for dramatic effect and scanned the group until he met Jayne's eyes. "Jayne."

Jayne thought her ears were playing tricks. The grandparents with their grandchildren smiled and nodded. The Brazilian couples started clapping. Natalie stared down at the hat in her hand. And Rosa puckered her face as she stood at the outer edge of the gathering. The newlywed couple were so intent on each other that Jayne didn't think they remembered where they were.

"What's going on?" Jayne asked.

"You're going on a gondola ride with yours truly." Mason crumpled the piece of paper and shoved it in his pocket. "The rest of the group can do what they want with the next couple of hours, but you and I are heading to the Rialto Bridge."

She thought she heard a giant sigh from Rosa.

"Surely, someone else deserves this more than I do," Jayne protested. "What about the newlyweds?"

She heard another exaggerated sigh.

"Jayne, accept the gift graciously and let's go." Mason ran his fingers through his hair and then held out his arm for her. In a whisper, he added, "Everyone voted on it, so the drawing was fixed. Everyone except one, of course."

What a touching gesture, she thought as she walked with Mason and reveled in the atmosphere, leaving all other "sighs" behind.

She marveled at the architecture, supported by pylons, stretching out in front of her. The walkway was only about twelve feet wide and then there was water. She looked up and recognized the famous Rialto Bridge, arching over the Grand Canal, from her reading. Arches led to a central peak that resembled a little house.

"I can't believe I'm really here." She gazed at the bridge as people crossed it and silently added, "With you." At the base of the bridge, gondolas were tied in groups like fish from a fruitful morning's catch. The boats' black lacquered finish accentuated the bronze tips. They were sleek. Jayne wondered if they rocked too easily.

Mason motioned to one of the gondoliers, who was dressed in black pants and the traditional striped shirt. He was a stout man with short gray hair and a very red face.

The gondolier reached out to help her, but she paused. "I'm not going to get sick, am I?"

Mason laughed, a deep rumbling sound that made her laugh too. "No, I think you'll be fine on this boat."

She climbed in and took a seat. Mason sat next to her on the bench. The gondolier poled away from the quay. As Jayne turned to watch the old man, the muscles in his arms strained as he dug the pole deep into the canal. His straw hat lay at his firmly planted feet.

"You can sit back and relax." Mason put his arm around her shoulders and pulled her back.

It was only then that she realized that every muscle in her body had been as rigid as steel. Guilt tried to tug at her, but the feeling of his arm calmed her. She settled back, melting into his embrace.

The gondola floated under the Rialto Bridge. Crowds on the bridge gawked at them.

"This is not quite what I had imagined," Jayne said as the eyes from above seemed to penetrate beneath the surface. *Do they think we're a couple?* The thought intruded like a nagging mother. Tensing, she moved forward a bit.

"It will get better as we move along." Mason waved at some of the people on the bridge. They waved back. She relaxed back into his arm.

The gondola turned down a narrow canal. The crumbling stucco skin of the homes showed the skeleton of red brick underneath. All the windows were shuttered and peeling. Jayne's romantic illusions slowly took a backseat to reality.

"It's a shame," she said. "The slow decay."

"It can't be helped," Mason replied. "Everything eventually crumbles."

"Maybe so. But does it have to?" She leaned back, now assured that her stomach wouldn't react to the boat ride.

The canals snaked through the city along homes, shops, and businesses. When they floated under some of the bridges, the gondolier had to crouch down to get through. After one such ducking, the gondolier said something to Mason.

"What did he say?" Jayne asked.

"He wants to know if we want him to sing."

Jayne thought for a moment. "That would be lovely."

Mason replied to the gondolier.

The stocky gondolier looked more like a retired prizefighter than a singer, so she prepared for the worst. But his mouth opened wide and emitted the most beautiful operatic tones on earth, full vibrato in a lush baritone voice.

Jayne looked at Mason.

He looked at her.

They both erupted in laughter and clapped their hands. The gondolier took a short bow without missing a note. More people from the sides of the canal waved at them because of the singing. Mason put his arm back around her and she liked it. She knew she shouldn't, but she snuggled deeper into him. Here she was in Venice, on a gondola, with a gorgeous man. A caring, sensitive man. At this moment in time, it didn't matter to her that he wasn't her husband.

After the gondolier finished his song, he turned the boat into another canal, passing under a limestone archway rimmed with stone faces that spanned two buildings. Two latticed windows were set into the sculpted exterior. The top looked like the scrolls on a violin.

"It's the Bridge of Sighs." Jayne leaned forward to get a better view. "What was it that Lord Byron wrote in *Childe Harold*? I think it was 'I stood in Venice, on the Bridge of Sighs; a palace and a prison on each hand...'"

"'... It was from out the wave of her structure's rise, As from the stroke of the enchanter's wand.'" Mason finished the quote.

She stared at him, a question fleeting through her mind. *Could he be my soulmate?*

"Did you know that Byron named the bridge because he thought you could hear the sighs of the prisoners as they took their last glimpse of freedom from the windows?" Mason looked up. "The locals call it Ponte Dei Sospiri."

"I thought it was a meeting place for lovers and that the sighs were from them as they took their gondola rides underneath it."

Jayne watched as they neared the bridge. She couldn't take her eyes off the baroque designs and the scrolls carved into the top of the covered bridge. *Mason knows Byron's poetry,* she thought. *By heart.*

"It's beautiful." She leaned back as they started to float underneath it. Just as the bridge was overhead, Mason bent over her and kissed her lightly on the lips.

It felt like the soft fluttering of butterfly wings, promising and full of life.

"That … was sweeter than any chocolate." And she sighed.

Jayne laughed nervously and knew she should protest, but she didn't have the strength. She liked the way she fit in his arms. She enjoyed the kiss. Instead of obeying the tiny voice in her head, she laid her head on his shoulder and relished the moment. No mantra needed.

"So, you like Lord Byron's poetry?" Mason pulled her closer. "The Byronic hero and all that?"

"Yes, I know," Jayne said as the gondola continued down the narrow canal. "He's much like Hemingway, I suppose. On paper, I'm drawn to the masculine, brooding type."

"Just on paper?" Mason cocked his head and lifted an eyebrow.

"Maybe I thought I could save them." Or, she thought, maybe they were safe because they were unreachable. She thought about Byron with his deformed foot and beautiful face. For as long as she could remember, she had fantasized about the romantic poet. His exile must have been painful. His poetry was full of emotion and passion. What her real life had lacked, she had found in reading. Now, she was floating down the same canals that had inspired some of her favorite poems and living her fantasy with Mason.

"They lived such short lives." Jayne's thoughts were drifting toward melancholy. "Keats and Shelley were only in their twenties when they died. Byron was in his thirties.

How could they have lived so much life in those short years?"

Before Mason could respond, the gondola returned to the Rialto Bridge and docked. Mason tipped the gondolier. They exchanged a few words in animated Italian.

"What did he say?" Jayne asked as they started to walk back to the hotel.

"He said, 'You are a lucky man to enjoy Venice with such a beautiful woman.'" Mason reached out and took her hand, looping it into the crook of his arm. "Wait. I have an idea. I'll take you to a place where Byron and Shelley used to share coffee and talk."

She picked up her pace, glad her time with him wasn't going to end right away. It must be the place, but all she cared about was this moment. Now. The present. She could worry later.

"Let's take a water taxi and I can show you something on the way," Mason said.

They boarded the taxi and made their way down the Grand Canal away from the Rialto Bridge and toward St. Mark's Square.

"Look quickly to the left at that sharp turn in the canal." Mason pointed. "That's Palazzo Mocenigo, where Byron lived and Shelley visited."

Jayne craned her neck, her mouth parted slightly. "You have to enter by the canal?"

"You can just picture Shelley arriving late at night during a rainstorm. His gondola pulls up to the door where Byron and his current mistress, who happens to be the baker's wife, meet him. The sounds of a monkey, fox, dog, and other animals cavorting in the background complete the scene."

Jayne laughed but cut it short when she thought about the mistress ... the baker's wife. She shook off the thought and kept her pledge to live in the moment. "Byron had animals at his home in Ravenna, too." She gazed at the dingy three-story façade. "This taxi is going too fast. I think that's a coat of arms sculpted between the windows on the second floor."

She had almost turned around in her seat to keep the villa in view. She squeezed his hand. Dreams coming true made her heart beat erratically. Her breathing shallower. Maybe that was why her head seemed to be floating high in the clouds.

Within minutes, they arrived at St. Mark's Square, where they landed and walked to Café Florian. There were tables and chairs in front of the restaurant. She shivered with excitement.

"We can go inside if you think it is too cold," Mason said.

"No, I'd like to stay out here." Jayne gazed out at the tower and the square.

"What do you think?" Mason pulled out her chair and she sat down.

"It's beautiful." She shifted her chair closer to the table. "Just think, Byron and Shelley sat in this very same spot. Drinking and talking. Creating masterpieces. It's unreal."

"Not only Byron and Shelly, but Stravinsky, Goethe, Proust, and many others sat here and talked." Mason ordered two coffees from the waiter.

"How do you know so much?" Jayne asked as she shifted her seat forward.

"My parents didn't think I could make it as a musician, so they sent me to the university. In fact, after my music career failed, I went back and earned my doctorate in social history."

Her eyes widened and her mouth dropped open. "Then why are you doing this? You could be teaching."

He shifted in his seat and put his elbows on the table. Leaning forward, he stared into her eyes. "I don't know. It just didn't seem to be the right thing for me at the time."

"What a waste," she smiled at the waiter as he placed coffee in front of her.

"I wouldn't have met you," he replied as he blew on his coffee to cool it.

As they both sipped their coffee, she thought she heard her name being called. She cocked her head and listened.

"Jayne … Jayne."

Mason must have heard it too because he was glancing around the square.

"Over here." Lynn stood beneath the Campanile as it started to ring. She waved her hands over her head. She was dressed in red from head to toe, and her blond hair glistened in the sunlight. A brilliant scarf of red, black, and gold draped around her neck.

"You know someone here in Venice?" Mason continued to stare at the woman who approached them.

"No, of course not," Jayne said as she stood to meet the woman in red. "Mason, I would like you to meet my cousin, Lynn."

Mason stood and shook Lynn's hand. Lynn's eyes roamed from the top of his head to his shoulders and slowly down to his toes as she checked him out. She was like a whirlwind. Without an invitation, she joined them at their table and ordered her own coffee in Italian.

"They told you I was coming, didn't they?" Lynn thanked the waiter as he brought her espresso.

"Jayne did." Mason sipped his coffee.

"It's good to see you, Jayne." Lynn held her espresso cup, but she didn't drink it. "You look wonderful."

"I can't believe you're really here," Jayne said, but she looked at Mason over the rim of her coffee cup.

"It's me, all right." Lynn took a sip. "Now, where are we going next?"

CHAPTER 14

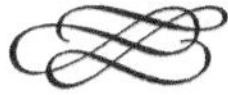

onday evening, October 22, 2012

"Can you believe it?" Lynn stood by the hotel window. "Imagine having your front door dump directly into a canal." She turned from the window and walked over to her bed. She propped up some pillows and flopped down, crossing her legs.

"Why did you decide to come?" Jayne sat in a chair poised in the corner of the room, her feet resting on a footstool. Her reaction to Lynn's arrival confused her. She should have been ecstatic, but she wasn't. She struggled with the green-eyed beast for the first time ever regarding Lynn's reaction to a man. It felt as uncomfortable as an itchy wool sweater. She hated wool sweaters.

"When you told me about the death of the old man, I thought that maybe you could use a friend." Lynn shifted a bit as she fell deeper into her pillows.

"His name was Floyd Parks," Jayne replied with more bite in her tone than she wanted.

"I'm sorry, Jayne," Lynn said. "It must have been awful to watch."

"I thought you had commitments at work." Jayne got up and went to the window, her back to Lynn.

"My commitment to you is stronger, especially now." Lynn got up and stood next to Jayne. "Is something else the matter?"

Jayne just stared out the window. Boats floated back and forth between the hotel and the other side of the canal. Tourists, with shopping bags bulging, lined up to be ferried across. The sidewalks were jam-packed with people milling about.

"Let's go for a walk before it gets dark," Jayne said. "We're in Venice, for God's sake. Let's go explore." She smiled, fighting her itchy feelings, and picked up her jacket from the back of the corner chair. For heaven's sake, she thought, Lynn is my best friend.

"I'm all for exploring." Lynn went to the closet and slipped on her red coat, exchanging her heels for flats.

As they passed the mirror above the desk, Jayne noticed the stark contrast. Lynn was vibrant, full of energy and life. Jayne paled in comparison, even in her own eyes. She always had. Somehow, it felt more intense this time. Her mind drifted back to the gardens at Chateau Caen. The faded flower next to a vibrant, colorful blossom.

They entered the bustling activity on the sidewalks and the crowd swept them away. They crossed several bridges as they zigzagged through the narrow streets.

"It's like a giant maze," Lynn exclaimed. "Look at that." She stopped in front of a shop window displaying masks of every variety imaginable.

"They're exquisite." Jayne bent to examine one. It was a full facemask of white, trimmed in ripples of elaborate gold. The full lips were crafted in solid gold. The chin was etched in light gold *fleur-de-lis*. The empty eyeholes formed the center of intricate golden designs. The crowning glory was an enormous plumage of black feathers like a lion's mane.

"Let's go in," Lynn said as she pulled the shop door open.

The shop was like a dream menagerie. Masks stared, vacuous from every wall. In the corner, a mannequin loomed, dressed like an empress in a glittering purple and gold gown. It was a work of art. The bosom was extremely low-cut and fitted to the waist. Swirls of gauzy fabric flowed from the waist to the floor. The frozen mannequin's hand held the facemask, embossed with more gold.

The shopkeeper approached and spoke in slightly accented English. "That is the Volto Versailles Baton Mask. As you can see, it has diamonds and emeralds."

"It's lovely," Jayne explored the complexities of the design. "What is it made of?"

"Papier mâché as the base and then an overlay of gold or silver leaf." The shopkeeper pulled another mask from a shelf and showed the inside. "See."

"Look at this one, Jayne," Lynn picked up the mask and held it in front of her face.

Jayne laughed as the half-mask with the extraordinarily long nose framed Lynn's face. "You look like Pinocchio."

"This could be kind of fun," Lynn said suggestively as she put the mask back on the shelf.

Jayne turned to the shopkeeper. "I know these masks are for Carnivale, but exactly what is the celebration all about?"

The shopkeeper seemed delighted by the question as she explained the festival's origins. The history of Carnivale went back to the eleventh century. Mutating throughout the centuries, by the eighteenth century, it was a time when social class barriers faded behind the masks.

The shopkeeper added, "After all, Masquerades, Mardi Gras, Carnivale, and Venice Masked Balls were events originally designed to allow the identity of the person to be hidden, so that they could interact with anyone they wanted, for a variety of reasons." She smiled broadly.

"So, you could basically do whatever you damn well pleased,"

Lynn said as she picked up a half mask of verdant green trimmed in gold.

"Well, you know what Oscar Wilde said about masks," Jayne added.

"No, Jayne," Lynn said. "What?"

"He said that 'Man is least himself when he talks in his person. Give him a mask, and he will tell you the truth.'" Jayne picked up a full facemask of pink, purple, and gold. "I think I'll get this one for Kim. It will fit in my suitcase."

"I'll get this one for myself," Lynn said. "Who knows, it might come in handy during this trip. All I need is a green negligee to match."

For the first time, Lynn sounded crass to Jayne. They made their purchases and hit the streets of Venice again.

"What a wonderfully decadent place," Lynn continued. "I wonder why I never thought about coming here before."

"You're so tacky," Jayne blurted out before she could stop herself.

"What?" Lynn stopped walking and the couple behind her ran into her. She apologized and stared at Jayne. "What's wrong with you? You're acting weird."

"I'm sorry," Jayne said. "I think it's just everything getting to me."

They started walking when Lynn stopped short again. "This will help."

They had stopped in front of a gelato shop. "Mocha gelato," Lynn said. "I've had gelato in some of the Italian restaurants at home. It's ice cream, but better."

They wewnt into the shop where a rainbow of colors greeted them. Greens, pinks, creams, and buttery brown were in deep containers behind refrigerated glass. Jayne focused on something called "stracciatella" that looked like fluffy chocolate clouds with huge chocolate chips floating in them. She didn't need a translator as she pointed to the confection. Lynn ordered a pink one.

"This looks like a chocolate dream," Jayne said as she sat at a round table in the corner of the gelateria. She dipped her spoon slowly across the top of the mound and captured a chip. "Oh my God, this is scandalous." Bliss melted in her mouth.

"Ditto." Lynn scooped up a second bite quickly. "This is living." She paused and plunged her spoon down into the gelato. "I'm sorry."

Jayne just continued to eat her gelato and shook her head. *No pity. Not now.* She waved it off with one hand.

"Where do you want to go next?" Lynn picked up her spoon and began to eat again.

"Let's just go back to the hotel. We're supposed to have dinner with the group. You can meet some of the people you're going to tour with." Jayne scooped up a huge bite and stuffed it in her mouth.

"We should have done something like this a long time ago, Jayne," Lynn said as she scooped up the last bit of her gelato.

"At least we're doing it now," Jayne replied as she dropped her spoon in the empty container and dropped it into a receptacle.

They walked silently through the labyrinth of narrow streets and back across arched bridges to the hotel. The group was going to have dinner together in a reserved space just off the main dining room.

A large rectangular table dominated the area. Each place setting was arranged faultlessly. The Brazilian couples were already seated, and they called Lynn and Jayne to come sit with them. Jayne went on one side of the table and Lynn sat directly across from her. Without Mason there to translate, the only communication that took place was in exaggerated sign language.

The grandparents entered with their grandchildren,

followed closely by Mason. The grandparents took seats at the far end of the table and Mason pulled out the chair next to Jayne and tilted it forward, showing the place was taken. Jayne tensed as she watched Lynn checking Mason out as he bent to say something to the other people around the table.

"I just told everyone that we will introduce our newest member of the group when everyone gets here." He smiled at Jayne. He wore what had become her favorite grayish-blue sweater.

"I'm looking forward to getting to know everyone," Lynn said, her gaze fixed solely on Mason.

"They don't all speak English, Lynn," Jayne said.

"Who needs English?" Lynn replied and took a sip of her water.

Rosa entered with Natalie. Rosa sat on the other side of Mason and Natalie took the seat next to Lynn. The newlyweds took the remaining seats.

"Okay, it looks like we are all here." Mason stood behind his tilted chair and spoke in Spanish, then Portuguese. He motioned to Lynn, who stood up. She lifted her glass of water in acknowledgment of everyone.

"I'm happy to be here enjoying the trip with my cousin, Jayne." She saluted Jayne with her glass before she sat down. Then, she turned toward Mason. "Thank you for such a warm reception."

Mason nodded as he pulled out his chair and sat down. Waiters began filling wine glasses and bringing in the first course of the meal.

"So, where did you two go this afternoon?" Mason asked as he sipped his wine.

"We wandered around and found a wonderful mask shop," Lynn offered.

"Really?" Mason shifted to one side as the waiter placed a salad of mozzarella, tomatoes, and basil in front of him.

"Yes," Jayne interjected. "The shopkeeper was kind enough to share some of the history of Carnivale with us."

"She shared some of the basics, but I know there must be more to it," Lynn said as she cut into a thick slice of tomato. "I think she left out a lot." She chewed slowly and looked only at Mason.

"I thought it was very informative." Jayne sipped her wine too fast and coughed.

"Went down the wrong way?" Mason asked as he lightly patted Jayne between the shoulder blades.

Jayne just nodded.

"It might have started out as part of a pagan ritual, but when the Roman Catholics got hold of it, the meaning expanded." Mason focused on Jayne. "You know that it comes just before Lent, right? Like Mardi Gras?"

"Yes, the shopkeeper told us that," Jayne took another bit of mozzarella and tomato and tried to divert the conversation. "This salad is really good. Is that olive oil and balsamic vinegar drizzled on the top?"

"You know that the masks are integral in the celebration," Mason continued. "They offer anonymity so everyone can indulge in their fantasies and then repent for their excesses during Lent."

"Now that's more like it," Lynn said as she eyed Mason over the rim of her wine glass. "The shopkeeper told us the G-rated version with something about equaling the social classes so they could talk."

"Well, I guess the social classes were equal in all respects during Carnivale." Mason laughed softly.

"So, Lynn, that is your name, *si?*" Rosa glared across the table. "Why did you decide to join this tour so late?"

"It sounded like fun when I talked to Jayne, so I decided to join my best friend. Why do you ask?"

"It just seems odd." Rosa leaned as the salad plate was taken away. Her low-cut sweater gave those on the opposite side of the table a full view.

"Life is odd, isn't it?" Lynn raised her glass to Rosa and dismissed her as she took a sip and looked at Mason again.

"Are you married?" Rosa continued her interrogation.

"No. Why?" Lynn parried. "Are you interested?"

"Of course not. Mason just might have his hands full with more women to entertain on this trip than he is used to." Rosa took a healthy sip of wine and motioned to the waiter for a refill.

"I'm sure Mason can live up to the challenge." Lynn raised her glass to the waiter for a refill as well.

"Maybe he can focus on the single women in the group," Rosa continued.

"I'm sure Mason will take care of everyone in the group according to their needs." Lynn set her glass down and focused on her meal.

As Jayne watched the interplay, she lost her appetite. These two women were like piranha circling their prey. *Am I that obvious?*

Mason seemed oblivious to anything but his entrée until his leg moved closer to hers. The warmth sank through and melted her qualms temporarily.

"You know Mardi Gras and Carnivale have been sexually decadent for centuries now." Mason slowly twirled his spaghetti with his fork. "Guilt-free sex with any willing partner."

Jayne froze with her glass midway to her mouth and glared across the table at both Lynn and Rosa. Their eyes were full of possibilities, all centered on Mason. She tensed, seething as she moved her leg away from Mason's. He was toying with all of them.

She had been a fool.

"I'm sorry, but I just remembered something and I have to go," Jayne said, abruptly setting her glass down. "I'll see you all in the morning." She pushed away from the table and walked briskly to the door. She was almost running down the hallway when someone caught her by the arm.

"What's wrong?" Mason pulled her around to face him.

"You're a ..." Jayne began and shook loose from his grasp.

"What?" Mason leaned down closer to her.

"You were playing with us the whole time." She couldn't help that her voice was breaking. "You kissed me."

"Yes, and I enjoyed it," Mason said.

"And that's it?" Jayne looked into his eyes, her body shaking.

"No, it's not just it." Mason moved closer. "I'm sorry, but I couldn't resist taunting those two a bit. They are so obvious. So ordinary. I didn't think about the effect it might have on you. You're different."

"Lynn is my cousin and my friend," Jayne replied. "I don't like to see her belittled."

"I'm really sorry, Jayne," Mason said, drawing out the vowel as he put his hands on her shoulders. "I fell into an old habit. I won't do it again." He gave her a hug. "Good night. I'll see you in the morning."

Mason turned and walked back to the dining room.

Is he really sorry, or is he just placating me? She had already been confused about her reaction to him, but now it was utterly vexing. She made her way slowly back to her room, thoughts storming through her head.

Was he toying with me like the others? Her warring thoughts tasted like bile rising in her throat. *Did everyone on the tour hide behind a mask? Ready to act on instinct? Have I fooled myself into thinking it could be more?*

In her room, she decided to take a shower. First, she washed off her makeup at the sink. Blotting her face dry with a towel, she stared in the mirror. Was her mask off? Was it jealousy that reared its ugly face in response? She didn't know. She had never had this clash of emotions before. She shook her head and stepped into the shower.

She was just getting into bed when Lynn returned. "Hey, are you all right?" Lynn asked softly as she locked the door.

"I'm fine," Jayne said as she propped up her pillows and lay on her side.

"Boy, that Rosa's a piece of work, isn't she?" Lynn opened her suitcase and pulled out a negligee.

"I think she slept with Mason at the beginning of the tour," Jayne replied. "She was a bit possessive of his time then."

"I thought he would have had better taste than that." Lynn went to the sink and began her ritual with special cleansers, toners, and other items. "He is a great-looking guy. The streaks of gray in his hair are really sexy. And his eyes, off the scale gorgeous."

Jayne's gut twisted as Lynn continued to talk about Mason. She closed her eyes and tried to stop listening, pulling the pillow over her head. She had no right to feel this way. After all, she was married and Lynn was not. She pulled her head out from under the pillow and pummeled it. Mason was not forbidden fruit for Lynn. But why was it forbidden to feel alive in someone's embrace? She rested her head on the abused pillow and squeezed her closed eyes tighter as if trying to close out the world.

"Oh, I'm sorry." Lynn's voice was closer. "Are you asleep?"

"Yes," Jayne lied.

"Right," Lynn said. "I'm just excited to be here."

"Why?" Jayne opened her eyes and sat up, staring at Lynn.

"Isn't it obvious?" Lynn pulled the covers up and tucked her arms down at her sides.

"Have you always been so self-centered?" Jayne couldn't believe the words that lingered for a moment between them.

"Self-centered?" Lynn sat up abruptly. "Are you kidding me? Where did that come from?"

"I don't know," Jayne said. "It was just disgusting to watch you and Rosa catfight over him."

"Honey, that was not a catfight," Lynn said. "That was just sizing up the competition."

"I thought you came over here to help me out," Jayne replied.

"You don't need any help from me," Lynn said. "I thought you would be depressed from the loss of Floyd." Lynn stressed the man's name. "But you seem just fine."

"I'm just confused," Jayne said as her thoughts returned to Mason.

"I can understand that," Lynn replied. "Watching someone else die had to have been the pits."

Jayne nodded and let it go.

"You are just stressed out from everything," Lynn continued. "I'm sorry. You're right. I should be focusing on you instead of man-hunting."

"Are you happy, Lynn?" Jayne twisted the sheets in her hands.

"What's happy?" Lynn leaned forward.

"Content," Jayne said.

"No, I'm never content," Lynn replied. "And I must confess something. I've always been a bit jealous of you."

"Me?"

"Yes, you always seemed content, especially after you had your children." Lynn pulled her knees up and wrapped her arms around them. "You have children. Part of you will continue through them. With me, it all stops here."

But, Jayne wondered, was that enough to satisfy a reason for being?

"Well, let me be clear," Lynn said. "I don't mean that I'm envious of your marriage."

"Without the marriage, there would be no children," Jayne replied.

"I just couldn't make that much of a sacrifice," Lynn said. "Was it worth it?"

"For the children," Jayne admitted. "Definitely."

"But what about you?" Lynn straightened her legs.

"In my marriage, the children were enough," Jayne said quietly.

"You didn't answer my question," Lynn pressed.

"Good night, Lynn." Jayne turned on her side and burrowed under the covers.

"Night, Jayne." Lynn turned off the light on the nightstand.

Jayne did not fall asleep quickly.

CHAPTER 15

uesday, October 23, 2012

Jayne turned her face toward the morning sun as she stood beside Lynn in front of the hotel. She decided to enjoy every moment of this beautiful day. She wouldn't waste time focusing on Mason. Venice had much more to offer. She had succumbed to her romantic images of the place yesterday, but now she would steep the rest of her visit in the history of the area.

Mason led the group to St. Mark's Square, where Jayne's new resolve took a hit as she looked at the Café Florian. Thoughts of Byron and Shelley discussing the latest stanzas of *Don Juan* fluttered unbidden. Memories of her time there with Mason took center stage. *Could it have been real?*

"God, look at all of these pigeons," Lynn said as she cringed a bit. "They are filthy little creatures."

As the group continued across the square to the cathedral, a flock of pigeons took flight. Lynn screamed and Mason turned around. Lynn ducked behind Jayne, who simply shrugged. Mason shook his head and began to talk about the church facade.

"The exterior is decorated with Byzantine, Romanesque, and Gothic art. You'll notice that there's a mosaic on the surface begun in 1260 and completed ten years later." Mason continued talking about how relics had been brought from all corners of the world to be housed in the cathedral.

The group followed Mason inside. They found themselves ensconced in a golden orb. "The walls of the altar are inlaid with precious jewels and twenty-four-carat gold. In fact, Napoleon helped himself to a few of those jewels while he was here."

Mason then pointed to the ceiling. "The ceiling is composed of mosaics that depict Genesis, and the gilded mosaics directly above show the transfer of St. Mark's body. The gold is supposed to show the light of God within these walls." Mason paused as everyone looked up. "Now, please look around on your own and we'll meet out front in about a half hour."

Rosa started to approach Jayne, but Natalie headed her off as the rest of the group went their different ways. Mason joined Lynn and Jayne.

"It's magnificent," Jayne said, mentally thanking Natalie.

Wherever Jayne focused, there was a feast for the eyes. She noticed the marble floor was buckling, creating a wave of sorts. The physical evidence of Venice's sinking made her heart drop.

"Are these curves in the floor the pylons?" she asked Mason.

"Yes, unfortunately they are," Mason replied.

"What a tragic waste," Jayne said. "They have to do something to save this."

"Sometimes, tragedies happen despite everything," Mason replied as they walked slowly.

Lynn maneuvered herself next to Mason.

"Just think of the jewelry that this gold could make," Lynn said.

"Jewelry?" Jayne frowned and wagged her index finger. "Think of the years of work these artisans gave to create this masterpiece. It's incredible. Think of the precision of placing each bit of tile to create the mosaic. What patience." Jayne began to walk and look closer at her surroundings.

But she was close enough to hear Lynn talking with Mason.

"She has always been the dreamy one. Always had her nose stuck in a book, dreaming about people and places," Lynn said.

Jayne bristled. *It sounds like I'm a child.*

"She seems to feel things deeply," Mason said.

Good. He doesn't think I'm a child. Jayne leaned to pretend like she was concentrating on the blue bits of the mosaic in front of her.

"Yes, she has always been sensitive," Lynn replied. "I'm more of a realist. You know. Take what's yours and damn the consequences." She touched Mason's arm and smiled seductively.

She's flirting with him. I can't believe this. Jayne edged closer to a statue opposite the mosaics. Her shoulders tensed as anger tugged at her.

"I don't live in the past or dream about what could have been." Lynn shuffled closer to Mason.

Really, Lynn? Jayne moved further away but still listened. Her head pounded as she continued to watch out of the corner of her eye.

Mason stepped back. "It's hard to believe that you two are such close friends."

"Why?" Lynn reached out and touched Mason's arm.

"You're so different." Mason pulled his arm back.

Jayne clenched her hands into fists and slightly pummeled her sides.

"Why is she here by herself?" Mason ventured.

Jayne froze and unclenched her fists while beads of sweat formed on her forehead. *Don't tell him, Lynn.*

"She's not," Lynn replied as she reared her head back. "I'm with her."

Jayne tried to focus on the blue bits of tile in the mosaic again.

"Where is her husband?" Mason asked boldly. "Why isn't he here with her?"

Oh God, don't talk about Tom to him.

"Tom is working," Lynn replied. "He always works. He is a self-centered man who thinks only about number one."

"A working man is a self-centered man?" Mason quirked an eyebrow.

"No, that's not what I mean," Lynn smiled. "He just makes decisions based on himself and expects the family to simply follow his lead."

"That still doesn't sound horrible." Mason moved closer to Lynn.

"He just doesn't care about Jayne's feelings," Lynn said.

Jayne's shoulders tensed up so tightly that her neck disappeared. She hoped no one was noticing her.

"How do you know?" Mason continued.

"Why do you want to know about Jayne's husband?"

Jayne swiped at her upper lip and decided she needed to stop this conversation right now.

"Look at this blue," Jayne called out to Lynn and Mason. "It's almost fluorescent. How did they create such patterns from bits of tile?" She held her breath, hoping they would respond.

"Have you ever seen anyone get so excited about bits of color?" Lynn said and looked intently at Mason. He walked over to where Jayne was standing.

"No, I haven't," he replied. He leaned close and his face showed a mixture of admiration and intelligence. Jayne exhaled as her shoulders relaxed and she enjoyed another mini lecture about the mosaic, punctuated with light touches on the shoulders and reciprocal touches on the arm. Subtle laughter broke the hollow silence of the cathedral.

As she glanced away from Mason, Jayne noticed that Lynn

stood in the background with brows furrowed, leaning against a pillar.

"I'd better spend some time with Lynn," Jayne said. "And you should join the rest of the group. I've been monopolizing you again."

His head was slightly angled as if weighing each of Jayne's words. As he began to straighten his head, his eyes sparkled. "I love being monopolized by you."

She looked back at Lynn and sighed as Mason walked toward the rest of the group, congregated at the entrance. He pointed to the ceiling and resumed his tour guide persona.

"Lynn, how could you?" Jayne walked over to Lynn, still leaning on the pillar.

"What?" Lynn shrugged her shoulders and stood up straight.

"Talk with Mason about me."

"Oh, you heard?"

"Clearly."

Lynn smiled and patted Jayne on the shoulder. "You little devil."

"What?"

"I've been such a fool," Lynn said. "And Rosa was, too."

"You've lost me," Jayne said as they started to walk slowly toward the group.

"He's head over heels in love with you," Lynn said. "It's written all over his face every time he is near you."

"Stop," Jayne said, fumbling with her purse as if it were slipping off her shoulder. "There is no way a man like Mason has fallen for someone like me. Besides, I'm married."

"I've never seen you so full of life, so in tune with your surroundings ... and especially with Mason." Lynn stopped walking and put her hands up on Jayne's shoulders. "His eyes actually sparkle when you talk. Something inside him lights up when you are near him." She paused. "No man has ever looked at me that way."

"You're being dramatic," Jayne said as she shook her head. "No way."

"I'm telling you there is something special there," Lynn said as she turned and began to walk toward the group.

Mason looked at them as they approached.

"See," Lynn smirked as Mason smiled.

And yes, Jayne saw the sparkle in his eyes as they connected with hers. *Could Lynn be right?* She pushed the thought away, telling herself to just focus on the next place on the day's itinerary.

The next stop was the Murano glass factory. The group boarded a water taxi and arrived on a separate island about nine minutes later. It was such a short ride, Jayne didn't have time to feel sick, or maybe she was just getting used to boats.

"All of the glass factories in Venice were moved to this island in 1291 because of the risks of fire," Mason said. "This consolidation made the island the center of glass production for many years."

"I've seen some beautiful glasswork in Las Vegas," Lynn said to Jayne as they moved toward the exit of the taxi. "It covers the ceiling in the Bellagio hotel."

The tour group followed Mason to an older building. "There are only three to five artisans with about fifty to sixty helpers. Each glass factory used to have its own special recipe, but now the secret has been cracked, no pun intended, by computers."

They entered the workspace and were hit with stifling heat. The blast of the furnaces filled the studio and roared like greedy beasts wanting to be fed. There was no extra machinery in sight, just three men wearing T-shirts and jeans. The tour group sat in bleachers across from the furnaces. Jayne focused on a glowing orb nestled in the mouth of one of the furnaces.

"Giuseppe is the master craftsman, and Piero is his apprentice." Mason nodded to the two men and they began their demonstration.

Jayne watched intently, squinting her eyes, as Giuseppe picked up a giant rod and prodded the unshapely piece of glass. He had silver hair, slicked back. His bronzed biceps flexed as he focused on his work. The glob of glass continued to glow like the sun as he removed it from the furnace and began to roll the pole back and forth. Piero, a younger man with his hair tied back in a ponytail, used mitts to caress the glass into an oblong shape. His lats flexed in his tight white T-shirt as he moved around. Then, they placed the glass back in the furnace.

Using a large pair of tongs, the master artisan pulled the glass from the furnace once more. As he rolled the pole slowly, he worked quickly with the tongs. Like a magician working his magic, he transformed the blob of glass into an animal's head with a couple of quick pulls. Piero watched intently.

"The artist has to work fast before the glass begins to cool and harden," Mason added.

The mane of a horse materialized, followed swiftly by legs with hooves. With a flip of the wrist and a poke of the tongs, the mane flowed and the legs curved. With a finishing flourish, Giuseppe pulled a tail from the sleek body of the horse.

"The real test," Mason said, "is whether the horse can balance on its hind legs."

Giuseppe added a few more tugs on the horse and set it on the worktable. It balanced with front hooves midair in perfect alignment. No pattern to follow. No adjustments needed. A perfect work of art in glistening glass.

What a gift, Jayne thought, to be able to leave something like that behind.

Mason asked if there were any questions.

"How do they get different colors?" Natalie asked.

"They use different minerals. Red and yellow are the hardest colors to keep consistent." Mason continued to field questions.

"It's hot in here," Lynn said.

Jayne just shook her head as she continued to watch the

glassblower move on to another project. This time, he blew into the orb and began to create a vase. Within that vase, he placed another piece of glass with different colors. It was like watching God create the earth. Just like painters and sculptors, the human capacity for creativity was on display for all to admire ... all who cared to admire.

Giuseppe dropped his silver head down as he put some extra finishing touches on the piece. He wasn't on this earthly plane as his eyes focused on the glass. Jayne thought that he must be in perfect tune with God, who used the artisan's hands to bless this world with beauty. She could have watched this miracle all day, but the group shuffled out of the workshop and into the gift shop that was nothing less than a glass menagerie.

"Can you believe this?" Lynn said. "I'm going to look at the beads and jewelry."

"Fine." Jayne looked at the chandeliers hanging overhead and the shelves bulging with glassware. She passed by the cups, goblets, and 24-carat filigreed platters. She walked back to the figurines. There were horses like the one Giuseppe created. But as she looked through the giraffes, elephants, cats, and fish, a special figure caught her eye. She looked at it closely and saw its reflection in the mirror behind the shelves. It was a ruby-red unicorn. Like the horse, it reared up on its hind legs with its forelegs arched in the air. A golden horn pierced the mane and twisted to a precise point. She reached out to touch it but pulled her hand back slowly. The fragile legs tapered to hooves that squared off into the air.

"Do you see something you wish?" a salesperson approached.

"Yes," Jayne pointed to the unicorn.

"Fine choice," the salesperson said. "You can see the ruby red is flawless. If the artisan sees a flaw in the color, he must toss it back into the furnace. The gold is added later and must be precisely centered so it looks like it is one piece. Much skill is needed to make this unicorn."

"Can you wrap it up for me?" Jayne said, still in awe of the piece and unwilling to touch it.

"Yes, do you want to know the price?"

"No, I'll take it." Jayne followed the salesperson to the front desk.

"That's beautiful," Mason said. He stood by the checkout desk. "So, you believe in miracles."

"No, but I do believe in fairy tales and myths," Jayne replied. "And with them, the possibility of true love."

"Look at this, Jayne." Lynn came up to the checkout wearing a beaded bracelet that glittered like diamonds. She had a bag with her as well. Reaching into the bag, she pulled out a beautiful wine stopper. "I bought a bunch of these for my friends. They'll love them. I also have a few earrings and a necklace. Did you look at the jewelry?"

"No, I have what I want," Jayne said. "Can you believe this place? Look at what the artisans give to the world."

"It's a business, Jayne," Lynn replied.

Mason was quiet.

Jayne continued, "Artists do have to live and that means they have to make some money. They always have. Think about Michelangelo working for the Medici family and the Church. Look what he produced. Just because he made money doesn't make it any less of a work of art. Think of what they left behind. We know their names because of it."

"Wow," Lynn replied. "That was something."

Mason just kept looking at Jayne.

"What do you think?" Lynn asked Mason.

"I think I had better start rounding up the rest of the group," Mason replied as he turned to scan the shop for the others.

"Ready, ladies?" he asked as the group had gathered just

outside of the door. He glanced around the store and then looked at Jayne. "You know that you did it again."

"What?" Jayne asked, shifting her stance and noticing that Lynn had moved outside to join the rest of the group.

"I have been to these places more times than I can remember," he said, moving closer to her. "And I believe that I'm seeing them for the first time in my life."

She didn't know what to say and glanced at Lynn, who had a huge smile on her face.

"Come on, let's not keep everyone waiting," he said. Jayne got the distinct impression that he enjoyed her confused silence. He led her to join the group with a light touch on her elbow. Lynn stepped up to meet her as Mason went to the head of the group to lead them back to the water taxi.

"This is our last day in Venice," said Lynn. They lingered behind the group.

"Yes, next is Florence," Jayne said, recovering her wits. "I can't wait. I want to see the place where the Brownings lived."

"You and your English writers," Lynn said.

"Poets, if you please," Jayne said and smiled. Visiting Florence had been a dream since she first became aware of the poets' love story.

"You have a chance here," Lynn said.

Jayne frowned and inclined her head to one side.

"You know what I mean." Lynn nodded toward Mason, who was leading the group and glanced back as they neared the water taxi.

"The rest of your time in Venice is free for you to use as you wish. We will leave bright and early tomorrow morning. Florence is our next stop." Mason motioned everyone toward the water taxi.

"Florence could offer you more than you ever dreamed of," Lynn said.

"Oh, stop it, Lynn." Jayne walked faster.

"Okay, what do you want to do with the rest of our time here?" Lynn changed the subject temporarily.

"Let's find a special place for dinner," Jayne said. "Just us."

"Sounds good," Lynn replied. "Let's ask Mason for a recommendation."

Lynn smiled smugly as Mason took a seat next to Jayne on the taxi.

"Mason, Jayne and I would like to go out for dinner tonight," she said. "Do you have any suggestions?"

"Venice is not really known for its great food. In fact, it's just the opposite." Mason shifted in his seat. "But if you want a unique experience, try one of the cicchetti. It's like a tapas restaurant. You get plenty of wine and plenty of variety with little plates of tidbits that will eventually fill you up. Some places only have standing tables, but there are others that have tables where you can sit."

"Would you like to join us?" Lynn asked.

Jayne glared back at her cousin. *What was she doing?*

"That would be great," Mason replied. "I'll meet you in the lobby at six."

"Wonderful," Lynn replied and looked at Jayne.

THAT EVENING, Lynn and Jayne met Mason in the lobby.

He smiled. "Ready?

"Actually, I'm really tired," Lynn said. "I think I'll just stay here and order room service."

"What?" Jayne exclaimed. *What was my cousin doing?*

"Really, you two go and enjoy yourselves," Lynn said as she turned back to the stairs. "Ciao."

Jayne just looked at Mason. *I'm going to kill her.*

"She's *your* cousin," Mason replied, shrugging his shoulders.

They walked out into the cool evening with the stars shining off the water. The moon was full, bathing the streets in a warm glow. The cicchetti was not far away. It hummed with activity. Lively conversations collided with boisterous laughter.

Mason found a table nestled in the corner and attracted the attention of a waiter. He ordered a variety of dishes and a carafe of wine. Mason blended in with his surroundings as he used sweeping hand gestures to accentuate his words.

He nodded to a couple seated next to them. "*Ciao come stai questa sera meraviglioso?*" he asked.

The man responded, "*Meravigliosa e voi?*"

"*Eccellente. Meravigliosa.*" Mason added emphasis with his hands again, bringing them to his lips and kissing the air with a flick of his fingers.

The waiter returned, balancing the carafe and a couple of small dishes.

"You are a chameleon," Jayne said as she sampled a delicacy from one of the many plates that soon filled the table.

"You think so?"

"Definitely." She sipped her wine. "Who is the real Mason?"

"Stick around." Mason held his glass up for a toast. "To finding out what's real."

Jayne laughed as their glasses clicked. "To looking behind the mask."

She watched his lips caress the wineglass and then followed the journey of his sip by watching his neck pulse and still. He was silent as he set his glass down.

"What are you thinking about?" she asked.

"Mysteries of life," he answered. "Are you ready for more food?"

"No," she exclaimed. "I want to take my time and enjoy each bite. I'm afraid you might be in for a very late evening."

"I like to eat, too." He sopped up the remnants of one dish. "Let the feast continue."

She chewed deliberately and decidedly. If she liked something, her head tilted ever so slightly. If it was exceptionally good, she closed her eyes briefly. Nothing came close to the chocolate scale, but she did enjoy a lot of the specialties. She was mid-bite when she noticed his intense stare.

"Do I have food on my face?" she asked, swiping around her mouth with her napkin.

"No," he replied. "I'm sorry. I'm just enjoying the show."

"What show?"

"I've never seen anyone enjoy food like you do," he laughed.

"Really?"

"No, I don't mean that in a bad way." A crease appeared along with a frown. "You show your enjoyment in your body language. I just love watching."

He loves watching me eat? What is that supposed to mean?

As if reading her mind, he said, "I just love being with you. You make every moment a new experience. Even just eating."

Mason signaled the waiter to bring on another tray.

In this moment, she felt like Cinderella finding her prince. Elizabeth with her Robert. Special. Celebrated. Loved. The glow of it warmed her from head to toe.

As usual, time went by much too quickly, and before she knew it, they were back at the hotel, saying good night. She lingered for a moment, and when he began to lean in for a good night kiss, she turned her back and went into her room, leaving him standing in an empty hallway. She still wasn't sure it was real. Thoughts about the way he had played Rosa and Lynn wafted through her head.

Lynn popped up as the door closed. Jayne gave her cousin a stern look.

"Don't look at me that way," Lynn said. "You had a great time, didn't you?"

Jayne smiled, her momentary irritation dissolving into a pool of helplessness. "Yes, of course I did. But it's wrong and you know it." Jayne shrugged out of her coat and pulled a hanger from the armoire. She shut the doors softly and turned back toward Lynn.

Sitting on the edge of the bed, Jayne slipped off her shoes and crossed her legs up on the bed. "Please don't do that again. It's too hard."

"What's so hard?" Lynn sat up. "He's perfect for you."

"I'm married," Jayne said, rubbing the temples of her forehead. "And you know the complications."

"Have you ever felt this way before with any other man?"

"No, but that doesn't make it right." Jayne's voice rose slightly, like it did when she had disciplined her children.

She had always done the right thing before. Her Southern Baptist upbringing had made sure of that. Now wasn't the time to do otherwise. Plus, she had her doubts.

"What harm can being happy do?" Lynn argued.

"It's not fair to anyone except me," Jayne replied. "I would be the only one that was happy for however long it lasted."

"What's wrong with that?" Lynn persisted.

"It's selfish," Jayne said.

"Is Carnivale selfish? Is loving someone selfish? Maybe being selfish is human nature. Do you really think you are better than the rest of us?" Lynn stood up and began to pace. "Jayne, for God's sake, take this chance to be happy for a few days out of your entire life. There won't be another chance."

"Why this sudden change?" Jayne asked. "I thought you wanted him for yourself."

"That was until I stepped back and watched the way he looks at you." Lynn stopped pacing and stood in front of Jayne. "It's you he wants."

"What about the complications?" Jayne asked.

"It's an affair. A fling. Not a lifelong commitment."

Jayne froze for a moment as if her blood had coagulated throughout her body. *Am I capable of just having an affair or a fling?*

"I'm sorry, Jayne," Lynn said. "I didn't mean it that way. Anyway, Mason doesn't have to know about your…complications."

"I'm not sure I can do that," Jayne said. She tucked herself under the covers. "I don't know if I can let go, so it is better if I never start. Maybe it is not fair to him."

Lynn turned off the light and slipped into her bed. "Just think about it, Jayne."

That's all Jayne did, on and off, through a very restless night.

CHAPTER 16

ednesday, October 24, 2012

Jayne soaked in the panoramic view like a child ogling FAO Schwartz. The vista spread before her, thick with cupolas topped with red tiled roofs, and bell spires crafted from red, green, and white marble. Patches of trees dotted the city of Florence and hills loomed in the distance. She had dreamed of this place for a long time. It exceeded her expectations.

She shifted in her seat and started pumping her leg. Brunelleschi's dome and the Duomo dominated the central landscape majestically. The bus pulled to a stop on a hilltop that overlooked the city.

As she disembarked, Jayne knew it wasn't her imagination. The light was different here. It seemed to illuminate multi-dimensionally. She took a deep breath and continued to stare at the view. She had watched the movie based on Forster's *A Room with a View* so many times that she thought she knew what to expect. The photography in that movie had mesmerized her. But now, she understood that it was a second-rate reproduction of the original. Her soul opened in response.

"Hey, Jayne," Lynn called from the other side of the bus. "You have to look at this."

Reluctantly, Jayne pulled herself away from the view and walked around the bus. There in the middle of a grass circle was a statue. Not just any statue, but Michelangelo's *David*. She couldn't believe it was out in the elements and not protected in a museum somewhere. The alabaster marble glistened. The young David's chest was carved so intricately that the muscles gave the illusion of expanding and contracting. The neck seemed to have a pulse. Jayne came closer and focused on the hand that was hanging by his side. The nails showed growth. And the veins. She was sure they pulsed with life.

"He's not well endowed, but he's hot," Lynn said. "Look at those abs." Jayne saw Mason watching them off to the side and grinning at their actions.

"I can't imagine how someone created something like this from a slab of marble. It looks alive." Jayne continued to walk around the statue to take in every angle.

"Michelangelo said that the piece was already there. He just released it from the marble," Mason commented as he joined them.

"But the artist must have the gift to see what's there, right?" Jayne replied.

"Apparently so," Mason said.

"Well, this is Tuscany," said Lynn. "It's beautiful. I could stay here forever."

Jayne was quiet. She had thought the trip had been fascinating so far, but she couldn't wait to delve into life in Florence. She had imagined being here so many times. The Arno streamed just below them from the Piazzale Michelangelo. The covered bridge spanned the river with Vasari's Corridor arching in the middle. On each side were actual homes built into the bridge. "This bridge is the third one built in the exact same place. The first was built by the Romans." Mason's tour guide persona was in full swing.

Jayne took in the view one last time before getting back on the bus. She looked at the houses clustered together and wondered which one had been the Browning's Casa Guidi. She could understand fully why writers and artists had been drawn to this place. There was something otherworldly here. She could feel it.

"Paradise is not lost anymore," Jayne said in a whisper. "It's right here."

The tour bus dropped the group off one more time, and they followed Mason. He didn't tell them what they were going to see. They walked through the streets that had shops and homes. But when they turned the final corner, everyone sighed audibly. There was a collective gasp as the Cathedral of Florence and Duomo Square burst forth like a multi-tiered wedding cake with flourishes of intricate designs. There were actual layers of marble that created the exterior.

"It works every time," Mason said. "I always bring my group through the back streets to get the full impact of the cathedral."

"It's incredible," Natalie said. Rosa was at her side but remained silent.

"It's made from Carrara white, Prato green, and Maremma pink marble." Mason noted the three portals and the pediment over the central portal. Statues of the apostles and Mother Mary peopled the arches. A giant rose window stood over the middle portal as well. Even the doors of the cathedral were works of art made of bronze.

The inside was not as ornate as Jayne had expected. It had smooth lines and buttressed ceilings, and the floor was amazingly intricate. The big surprise for her was what was hidden in the lower levels. The new cathedral had been built over an old one that was again built on the ruins of a Roman *domus*. Roman ruins lay beside frescoes that once decorated the ancient church. The old replacing the new, she mused. It's the natural order of life.

"What foresight they had to keep these ruins intact," Jayne said. "I never dreamed."

"There is one more surprise still," Mason said. "Wait until you see the Baptistery next door."

He seemed more animated today to Jayne. Maybe this place had a special impact on everyone. The people they passed by on the streets smiled and nodded. The Baptistery was just across the way from the cathedral and was made from the same layers of green and white marble, with the notable exception of the pink. It was octagonal, and people seemed to swirl around it continuously.

The group followed Mason to the east door of the Baptistery of San Giovanni.

"There are three doors to the Baptistery," he said, pointing to the other two doors. "This one is called the 'Gates of Paradise' and has ten panels that depict events from the Old Testament."

The gilded bronze glistened with evidence of frequent polishing and exquisite care. Jayne moved closer as Mason continued to talk about the doors. The texture of the illustrations seemed to be coming out of the door, creating a 3D effect. The Creation of Adam and Eve was opposite Cain killing his brother. The next panels showed the extremes of Noah's life, from his thankfulness for the reprieve from the flood to his drunkenness. Further panels brought the story of Jacob and Esau to life. Opposite this story was Joseph's, and below that, Moses received the Ten Commandments beside the Fall of Jericho. At the very bottom of the door, the two last panels illustrated the battle between David and Goliath next to Solomon receiving the Queen of Sheba.

The images cast moving shadows. The folds of the clothing, the fur on the dogs, and the hair on the heads of the characters were finely crafted in each panel. Movement and perspective made the figures life-like. The moral of each story was palpable, frozen in bronze for all time.

Jayne stared, succumbing to the masterpieces' spell.

"They are amazing, aren't they?" Mason said at her side after sharing some insights into the doors with the group. "Michelangelo called this 'Heaven's Door.'"

"I have never seen such artistic creativity on display in any one place in my life," said Jayne, reaching out to trace the contours of a child at the edge of one panel. "It is heavenly."

"The mosaics inside are phenomenal, too," Mason commented. "Let me show you."

"I think I'm on sensory overload," Jayne replied. "I don't know if I can take any more. This is almost as good as chocolate."

"It is beautiful," Lynn said as she moved from the outer edge of the group to Jayne's other side.

"Just think of all the great artists that were influenced by Florence," Jayne said. "Leonardo, Donatello, Giotto, the Lippis, Masaccio, Botticelli, Pontormo."

"Gucci and Ferragamo," Lynn added.

"The Tuscan area of Italy is filled with great sights," Mason said. "Maybe we can go on a side trip to Siena. I think you'd like it there."

Life here seemed stoked with energy. Everything smelled better. It looked better. It sounded better. She belonged here for some reason. She felt it from the inside out.

"I'm starving," Lynn said. "And I hope we find the Gucci shop. I see an amazing handbag in my near future."

"Come on, everyone," Mason announced to the group. "We're going to the best pizza place on earth." He then translated what he said and was welcomed with oohs and aahs. "The local Chianti goes great with it."

Not far away, in one of the many piazzas, they learned that a restaurant did indeed have the best pizza in the world. Jayne stood with Lynn at a tall table without chairs, holding a huge slice of pizza. The rest of the group sat scattered at outdoor tables, each with a jug of Chianti. Even Rosa seemed to be coming out of her funk. She laughed with Natalie as the cheese from her pizza strung out from her mouth.

"I'm too excited to sit down," Jayne said. She blew on her pizza.

"I've never seen you like this," Lynn replied as she tipped the jug of Chianti to fill their glasses.

"Can't you feel the energy here?" Jayne took a huge bite of her pizza. "God, this is really good."

Lynn took a bite of hers and nodded.

"You look great. Your hair is not as straight as it usually is." Lynn wiped her mouth with a napkin.

"It's something in the air here," Jayne said.

"It's just amazing," Lynn continued. "You don't look sick at all."

Jayne stopped eating, a piece of pizza lingering near her mouth.

"I'm sorry," Lynn said. "I'm sorry."

Jayne put her pizza down and took a healthy swig of Chianti. "I'm on vacation. The only real vacation of my life. A vacation from everything except my dreams. That's all I'm dealing with right now." Jayne took another large bite, chewing slowly to savor the different cheeses, tomatoes, oregano, and basil. Her tongue was alive with sensitivity. Sweet with sharp. Tangy combating the bland dough. She washed it down with another drink. Full-bodied sweet Chianti.

Pigeons fluttered about and cooed. She watched a couple arguing across the piazza. The woman yelled and flung her hands wildly. The man looked like he was begging for forgiveness, hands clasped.

The diversity of languages she could hear—Portuguese, Spanish, English, and Italian—sounded normal and melodic.

Maybe this is what heaven is like, she thought. She was suffused with a deep, deep serenity and joy, all of it touching her soul, the center of her being.

Jayne experienced the moment more intensely than any other in her life. *Why hadn't I lived like this more during the last thirty years?* Just looking at the different shades of blue in the sky was life-affirming. *How many days had slipped by, barely noticed?* She realized that she had only existed before. Existed within a confined notion of a life.

She continued to watch the shopkeepers come out to the piazza to entice passersby with full voices and gestures. They were animated in a way she had never witnessed. She could tell the tourists from the locals by their reactions. Equally animated responses indicated locals. Tourists seemed to be drawn in by emotion.

"Jayne, I said I was sorry," Lynn said as she finished her pizza. "Can you at least talk to me?"

"Oh, sweetie, I am fine. I don't think anything can bother me right now. I'm just taking it all in," Jayne replied. "It's fascinating to just watch the people here."

"Okay, as long as you're not mad at me," Lynn said, wadding up her napkin and clearing off the table. Jayne shook her head. Lynn smiled, the furrow between her brows relaxing, then walked over to the waste can and dropped it all in.

When everyone had finished their pizza, Mason led the group back to the hotel, where the bus stopped for them to unload. The rest of the afternoon was open for people to explore the city individually. Mason offered a couple of suggestions that included a visit to the Gucci store, a tour of the Uffizi Gallery, or the Boboli Gardens. The grandparents with their grandchildren chose the gardens. The Brazilian couples, along with Natalie, Rosa, and Lynn, wanted to delve into the Gucci adventure, while the newlyweds decided on the art gallery. Mason had made arrangements with local tour guides and showed everyone where to meet as he distributed room keys. Jayne and Lynn were the last in line.

"Which tour are you two ladies going to take?" Mason asked.

"Gucci, of course," Lynn offered. "But I know Jayne isn't interested, so she will be all alone."

"She has the other two options," Mason said.

"I'm not sure I'm up for either of them," Jayne replied. "What I would really like is to find the areas where Elizabeth and Robert Browning lived or found inspiration."

"I think I can arrange that," Mason said, smiling and tipping his hand in a mock salute. "I just happen to know where Elizabeth is buried. It's not far from here."

Lynn gave Jayne a self-satisfied smile. "I'm off to mine for Gucci treasures. Enjoy your afternoon."

"I'll meet you down here in ten minutes," Mason said. "We'll just walk, if that's all right with you."

"Perfect," Jayne replied as she followed Lynn to their room.

Lynn smiled but didn't say anything. Jayne changed into comfortable walking shoes. As she was leaving, Lynn called out to her.

"Enjoy yourself. Relax and don't fight it."

Jayne closed the door and went downstairs. Not seeing Mason right away, she turned to study the artwork on the lobby walls.

She heard a hiss and turned around to find herself face to face with Rosa.

"Eres una mujer casada que engaña, así que eres una puta."

Rosa spat the words out at Jayne, who reared back against the verbal assault.

"Eres egoísta y desconsiderado."

The last time Rosa had gone on a tirade against Jayne in her native language was at the group dinner. No one would tell Jayne what Rosa had said. This time was going to be different. Jayne stood up straight and leaned into Rosa. "If you are going to insult me," Jayne said and wagged her finger in front of Rosa's face. "Please have the decency to say it in a language I can understand."

Lynn popped up behind Rosa, but Jayne waved her off.

"Just say it," Jayne demanded.

Rosa crossed her arms and repeated, "You're a married woman cheating on your husband, so you are a whore."

Jayne's eyes bulged and her mouth dropped open.

"And you are selfish and inconsiderate."

Jayne spat back the words. "You're a jealous, sad woman, and I feel sorry for you."

Rosa stepped back, unfolded her arms, and glared at Jayne.

"I'm sorry that you are not happy," Jayne continued. "Some things can't be helped, but you probably would not understand that. I don't expect an apology, but I do expect you to stay out of my face for the rest of this trip."

Jayne heard some clapping behind her. Mason, Lynn, and Natalie were standing there. They continued their applause until Rosa ran back up to her room.

"Guess she won't be joining us for the Gucci excursion," Lynn said. "Natalie, will you join me?"

Natalie followed her out the door.

The confrontation over, Jayne shook. Her heart pounded so hard she heard it. Taking a few deep breaths, she started to follow Lynn and Natalie.

"That's the wrong way," Mason called out.

She turned and came back to his side.

"This way, *cara mia*," Mason said as he tucked her arm into the crook of his.

Her nerves calmed as she repeated her mantra. Rosa was not going to ruin another moment. She squelched her mother's voice welling up in her consciousness. *Not today*, she repeated to herself. *Not today.*

The sun glittered off the brickwork as they crossed the

piazza and entered another labyrinth of shadowy, narrow streets.

"How do you not get lost in these streets?" Jayne asked, her sense of direction totally obliterated.

"I guess I'm just used to them," Mason replied. "What triggered your interest in the Brownings? They're not exactly trendy reading."

She relaxed as the confrontation gave way to her excitement about the poets.

"I took a class that focused on Robert Browning, not Elizabeth, although she was much more popular during their careers." Jayne thought about the way the story of their relationship had crept into her soul. She had fallen in love vicariously with Robert Browning because he had seen much more than an invalid when he looked at Elizabeth. He had fallen in love with her intelligence. They were soulmates. It was possible. "They were gifted poets and my professor brought them to life for me. It was a class that affected me profoundly."

"She certainly wasn't drop-dead gorgeous," Mason said. "I have read her poetry, but I like Robert's work better."

"He was a very intelligent man. His poetry was on a higher level of thought, and he assumed that his readers were as well-read as he was. His father had a vast library and Robert read every book in it." Jayne looked at Mason as they turned down another street. "He saw beauty in her poetry first and fell in love with her through that. You do realize that she was an invalid when they met?"

"Yes, I did. Her father was a bit twisted, wasn't he?" Mason continued leading the way as they passed by the train station.

"He was very protective," Jayne said. "You can't blame a parent for being over-protective of a sickly child. She had some sort of lung ailment that was never fully diagnosed."

"I guess not," Mason said. "We're almost there. She is buried with a few other English expatriates in the Cimitero Accatolico.

I believe Anthony Trollope's mother is buried here, as well as Arthur Clough and a couple of Americans."

"I think it's very sad that she's buried here so far away from Robert," Jayne said. "It's not right."

"Here we are," Mason said as they navigated traffic and approached a wrought iron gate braced by two pillars. A bronze plaque on one pillar listed the names of famous people buried in the cemetery. Elizabeth's name was first. The graveyard seemed to reach out and obliterate Jayne's energy, her thoughts swirling with the macabre.

Did Robert pass through these gates with his grief on full display?

Her heart sank as they walked up the crumbling stairs and passed through the gates.

What was his final goodbye to his soulmate?

Her body tensed, then shook from her shoulders down through her legs.

How could he keep on going and just leave her here?

An archway led through a stucco building with red tiles stacked neatly on the roof. Jayne looked at the pathway that rose from the arch, abutted by green bushes leading to monuments. She concentrated on breathing in and breathing out.

Large stone crosses mingled with smaller gravestones. Age had worn names and dates, almost erasing some. Jayne held Mason's hand. She thought about all that was left of a person when they died. Just a name and a date. That was the equalizing factor in graveyards. Still, the size of the monument proclaimed social status.

"Here she is," Mason said as they neared a large monument unlike any others in the cemetery.

"This is incredible," Jayne said as she gazed at the tomb. A short, wrought iron fence surrounded it. There, on six Corinthian pillars, a marble coffin seemed to float into the air high above any other tomb. A profile was carved into all four sides of the coffin.

"They were married for fifteen years before she died," Jayne said quietly. "You know, they eloped to get away from her father."

"Yes, I do," Mason replied.

"They courted through letters for a long time before Robert visited her. She was bedridden. What kind of man falls in love with an invalid?" Jayne looked expectantly at Mason.

"One who looked from the inside out." Mason squeezed her hand.

"She wrote her *Sonnets from the Portuguese* for him." Jayne let go of Mason's hand and began to circle the grave. "How do I love thee. Let me count the ways."

"I love thee to the depth and breadth and height my soul can reach ..." Mason quoted.

Stunned by the knowledge that he knew the poem, she paused and then continued. "... when feeling out of sight for the ends of Being and ideal Grace. I love thee to the level of everyday's most quiet need, by sun and candlelight."

Mason closed his eyes and then continued, "I love thee freely, as men strive for right; I love thee purely, as they turn from Praise."

Jayne completed circling the tomb as she continued the recitation of the sonnet with Mason. "I love thee with the passion put to use in my old griefs, and with my childhood's faith."

Mason reached out and enveloped Jayne's hand in his. "I love thee with a love I seemed to lose with my lost saints."

Jayne finished the sonnet, looking straight into Mason's eyes. "I love thee with the breath, smiles, tears, of all my life! — and, if God choose, I shall but love thee better after death."

They stood face to face with the words of one of the greatest love poems still lingering in the air. Mason cradled Jayne's face in his hands. Their bodies fit snugly together, fused by a lingering kiss.

How odd to feel so alive and in love in the midst of a cemetery.

Her soul soared.

Time had no meaning, but when the kiss ended, Mason put his arm around her. They stared at the gravesite for one more moment together and then began a slow stroll away.

"He must have loved her beyond belief," Jayne said.

"I can understand that," Mason replied as he squeezed her shoulders.

"Have you ever taken care of an invalid?" Jayne inquired.

"No, not really." Mason removed his arm and held her hand. He looked at her as she continued to talk.

"It's a lot of responsibility to look after someone who's not well," Jayne said. "It's like taking care of an infant, but worse. You have to watch them decline without the hope that they will grow out of it."

"I guess you're right. I never really thought of it." Mason held the gate open for Jayne.

"When Robert made the decision to elope, he didn't know if she would get better or not," Jayne said. "He gambled on Italy's climate and love to heal Elizabeth."

"It worked for fifteen years," Mason said. "And she even gave him a son."

"You see," Jayne said with a smile. "Love can be strong enough to heal."

"I see." Mason stopped, pulled her into an embrace, and kissed her again.

The kiss ended abruptly when some Italian men passing by hooted encouragement.

"I don't even know who I am anymore," Jayne laughed nervously.

"I am beginning to." Mason tucked her shoulder under his arm again as they continued.

They remained silent for the rest of the walk back to the hotel. Jayne wondered whether Mason was anything like Robert

Browning. *Did he have the capacity to love no matter the cost or the length of time? Whether it was fifteen years or fifteen hours, was it worth it to love someone so deeply? Was the pleasure of love worth the pain of parting?*

She thought that it was indeed worth it for her, even if her soul went to hell. She wasn't equally sure that it was worth it for Mason. All she knew right now was that this didn't feel like an affair or a fling, to use Lynn's words.

But she was married to another man. Rosa had reminded her of that fact. Mason was so different from Tom in almost every way. Looks, temperament, intelligence. *No, that's not fair.* Tom was intelligent in his own way, with numbers, facts, and figures. He had never appreciated anything poetic, but she had accepted that limitation years ago. Now, she cavorted in public with another man. She really was going to go to hell. Maybe she was selling Tom short. Maybe …

As they entered the hotel, the desk clerk waved them over. He told them that someone was waiting for each of them in the bar. Mason led the way, and when they entered, Jayne saw Lynn. Mason looked around. Suddenly, a loud shout filled the room.

"Mason, Mason."

A beautiful Italian woman stood and moved toward Mason with arms outstretched. She kissed him and hugged him in a more than friendly manner. She wore high heels and a tight-fitting dress accented with gold jewelry. A mass of beautiful black hair was piled on her head and spilled over her shoulders. She looked like a Roman goddess. *Another Rosa?*

"Whoa," Lynn said as she pulled out a seat for Jayne. "That's some gorgeous woman."

Jayne didn't reply as she banished all thoughts of Tom and just watched. Mason looked happy to see this woman, but when he looked over at Jayne, he seemed nervous. Jayne turned her back and ordered a drink, prickling with questions. *Were his women stashed in every nook and cranny? I'm a fool. I deserved what Rosa said.*

"How was your trip?" Lynn asked, obviously trying to divert Jayne's attention.

"Fine." Jayne picked up her drink and took a large swallow. She watched Mason talking with the woman, both of them gesturing wildly with their hands and arms. The woman looked in Jayne's direction a couple of times.

"I wonder what that's all about," Lynn said. "Oh, no. They are coming this way, Jayne."

Jayne tensed and took another sip of her drink.

"Jayne and Lynn," Mason said, "I would like to introduce you to an old friend of mine, Sophia."

"Pleasure to meet you," Sophia said. "Welcome to my country. How do you like it?"

"It's beautiful," Jayne said. "You are lucky to live in such a wonderful place."

"Yes, it is home," Sophia said. "Mason, where are your manners? Order more drinks for us. It is rare that you get to entertain all these beautiful women, *no?*"

Sophia sat between Jayne and Lynn, leaving an empty seat beside Jayne. "Life is too short to waste time, *no?*" Sophia smiled.

Jayne relaxed. Up close, Sophia looked older than she had from a distance. Her mannerisms toward Mason were more maternal than sexual.

"So, Lynn," Sophia turned, "you want to meet some beautiful Italian men?"

Lynn's jaw dropped. Mason smiled as the bartender placed more drinks in front of them. Mason winked at Jayne.

"Of course. To finding beautiful Italian men," Lynn said as she raised her glass. Sophia joined the toast.

Jayne just sipped her drink and smiled, banishing all thoughts and tiny voices that fed doubts and guilt.

CHAPTER 17

Thursday, October 25, 2012

Arriving in the lobby the next morning, Jayne learned that Sophia was going to be the tour guide for the day. Sophia had planned a series of walks and trips to gardens and museums. Her buoyant personality soon enthralled everyone in the group. As she described the schedule, she accented each event like a circus ringmaster introducing another fantastic feat.

Lynn was still nowhere in sight as the group started out the door. Sophia lagged and turned to Jayne.

"Jayne," Sophia said, her smile deepening the laugh lines in her face. "Mason has arranged a special tour for you today."

"What about Lynn?" Jayne said. "I left her in the room."

"Miss Lynn has been taken care of, don't worry. She also has a special tour guide." Sophia turned and waved over her shoulder. "*Ciao.*"

"*Ciao,*" Jayne replied in her best Southern-tinged Italian accent. She took a seat in the lobby and waited, wondering what was in store. She crossed her legs, leaned back, then rocked forward, switching her legs to cross the opposite way. Her foot pumped out the seconds until Lynn came bounding down the stairs on the arm of a beautiful Italian man. Raven hair, olive skin, and Adonis body.

"Jayne," Lynn said as she stopped on her way out. "This is Antonio."

"He certainly is," Jayne replied. "Enjoy your day."

"Ditto," Lynn replied and then whispered, "Don't wait up for me."

Jayne laughed and shooed her away just as Mason strolled into the lobby.

"I see all is in perfect order," Mason said as he waved at Lynn and Antonio.

"Seems that way," Jayne said. "So, what's this special tour you have cooked up?"

"I paid Sophia to take over my tour duties today so we could visit Casa Guidi and then enjoy a private picnic in the countryside."

"Perfection." Jayne fought the urge to jump up and down like a youngster. Her palms grew sweaty and her heart raced. "I can't believe I'm going to see where they lived." She hoped the place pulsed with the energy from the love that this amazing couple shared.

They took a quick taxi ride and disembarked into a piazza, where a corner building angled out in a V-shape.

"The residence was built by the Ridolfi family, who wanted to be near the Pitti Palace across the street." Mason pointed as he continued, "That was in the fifteenth century. Count Guidi purchased it in 1618 and enlarged it by putting two buildings together." Mason stopped and cocked his head sideways. "I sound like a boring professor, don't I?" He smiled and looked sheepish. He shifted his stance and swiped his hand through his hair.

"Never." And she meant it. She loved that nervous habit and fought the urge to run her own fingers through his hair. "I love it. Please don't stop." She squeezed his arm.

He resumed his lecture. "By the time the Brownings took residence, it had been purchased again and divided back into two apartments. They rented seven rooms that had been ornately decorated by a Russian prince when they leased them."

"How do you know all of this?" Jayne said as she eyed the outer walls. It had a few windows on the ground floor and a series of arched windows on the second floor. Balconies lined one side of the building.

"I knew a little, but I looked up the rest last night." Mason looked proud of himself as his chest puffed out and he motioned toward the entrance. "Let's go in."

This is the end of a pilgrimage, she thought. One that had started years ago and been fueled through her extensive reading. Words were going to be translated into reality.

I'm here. Really here. She had not felt this excited since she had attended her first birthday party as a child.

She had imagined the place as light and airy, but as they entered, the shadows descended into a very dark and gloomy hallway. *Am I ready for the reality?* A bronze bust of Robert Browning haunted the hallway.

Her mind reeled until lines from Robert Browning's *The Ring and the Book* peppered her thoughts: "Under the doorway where the black begins / With the first stone-slab of the staircase cold."

Okay, that makes sense now.

Jayne followed Mason up the stairs to the first door on the left. She entered the Brownings' domain reverently and walked quietly into the drawing room. It was painted a light green like the leaves of a water lily. Heavy wood furniture with red upholstery filled the room, and pictures covered the walls. A weathered, gold-leafed framed mirror hung over the fireplace.

"My God," Jayne said as she moved closer to the mirror. "It was real."

"What?" Mason asked.

"The mirror in one of his poems, *The Ring and the Book*." Jayne began to recite:

> *"The book was shut and done with and laid by*
> *On the cream-coloured massive agate, broad*
> *'Neath the twin cherubs in the tarnished frame*
> *O' the mirror, tall thence to the ceiling top."*

"See," she pointed, "there are the cherubs." Jayne saw her reflection in the mirror, with Mason just behind her. She wondered how many times Robert and Elizabeth had looked into this same mirror. *What did they see? Did it reflect their love? Was it still there to reflect on others?* She watched Mason come closer and put his arms around her waist.

"You are really enjoying this place, aren't you?" Mason whispered in her ear.

"It's the best tour by far, and I've only seen one room." Jayne relaxed into his embrace. "Just think of the parties in this room. The conversations. I wonder if they wrote in this room."

The docent answered her musings as he entered the room. "Yes, this was the heart of their home. Everything was celebrated in this room." The docent was an elderly man with amazingly alert blue eyes. His English flowed with an Italian lilt. Syllables accented with vowel sounds, more British than American. "The other side of this room is the dining room. The Brownings had a cook who used the small kitchen to prepare meals. You can go out on the terrace from either room." He pointed to the doors.

The terrace hung over the streets below and provided a perfect vantage point to watch passersby without intrusion. It was filled with potted plants and plenty of seating.

"This must have been wonderful in the evenings after dinner and a busy day of writing," Jayne reflected.

"Look at this," Mason pointed to something written under

the glass on a table. "It's more from *The Ring and the Book*. I'll read it to you:

'And from the reading, and that slab I leant
    My elbow on, the while I read and read,
    I turned to free myself and find the world,
    And stepped out on the narrow terrace, built
    Over the street and opposite the church,
    And paced its lozenge-brickwork sprinkled cool;
    Because Felice-church-side stretched, a-glow
    Through each square window fringed for festival,
    Whence came the clear voice of the cloistered ones
    Chanting a chant made for midsummer nights ...'"

Jayne scanned the view from the terrace, channeling Robert. "I can just see him out here, listening to the music that came from the choirs in the church."

They went back inside to a room where tapestries hung on the walls. There was pattern and muted color everywhere. Jayne knew some tapestries had inspired Robert's poetry, but she couldn't remember which ones.

They followed the docent to the bedroom. "We rent this out for people to stay."

That seems sacrilegious. The thought hit hard as her hand moved toward the neckline of her blouse. She tugged at it as if it were too tight. Elizabeth had died here. In this room. Now, people paid to sleep in that sacred space. The muscles in her face tightened.

A large four-poster bed with thick curtains dominated the bedroom. It didn't seem as authentic as the rest of the house. Still, she couldn't help feeling gloom push down on her. No matter the furnishings, this is where Elizabeth died in her husband's arms.

She didn't need a vivid imagination to understand the

feeling of not being able to breathe. *Did the comfort of dying in someone's arms, whom you know without a doubt loves you beyond life, make it any easier? No. It had to have made it even harder to say goodbye.*

Jayne had never been good at saying goodbye. She had wept on family vacations after spending a month with her parents. She had cried when the kids started school, even though she knew they'd be home within a few hours. She had fought back tears when she moved from one state to another as she recalled friends left behind and places that would probably never be seen again. *Would Tom be there when I die?* The thought offered no solace.

A shiver rippled through her.

Sniffing and swiping at her eyes, she let gloom consume her. She wished Elizabeth could tell her how she did it. How she let go. If there was a good way to die. She fumbled in her purse for a wadded-up tissue. *It's leaving everyone behind that makes it difficult.*

"Let's get out of here," Jayne said suddenly. Her lungs seemed to be constricting. *Is the room spinning?* She squeezed the tissue in her hand, mashing it into pulp.

"What?" The lines in Mason's forehead deepened. "But I thought you wanted to see this place."

"I just don't feel comfortable in this room," Jayne said and walked out the door.

She turned and felt Mason close behind.

"I'm sorry," he whispered. "But I thought…"

"It's not you," she replied as she re-entered the main living area. "It's me."

She ran her fingers across the desk, nestled in the corner. "I wonder if this was her desk." Jayne anchored her thoughts to this space instead of the bedroom.

The docent stood in the doorway. "No, unfortunately. Most of the original furniture was sold. The Trust has purchased pieces similar to the originals, with a few exceptions such as the personal items you see in this room."

Jayne looked at the delicate black lace gloves perched on the end of the desk. They were very petite and she doubted that her fingers would come close to fitting into them. On the wall hung a black fan, spread out and mounted under glass. Jayne could imagine Elizabeth and Robert on the terrace. Elizabeth would be gently swaying the fan, perhaps flirting a bit during their conversation.

She could not imagine a similar vignette with Tom. With Mason, she was living it.

"Look at this, Jayne." Mason motioned to her to join him in front of a display case. It held a beautiful piece of amber jewelry that had been a gift from Robert.

"You know, she was quite a few years older than Robert," Jayne said as she looked at the amber glowing underneath the glass. *Had it captured some of the love that had fueled this couple's life together?* "She wasn't impressed with his first love letters."

"Really?" Mason replied. He stood very close to Jayne, looking over her shoulder at the necklace. "Or was she just playing coy?"

Jayne smiled. "This has been wonderful, but I think I'm ready to go now."

They left Casa Guidi and slowly walked down the street. She stopped once and turned to get a final look at the corner residence that had contained so much happiness and eventual sadness. It held the essence of the lives that left something behind to help humanity see the beauty in life. Satisfaction melted deeper into her. *So, this is how it feels to realize a dream ... to make it real ... to replace it with a tangible memory.*

"It's a beautiful day," Mason said. "Let's go to the Boboli Gardens before we go out for our picnic."

"Lead the way," Jayne said, thinking that this was probably the most beautiful day of her life. She looked at Mason and saw not only a handsome, slightly younger man, but a man full of caring and sensitivity. When she first met him, a tough coat of armor shielded the man she now watched smiling and holding her hand. His touch was light but firm. Something fluttered deep within her when she was with him. Something that had been dormant until a few days ago. Instead of bemoaning the fact that it had been asleep for her life until now, she decided to thank God that it had awakened at all.

They walked by the Pitti Palace and into the immense Boboli Gardens. The cultivated landscape stretched as far as Jayne could see. They continued walking as the sidewalk began to incline.

"This is the way to the amphitheater where one of the first operas was performed," Mason said as his tour guide mantra kicked in. "They made it from the quarry where they took the stones that built the palace."

With each step up, Jayne labored to keep her breath steady. Halfway up the path, she had to stop. Despite her efforts, she began to wheeze. She stopped walking and bent over.

Mason put his hand on her back. "Are you all right?"

"Just winded a bit," Jayne lied. "Give me a minute and we'll make it to the top."

She looked at Mason and hated the fact that she had caused him pain. He was obviously worried, but she knew this wasn't the right time to tell him. She couldn't take the risk. Not now.

He looked at her with such concern, his hands cradling her back and arm. She fell completely in love with him at this moment. She couldn't fight it. It just was.

After a few minutes, she started slowly to resume her climb. This time, Mason walked much more slowly and made her take breaks every few steps. He seemed to want an explanation, but she wasn't ready yet.

When they got to the top of the hill, a maze of green met them. The view of the surrounding area was magnificent. The

Tuscan hills, scattered with homes and vineyards, reached toward the sun. A living picture postcard, undulating with nature. Vibrant with life.

"This is gorgeous," Jayne said as she leaned on Mason. "I can't believe this is real."

"It's real," Mason said as he turned her in his arms and held her. As she kissed him, her mind soared. She lived and loved under the Tuscan sun. It was leading to a pivotal moment in her life. She knew that.

"You realize that I'm falling for you," Mason said as he looked into her eyes.

"Let's go on our picnic," she said, not ready to share everything just yet. "Where are we going, anyway?"

The corners of Mason's mouth turned down, but he took her hand as they walked back across the garden. "Sophia has arranged everything."

"Sophia?"

"Yes, we've been friends for a very long time," Mason said. "She has a villa on the edge of her parents' vineyard. She keeps it for guests and insisted that we go there."

"It sounds wonderful," Jayne said as she leaned her head on Mason's shoulder. As they continued walking in silence, taking in the beauty that surrounded them, she couldn't shake a slowly growing feeling of guilt. She didn't know what Mason expected from the relationship. Maybe she was worrying about nothing. Maybe it was just another tourist fling for him. Just because it meant so much to her didn't mean it was the same for him. Or maybe Lynn was right. Jayne let her thoughts settle temporarily as she just enjoyed feeling her senses come alive. Every fiber of her being tingled with potential.

A car with a driver waited for them at the hotel.

"Is Sophia wealthy?" Jayne asked as she slipped into the back seat of the car.

"Her family owns one of the largest vineyards in Tuscany," Mason replied.

"She doesn't seem wealthy," Jayne replied.

"You mean she's not a snob," Mason laughed.

"Yes, that's exactly what I mean," Jayne said.

"She's just a wonderfully spirited and giving Italian woman," Mason said as he pulled Jayne closer to him. Jayne snuggled in and enjoyed the view of the countryside on the way to the vineyard. The streets curved through the landscape without a logical reason for the sharp turns that almost doubled back on themselves. Perhaps the road builders wanted travelers to experience everything more than once during their journeys.

"What are those beautiful tall trees that I see everywhere around here?" Jayne asked.

"Those are the famous cypresses of Tuscany," Mason said. "Actually, there is an interesting history about them. They're not indigenous to this area but were brought here by the Etruscans, who thought the trees had mystical powers. Each tree lives for about 2,000 years and never loses its leaves. The ancient tribes thought that made the trees supernatural."

"Amazing," Jayne said.

"The Etruscans even planted the cypress trees in their necropolis to keep demons away and help the spirits make it safely to the afterlife. The trees produce oils that are very fragrant and protect the wood. They even made coffins from them because the wood didn't decompose quickly." Mason shifted in his seat and pointed to a church in the distance. "Churches plant the cypress trees in front of their entrances to welcome people and ward off evil. Homeowners also plant cypress trees near the entrance to welcome visitors."

Jayne trembled and snuggled closer to Mason, while the duality of the cypress trees was not lost on her imagination. A welcoming abode, and a transit of souls to the other side. Maybe not such a duality after all, she thought.

They passed wave upon wave of grape vines, twisted carefully around wire trellises like nouveau art sculptures. The car turned slowly into a narrow gravel driveway that led to a stucco villa. It oozed charm amid slow decay. Some of the stucco had crumbled away, but what was left was a peach color. The now familiar red tiles covered the roof, with a few out of place that just added character. Cypresses towered on either side of the front entrance. Shutters with flaking green paint braced the sides of each window. One hung askew.

The driver opened Jayne's door and smiled. Mason rounded the car and took her arm as they walked up to the entrance. A full-figured older woman opened the door just as they reached it and held up her arms, shaking her head and talking rapidly.

"This is Gina. She has been the housekeeper here for as long as I have known the family." Mason hugged the old woman and introduced her to Jayne. She hugged Jayne and kissed her on both cheeks. The intensity of the woman filled the foyer.

"She has our picnic set up on the back terrace," Mason said as he led Jayne through the villa. Its décor was typical of Tuscany, a mixture of old and new. When they walked through glass-paned doors to the terrace, Jayne thought she had walked into a painting. The landscape spread out in undulant hills carpeted with trees and vineyards. Red wild flowers covered the area near the villa. Bushes and flowers accentuated the stone section just below them.

Her overwhelmed senses clouded her ability to say a word. Her eyes scanned and darted everywhere.

A wrought iron table and two matching chairs stood to the left of the doors. The table was set with an open bottle of white wine, bruschetta on a wooden board, a colorful salad piled high in a ceramic bowl, and a plate of assorted cheeses in various shapes and hues. Mason pulled out her chair and she sat down, her mind reeling as a fantasy came to life.

Mason poured their wine and Jayne served the salad.

"To us," Mason said as he raised his glass.

"To us," she replied, wondering how or if "us" was going to begin. Doubts tugged at her conscience. She pushed them back, determined to move forward.

The salad was fresh beyond belief. The tomatoes were tangy and the cheese just a little sharp. It was the perfect combination. She tasted the crisp bruschetta, and the olive oil was luscious. She chewed and swallowed slowly, savoring the flavors.

"Is it my imagination or is every aspect of life more intense here?" Jayne couldn't help saying aloud.

"What do you mean?" Mason asked as he sipped his wine.

"This is the best food I've ever had, and it's just salad. But it tastes fresher, fuller, more intense than any other salad." Jayne paused and sipped her wine. "The light even seems different here."

"Tuscany is one of my favorite areas in Italy," Mason replied. "The Italians do live differently than the rest of us. Maybe it's because the place has influenced the people instead of the other way around."

"I always thought I had a vivid imagination, but it never came close to this," Jayne said as she continued to enjoy her meal. "This was a wonderful idea. I know what Robert and Elizabeth must have felt like, sharing their lives in this wonderful place."

They finished the meal in silence, punctuated with the songs of birds and the wind through the trees. The air felt cool, but the wine warmed Jayne. The soft breeze caressed her face. She watched Mason eat his salad the European way, with his fork upside down and prodding with his knife. It seemed so much more natural than the way she was used to eating. She tried it. It was awkward with the first bite, but soon she was plunging her fork upside down into the salad and piling tomatoes on the underside of her fork easily. Finally, after all these years, she knew what it felt like to be completely happy. With a shallow sigh, contentment infused her body, right down to her bones.

After they finished, Gina quickly removed the plates and placed another bottle of wine on the table with the cheese.

"This has been a perfect day," Jayne said. "Thank you." She stood at the edge of the terrace with Mason closely behind, his arms wrapped around her.

He turned her slowly around and kissed her deeply. She released any apprehension and met his kiss with equal fervor. Her rapid heartbeat drowned out the sounds of nature. She felt the muscles in his shoulders tense as he pulled her closer. She lost herself and she didn't care.

They held each other in a trembling embrace and time ebbed away.

"You know we can stay here the night if you want," Mason said breathlessly. "Sophia will take care of everyone else."

Jayne thought about spending the night in his arms. She knew she loved him. And because she loved him, she knew what she had to do next.

"Mason, I have to tell you something," Jayne said as she put herself an arm's length away from him. Her breathing quickened and she fought the sinking feeling in the pit of her stomach. It had been such a perfect day.

"I already know that you are married," Mason said as he tried to pull her back into his arms. "And I know that it's not a happy marriage."

Jayne broke away, went back to the table, and sat down. She poured another glass of wine for each of them. The bottle clinked on the edge of the glasses as her hand shook. Mason took a seat across from her. His brow furrowed as he leaned forward.

"That's not the whole story," Jayne continued. She handed him his glass and took a deep swallow of her wine. Her hand still shook as she sat her glass down.

"What is it?" He tried to reach for her hand.

"Lynn said that I shouldn't tell you," Jayne confessed. "But I'm not like Lynn."

"You are scaring me, Jayne."

"First of all, despite not wanting to, I have fallen in love with you," Jayne said.

Mason smiled broadly. "I love you, too."

"I shouldn't have, but I did and it's not fair," Jayne said. Mason started to talk, but she put up her hand. "Please let me finish while I have the nerve." She gulped the rest of her wine, the glass clinking against her teeth. "I'm not well, Mason."

"What do you mean?" Mason said. "I don't care. We'll take you to a doctor."

"I've already been to doctors and they can't help," Jayne said as her stomach rolled and twisted into a knot. *God, this is hard. Impossible.*

Mason was silent as all color drained from his face.

Guilt stabbed at her. *I'm hurting him. I can't stand it.*

"But there has to be something." He leaned forward and swiped his hair back with both hands. "Modern medicine has come a long way."

She shook her head, her nerves pinging like an arcade game.

"But you look fine," he said, shaking his head. "You don't look sick at all."

He stood and paced back and forth, pivoting on his toes. With each pace, her heart seemed to skip a beat. Her breath became shallow as she watched his face harden into deep furrows. Time ceased in a nightmarish eternity. *Oh God ... oh God.*

"How can you look so healthy?" He pivoted, swiping his hair. "What is it? What's wrong?"

"Lung cancer," she puffed out the words as she watched him stop mid-pace.

His features softened slightly as understanding dawned, but

the furrows remained. "The shortness of breath. The altitude sickness."

"I have less than a year left." Jayne looked at Mason and waited, not knowing what kind of response was coming. Her world shrank into the silence as she chewed on the inside of her cheek. The pinching pain would keep her from fainting. She tasted iron.

He looked right at her but didn't seem to see her. His mouth opened, but nothing came out. The warring emotions flitted across his face, concluding with a momentary cease fire.

"Mason?" She felt hollow, like her insides had evaporated. Maybe she was disappearing.

Mason turned away from her without a word and walked into the villa.

She watched his wide shoulders slouch and his head bow as the doorway swallowed him. The moon seemed to disappear and the night sounds deafened. Time lingered excruciatingly from second to second. Her heartbeat mocked each second. She just sat at the table, not sure whether she had the strength to stand.

She held her breath when she finally saw movement at the door. But instead of Mason, it was Gina who emerged and said, "The car is waiting for you to take you back to your hotel."

Jayne exhaled slowly.

CHAPTER 18

ate Thursday night, October 25, 2012

On the third shaky attempt, Jayne succeeded in slipping her key into the door. The room was pitch black. No Lynn in sight. It was just as well. For the first time since her diagnosis, Jayne didn't mind being alone. Anything had to be better than what she had experienced in the last few hours. There were no more tears. She had cried them all out during the tedious drive back to the hotel. *Have I sabotaged myself again?* A perfect day turned into a perfect nightmare. *What did I expect?* Fantasy was not reality. She should know that by now. Stupid dreams. Fiction. *Where has it gotten me?*

She didn't bother washing her face or even changing into pajamas. She propped her pillows up and lay on top of the covers. In the distance, she heard bells chiming. She thought of the cathedrals and chastised herself. Perhaps her soul was safe from damnation now. But her heart felt shattered into splinters. Splinters like those her mother gouged at with tweezers when she was a child. Her mother's voice chanted admonishments. *How could you be so stupid? What have you done now?*

Jayne shifted in her bed, tossing thoughts about her mother away.

Where was the benevolent God in her life? She had not done anything to deserve this. Anger spewed through her, aimed at scattered targets. Tom. Lynn. Mason. God. It reared and attacked like a tiger, shredding each victim unfairly, gnawing voraciously. She pitched back and forth, throwing one of the pillows across the room.

Her head popped up at the sound of a light knock at the door. She tried to ignore it by shoving her head under her remaining pillow, but the knock became more insistent. She got up and thought her knees would buckle. Her hand quivered as she opened the door.

"*Il mia povera piccolo*," Sophia said as she reached out and hugged Jayne. "*Uomini stupidi.*"

Jayne didn't understand a word but soaked in the warmth of the arms surrounding her. Sophia's perfume filled the air with a flowery scent.

"Come on, my poor little one," Sophia said as she guided Jayne back into the room. "Men can be so stupid, *no?*"

Jayne hiccupped as she nodded. "What time is it?"

"Past midnight," Sophia answered as she glanced at her watch. "But I could not wait until morning. I had to see you."

"Come in and sit down." Jayne pulled a chair out for Sophia, then perched on the edge of the bed.

"I left Mason with his third bottle of wine." Sophia shook her head. "But I told him what I thought. Gina told me everything."

"It's all my fault," Jayne said. "I shouldn't have led him on."

"Nonsense," Sophia said. "Love is not wrong. It may surprise you, but it is never wrong."

Sophia reached out and held Jayne's hands in hers. "We all live and we all die, *il mia amica*. Why not live and love while we can?"

Jayne shook her head and fought another onslaught of tears.

"Let me tell you a story," Sophia continued. "A young man once thought he was in love. He was handsome and a talented musician. His woman was his muse. She stoked his career into one of moderate fame and fortune. He gave her everything, and she left him with nothing. One day, after the music career had faded, the money and spotlight were gone. She left without a word and wounded his soul." Sophia shrugged. "After all these years, I finally saw his soul again."

"Mason?" Jayne asked.

Sophia nodded.

Jayne slumped against the weight of her guilt. "I'm so sorry,"

"He is afraid," Sophia said. "Stupid men. They can be cowards in love."

Sophia stood and put her hand on Jayne's shoulder. "Is there anything I can do for you?"

Jayne just shook her head and wiped her nose with her fingers.

"I gave him my advice before I left," Sophia said. "I don't know if he heard it, but Italians live and love … even if it's just for a day. Remember that, *il mia amica*." She hugged Jayne again. "*Buonanotte.*"

As the door shut softly, Jayne got up and went to the bathroom. She looked in the mirror. Puffy eyes receded desperately into their sockets. Dark circles ringed below her eyes. Her nose was red, chapped slightly from too many swipes of her fingers and rough bathroom tissue.

She couldn't look any longer at the stupid woman in the mirror. She turned on the cold water and splashed it on her face. It didn't help. When she looked in the mirror again, a dying woman looked back. "What did you expect?" she said to her reflection. "Robert Browning?" She splashed her face again. "You selfish fool. You deserve to feel exactly like you are feeling. You should have done the right thing sooner. You idiot."

Jayne heard the door to the room open slowly.

"Are you alone?" Lynn asked.

"Very much so," Jayne replied as she turned the water tap off. "Where were you?"

"Antonio." She said his name with ultimate satisfaction. Jayne heard her pull out the desk chair. "What about you?"

"Don't ask," Jayne put her hands on the sink and slumped down. If she could have gone down the drain, she would have.

"What did you do, Jayne?" Lynn asked.

Jayne slouched into the room.

"You look awful."

Even though her cousin had obviously spent most of the night making love, she looked refreshed. Her cheeks were rosy and her eyes bright.

"I told him," Jayne said as she turned to face Lynn.

Lynn's mouth dropped open. "For God's sake, why?"

"I had no choice." Jayne walked to the edge of the bed and sat down across from Lynn.

"There is always a choice," Lynn argued.

"No, there isn't," Jayne said. "I know that better than anyone."

Lynn was quiet for a change.

"I told him because I love him," Jayne said. It felt good to say it. "I couldn't be with him and not tell him."

"What did he say?" Lynn asked.

"Nothing really," Jayne choked out. "He just got up and walked away."

"He was in shock," Lynn defended.

"He hates me." Jayne rubbed her head. "Do you have any Tylenol? My head is splitting."

Lynn dug into her purse. "He doesn't hate you." She pulled out a bottle, opened it, and dumped four Tylenol into the palm of her hand.

"How do you know?" Jayne said as she reached for two of the Tylenol.

"You don't just stop loving someone," Lynn said as she

popped the other two Tylenol in her mouth and opened a bottle of water, washing them down. She passed the bottle to Jayne.

"I'm going to go home," Jayne said as she took another sip of water. "I can't face him on the rest of this tour. I'm just not strong enough." She knew this was what dying felt like. All the life she had experienced during the past several days drained into a black pit. Dwindling memories tinged with guilt. Oddly, she didn't feel guilty about Tom. Only Mason. "I am being punished," she said. "I'm married."

"That's ridiculous, Jayne," Lynn said.

"Oh, so 'God's in his heaven—All's right with the world?'" Jayne quoted Robert Browning.

"I don't know what that means," Lynn responded, "but I know that you are far from the horrid person you think you are. The world is full of real evil, and you just don't even come close."

Lynn got up and sat next to Jayne on the bed. "You've been a great mother. You sacrificed your life for your family. It was about time that you grabbed something for yourself. You did what your conscience told you to do. Just because Mason wasn't the man you thought he was, you don't need to punish yourself."

"You don't have to come home with me," Jayne said. "Stay and finish the trip. Maybe Antonio can take my place on the tour and go to Rome with you."

"Don't be stupid," Lynn said. "Now, let's try to get some sleep and talk more about this in the morning."

Lynn fell asleep while sleep evaded Jayne. She tossed and turned until a sliver of light pierced through the crack in the curtains. Friday morning dawned. She got up, went to her suitcase, and picked out an outfit. She took it to the bathroom and hung it on the back of the door. She turned on the water and tested it with her hand. Steam began to fill the room. She stripped off her clothes and stepped into the shower. She adjusted the temperature because she was having trouble breathing. She forced each heavy breath as the pellets of water hit her body.

Everything felt heavy. Gravity pressed down like a trash compacter, pushing until there was nothing but a lump of debris. In physics, there is always an equal and opposite reaction to something. Love was like that, too. The high of falling in love. The lows of love lost. *What is my lesson? What does God want me to learn from all this?* Now that she knew what it really felt like to love someone, she knew she had never really loved Tom. *What kind of lesson is that? Learning that I have lived a lie my whole life.*

She scrubbed her body vigorously. Her skin turned pink with the rubbing and hot water. She turned her attention to her hair, soaping it to a full lather. Her fingertips dug into her scalp. She scrubbed harder and rinsed out the suds. She stood under the water, holding her breath. *I should just die now if that's the lesson.* When her lungs burned like they were going to burst, she gulped in air and a bit of water. She coughed as she turned the water off. After drying herself, she wrapped the towel around her head and dressed.

"Your turn," she said as she left the bathroom.

Lynn picked up her stuff and went into the bathroom. "Did you leave enough hot water?"

"Believe me, there is hot water to spare," Jayne replied. She took the towel off her head and grabbed her flat iron. She held it in her hand and looked at her reflection in the mirror over the desk. Her hair was in soft ringlets. She put her flat iron down and picked up the dryer. She put it on the lowest setting and began to scrunch her hair, teasing the ringlets into life. They framed her face and gave some depth to her features. She took some extra time and even dipped into some of Lynn's makeup. At least the world didn't have to know how she felt. Her mask would be in perfect place. She found some bright coral lipstick to finish her new look.

"Wow," Lynn said as she emerged from the shower. "What happened?"

She stepped closer and looked Jayne over. "Your hair looks great. You look great. You are a regular quick-change artist.

"I borrowed some of your lipstick," Jayne confessed.

"Keep it," Lynn said as she began to put her own makeup on. "It never looked that good on me."

Lynn finished getting ready quickly. "Antonio is meeting us for breakfast downstairs. I will tell him to go. We still need to talk."

"I'm not really hungry," Jayne said. "You go ahead. I'm all talked out."

"No way," Lynn said as she grabbed Jayne's arm. "If you don't want to talk, you still need to eat, right? Let's go."

Jayne smiled and followed Lynn. They both jumped as Lynn reached for the door handle at the same moment that someone knocked.

"That must be Antonio," Lynn said. "He's probably anxious." She smiled at Jayne and lifted her eyebrows. Lynn yanked the door open.

"Mason," Lynn said as she inhaled.

"I need to talk with Jayne." Mason looked like hell. His face was tinged green. He hadn't shaved and his hair was disheveled. His jeans were ragged, and his sweater was pulled tight because of the guitar strapped over his shoulder.

"I'll be down having breakfast with Antonio," Lynn said as she strode by Mason, giving him a stark stare.

Mason stood in the doorway with one hand still holding the door open.

Jayne moved to the furthest corner of the room and sat in a chair.

"May I come in?" Mason finally asked.

Jayne didn't say anything as Mason hesitated and then stepped in and closed the door. He pulled his guitar off his shoulder and placed it on the bed. "I know I'm a shit." He grabbed the desk chair and yanked it out, twisted it backwards, and straddled it. "If it's any help, I feel like shit, too."

"You look like shit, too." Jayne couldn't help herself.

"You look beautiful," he replied. "You should fix your hair like that all the time. It's you."

Jayne's reserve began to melt, but she struggled against it like she used to when one of her kids did something wrong. "What do you want, Mason?"

"I'm sorry I'm not your perfect poet," he said. "I was in shock. It's not an excuse. I was selfish and thinking only of me, not you. I don't care how long we have. I love you."

Jayne didn't move. She didn't know what to say. She heard her heartbeat echo in her ears. Her dejection of the restless night dispersed, and in its place, a light began to slowly come back to life.

Mason picked up his guitar and sat on the edge of the bed. "This is for you."

He began to play, softly strumming the strings. The haunting melody filled the room. It floated like fairy dust, a mixture of notes lingering in the air. It was the personification of her soul. He reflected her perfectly in his song. Her song. No words. Just music. The notes wrapped around her heart and captured it, lifting her beyond the moment.

His eyes were closed and his head bent slightly. She watched his fingers strum, pick, and stroke the strings. He was making love to her through the music. The notes caressed and teased. The melody undulated. The phrasing built to a peak, then lulled. Wave after wave of music enveloped her in an intimate embrace.

When he finished, he opened his eyes and looked at her. It seemed like an eternity that he just gazed into her eyes. He had opened his soul to her through the music.

"That was the most beautiful apology on the face of this earth," Jayne said.

Mason leaned his guitar against the wall and came over to Jayne. She stood, wrapped her arms around him, and kissed him passionately.

He ran his fingers through her hair and cradled her head. "I want to love every inch of you." His touch was light, as if he feared he would break her.

How could this beautiful man love me?

His gaze gave her confidence. Those slate-colored eyes that had enchanted her from the very beginning. Eyes only for her.

She melted into his embrace. She paused for a moment to run both of her hands through his hair. Silk chestnut strands flecked with gray slipped through her fingers, exciting them. Caressing them.

They fell onto the bed. He consumed her slowly, delicately. She was being loved completely … finally.

She was alive. Never again would she see herself as a plain Jayne.

She basked in the afterglow and stroked the stubble on his face.

"I'm sorry," he said.

"What?" she looked up at him and stiffened.

"About not shaving," he said.

Jayne relaxed her shoulders and continued to bask.

"Did I hurt you?" Mason said as he rose on his elbow.

"I'm not a porcelain doll," she replied.

"I know, but …"

"Don't."

"I love you," he said as he traced her jawline and throat.

"I love you, too." As she said it, she knew that she had learned the lesson that God had wanted her to, however unconventionally.

"I want every inch of you to be familiar." He smiled as he added, "I want a better look at that tattoo."

She blushed and looked at the clock. "Don't you have to work?"

He grinned. "Sophia is taking over once again. I'll start back tomorrow when we head to Rome. But today, we are going to Siena."

"What?"

"Siena." He slipped out from the covers and went to the bathroom, picking up his clothes on the way.

Jayne got up and began to get dressed once again. Thoughts began taunting her. *How will I let him go? Time is running out. The trip will be over soon.* Her mind began to swirl so rapidly, she almost lost her balance. To squelch her thoughts, she repeated her mantra. *Live each day to the fullest, with no regrets.*

She made her way to a mirror hanging over the desk in her room. Her lipstick was gone and her mascara was smeared, but the woman in the mirror simply glowed. She was tousled and sexy. She ran her fingers through her hair and freshened up her makeup. She was glad Lynn had given her the lipstick. For the first time in her life, she felt beautiful.

"Are you ready?" Mason asked as he emerged from the bathroom.

"Let me get my coat," Jayne said as she went to the armoire. "Where's your coat?"

"We'll get it when I drop off my guitar in my room," Mason said as he put his guitar over his shoulder and held the door open for her.

After they stopped at Mason's room, Jayne's stomach growled.

"Do we have time to stop for some breakfast?"

"Of course," Mason led the way to the dining room after they got off the elevator.

Jayne's eyes widened when she saw Lynn and Antonio sitting at a table.

"Jayne," Lynn said, "join us."

"Why are you still here?" Jayne said as she nodded to Antonio. Mason pulled up a chair close to Jayne.

"I wanted to make sure you were all right," Lynn said as she sipped the remnants of her cappuccino. "But by the looks of you two, I could have been on my way a long time ago."

"I'm sorry, Lynn," Jayne said.

"For what?" Lynn stood with Antonio. "*Ciao*, lovers." She winked and tucked herself under Antonio's arm.

Jayne looked shocked. "How did she know?"

"How could she not?" Mason smiled and ordered their breakfast.

CHAPTER 19

Friday, October 26, 2012

It was like walking back in time to the Middle Ages as they entered Siena's Piazza del Campo. The medieval cathedral bells chimed the hour.

The drive had been leisurely with Italian music blaring from the radio in Sophia's car, which she had lent to Mason. It was compact, but not as small as some of the boxes on wheels they had passed. Nothing like the cars at home.

Mason parked in a very odd garage that looked like an ancient shed tucked away in the maze of streets outside Siena's walls. Jayne doubted that they would ever find it again.

The sun filled a blue sky. The sloping piazza's paving stones made it look like seven large slices of pizza, with the cathedral on one side and lines of restaurants on the other. People crowded together, some eating gelato.

Jayne and Mason walked slowly, arm in arm. She rubbed his back, enjoying the feel of warm muscle under his jacket. He squeezed her in response. She edged closer to him. A girl could get used to this, she thought. Solace surrounded her when she was with Mason.

How am I going to give this up? As soon as the thought crossed her mind, she pushed it away and repeated her mantra.

"You should see this place during the Palio horse race," Mason said, stretching one hand out to span the area. "People pack in here to watch each district race against each other."

"I've read about it," Jayne replied, rediscovering the moment through Mason's enthusiasm.

"You'll get to see some of the pageantry, anyway," Mason continued, his face becoming more animated. "Every day, the men parade through the streets with huge flags and drums to show off the different crests and colors of the original districts. They still make pottery based on the original colors."

Jayne loved the way he talked about places. He had a knack for bringing out the most interesting details. His voice modulated from serene respect to outright excitement, and she hung on every word.

The pace was much slower here than in any other place she had visited. No one appeared to be in a hurry. The piazza was the heart of the city. She looked across at the cathedral reaching up into the sky and soaked up the contentment as the sun warmed her face.

"Some of the best examples of medieval art are in that cathedral," he said. "We'll take a look in there after we get some lunch. You won't believe what we're going to have." Mason kissed her quickly as they walked across the piazza. The aromas of food mingled in the air, teasing her taste buds. Although right now, she still savored the taste of Mason.

"What's that?" Jayne asked as she thought she heard the beat of drums.

"Our timing is perfect," Mason said as he pulled her close and enclosed both arms around her. "Just watch over there." He pointed to a corner where a street poured into El Campo. The rhythmic drumbeating grew louder, echoing in her chest. As it crescendoed, men in colorful medieval costumes appeared, bearing gigantic flags. The myriad of colors coalesced into a rainbow as the men tossed the flags high into the air, the material fluttering like gossamer wings and collapsing as the men captured the pennons again.

"Amazing," Jayne said. "I can't believe someone isn't going to get impaled." Her imagination filled the piazza with a medieval mix of busy commoners and royalty looking down from the balconies. She snuggled deeper into Mason's embrace.

The men walked with obvious pride through El Campo, all in step and throwing their flags in unison.

"I'm sure the Brownings came here to watch this spectacle," Mason whispered in her ear.

She had no doubt and flushed with the knowledge of Mason's intuition.

The flash of color receded down another narrow street on the opposite side of the piazza. Jayne and Mason began to stroll again. She noticed light flecks of gray highlights in his hair. His eyes sparkled, and when they focused on her, she felt a flutter like the excitement of being at the top of a Ferris wheel.

"It's your choice, Jayne," Mason said. "Do you want some lunch or do you want to see some sights?"

"Let's walk around awhile before we eat," Jayne said.

"As the lady wishes," he said and bowed slightly. "This way."

They walked across the piazza to a fountain on the edge of the El Campo. "This is exquisite." Jayne put her hand on the warm tip of the fence and leaned in.

Three sides of the Gaia fountain were panels of carved marble. The front was partitioned off with black wrought iron gates. Water poured from a sculpted jug into the crystalline pool.

"It was completed in the 1400s and illustrates a mix of Gothic and Renaissance art," Mason said and laughed. "I really sounded like a tour guide again, didn't I?"

Jayne smiled and marveled at the longevity evident everywhere in this small city. Buildings, art, and the piazza itself had all stood through the centuries. The architects and artisans had achieved immortality of sorts. Traditions endured as well. Just not people.

"Okay, I can't wait any longer. You're going to be surprised," Mason said. "Let's go have lunch."

His face broke into a broad smile of anticipation as he reached for her hand and walked toward a restaurant behind the fountain. He greeted the waiter, who showed them to a seat next to the window. Mason ordered without a menu and wiggled a bit in his seat.

"What could possibly be so exciting about lunch?" Jayne laughed.

Mason moved his seat closer enough to touch her. Other than that, his only answer was a smug look, tempered with a smile complete with dimples.

The waiter brought wine and bread.

"Good," Jayne said. "Local wine and bread. That's exciting."

Still no answer from Mason as he tasted the wine.

Jayne followed his lead. It was unique, full of spicy apricot and pungent citrus flavors. "This is very good." Jayne nodded and took another swallow. She picked up a piece of bread and nibbled on it. "This is good too."

Mason still didn't speak. He shook his head, indicating that the surprise was not the bread or wine.

Salad followed the bread and wine, a beautiful array of tomatoes, cucumbers, and assorted cheeses with a wonderful vinaigrette drizzled on top.

Jayne lifted an eyebrow as she crossed her knife and fork on her now-empty plate.

Mason shook his head.

Finally, the entrée arrived. Jayne looked at the breaded concoction beautifully presented on her plate. She didn't have a clue what it was.

"Just try it." Mason had his knife and fork poised for action, but he waited, watching her intently.

There was a short stem at one end of the elongated entrée. Maybe it was a pepper of some sort. She cut into the mystery. It was crispy on the outside with thick breading, and cheese softly oozed out. She steadied her palate for a spicy assault. Instead, a smooth rich flavor filled her mouth and she moaned. It was unlike anything she had ever tasted. The cheeses were pungent and the breading a bit sweet, and it was definitely not a pepper.

"What is this?" Jayne couldn't even imagine.

"It's a pumpkin flower stuffed with homemade cheeses." He took a satisfied bite of his own.

"A flower?"

"Yes, a pumpkin flower," he cut another bite and poised it on the back of his fork.

"I'm eating a flower?" Jayne poked at the corners of the entrée.

Mason just smiled and nodded his head. A bit of cheese strung from the corner of his mouth. Jayne reached over and pulled on it.

"I can't take you anywhere, can I?" She chuckled as he licked the cheese from her fingers. Time disappeared. No past. No future. Just now, with her sitting in a restaurant in Siena with her lover, eating pumpkin flowers. She looked at Mason. The corners of his eyes crinkled slightly when he smiled. He had deep laugh lines and deep frown lines. He was a contradiction for sure. Her heart pounded for a moment as thoughts of the future interceded. She slammed them down, not willing to digress for a moment. She could almost hear Floyd saying, "Atta girl."

"What's for dessert?" she asked.

"Cappuccino and something chocolate," Mason replied. He put his arm around her and kissed her. His fingers tangled in her hair. She responded just as passionately, not caring that they were on display in the window of the restaurant. It was just natural, even for her.

After lunch, they headed away from El Campo toward the Duomo of Siena. As Jayne looked around, she noticed other couples draped around each other just like they were. She fit. For the first time in her life, she fit because she was with her soulmate. This truth tugged at her, trying to burrow down in comfort, but it lingered … unsteady and insecure at this point.

They walked past shops with magnificent window displays. Wine shops complemented bread and cheese shops. Pottery with brilliant persimmon orange, canary yellow, and azure blue hung in windows and even outside shop doors. Mason led her at a leisurely pace through the twisting streets with subtle squeezes or tugs.

They watched people as they strolled. Laughing at the old men ogling young girls and the subsequent reaction if they reached out to touch. Young men strutted like peacocks, checking their reflections in store windows. Jayne had to admit that there were some gorgeous people around. Some looked like models. All were dressed impressively. Despite everything, she felt just as beautiful as the people she watched. Her head held high and shoulders pushed back, she strutted with the best of them. Snug in her newly discovered sexuality. She watched a beautiful young man pinch a much older woman's rear end.

She looked at Mason and giggled.

He pinched her rear end in response.

She marveled at how easy it was to be with him. She was herself. No improvements to be made. No adjustments of thought. He loved her with all her imperfections. He even loved her curly hair.

Why now?

"Here we are," Mason said as they approached the Duomo.

"It's striped," Jayne said as they neared it. Different colors of brick made stripes right up to the roof.

"It does look striped from this angle," Mason said, "but the front is another beautiful facade."

As they walked around the side to the front, Jayne looked up at the building opposite the Duomo. "Look at that," Jayne pointed to the arched windows in the other building. Within the glass was the convoluted reflection of the Duomo, twisting the horizontal stripes into curves.

"I've never noticed that before," Mason said as he squeezed her around her waist. "There are a lot of things I've never noticed before." He looked down into her face and she could see love. It warmed her all over. "Wait until you step inside."

He hurried her up the front stairs and pushed her slightly ahead of him. She moved inside. When her eyes adjusted to the interior, she froze.

"Well?" Mason fidgeted like a young boy.

"I can't believe this," Jayne said as she slowly walked forward. Her eyes roamed everywhere, absorbing the beauty. The interior was stripes of marble like the outside. But the overwhelming magnificence was the intricate marble floor. The patterns reminded her of the brown, black, and rust-colored Grecian urns she had seen in the Louvre. The designs sprawled all over the space. The high ceiling and expanded naves created a vortex of color and light. Even the pillars had alternating stripes of black and gray that complemented the floor, rather than competing with it.

"I knew you would appreciate it," Mason said as he held her hand and went into tour guide mode. Enthralled by every word, she enjoyed her private tour.

"What do you really think about places like this?" Jayne asked as they made their way out of the cathedral.

"What do you mean?" Mason asked.

"What about the expense and the efforts to accumulate all this?" She pointed to the gold goblets littered about and the priceless paintings that lined the walls.

"I guess I just look at it as a museum. I'm glad that someone had the foresight to save all these things," Mason said as he pushed the door open for her.

"Perhaps," Jayne said. She tugged at his coat collar playfully. "Where to next?"

"I have no agenda," Mason said. Then one corner of his lip curved upward. "Well, at least no agenda for the day."

Jayne punched him in the arm and then tucked her arms around his. They left the Duomo and continued to walk by the apartments that were several stories tall. The windows were encased with green shutters. A couple of windows had laundry hanging from lines for all to see.

"What is in that building?" Jayne asked as they approached.

"That is one of the buildings of the University of Siena," he said. "Recently, the University has returned a lot of the buildings back to the city. There has been a university here since around the 1300s."

"Really?" Jayne thought about it and then continued. "Wouldn't that be a great place to teach?"

Mason looked and cocked his head to one side. The waves in his hair caressed his face as a slight breeze blew.

"Just think about the history," she continued. "What a great place to make a difference with today's generation."

Mason was still quiet, his eyes echoing a myriad of shades between gray and blue.

"You are basically teaching in your job as a tour guide," she said. "Except university students might be more receptive and not so interested in the next shopping stop."

Mason laughed at that remark. Jayne couldn't understand why he didn't seem to want to teach. He was intelligent and had so much to give.

"Why not teach?" She wasn't going to let it drop.

"It just seems so stuffy," Mason said. "I wouldn't fit in."

"You fit into this community. Look at you. You fit in

anywhere." She turned down another narrow street that Mason indicated, but she didn't stop talking. "This place is beautiful. It's steeped in old-world charm. There are plenty of places to entertain in the evening if you want to continue with your music. And then the opportunity to share all that you know with…"

"I'll think about it," he said. "For now, I think gelato is in our near future."

"If it's chocolate, lead the way," Jayne said as they took yet another turn down a street that looked just like the previous one.

After polishing off a double scoop of rich chocolate gelato, Jayne wiped her mouth and looked at the shadows starting to make their way across the piazza.

"I guess we'd better head back to Florence," Mason said as if reading her mind.

"I suppose so." Jayne sighed.

"We're off to Rome tomorrow," Mason said as he pulled her chair out for her.

"Rome," Jayne said as her heart seemed to plummet. She couldn't help equating Rome with the end of the tour. "I wish we could stay here."

"Maybe we'll come back," Mason said, and then his face dropped.

"Don't say it," Jayne said and put her hand up. "It was a beautiful day with memories I will cherish. Especially the pumpkin flower."

Mason laughed a short, forced-sounding laugh. It was a bit hollow to her ears. At least they had escaped for a short time. It was better than nothing.

As they drove along the winding roads, Jayne watched the play of shadow and light on the rolling hillsides. The light shimmered in its fading glory on the red tile roofs and the rust-colored stucco. The reflected color looked like bronze tans that so many Americans hoped for but never achieved. She watched the medieval city fade into the shadows.

"I'm going to take a slight detour," Mason said. "I can hear you thinking. The mood is taking a nosedive and it has to stop." He turned the car around and returned to the outskirts of Siena. Turning down a road, she saw a row of cars parked on one side. Mason slowed the car. As they passed some of the other cars, she noticed they were rocking slightly.

"What are we doing?" she asked.

"I'm showing you some of the non-touristy sights in Italy," Mason said as he pulled to the end of the line of cars and parked. He turned off the ignition. "Shall we?" He motioned toward the back seat.

"What?" Jayne asked. Then, it suddenly dawned on her as she looked at the car in front of them. It was swaying rhythmically and the windows were steamed up. "You've got to be kidding me."

"Most Italian men live with their mothers. They marry late and live with their mothers even after they get married," Mason said as he opened his car door. "This is where they go to be with their girlfriends or wives. They have to escape Momma to make love." He climbed in the back seat and slammed his door shut.

She shook her head as she followed suit. Somehow, Mason climbed over the seat and shut her door for her. He looked like a contortionist from Cirque du Soleil. She broke out laughing.

"What's so funny?" Mason said as he untwisted and sat next to her.

"A new type of foreplay?" She had tears running down her face from laughing so hard.

"Obviously, it doesn't pay to be a gentleman," he said.

Her shoulders still shook with laughter as he put his arms around her. He kissed her and she leaned back.

"Ow," she jumped as the seatbelt ground into her back.

Mason pulled back and just looked at her.

"The seatbelt," she said, shifting herself on an angle.

She initiated the kissing this time.

"Wait," Mason said as his knee got stuck between her and the seat.

Jayne started laughing again and this time Mason joined her.

"It was a good idea at the time," he said as he simply put his arm around her.

"You must have to be Italian for it to work," she said, laying her head on his shoulder.

"Or desperate," Mason said as he stroked her arm.

"Or younger and more flexible." Jayne laughed as Mason opened his door.

"Do you mind sliding over here?" Mason asked as he reached out for her hand. "I don't think my back can take twisting to open your door again."

As they resumed the return trip to Florence, the radio played softly. Jayne looked at her reflection in the window. Her hair glistened with softness, each curl unique. For once, she loved her curls.

Tomorrow was the second-to-last day of the tour. It was too soon. *What am I going to do?* She glanced at Mason and he looked totally lost in thought. *Is he thinking the same thing?*

"Where are you?" She looked straight at him.

"With you … always," he replied. She watched the color flush across his face and reached for his hand. It was cold.

"It was a beautiful trip," she said as she squeezed his hand. "Thank you so much."

"Believe me, I enjoyed it even more because I was with you," Mason said. She withdrew her hand slowly. A shadowy thought began to cloud her mind, or was it the sun setting that caused an illusion? It dipped behind a hill and resurfaced as the road turned.

Jayne leaned her head back and began to quote lines from one of her favorite poems:

"All we have willed or hoped or dreamed of good shall exist;
Not its semblance, but itself; no beauty, nor good nor power
Whose voice has gone forth, but each survives for the melodist
When eternity affirms the conception of an hour.
The high that proved too high, the heroic for earth too hard,
The passion that left the ground to lose itself in the sky,
Are music sent up to God by the lover and the bard:
Enough that he heard it once; we shall hear it by-and-by."

Mason was silent, apparently absorbing the words.

"That's from Browning's poem *Abt Vogler*, about a musician. In fact, it is rumored that Vogler beat Beethoven in an extemporaneous musical duel," Jayne added and opened her eyes. "Now who is the tour guide?" She chuckled lightly.

"Why that specific stanza?" Mason asked.

"I was reliving the day and remembered your song," she replied easily.

"It's your song," Mason countered.

When they arrived back at the hotel, Jayne followed Mason to his room. He made love to her again, and she experienced every fiber of his being. He consumed her soul and fused it with his. She would always be a part of him now. No matter what. The music of lovemaking filled her heart and she soared, the bard's lover.

CHAPTER 20

Saturday, October 27, 2012

After watching the landscape slide by the bus window, Jayne pulled out her notebook and her chocolate stash. With a smile tugging at the corner of her mouth, she thought that sex with Mason had been better than her beloved chocolate.

"What are you doing?" Lynn asked.

"Want some chocolate?" Jayne opened the bag and waved it under Lynn's nose.

Lynn reached inside and grabbed a couple of pieces. Jayne took out a piece and put the bag back in her purse. She picked up her pen with the other hand, popped the chocolate in her mouth, and opened her notebook.

"I mean that," Lynn said as she pointed to the notebook.

"I've been writing in it since the beginning of the trip," Jayne said. "I have to catch up on the last day."

"Why?" Lynn looked at her cousin expectantly.

"I don't really know," Jayne lied, not wanting to share the reason. "It just makes me feel good."

Jayne filled page after page as the bus continued to its last stop on the tour, Rome. Jayne continued to write and ignored the persistent thought that the best of the trip was behind her. Thoughts of Tom invaded her consciousness, but she pushed them aside once more. *Live each day to the fullest, with no regrets.* She should be ecstatic to see Rome in all its glory, but sadness slowly crept in as Tuscany receded into the past. A sadness for things that end. She wrote frantically in her notebook, trying in vain to stretch out memories of Siena. Trying not to let the hole in the pit of her stomach consume her. *Not yet.*

The traffic began to grow thicker like a hive of bees as the bus hit the outskirts of the city. Mason was back in his tour guide form, pointing out interesting sites and giving a short history of the area. The hyperactivity of a sprawling city snuffed out the tranquility of Siena.

The bus crept through the heavy traffic streaming toward the Coliseum, where they merged onto a road encircling the ruins. Across the street, they pulled off to allow the group to explore the Coliseum, Circus Maximus, and the Roman Forum before going to the hotel. Jayne put her notebook away and watched Lynn fidget with excitement.

"We are going to get off the bus when we get to the Coliseum," Mason said. "Then, we'll walk to the Forum and Circus Maximus." He smiled at Jayne, and her heart did a flip-flop like a teenage girl's.

Jayne marveled at Jacques' expertise in navigating the crowded streets. Vespas caused most of the distraction as they darted in and out of traffic. She wondered how many of those young drivers would live to grow old. *Did their mothers lie awake at night?* She thought about the worries she had survived while her own kids were teenagers.

"There it is," Lynn pointed.

The ruins of the Coliseum loomed larger than life, standing defiant as the bus pulled up in front. Shadows loomed and the arches looked out on the cars and mopeds buzzing past. Mason hurried everyone off so the traffic could continue. Horns honked, bellowing their displeasure. Once the group was together, Mason started his lecture.

"The holes that are on the exterior surface are where the stone was fixed to the edifice," he said. "Just imagine these crumbling ruins in their prime, all glittering with the pristine white travertine stone slabs reflecting the light of torches."

As he continued talking, he motioned for everyone to follow him. "The Coliseum was originally known as the Flavius Amphitheatre. Some celebrations would last for a hundred days. Over five thousand animals would be slaughtered during that time. Of course, there were gladiator fights as well. During the opening of the event, the arena was flooded to re-enact Rome's victories at sea."

"Incredible," Jayne said to Lynn. "And now all that's left is this crumbling skeletal frame."

Mason led the group inside the vast area. The floor was long gone, showing the vast lower chambers of the place. Jayne shuddered involuntarily as she scanned the wide space where so many people and animals died for sport. After dismissing the rest of the group to explore the ruins, Mason joined Jayne and Lynn.

"It's a remarkable place, isn't it?" Mason said as he leaned on one of the railings.

"Mind blowing," Lynn agreed.

Jayne shuddered again. "I can feel the ghosts. Can't you?" She looked at both Mason and Lynn. The sun made strange shadows over their faces. Mason left the railing and put his arm around Jayne's shoulders.

"Just for entertainment," Jayne said. "How could such an advanced people be so barbaric at the same time?"

"It's human, unfortunately," Mason replied. "They had advanced sets of pulleys and drops that made things move smoothly."

"All that technology wasted on games," Jayne said. "I think I've seen enough." She began to walk toward an exit.

"Wait a minute," Mason said. "I have to round everyone up and then we'll move on to the Forum."

Lynn caught up with Jayne. "I thought you liked history."

"Not this particular history," Jayne said and then tried to lighten up. If she kept this up, she would ruin the end of her trip like someone who wasted Sunday worrying about going back to work on Monday.

She shook her head. "I'm more of a romantic history lover."

Lynn laughed as she followed Jayne out. Before long, the rest of the group appeared. Rosa was talking with an Italian bystander whom she had picked up. Natalie looked left out. The Brazilians took pictures of the traffic while the grandparents tried to hold their grandchildren's fidgeting hands. The young newlyweds were locked in each other's arms.

As the group walked down the weathered brick pathway to the Forum, Jayne tried to shake her mood again. But the haunted feeling wouldn't budge. Strong metal fences kept the crowd from wandering through the ancient grounds where so many had walked their last steps on earth. She imagined she heard lions roar and anguished people scream. It was a tangible feeling like no other she had experienced before. She turned her face up to the sun, trying to see whether it would help melt the icy effect of the dark past.

Ancient pillars stood defiantly in the midst of rubble. A lone arch reflected the glamour that must have been superfluous in this former seat of government.

"This was where all the political action took place," Mason said. "It was also where the best shops and restaurants were located. You can take a few minutes for pictures, and then we will move on to Circus Maximus."

Jayne noticed that Lynn, Rosa, and some of the others drifting toward a few street-side vendors hawking designer knockoffs, like Fendi, Prada, Louis Vuitton. Jayne stood by the pillars that looked like a barren ribcage to her. Mason put his arms around her waist.

"Is this better?" he asked.

"Much," she said. She basked in his tenderness and then turned to face him. "What if the others see us?"

"Don't care," Mason replied and kissed her.

The group seemed to be gathered around one particular vendor. Lynn came away with her purchases.

"His knockoffs were the best," Lynn said. "I got these for some of my friends. Maybe they won't know the difference, or ask."

Jayne shook her head and smiled.

The group continued to the next stop. "There is nothing here," Lynn said, her jaw dropping. "It just looks like a track."

"They had chariot races here," Mason said. "So, it looks like a dirt racetrack. Most Italians today just look at it as a nice walking path."

On the far side of the ruins, the bus waited to take them to their hotel.

"My God," Lynn said as the bus pulled up to the front of the hotel. "It's a palace."

Jayne studied the red and gold flags that draped across the face of the building with the name of the hotel, Hotel Splendide Royal, emblazoned on them like regal banners of old. Between the banners, old-fashioned streetlamps adorned the smooth stone surface. The entryway was nothing short of art, with curved metal and glass creating a canopy shaped like a tortoise shell.

"We decided to go upscale for our last stop on the tour," Mason said. "This five-star hotel was a palace in the nineteenth century. Now, we peasants can live like royalty. At least for a day or two."

Everyone laughed as they followed Mason.

"Wow," Lynn and Jayne said as they entered the lobby.

"Luxury is an understatement," Jayne said as she tried to take it all in. The center of the lobby burst up into an atrium of glass, allowing light to shine in from the heavens. A large gold chandelier dominated the space beneath the atrium. The antique furniture had a royal flavor, lush greens and reds on a backdrop of sedate gold tones. Mirrors on each wall reflected this opulence back and forth. Huge potted palms flanked each corner of the room, giving it a final touch of grace.

"It's a fairy-tale palace come to life," Jayne said.

"I thought you'd like it," Mason said as he gave Jayne and Lynn their keys. "And remember, it really was a palace."

"I have two keys," Lynn said as she tried to hand one back.

"That's right," Mason said. "Jayne has a key to share my room, and Antonio will be coming, right?"

Lynn smiled and tucked the extra key in her purse.

"I assume that's all right with you," Mason said to Jayne.

She nodded and tried to feel guilty. Instead, she tingled with excitement. She felt like the heroine of one of her favorite novels.

They took the lift to Lynn's floor. "I left a message for Antonio at the front desk for you," Mason said. "The rest of the afternoon is free for everyone to explore. I already told that to the rest of the group."

"Thanks," Lynn said. "You two enjoy yourselves." She put the key in the door and turned. "I certainly will." The door shut softly behind her.

On the next floor, Mason led Jayne to another door. Jayne walked into a luxury suite beyond her imagination.

"It's stunning," she said as she walked across the red carpet with swirling gold medallion designs. The king-sized bed had a red and gold duvet that matched the curtains. Navy blue valances ran across the top of each window that provided views of the city framed with trees growing nearby. Gold-painted panels stood in sharp contrast to the cream walls. Gold leaf framed artwork hung over the bed.

She walked to the window and put her hands on the silk panels.

"I feel like I'm in a dream," she said as she turned to look at Mason. This was so perfect, she thought, that it couldn't be real. She walked out onto a terrace that had a beautifully set table for two. Mason joined her and put his arms around her waist, resting his head on her shoulder. The contours of their bodies fit … naturally.

"What would you like to do?" Mason asked as he turned her to face him. "We can have something to eat or we can go explore." He paused. "Or we can make love." He smiled seductively as he looked at her from head to toe.

Jayne knew she would not see anything outside of this room, gorgeous as it was, if she went to bed with him now.

"Let's go out and explore." She kissed him quickly and went back inside to get her purse. "We have all night to *explore* other things."

"Sounds great," Mason picked up his coat and shrugged into it. "Where do you want to go?"

"I want to see something other than buildings and museums," Jayne said. "Surprise me."

Mason held the door open for her. "I see. The gauntlet has been thrown down. The master tour guide will pick up the challenge."

Jayne had never laughed so much in her life. Mason was quiet in the elevator. She laughed again at his concentration, but by the time they exited the lobby, his face had switched from one heavy in thought to one that was smug in anticipated victory.

He hailed a taxi, and they were on their way. They stopped at a nondescript corner, where Mason asked the taxi driver to wait. They got out and stood in front of a mangled statue. The arms and legs were missing and the face had eroded so no features were left.

"This is it?" she asked.

"There is much more here than meets the eye," Mason replied and adopted his tour guide persona. "This statue has been around since the third century B.C. and became notorious between the sixteenth and nineteenth centuries. The Romans called it 'Pasquino,' and that name has several potential sources. All the sources have one thing in common. Satirical writing. The statue's popularity grew as satirical notes began to appear on it. Most of these notes criticized government officials. It was the first of many 'talking statues' in Rome. It was like the precursor of political cartoons."

"Bravo," Jayne said as she clapped. "This can't be one of the popular tourist attractions, right?"

Mason smiled as he helped her back into the taxi. She felt like a kid on a scavenger hunt, following the thrill of each new discovery.

Mason repeated the routine, but this time they stopped at a statue that was also a fountain. "This is the Fountain of the Porter. He talks in satire as well."

Jayne looked at the statue of an old man. His face was mired with age, yet the features were still there. He held a barrel of spirits and water poured from a hole in the front of the barrel. She was still laughing as Mason grabbed her hand and pulled her back into the taxi.

The next stop was another fountain.

"You'll like this one," Mason said as he pulled her from the taxi.

Jayne scrutinized the fountain that was carved into the shape of a deer's head mounted between two stacks of books. She ran her fingers over the edges and wondered how Mason could know her so well in such a short time.

"This is the Fountain of Books," he said. He made a flourish with his hands.

"No doubt," Jayne replied, falling deeper in love with him.

"There was a university close at one time that served as inspiration for it," Mason added. "We're off again."

Jayne recognized the next stop. It was a beautiful fountain with Neptune fighting an octopus as the central focus. It was much larger than she had thought. *It's funny how photos simply can't capture the true scope of some things.*

"This one is on the list of main tourist sites, so I'm not sure it counts," Jayne teased.

"What if I tell you that it had only the white marble basin for almost three hundred years?" Mason countered. "Then, in the 1870s, the statue of Neptune was added along with the sculptures of the sea horses, cherubs, dolphins, and sea nymphs."

"Ok, that's good for a start," she said.

"The Piazza Navona was built on top of an ancient stadium."

"And…" Jayne couldn't help prodding him along.

"And the name Navona means 'big ship.'" He tucked her hand in the crook of his arm and began to walk around the fountain. "Because they used to flood this area to reenact great naval battles."

"You are redeemed," Jayne said, squeezing his arm. "This is amazing."

The corners of his mouth turned up. "Shall we take a look at the other two fountains?"

Lined with restaurants and shops, the piazza had Bernini's Fountain of the Four Rivers and the Fountain of the Moor at the southern end. They circled each one, arm in arm, fitting in with the other people milling around.

"Would you like to stop for a while?" Mason asked as he finished talking about the fountains.

"No, I'm fine," she said, reveling in the history surrounding her.

"Then, you have a choice," Mason said. "Do you want to walk to the next place or stick with the taxi?"

"Let's walk," Jayne said.

He paid off the taxi and then tucked her arm around his and started walking. "I must admit that the final fountain on my list is a famous one and a must-see on any tourist's agenda."

"I'll let it slide, this time," Jayne teased. "You have surprised me enough to have redeemed yourself as the font of knowledge I have come to know."

As they turned a corner, she heard rushing water before the Trevi Fountain appeared in all its splendor. A giant Greek god dominated the scene that was constructed with Roman arches and majestic sea horses. A Roman building created a backdrop for the drama of a Titan ruling over the seas that shelved down from the main edifice.

"Most people think that the central sculpture is Neptune, but he is Oceanus, adjoined by Abundance and Wisdom." Mason put his arm around Jayne's waist. "The confusion probably stems from the number of fountains that do represent Neptune. Or, the fact that Neptune's son, Triton, is the one leading the chariot." He pointed toward the statue with its hand entwined in a horse's mane.

"It's miraculous," Jayne said, feeling insignificant in front of the masterpiece. Again, her favorite dream books did not come close to the reality spanning across her view.

"The water is funneled through an aqueduct created in 19 B.C. It carried water to all the fountains in Rome from a spring nearly twenty kilometers away." Mason leaned on the railing. "It's really quite an engineering feat."

"I think that the fountains bring nature into the midst of the city," Jayne said. "You can hear the sound just like a stream or river in the countryside."

"You're right," Mason said as he dug into his pocket.

"Looking for something?" Jayne asked.

"A coin, of course." Mason pulled his hand from his pocket. "Victory," he said as he raised a couple of coins for Jayne to see.

"What does the coin toss mean?" Jayne asked.

"It means that you will return to Rome someday," Mason said.

"Don't bother," Jayne said as she quickly turned away from the fountain and walked up the short flight of stairs. "Let's go."

Mason didn't say a word. He turned his back to the fountain and tossed the coins, then followed her up the stairs.

"Let's get a taxi back to the hotel," she said.

"Wait," Mason said as he pulled on her arm. "I have one more place to show you. It's really close, and I know you're going to like it."

Jayne nodded and walked away from the famous fountain. She fought away the melancholy that was trying to intercede.

I refuse to feel sorry for myself.

She was living a dream and had no time for nightmares right now. Putting her arm around Mason's waist, she twisted her finger through a belt loop. He responded by placing his arm around her shoulders.

Within a few blocks, Jayne knew exactly where they were.

"It's the Spanish Steps," she said as she looked at the wide flight of steps that fanned up. She glanced at the building flanking the steps and pointed. "Which one?"

"The Italians call it Piazza di Spagna," Mason said. "Do you see the red banners?"

"Yes," Jayne looked up at the second-floor window. She balanced precariously on her tip toes, straining to get closer.

"It's now called the Keats-Shelley House," Mason explained.

"He lived such a sad and short life," Jayne said. "He was so talented."

She climbed up a couple of steps and imagined Keats collapsing and being carried to his room. The stairs teemed with people. Life must have taunted him from his window view.

"A vale of soul-making," Jayne said in a whisper.

"What?" Mason leaned closer.

"He said that life was a vale of soul-making," Jayne repeated. "He distinguished between intelligence and the soul. He thought that the purpose of being in this world was to cultivate an individual soul. Everyone has a spark of the divine within him or her. But in order to cultivate individual identity, one has to experience pain and sorrow to return to God with more than when they visited this earth."

Mason looked up at the rooms. "He knew all that by the time he died at twenty-five years old." He looked at Jayne. "Astonishing."

"Do you want to visit his grave?" Mason asked. "Shelley is buried there as well. They are at the Protestant Cemetery."

"That would be nice," Jayne replied. "He also touted the power of the imagination," Jayne continued. "He coined the concept of Negative Capability—the idea that 'when a man is capable of being in uncertainties, Mysteries, doubts, without any irritable reaching after fact and reason.' In other words, he believed that some things are meant to be felt rather than fully understood."

"'Beauty is truth, truth beauty,'" Mason said, quoting from Keats's *Ode to a Grecian Urn*.

"That's my favorite Keats poem," Jayne said. She marveled at her connection with Mason. They were in tune on every level. Further confirmation that he was her soulmate. Time didn't matter. The truth of it soaked in. Her case had been proven personally. True love existed.

How am I ever going to let go?

Mason waved for a taxi and they drove to the cemetery. He spoke to the driver and they stopped in front of a giant pyramid.

"This isn't it, is it?" Jayne asked. "I didn't expect a pyramid in Rome."

"No, but I thought you'd like to see it," Mason said. The taxi pulled into a parking area and waited. "This is the Pyramid of Caius Cestius, who was a rich Roman magistrate around 12 B.C. It's made of white marble and has a burial chamber that was found in about the 1600s. This became a popular stop for the British on their Grand Tours."

"What's that?" Jayne pointed down the street to a building that looked like a castle.

"Oh, that's the Porta San Paolo, a castle-like southern gate in the third-century Aurelian Walls of Rome." Mason took Jayne by the hand. They walked to the entrance of the cemetery and made their way to a corner that was in the shadows of the pyramid.

"Look at all the cats," Jayne said. Dozens of cats walked around the cemetery, sat on graves, and poked in the bushes. "There's something eerie about cats and a pyramid." She saw a calico peeking out from behind a tree. "Something very Egyptian."

"Here we are," Mason said as he stopped in front of a grave. A cat snoozed in the shade of the tombstone.

Instead of the single grave she expected, Jayne saw two gravestones covered with violets in a marked-off square. "They were his favorite flower," she said, wondering who had planted them. The gravestones had a carving of a lyre with some of the strings missing. Very appropriate, she thought, as the image of the lyre brought Keats' words to mind. Without realizing it, she began to softly recite, "See, See the Lyre, the Lyre in a flame of fire upon the cradle's top, Flaring, flaring, flaring."

"Past the eyesight's bearing. Awake it from its sleep, And see if it can keep Its eye upon the blaze," Mason said, completing the quote.

She was no longer surprised when he finished both her thoughts and quotes. In fact, she expected it. Finding comfort in the rhythm of it.

"You know that you use the same imagination and inspiration in writing music, don't you?" Jayne replied, warmed again by their close connection.

Mason smiled and began to read the words on the headstone out loud: "This grave contains all that was mortal, of a young poet who, on his death bed, in the bitterness of his heart, at the malicious power of his enemies, desired these words to be engraved on his tomb stone. Here lies one whose name was writ in water, Feb 24th 1821."

"You know Keats only wanted that last part on his tombstone," Jayne added. "His friends were angry that the critics had been so hard on him, so they added that first bit." She sighed. "I read somewhere that they later regretted their decision." She squinted and couldn't read the other tombstone because of the sunlight that had dissipated the shadows. "Is that Shelley?"

"No, it's Severn," Mason curved his hand over his eyes. "That's the friend who took care of Keats until he died."

After looking for a moment, they found Shelley's grave. Jayne said, "You know he was cremated on the beach somewhere."

"Near Viareggio," Mason said. "His ashes are buried here." He read the inscription: "Cor cordium, heart of hearts. (1792-1822), Nothing of him that doth fade / But doth suffer a sea-change / Into something rich and strange."

He looked up at Jayne, his brow furrowing. "That's not one of Shelley's verses, that's Shakespeare."

Jayne smiled. "It's from *The Tempest* and seems most appropriate since Shelley died in a storm at sea." She looked down at the dates again. "They were both so young. How do you live that much life in such a short time?"

"We all have our moments," Mason said.

They walked back to the taxi.

"Let's go back to our beautiful room and have dinner out on

our terrace," Jayne said as she glanced once more at the cemetery.

Mason said something in Italian to the driver and then was silent.

"Well?" Jayne asked.

"I'm letting my imagination run free with thoughts and opening to Negative Capability, but mostly I'm thinking about being with you tonight."

Jayne leaned back and unleashed her imagination as well.

CHAPTER 21

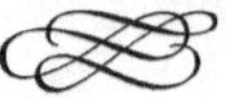

*S*unday, *October 28, 2012*

Jayne propped up on one elbow and watched Mason in the early morning light that filtered through the window. She stroked the rough shadow of his beard along his jawline. Each stubble aroused her. She should be ridden with guilt, but she wasn't.

She ran her fingers through her hair, which was tousled in a riot of curls. The covers were draped around her waist.

Brilliant gray-blue eyes opened, and he smiled, satisfaction suffusing into his now familiar dimples. He caressed her shoulder and traced her collarbone. Slowly, she responded to his teasing, scooting closer to him.

"Morning," she said drowsily, encircling her arms around him and pressing her body close.

"Cold?" he asked.

"No, not really," she replied, pushing away thoughts about the dwindling hours

remaining on the tour. "We'd better get ready."

"You're right," he said as he left the bed and headed to the bathroom.

She shivered again, fighting a gnawing sense of emptiness. Glancing at the clock, she quickly jumped up, wrapped the sheet around her, and toddled to the bathroom.

The shower was going. Steam wafting in soft swirls, clouding up the mirror. She had never showered with a man ... until this morning. She pulled back the shower curtain, and Mason extended his arms. The gnawing stopped ... at least for now.

He cradled her against him with her back to the water. He kissed her deeply as the water pelted her skin. His hands were soapy as he ran them over her body. Her skin was alive. As he rinsed the soap from her body, she reached for the soap dispenser and rubbed her hands into a lather. Soft strokes. Sinewy muscle.

His beautiful gray-blue eyes were full of passion. No more sadness. "You are incredible," he said as he caressed her shoulders.

She kissed him in response, wallowing in her newfound sexuality. *It will never be like this again. Never.* She stepped out of the shower and shivered again as she dried herself. Her skin was still on fire.

THE GROUP MET in front of the bus, where Mason usually gave his speech. Since they were running late, he skipped it this time. It didn't matter to Jayne. She had enjoyed the delay. Immensely.

Instead, he herded everyone onto the bus. Lynn wasn't going to be there. She had left a message that she was going to spend her last day in Rome with Antonio. Jayne wasn't surprised.

Mason relayed their destination in Portuguese and then in Spanish. "We're off to the Vatican today," he said.

Already writing in her notebook, Jayne glanced up to find Mason watching her. He went into his lecture mode. She reveled in it like a favorite song. His voice seemed to blanket her with softness.

"The Vatican is not part of Italy, but it is the smallest country in the world. The Vatican Museums house priceless artifacts and artwork that were collected or commissioned by popes. The museum began in the 1500s."

He moved from his seat and stood in the front of the bus. "We'll be stopping in the square where we will disembark and go through the ticket line." He glanced at Jayne. "Then, you have time to explore on your own, which I warn you will not be enough to see everything. We will meet back in the lobby in four hours."

Jayne loved hearing Mason talk about the places they were going to explore together. He was a gifted communicator. She knew he would make an astonishing teacher. He obviously respected history, even though he had come to take it for granted. Between his gift of music and oratory, he should be doing more, she thought as she followed the others off the bus.

She took a deep breath that was cut short, which was happening a lot more during these last few days. She had been popping more pills every morning. She hauled in another breath before meeting Mason outside the bus.

Vatican City spread out in an arc before them. He kept the group together, with her by his side, and talked about the statues that lined the semi-circle. They seemed poised to protect the space as they looked down on the humming crowd.

They passed by a Swiss Guard dressed in a brightly colored uniform that reminded Jayne of the Three Musketeers. "Why is he here?"

"Remember the Lion Monument that was carved into the hillside?" Mason asked.

"Of course," Jayne replied. A quick jab of sadness brought memories of Emma and Floyd. The sadness evaporated as she remembered the gift they had not even realized they had shared with her. Love was real. They lived it until the end, and maybe even beyond. Just like the Brownings.

"These are the soldiers who died for the pope over 500 years ago, and they are still protecting the current pope." Mason led the group to the ticket line, where the rules for proper dress were repeated in different languages over a loudspeaker. Women had to have their arms covered and men couldn't wear shorts. Even Rosa was dressed conservatively.

"During this time of year, the dress code isn't a problem," Mason said. "But you wouldn't believe the issues we run into in the summer."

The group was going to tour the Basilica first and then split up and go to the different museums. "We won't be able to see everything," Mason warned everyone again. "Make sure you pick up a map and make decisions."

The Brazilians and the Spanish in the group fidgeted and shuffled their feet as they entered St. Peter's. To Jayne, they acted as if this was the end of a pilgrimage. Their expressions were the same. Eyes wide, mouths agape, heads slightly bowed.

Mason began talking. The hushed whispers showed devout reactions to whatever he was saying. When it came to the English translation, Jayne realized that the Basilica was built on what was believed to be St. Peter's final resting place. A tomb represented the descent from the cross, a sobering reflection of sacrifice.

Leading the group towards the entrance to the Chapel of the Pieta, Mason relayed the story behind Michelangelo's famous sculpture. The artist had only been twenty-four years old when he created the masterpiece. Close in age to Jayne's children.

Maybe it just took more time nowadays for kids to mature. Kim was a talented teacher, but she hadn't reached her full potential yet. Maybe art was different. John was further ahead, but his passion was self-centered, focused on getting ahead in business to make more money. At least Kim was shaping young lives. Shaping the future. Making a difference.

Jayne stood in front of the statue as Mason translated and looked at the intricacies of the sculpture. Mary cradled the body of her Son, draped lifeless in her arms. The intricate folds of the clothing were so lifelike that Jayne fought the urge to reach out and readjust the cloth that was slipping off the body. Sinewy muscles and flexed feet preserved in marble were nothing short of miraculous.

But to Jayne, the most striking impact were the faces of both mother and son. The resolution from the mother, with one palm of her hand poised upward, releasing her child to God. It wasn't what Jayne had expected. She thought Mary's face would be twisted in grief. It wasn't. It portrayed solemn sadness and acceptance simultaneously.

What is a mother's responsibility to her child?

Jayne thought about Kim and John again. *When is it time to truly let go?* Sadness and acceptance were part of it. Sadness when they leave to go to their first day at school. Sadness when the center of their lives shifts away. Acceptance that there has been a change that continues to grow as children grow into adults.

"Jayne," Mason called, "we're going down to see the tombs of the popes."

"I think I'll just wander around here," Jayne said. "Can you meet me here after you're finished?"

"I'll bring the group back and we'll walk over to the museum," Mason said. "Then we will split up." He came over and gave her a quick kiss.

"I'm sure that was sacrilegious, Mason," Jayne teased.

"Only if you're Catholic … and I'm not." He laughed and walked toward the group easily switching languages, as usual.

She strolled slowly through the magnificent church. The

curved domes were covered in gold and blue. Bulging with grandeur, it was more ornate than any palace she had seen.

A side dome was painted with a heavenly scene. The light illuminated it like a spotlight. She walked from the smaller domed area, looking at monuments to popes, when she was drawn to a majestic display in the front of the cathedral. A round window blazed yellow like the sun itself above a wooden throne. Sculpted rays dramatically enhanced the effects of light.

Jayne couldn't help but think about the real person who inspired it. Peter, a disciple of Jesus, had been a humble fisherman. *What would he think of this extravagant monument created in his name?* It seemed to Jayne that the money used to create these beautiful works of art could have been used to help the needy throughout time. But, on the other hand, if these works had never been created, people wouldn't be able to enjoy them. One cause seemed fleeting, like the passing nature of human need, while the other led to immortality.

As she walked back to the entrance, she pondered the notion of immortality. *Does it require something tangible to be left behind? Or is it a fallacy? Will I be immortalized in memory first, and then through successive generations? Does immortality have to be intertwined with a specific memory?* In the end, she realized that everyone was going to die, and how they were remembered didn't really matter. What mattered was how they lived their lives.

"There you are," Mason said as she neared the entrance. "I thought we were going to have to send out a search party."

"Sorry," she said. "I lost track of time."

"This way, everyone," Mason said in English, but motioned so the group understood. They followed him like unruly soldiers on a chaotic march. The entrance to the museum was surprisingly modern. "This entrance was renovated in 2000," Mason explained.

The expanse held three floors. Mason went to the desk, paid

the entrance fee, and picked up a pile of maps. As he handed out the maps, he said, "This will help you choose what you want to see. Remember, we will meet in two hours to tour the Sistine Chapel together."

Everyone nodded and the group dispersed. The Brazilians and the newlyweds walked off to the left, while the Spanish, including Natalie and Rosa, went to the right. Mason and Jayne were left standing alone.

"Where to?" Jayne asked as she looked over his shoulder at the map he had opened.

"You tell me." Mason shifted the map so Jayne could get a better view.

She scanned the long list. Too many choices. So, she simply closed her eyes and pointed.

"The Pius-Clementine Museum it is," Mason said. "It was a random but great choice."

Jayne put her hand through his arm and slid it down to hold hands. As they walked, Mason talked about the museum. "The museum was commissioned in the 1700s by Popes Clement XIV and Pius VI to collect the most important Greek and Roman masterpieces in the Vatican."

Entering the museum, they were greeted by a huge Greek statue of an athlete after the race, scraping the sweat off his body. A vision of beads of water in her morning shower with Mason made Jayne blush.

The artistic majesty tantalized her eyes as they walked from room to room. Perfection reached out from every corner. A spiral staircase leading up from an octagonal courtyard was the widest that Jayne had ever seen. Roman emperors filled other rooms, while statues of animals filled still more. Sculpted perfection. Never any flaws.

"This is the Room of Muses, who were associated with creative passion and poetry," Mason said as he led Jayne into another room.

The ceiling was a beautiful fresco of the muses in action. Color illuminated the room and dripped down to red walls that provided the perfect backdrop for the statues on display.

"The fresco tells the story of Apollo and the nine muses," Mason said.

Jayne approached the remains of a statue. The head and arms were missing, but the abdomen and back were chiseled to muscular perfection.

"I wonder what the rest of him looked like," Jayne said. Again, visions of Mason's body filled her thoughts. *I'm becoming quite salacious. And I like it.*

"This is the famous Belvedere Torso that dates back to the first century B.C." Mason rubbed Jayne's back as he continued. "It inspired Michelangelo, who thought it the embodiment of the ideal of a powerful representation of the male body."

"Look at the way the light and shadow dance across the muscles," Jayne said as she walked around the statue. The complexity drew her in. "What an amazing gift," Jayne said. "I believe that God grants this creativity to help us get through the rest of the stuff we have to endure in our lives. We see perfection represented, but we can never attain it."

"I never thought of it that way," Mason said. "You make me see everything differently. That's one of the things I love about you."

"It's a shame to waste it if you're given such talent," Jayne said, looking directly at Mason.

"I know. I'm thinking about it." Mason's mouth twitched. He ran his fingers through his hair.

They spent the rest of the time trying to take in all the rooms in this museum, which was only a part of everything there was to see. Maybe this was the Church's way of giving hope to the people. If the capacity to create such beauty exists within humanity, there is hope for a better future.

Time passed quickly until the group met for their tour of the

Sistine Chapel. The intimate crowd created a procession that marched through several rooms to get to the entrance of the chapel.

"The Sistine Chapel was built between 1475 and 1483, the time of Pope Sixtus IV. In 1508, Pope Julius II commissioned Michelangelo to repaint the ceiling. The work was completed between 1508 and 1512." Mason continued to translate bits of information about the simple architecture of the chapel itself and all the ceremonies that had been performed over the years. He added that Michelangelo was commissioned again, between 1535 and 1541, to paint the Last Judgment over the altar.

Everyone chattered back and forth, but when the doors to the chapel opened, silence spread only to be broken within seconds by awed sighs and inhalations.

Everywhere she looked, she saw bursts of color animated by small windows that filtered the light. She craned her neck to see the creation of man reenacted, man's and God's hands outstretched, nearly touching. Another section showed Adam and Eve in the Garden of Eden, the snake wrapped around the Tree of Knowledge, despair showing on the faces of the transgressors.

The brilliance in the room overshadowed her, making her feel like a slight human stain with frailties, under a canopy of God. Pillars separating the biblical scenes gave the paintings dimension. Jayne could almost hear the angels' trumpets and the apostles' words. She had never experienced such intense spirituality in her life. She felt like falling to her knees in prayer. If one man could create such magnificence on earth, God's creation of heaven must be unimaginably beautiful.

As she moved from the ceiling to the wall behind the altar, tears blurred her vision. The visual and spiritual connection filled her soul. From the top, she saw the multitudes looking at Jesus and Mary in the center, with smiles and faces full of happiness. As her view lowered, she saw the tortured souls in the shadows grimacing in the pain of payment for sin.

She began to pray for her soul. *Am I going to be one of those in the shadows?* She prayed for solace. She prayed for forgiveness. She acknowledged her sins. Still, she couldn't believe that the love she shared with Mason had been a sin. God would not be so cruel as to bring them together only to penalize them. As she prayed, she felt a connection, a lightness, that seemed to communicate in a unique voice she had only heard a few times in her life. She would never be alone again. Browning's words floated to her, "God's in his heaven—All's right with the world." Although she had read those words many times, this time she understood completely.

She pulled a tissue from her purse and dabbed at her eyes. No one spoke in the chapel. There were no words that would match what they saw. However, once they filed out of the chapel onto a road outside the wall of the Vatican, everyone broke into conversation, but only in whispers.

The Brazilians and Spanish wanted to stop in the Vatican gift shop before getting on the bus, so Mason led them while Jayne and a couple of others boarded. When the group returned, they looked satisfied with their experiences and sacramental items.

Instead of sitting in the front, Mason sat next to Jayne. Everyone seemed content to bask in the afterglow of their own experience. Still, the conversations were subdued.

"Thoughts?" Mason said as he sat close to Jayne and picked up her hand.

"Beyond description," she replied, squeezing his hand. She ran her fingers across his. His hand completely engulfed hers. She stroked his palm and thought about his music. He had gifted hands.

"You need to go back to music," she said.

"Where did that come from?"

"It's a sin to be given such talent and waste it."

"But it wasn't good enough before."

"Maybe you didn't stick with it long enough," she replied, not letting him off the hook this time. "Michelangelo argued that he wasn't a painter and look what he produced. It didn't come out right the first time, so he started over."

"It's too late now," Mason said.

"That's an excuse," she said. "You might not produce on a grand scale. Then again, you might. Either way, if you write and play to make just a few people enjoy part of their day, it's sharing the gift." She let go of his hand and clasped his arm. "It's sharing the gift that's important. You also have the gift of communication. You could teach, as well. Maybe you will have to do both, like Michelangelo sculpted and painted."

On the way back to the hotel, Mason gave a goodbye speech, first in Portuguese and then in Spanish. He didn't bother to translate for Jayne. She wasn't sure what that meant. It was the end of the tour, and everyone was free to go their separate ways.

The group mingled in the lobby, hugging and bidding farewell. The Sistine Chapel seemed to have affected them all. Even Rosa approached Jayne as she stood in the corner, gave her a brief hug, and said goodbye. The newlyweds were the last to go and waved at Mason and Jayne as they entered the elevator.

Mason checked for messages at the front desk. "Lynn says that she will be back very early in the morning," he read from one of the notes. "Everything else is just turning in reports and that can wait."

Jayne was quiet as they entered the elevator, slowly filling with dread and depression. The gnawing returned. *This is it.* Her time with Mason was ticking away. She had pushed it to the back of her mind throughout the trip. *Living each day to the fullest, with no regrets.* There was no way to hide from it now. She would simply squeeze every moment until it was dry. Wringing it out so nothing would be left to regret. Just as her books had sustained her before, memories would sustain her now. And for the rest of her short future.

Mason held open the door to their room and she took in the fantasy of the majestic surroundings for the last time.

"Come here," he said as he opened his arms to her.

She responded to his invitation, feeling the warmth of his body, melting into the embrace.

"I have a surprise," he said as he led her to the terrace.

A sumptuous meal spread across the table, with wine chilled in a stand beside it. The lights of the city twinkled in the distance. A candelabrum flickered across the gold-edged plates. Jayne touched a beautiful shawl draped across one chair. Reds, yellows, blues, and purples swam together toward the fringed ends.

"This is gorgeous," she said.

"I thought it might get chilly out here," Mason said as he draped the shawl around her shoulders. She felt cocooned in his love as his fingers gently caressed her. "I was hoping you'd like it."

"Just a minute," she said as she went back into the room. She returned with a box. "This is for you."

Mason took the box in one hand while pulling out her chair with the other. He took his seat across from her and slowly opened the box.

"It's the unicorn," he said. "I can't take this."

"I bought it for you," she replied. She took it from him and held it by one of the candles. "See how the red glows. It's full of the possibilities of dreams coming true." It seemed to pulse with life as she held it. "I've lived my dream on this trip, and I want you to live yours." She handed it back to him. "I will always love you."

He held it up and looked at it. "What makes you think that I haven't lived my dream, too?" He placed it on the table where it balanced perfectly on its tail and hind legs. The forelegs leapt into space. He reached out for her hand. "Don't go. Stay here with me. I'll take care of you. We'll settle in Siena."

The words came at her with a rush of intensity, pelting her like a hailstorm.

She was silent as she stood up on shaky legs. Her heart pounded in her chest. She had pushed it back in her mind. The main stumbling block for her. "Just a minute." She went back into the room and returned with her wallet. She opened it and handed it to him. Tears threatened, so she swiped at the corners of her eyes.

She watched as he looked at pictures of a young man and woman. Her children had been her life. Thoughts of being so far away from them made her heart sink and her stomach lurch.

"She has your eyes," he said, running his finger across the photo. "And he has your nose."

"They are real, Mason. They have been my life. How can I leave them?" Her hands were shaking.

"We could have them over, too," Mason said. "I would love to meet them."

Tears rolled down her cheeks. *Would it be possible? Can I have both? Do I have the strength to choose?* The questions kept coming like violent waves pummeling her against the rocks in a high tide.

She reached for her wallet and snapped it shut. "We have tonight."

He stood and she met him, leaving the meal untouched. He wiped away her tears before kissing her. He wrapped his arms around her as they entered the room where she began to memorize every touch, every feeling, every emotion related to Mason.

Time melted into passion as the evening turned into night. Satiation was the aim, but it could never be achieved. Exhaustion gave way to sleepy embraces. Night gave way to early dawn.

Mason looked like he was deep in a dream when Jayne woke. She tumbled out of bed and took a last look before she slipped into her clothes, packed, and left.

Jayne knocked lightly on Lynn's door, her suitcases by her side. *Please be there. Open the door.* Her silent pleas were answered when a sleepy-eyed Lynn cracked open the door.

"Are you alone?" Jayne asked.

"Yes, in fact, I just got back," Lynn said as she opened the door and let Jayne in. Her shirt was halfway tucked into her underwear. She padded over to the bed, slipped under the covers, and looked at Jayne.

"Well," she said, "what in the hell are you doing here?"

"He asked me to stay." Jayne sat on the edge of the bed.

Lynn perked up. "Wonderful."

"What?"

"That's wonderful," Lynn repeated, leaning forward. She bobbed up and down on the bed. "He's perfect for you."

"Are you crazy? I can't stay." Jayne said.

"Why not?" Lynn looked genuinely puzzled.

"The kids, of course." She couldn't believe Lynn didn't realize it.

"You have got to be joking," Lynn laughed.

Jayne stood up and headed toward the door.

"Wait," Lynn called to her as she jumped out of bed and followed her.

"Jayne, look at me," Lynn said as she put her hands on her cousin's shoulders. "Your 'kids' are grown adults. They are on their own now."

Jayne just looked at Lynn.

"There is only one question you have to answer here," Lynn said. "Do you love Mason?"

Jayne froze. Motionless. Unable to speak. Mind swirling. Love conflicting.

"You and I both know that your marriage has been over for years. Maybe it never really existed." Lynn pulled Jayne over to the edge of the bed and pushed on her shoulders, forcing her to sit down. Lynn picked up Jayne's hand as she sat next to her. "Do you remember when we were kids and we would go to the corner store?

"Yes," Jayne responded.

"Do you remember the basket with the grab bags in it?" Lynn continued.

"Yes," Jayne smiled as she remembered the little brown bags stapled shut. "They were all the same price, but each bag was filled with something different."

"Right," Lynn said. "Some of the mystery surprises were crap with cheap toys and candy."

"I know." Jayne wasn't sure where this was going.

"Yes, but remember the time you got the matching ring and necklace?" Lynn said. "I was so mad. I couldn't believe it."

"Oh, I get it," Jayne replied. "I understand."

"You have much more than that now." Lynn stood.

Jayne sat as conflicting thoughts speared through her mind. Guilt parried with desire. Time seemed broken. She was displaced. Love for her children pierced love for Mason. It was late fall, and she was headed into a winter without hope of spring. Could she stay? Each moment with Mason would be a foil to counteract the loss of time.

Should I stay? The question hovered in her mind.

Then, mysteriously, Floyd's voice prodded and teased her. *Come on, girl.*

But what if I lose my children ... their respect?

Then they never really understood you, or love. Love is all, my dear. Love is all. Floyd's voice echoed with a chuckle. His voice faded, but the warmth of it lingered.

She made her choice.

"I'll leave my luggage here," Jayne said as she ran to the door.

"That's my girl," Lynn said.

Jayne heard Lynn laughing as the door slowly closed. She ran down the hall and pushed frantically at the elevator button. God, she thought, what if he's gone? Then, what? The door opened slowly. She jumped in and pushed the buttons repeatedly.

She had left her key in the room, so she pounded on the door. "Mason?"

The door didn't open. Her heart dropped to her toes. Her indecisiveness had cost her once again. This time, books were not going to be enough. Neither were her memories. She leaned her head on the door and closed her eyes.

Before she could react, the door swung open, and she fell into Mason's arms.

"I thought you were gone," she said as she kissed him, falling deep into those beautiful gray-blue eyes. Eyes she thought she might never see again.

"I was getting ready to come and find you," he said as he pulled her closer in his arms. "You should know that I would never let you go."

"It's not going to be easy," she warned. "I'm going to have to call Tom."

"Life isn't easy," he replied as he traced her lips with his finger. "I want you with me always, for better or worse." He kissed one cheek. "To love and to cherish?" He kissed her other cheek.

"In sickness and in health?" she countered, kissing his cheek.

"Exactly."

"Do I win the argument for the existence of true love?"

"Hands down," he said. "You win."

"We win," she said as the door closed softly behind her.

~

Jayne sat in the hotel business room in front of the phone. It was midnight. She rubbed her temples and closed her eyes. She chewed her bottom lip as her pulse quickened and her breath shortened.

She wiped her sweaty palms across her thighs before picking up the phone and dialing. Mason had scrawled out the numbers she needed to make an international call.

Ring ... ring ... ring ...

"Hello."

Her stomach lurched at the sound of Tom's voice. Familiar, but distant.

"Hello, Tom," she said, her mouth suddenly dry.

"Aren't you supposed to be on your way home?" he asked. "I got the promotion and things at work are crazy. I'm afraid that the house is a mess. I've just been swamped."

Jayne ran her tongue over her teeth, trying to get some moisture to help the words slip out.

"Jayne, are you there?"

"Yes, Tom. I really don't want to do this over the phone, but it's better than an email."

"What?"

She waited for another second and just plunged in.

"I'm not coming home."

Silence crackled over the phone.

"And the reason I took the vacation was to think about how to tell you and the children. Some news. Some bad news."

Tom's labored breathing was all that she heard before continuing.

"I have terminal cancer. Stage four. The doctor said I've got about a year. Less than that now."

Her soft southern accent drew out each word.

"Just a minute. What are you saying? I don't understand."

"I've met someone. I want to spend the rest of my days with him. However long that might be."

Silence made the back of Jayne's neck itch.

"This is ridiculous, Jayne," he said with an edge in his voice. "You've read too many of those novels. Unrealistic. You can't really want to stay with someone you just met. Come home and we can discuss this as a family. I don't have time for this. We can get second opinions."

"You've never had time for anything but your work, and I've already had second opinions. It's real. I've made up my mind. It doesn't take that long to know someone. Really. If it is the right someone."

"So, you want a divorce? Is that it? Haven't I worked and slaved for you enough? A beautiful home. Most anything money can buy. I really don't understand how everything changed in a couple of weeks."

"I never asked for anything but your love. Please don't hate me. Our marriage has been over for a long time. We just didn't realize it. It became convenient for both of us. This is the last thing I'll ever ask."

"You mean until you try to take half of everything?"

"Didn't you hear me, Tom?" Her voice broke. "I won't be here much longer. I don't want anything from you."

"I can't believe any of this. How am I supposed to go to work this morning?"

"Work has been your partner for years. You will be fine. I'll call the kids and tell them as soon as I hang up."

"It's not fair."

"Life's not fair, Tom."

Jayne's hand shook as she hung up the phone. Tom had always measured love by material things. She realized that now. She should have acted sooner. Found Mason sooner.

Shaking her head to scatter her regrets, she focused on dialing Kim's number.

An hour later, she returned to the room. Mason was awake and opened his arms to her. With that simple gesture, she broke. Tears streamed.

"I'm sorry," Mason said as he held Jayne. She was in a fetal position, curled up next to him in bed. She sniffed and swiped tears away with her fingers.

"He sounded so much like his father," she puffed out between sniffles. "He was furious. Told me it was crazy not to tell them about my diagnosis and run off on a silly trip."

Mason held her tighter.

"I've lost my son, Mason," she said as she sat up. "He was cold. The hairs on the back of my neck stood up as he said unbearable things."

"It's all my fault," Mason said as he shifted to face her. "I don't like to see you in pain."

"At least Kim was a little better. She wants to fly over and talk."

Jayne scooted off the bed and went to the window, rubbing her arms. Rain pelted the balcony, leaving inky whirls of water on the tabletop. There was always a cost to love. She knew that. She was willing to pay it. For him. For his love.

EPILOGUE

lmost a Year Later, September 28, 2013
The Piazza del Campo buzzed with life. Sitting at an outside table in front of their favorite café, Mason sipped his cappuccino, cringing at the bitterness. He added another scoop of sugar and stirred, watching as tourists, locals, and lovers walked in the piazza. Taking a deep breath, he held his cup as his gaze focused on an older couple. Arm in arm, just like he used to do with Jayne. He sipped as loneliness gripped him. Deep and profound. An ache in the hole left in his heart. He thought he could hear Jayne's voice. The rhythm of her southern accent chided him, telling him to live each day to the fullest, with no regrets. Just as they had over the past several months.

He shifted in his seat to catch a last glimpse of an older couple as they laughed, resting their heads together to form a heart.

Had it just been a month?

Time was a funny thing, he thought. The months with Jayne flew by. Trips to neighboring towns. Assisi where Jayne found a deep connection with St. Francis. Chianti tasting in Monteriggioni and exploration of a castle. Multiple trips to Florence and Rome.

He looked around the piazza, remembering the thriving Christmas market, bustling with activities, and aglow with huge trees strewn with colored lights. Wooden stands had filled the space with a vast assortment of hand-crafted items. The air had been pungent with smells from the food stalls. Roasted chestnuts. Mulled wine. Cheeses and salami. A smorgasbord of delightful sweets. Jayne had reveled in all of it. Her favorite holiday. Purchasing a small, scraggly Christmas tree. Her eyes lit up when she found the roughhewn nativity scene to go with it.

Their Christmas day had been filled with laughter and tears. The next day, Kim had arrived, giving Jayne a boost of energy that fueled several day trips. Each day had passed in a flurry of activity and had brought Mason and Kim closer. By New Year's Day, Kim had confided to Jayne that she could see why her mother made the choice. Kim had promised to talk to Tom and John to plead her mother's case. Their goodbye at the airport had been filled with tears even though Kim had promised to return for the summer.

Spring held short strolls through the curving streets. Dining at their favorite restaurant. Long drives in the countryside. Flowers blooming in their own flowerbox on the balcony. Jayne spent time each day in a church, not far from the flat. She told him that, in an odd way, it had felt like her childhood Baptist church on the hill. It was a smaller church with a weathered stone exterior. Inside, ancient paintings flanked the walls as the view toward the altar glittered in gold. The organ pipes fitted against red fabric as heavenly music floated down. Sitting in the pews, Jayne had met Francesco, a Catholic who always seemed to appear whenever she had visited. Over time, he became her confidant. Her friend. And later, a friend of Mason's, too.

Enough, he thought, shaking his head. Mason finished his cappuccino and signaled the waiter. As he left the café, someone called out to him. A student from the summer term. Mason managed a tight smile and waved. Jayne had insisted that he teach the summer term on a trial basis, "Just to see if you like it." He hadn't wanted to spend any time away from her, but when Kim returned and sublet a flat across from theirs for the summer, he had no excuses.

And he did love it. She had known it all along. *She knew me better than I did.* He contracted for the next academic year. Classes would start in October. A good diversion. If he could make it a few more weeks.

He continued across the piazza, glancing at the restaurant where he and Jayne had enjoyed eating. The pumpkin flower had become a staple in their diet. She had worn her little black dress many times, his favorite because she shone in it.

His heart dipped and sank. Her declining appetite and weight loss were two of the hardest parts.

In his flat, he found the silence jarring. The clutter of her illness, pill bottles, oxygen tanks, piles of pillows and blankets, gone with things back to normal. Normal feels so empty now, he thought. He strived for consolation with the good memories that surrounded him.

Jayne had created a comfortable home for them. The walls were full of photos of them in their favorite places. The oil painting from Paris hung over the fireplace. She also framed some posters of his concerts at area bars. His unicorn stood on the windowsill where the light made it seem alive.

Mason opened a window about an inch. A crisp breeze floated in and fluttered against some papers, anchored by Jayne's red reading glasses, on top of the bookshelves. Books had been the only things that she had sent for from home. They were combined in no particular order because they had read them all many times. At the end, Mason had read to Jayne for hours as they cuddled in bed or in a chaise lounge on the balcony.

In the corner, next to the books, the silk shawl hung on a hook on the wall. Jayne had said that when she wasn't wrapped in it, she liked to look at it. The breeze from the window rippled the tassels. He went to the balcony doors and pulled the sheer curtains back. A lark balanced on the wrought iron banister. It looked at him and began to sing. Notes with a pitch and tone that felt like balm for his aching soul. The bird twittered for a while, took a quick bow, and flew away.

Someone knocked softly on the door. When he opened it, there was Francesco, wearing a blue and green plaid button-down shirt with blue pleated slacks. His brown leather belt matched his soft loafers. Average height and slim waisted. His hair stood in tufts of white. Pure like fresh fallen snow. His brown eyes bright and clear. Twinkling with love for everyone.

"*Ciao*, Mason," Francesco said as he wrapped Mason in a huge hug.

"Good morning," Mason said as he motioned him through the door into the living room. "How are you?"

"More important, how are you, my dear friend?" the elderly man asked as he touched Mason on the shoulder. They sat next to each other on the couch. "It is an important day, is it not?"

"Yes, I will meet Kim and Lynn in Florence," Mason said, swiping his fingers through his hair. The chestnut locks had given way to more gray, almost half-and-half now. "Thank you for helping me arrange everything."

"My pleasure. As a volunteer at the church, I have a few connections, you know." Francesco said, patting Mason on the knee. "She was a special woman. A friend. She shared her fears, as you know. I listened and offered her what I could. I gave her prayer books. She loved to read them out loud in the church. Her soft pleas echoed her spirit. If she'd had more time, I'm sure she would have become a devout Catholic."

"I know guilt haunted her," Mason said. "I feel guilty about making her so guilty."

"Oh no, my friend, no time for guilt. Love like yours has no room for it. Sometimes, God works in ways we cannot understand. I pray for the repose of her soul every day. I promised her I would."

"She changed my life. Even more, she ignited my spirit. I didn't deserve such an angel."

"Pray for her. Pray for you. She is with you still. Love works that way. God is love, so it can never go away completely. It is never too late for forgiveness, my friend. Just remember all the things that Jesus forgave."

Mason's attention diverted back to the balcony. The lark had returned and was in full song again. He remembered the gondola ride with the sonorous voice of the poleman.

"Ah, a lark," Francesco said, standing and walking to the balcony doors. He pulled back the sheer curtains. "Did you know that larks are symbols of joy, hope, and laughter? Their singing certainly brings joy. I think our Jayne has sent us a message, my friend."

NAVIGATING THE TRAFFIC, Mason entered the English cemetery in Florence. The green and marble "Isle of the Dead," as the locals called it, loomed over the street. Cypress trees grew among the tombstones. The light cast long shadows through some wrought iron fencing. Memories of his visit to this famous graveyard with Jayne floated like ghosts. Francesco had helped him arrange for the burial of Jayne's ashes in a small corner of the famous cemetery.

He walked along the hedges with a heavy heart, feeling disconnected from life. Without Jayne. The final goodbye. *Or was it?* She had made him promise not to stop living, but continue for both of them. To keep moving forward. She repeated her mantra and said it would be his now. A lifetime squeezed into bittersweet memories. Jayne always chose to focus on the sweet.

Her weakness and exhaustion during the last months kept her bedridden. During her lucid moments, they had talked, read, and he played music for her. Music he had written. Sometimes, as she drifted off, her breathing had become slow with long pauses. He found himself trying to breathe for her. On her last night on earth, she had asked Mason to carry her out to the balcony. He wrapped her in her shawl and then spooned with her on the chaise lounge. They both fell asleep in the cool night air after bathing in moonlight and watching stars shoot across the sky.

He had jerked awake in the wee hours of the morning. Her lungs rattled as she tried to talk. A whispered, *I love you ... forever*. Her dying words. He hugged her closer, cradling her. Tears glistened in the dawn.

He swiped his eyes as he remembered. A clergyman from the cemetery approached with Kim and Lynn close behind. Francesco had arranged a short ceremony with the local Protestant clergy.

He nodded at Lynn. Kim, looking so much like her mother, hugged Mason. They held hands as they followed the clergyman to the burial site. Lynn walked a few feet behind them.

"I read the letter," Kim said, squeezing Mason's hand. "It was more than beautiful. Heartfelt. Loving. I didn't know she could write so well."

"She was a woman of many talents. Brighter than she even realized."

"I gave the other letter to John," Kim said, shaking her head. "He didn't even open it. I hope he didn't destroy it. He's still angry."

"He will come around," Lynn said, pushing her sunglasses up. "I promised your mother that I would take care of both of you. She knew that choices had consequences."

Mason felt a familiar guilty tug. Loving him had cost her so much. Her son.

"Maybe Dad will be able to help him," Kim said, patting Mason's arm. "He was in denial for so long. He just hired a housekeeper and kept working. He thought she would come back. He didn't believe she was sick." They stopped before they reached the burial site. "I think I finally broke through when I asked him about paying for the funeral. I know you didn't want me to, but I did. He didn't even blink. He agreed and said it was the least he could do. I couldn't get him to come with me, but I think this is a start."

Lynn crossed her arms and opened her mouth. No words came out. She just shook her head.

The clergyman motioned for them to approach. A carved stone marked the spot where the ashes had been buried earlier in the morning. *Jayne Thompson 1960–2013*. And underneath a quote, *Love is all and Death is nought!*, from one of her favorite Robert Browning poems.

The ceremony proceeded. Mason had pictured reading the entire poem *Fifine at the Fair* many times. It was more like a novel written in poetry form. It was about life and death. It was about love.

She had adored the rhythm of the words and had teased him about his flat Canadian vowels. The layers of meaning peeled away with each rendition.

"That was beautiful," Kim said, bringing Mason back to reality. "She would have loved it." Tears glistened in her eyes.

Eyes so like her mother's. A hollowness filled his body. The same feeling that night a month ago. When he had to tear himself away from Jayne's lifeless body to call Kim to come quickly before he called the authorities. He had watched Kim buckle under the pressure of seeing her mother, inside on the couch. He couldn't leave Jayne outside in the cold.

They thanked the clergyman and began walking back toward the entrance.

"I am so glad I got to see her last month," Lynn said. Her voice shook with a throat full of emotion. "You two took wonderful care of her. The hospice nurses told me how you catered to her every need. Even chocolate gelato."

"She gave me more than I could ever return," Mason said. Their pace slowed. "I loved every single moment I got to spend with her."

Kim nodded. "She was different with you, Mason. It was beautiful to watch."

They neared the entrance. Lynn turned to give Mason a quick hug. "Well, I'm off to see Antonio. Thank you for bringing him into my life. If you ever need anything, please just reach out. I promised Jayne I would take care of you, too."

"What are your plans?" Mason waved to Lynn and focused his attention on Kim.

"I need to get back tomorrow," Kim said, looking down. "School has started. I have to get back to my students."

"Okay, I get that," Mason said, swiping his hands through his hair.

"Are you going to be all right?" she asked, her brow furrowed. "If you need me to stay longer, I can arrange it."

"No, no," Mason said, putting her hand on the crook of his arm. "I'm glad I remembered to bring them."

"What?"

"Wait here," he said as he made his way through traffic to his car, picked up some notebooks, and returned.

"Here," he said, carrying a big tote. "These are your mother's notebooks."

"Notebooks?"

"Yes, she wrote constantly during the tour and afterwards. I think she wrote for every situation that life could possibly throw at you or John. She shared some bits with me. A few sections are written to her grandchildren. In her voice. In her way. These pages will keep her with you. Along with your heart. Forever. As long as you need her."

Kim burst into tears as she opened the tote and glanced inside.

"Thank you for loving her and taking care of her," Kim said. "She finally lived her dream instead of just reading about it."

"She resuscitated me. Gave me life. She was my light in the middle of a dark existence." Mason said as he reached out and enveloped Kim in a hug. "Do you have a place to stay?"

"Yes," she said as she shifted the tote to her shoulder. "Just help me flag a taxi and I will be on my way." She looked him straight in the eye. "I loved being part of your lives this summer. I hope I can remain in yours now."

"Always." Mason started to wave for the taxi. When one stopped, he opened the door for her. "Thank you for helping me take care of your mother. Because of you, I could let your mother see some of her plans for me in action. Teaching social history. Playing music."

She reached up and kissed him on the cheek. "Love you."

"You too." He watched until the taxi was out of sight.

Shadows dipped in silhouette and night fell as Mason entered the flat. For a moment, he thought he could hear Jayne whisper. *Love you, forever.* She was still here. With him. He knew that now.

Mason put a CD in his stereo. He smiled as he remembered Jayne insisting on CDs because they were tangible. Real. Not like the downloaded stuff.

He skipped to the last song, "High Hopes." The sound of bells filled the flat, soon followed by the soulful notes. He lay down on the couch, closed his eyes, and let the words he and Jayne had listened to wash through his soul.

She had been his muse, encouraging him to write his own music and lyrics. Their time together had been prolific for him. He still couldn't believe how the music seemed to just come. He played every line for Jayne. It seemed to help both of them. But Jayne wasn't satisfied with the small audiences or in the local bars. She had made him rent a studio, make a demo, and send it to producers. She had made him check his email every day.

When the song was over, he opened his eyes and went over to the desk, flipping on his computer. He scrolled through the list, mostly communication from the university about the upcoming semester. He stopped scrolling when he saw an email from a recording company.

Okay, Jayne, let's see what we have here.

His stomach knotted.

Click.

He read. His heart pounded. Hands shaking. Tears streaming.

An exclusive artist recording agreement. Terms and commitments. Options. It was bittersweet. *You are right again, my love.* She had opened a new world for him. Everything he saw now was through her lens. Bright. Full of promise.

Robert Browning and Pink Floyd. Only his Jayne would find the connection. Only his Jayne. He read the email again. His muse had come through for him. He was going to record their music. He'd call the album *Love Is All.*

The End

ACKNOWLEDGMENTS

A heartfelt thank you to my husband, Rod, who believed in me when I doubted myself, and to my children, Ian and Janna, for their steady support and encouragement.

I am immensely grateful to my mentors in the University of Nebraska MFA in Writing program, Charles Wyatt and Patricia Lear, who read this manuscript in its many stages—again and again—with insight and generosity.

A special thank-you to Meredith Alder, who devoted a summer to reading the manuscript and meeting with me weekly at Scooter's Coffee for caffeine-fueled discussions.

I'm also grateful to the editorial team at Old Fort Press for their thoughtful work polishing the prose. And finally, thank you to Leigh Ebberwein, publisher at Old Fort Press, for your tireless efforts to bring this novel to readers. Your belief in this story has meant the world to me.

www.ingramcontent.com/pod-product-compliance
Lightning Source LLC
Chambersburg PA
CBHW021026310726

48969CB00006B/1555